Mandy Bagg ....... winning ....
She loves the Greek island of Corfu, white wine, country music and handbags. Also a singer, she has taken part in ITV1's *Who Dares Sings* and *The X-Factor*.

Mandy is a member of the Romantic Novelists' Association and the Society of Authors and lives near Salisbury, Wiltshire, UK, with her husband and two daughters.

# Single for the Summer

## Mandy Baggot

EBURY
PRESS

1 3 5 7 9 10 8 6 4 2

Ebury Press, an imprint of Ebury Publishing
20 Vauxhall Bridge Road,
London SW1V 2SA

Penguin
Random House
UK

Ebury Press is part of the Penguin Random House group
of companies whose addresses can be found at
global.penguinrandomhouse.com

First published in the UK in 2017 by Ebury Press

www.penguin.co.uk

A CIP catalogue record for this book is available from
the British Library

ISBN 9781785036729

Typeset in India by Integra Software Services Pvt. Ltd, Pondicherry

Printed and bound in Great Britain by Clays Ltd, St Ives PLC

Penguin Random House is committed to a sustainable future for our business, our readers and our planet. This book is made from Forest
Stewardship Council® certified paper.

MIX
Paper from
responsible sources
FSC® C018179

*For Jenny, thank you for your never-ending support. This book couldn't have been written without you xx*

# One

# Gianni's Trattoria, London

There were flowers, and not the corny, wilting garage roses boyfriends think will do when they've forgotten an anniversary. These were bright pink, the colour of Hubba Bubba, and they were peonies, Tess's absolute favourites.

There were also candles, giving off a gentle scent of soft sands and vanilla, and a bottle of champagne in a silver cooler next to the table. Tess breathed in, taking in the table setting, soft Italian guitars playing familiar background music. She needed to calm, still her beating heart. She smoothed one trying-not-to-be nervous hand over her Stella McCartney trousers, closed her eyes and inhaled, tipping her head slightly, until her shoulder-length waves of blonde hair touched the middle of her back. It was only five weeks and two days. It was nothing more than Tony making an effort. Perhaps it was his birthday? Should she know when his birthday was after five weeks and two days? They had had fifteen little dates. Several dinners, a trip to see the latest blockbuster, and a lunch on the Thames. Simple. Enough.

She looked away from the table, catching the eye of the restaurant's owner, Gianni. He was smiling at her as he polished champagne flutes and then … he winked. Fear began to spread through her like a rampaging bush fire.

'Bae!'

Tony appeared from the direction of the toilets, wiping his hands together. She swallowed. Dressed in his trademark three-piece M&S work suit, dark grey trousers, waistcoat fully buttoned up, jacket a little too big for him. His skin tone said St Tropez – the fake tan, not the region in France – hair dark and plentiful and the smile that had caught her attention on Tinder. He had looked handsome on her arm at the last work dinner. Everyone had said so. But Tess wasn't sure if that was entirely good when things were always destined to stay casual.

She smiled. 'Hello.'

Tony slipped his arms around her, drawing her close and she breathed in the scent that had become almost familiar over the past five weeks and two days: Turtle Wax car polish and Spearmint Extra gum.

Tony *was* nice. Tony was really, *really* nice. He didn't belch or fart in front of her, he didn't pretend he could cook, and he had never, ever accidentally left any item of clothing or personal paraphernalia in her apartment. He turned up when he said he was going to. He didn't make a fuss when she had to work late. But now there were flowers! Champagne! Candles! It was ridiculous to worry though, wasn't it? After all, it was only five weeks and two days.

She let Tony go and steadied herself, one hand on the back of the nearest chair. 'This is lovely.' She nodded towards the floral display and the champagne. 'But ... I only have an hour for lunch, Tony. I have a client coming in at two thirty.'

He touched a finger to his nose and winked. 'Don't worry, bae, it's all sorted. This is a special occasion.'

He pulled out the chair for her. Prickles spiked down her back like a dozen baby hedgehogs doing the Macarena along her spine. *Special occasion.* She really, *really* hoped it was his birthday.

'Sit down, Tessa, or we'll have to skip the starters. And believe me, you won't want to miss them.'

*Tessa.* Yes, that was an annoying trait he had. He might not fart or belch but he did call her Tessa, which she hated and really should have told him during at least one of their fifteen dates. It wasn't even her name. She was Tess. Just Tess.

She sat down, straightaway pulling her iPhone from her handbag and placing it on the table. A quick press of the home button, but no sign of a work emergency, only the wallpaper photo of her and best friend Sonya. High on vodka shots and a late-night kebab they had suffered the effects of for weeks, both of them gurning at the lens from beneath giant, pink furry sunglasses. That was one weekend in Brighton Tess would never forget. She had even met the fish and chips guy. Uncomplicated one-night-of-sex-and-a-fish-and-chips-lunch-the-next-day-guy.

She waited for Tony to take his seat then couldn't help herself. 'Tony, is it your birthday?'

'What, bae?'

*Bae* was also a pet name that got on her nerves. And, if eavesdroppers didn't keep up with the latest slang, they might assume she was being referred to as *a body of water with a large mouth.* Not exactly flattering.

'Well, the flowers and the champagne ...' She swallowed. 'The *special occasion.*'

Tony reached across the table, taking her hand in his and smoothing his thumb across her palm. 'All in good time.'

The bush fire was spreading through her again. It was getting very near to being hotter than Idris Elba. This burning, bubbling, hellfire was close to needing water to be dropped from a squadron of planes.

'So ... it's not your birthday?' Tess asked, pushing the champagne glass forward a little in a move she hoped would spark action. She needed fortifying. And then she needed an escape plan.

'No,' Tony responded. 'I'm a Sagittarius, bae. The archer.' He acted out pulling back the string from a bow and shooting an arrow into Gianni's Renaissance paintings on the ceiling.

*Impromptu mime.* He did that a lot too. And he cracked his knuckles as often as other people breathed. But that was OK. Everyone had their quirks. And she had dated a lot worse. A *lot* worse.

'Could I have some champagne?' Tess asked, her voice a little hoarse.

'Where's my manners, eh? Not getting my lady a drink.'

*My* lady. Ownership issues. It was like the sadist from Wapping all over again. She closed her eyes for a second.

Recovering a little and refocusing, she watched Tony take the champagne out of the cooler, tear off the foil top and begin pressing and working the cork with his hands. One large pull and it popped, Tony adding the noise of an explosion for maximum effect as the frothy, bubbling liquid spilled over the top of the bottle. She could smell it. She could almost taste it. Right now, Tess had never craved a drink more. Tony had barely finished half-filling her glass when she picked it up, nuzzling the flute like a parched thoroughbred, and taking a hearty swig.

'So,' she began. 'How's work?'

'Well,' Tony answered, leaning a little over the table. 'That's partly why we've got champagne for lunch.'

Relief drenched the bush fire like a large, full-to-the-brim reservoir had been dumped on top of it. He was celebrating something to do with work! Yes! He wasn't going to ask her to move in with him. She wanted to kiss his minty breath. Sweet, very tanned, easy-going Tony. He might still make the *whole* six weeks after all. They could maybe fit in a final trip to the West End.

'You, bae, are looking at the new manager of the Hackney branch.'

'Oh, Tony,' she exclaimed. 'Your own showroom!' She was pleased for him. That was another thing about Tony. He worked hard. He understood *her* need to work hard too. She smiled and raised her glass. 'Congratulations.'

'Thanks, bae. I know it's Hackney and not the one I'd set my sights on, but it's a big ol' showroom and it's a step up the ladder.' He smiled. 'Bigger and better things are coming.' He put his hands together then blew them apart with another 'boom'.

'Your starters.'

It was Gianni, bringing scallops. Up until recently she would never have entertained eating that particularly dish but now Tess settled back in her chair, sipping some more champagne. She did so love scallops. Expensive, pint-sized, protein and cardiovascular health heavyweights that now reminded her how far she had come. Here Gianni did an amazing scallop, mushroom and parmesan recipe all parcelled back up in the shell.

Gianni put a plate down first in front of Tony and then slid a serving in front of Tess.

'Thank you, Gianni,' she said, looking up at the restaurant owner.

'Enjoy,' he replied, smiling.

And then it happened. Gianni winked again. Was there something in his eye? A sliver of unease edged back into Tess's psyche. She looked across the table at Tony, only to find he was paying far more attention to *her* than he was to food. He usually ate with the gusto of a famished chocoholic let loose in Cadbury World.

Now, as she studied her plate, it wasn't just the wink that was worrying her. It was the scallop shell. And somehow, today, the shells in front of her looked bigger than ever. If a shell had the capability of looking poignant it was utterly doing its very best right now.

Tess had found out two years ago that shells were very good for hiding things in. Romantic things. Sparkly, diamond and gold romantic things. Rings. *The* ring. An *engagement* ring. But, right now, here, it just wasn't possible. It had only been five weeks and two days. Tony wouldn't. He couldn't. It was absurd to even think it. And she was so over it. She was changed.

'All right, Tessa?' Tony asked, a smile on his lips.

'Yes,' she answered, slugging back some more champagne. 'Lovely. Mmm, scallops.' She inhaled the sea aroma mixing with the garlic and herb dressing.

'You going to eat them then?' Tony asked. 'Or just sniff them?'

She laughed. 'You first.' She looked down again at the plate. When she opened the shell there was going to be a diamond solitaire leaping out at her like a jack-in-the-box, only twice as scary. She checked herself. She was being mad. This was Tony. Tony had never even stayed the night at her apartment. *She* had stayed over with *him*, and there had been two lovely hotel breaks, but he never pushed. He seemed to know instinctively the limitations of the relationship. Which was one of the reasons why he had lasted this long. He had never got clingy or asked too much.

Tess put her fork to one of the shells on her plate, then, closing her eyes and taking a deep breath, she flipped off the top. Waiting half a second, she then opened her eyes. Anxiety evaporated. Nothing. Nothing but the scallops, mushrooms and cheese. Sweet relief!

'Oh!' she exclaimed. 'Oh, I do love these.' She dug her fork into the shell and put the contents into her mouth, letting the intense flavours coat her tongue. Gorgeous, gorgeous food. Just high levels of succulent taste sensation, and no engagement ring. She almost felt like she'd won the Postcode Lottery.

'So, when do you get to move to Hackney?' she asked.

'Well,' Tony said. 'There's going to be a transition period with the manager who's retiring, but it could be as soon as next month.'

'That's great,' Tess said, smiling. 'Will you move over there? Or commute?'

'Well … that depends,' Tony answered.

'On whether you can find a nice apartment?' God, these scallops were extra divine today. She put the last morsel of the first one in her mouth.

'Yeah, maybe a house, bae. Time to move on from the ol' bachelor pad methinks.'

Tess smiled. 'I hope you're going to keep Tony's Bar though.' The retro eighties bar in Tony's living space had optics, a flashing sign and a signed photograph of Rylan behind it.

'Natch, bae.'

Tess flipped the top off the second scallop shell and dug in her fork.

'Tessa,' Tony said.

'Yes?' Tess replied. She put the fork into her mouth and bit on something hard. Fuck. What the hell was that?

'Christ, don't swallow!' Tony ordered.

No man had ever said that to her before. She took his advice though and spat onto the plate. For just a millisecond, she realised swallowing would have been her preferred option. Or choking. Choking might have involved a nice, dramatic, hopefully quick ride out of here in an ambulance. As it was, she was breathing – just about – and staring at a ginormous diamond ring encased in saliva-coated parmesan.

Tess looked up, a hot flush already on her cheeks, just in time to see Tony slide from chair to parquet floor, dropping down on to one knee.

'Tessa. Bae. Will you marry me?'

This was a disaster. Maybe this wasn't in the same league as child labour in India or Boris Johnson becoming foreign secretary, but it was close. Tess couldn't speak. Her eyes flitted from Tony – one knee at a right angle to the rest of his body, the other suctioned to the floor – to the plate and that ... *foreign body*. The ring that had been in her mouth.

The sensory memory at the back of her throat was telling her it was still there. She swallowed, half-expecting to feel the giant diamond rolling over her airway like an Indiana Jones-style stone across an ancient tomb.

'Bae?' Tony said, dark eyes morphing into the sad, desperate eyes of an abandoned stray advertising Dogs Trust.

She still couldn't speak but she really didn't want him to speak either. The less he said the better. Perhaps she could pretend she hadn't heard him. She could pluck the ring from the plate and declare her angst that she had almost met her maker because of Gianni's lack of hygiene in the kitchen. But the problem with that course of action was that Tony was still on the floor in a position that could be one of only two things: he was either proposing or taking an inordinate amount of time to tie up his shoelaces.

She had to be brave here. Brave and kind. Let him down gently.

'Tony,' she said, her voice barely more than a whisper.

'Yes,' he answered. He looked so expectant, so hopeful. Why hadn't she seen this coming? She drew in a breath. Because she had only been dating him five weeks and two days and any *sane* person would not be considering marriage after only three Italian dinners, Tom Cruise and a couple of nights at a Radisson.

'Tony, please, sit back down.'

He smiled then. 'Oh no you don't. I want to do this the right way, Tessa. The traditional way.'

And that was near enough what Adam had said. Another time, another plate of scallops, the metallic taste was in Tess's mouth before she could do anything about it. *That* ring had been Adam's grandmother's, passed down that side of the family and apparently originating from the Mozambique diamond mines. That time she had cried. Cried so hard she thought her eyeballs were actually going to burst and shower the entire restaurant with the crop of tears she'd unknowingly cultivated. She had felt so totally, completely *happy. Love Actually* happy. Love was possible for her. Love was real. She was not going to be another daughter from divorced parents who couldn't make a relationship work …

'Tony,' she tried again. 'Please get up.' She chanced a glance at the other diners, not wanting nice, decent, slightly Ambre-Solaired Tony to be embarrassed. She narrowed her eyes at the woman in blue who had a baby plum tomato on her fork midway between salad bowl and mouth, until the diner had the good grace to get on with her eating. Looking back to her date, she saw that Tony remained unmoved, like Angela Merkel on the subject of migration.

'Tessa.' Tony cleared his throat. 'Will you—'

She couldn't hear the words again. It was no good. She was either going to have to inflict blunt force trauma to the ear canal or use a desperate lie. What to do? Make it crystal clear and break his heart? Or tell a fib?

Tess leapt from her chair, phone in hand, like she'd just sat on a nest of wasps. 'Oh my God, no!' She put a hand to her chest where her heart was truly palpitating with shock and adrenalin.

'What's wrong?' Tony asked, finally shifting his position, preparing to stand up.

'It's ... my ... cousin ... she ...' She glanced first at her phone, then over at the ring, letting the engagement dread do its work on her. The sob was completely real. 'She's at the hospital.'

'What?' Tony said, standing up. He was up!

'She's ... I need to go,' Tess said, picking up her handbag and pushing her chair into the table.

'Can I do anything? Drive you? Call you a cab? Come with you?' Tony asked.

She shook her head, feeling immensely guilty. What was she going to do when he called her later to ask how her cousin was? Should she invent rapid childbirth or a small non-life threatening accident? What exactly was she going to do when he arranged another dinner to do this same thing all again? She swallowed. She could just say the words. She could just say, very, very quietly, quiet enough so the woman in blue with the Caprese salad didn't hear, that she couldn't marry him.

No, it was better this way. No public humiliation. No answers to the whys and wherefores. Tony didn't know where she lived, or where she worked. She would just get rid of the phone number he used to call her on and ... disappear. In the long run he would thank her, she was sure of that. He would find someone new. The new bae would jump at the chance of moving to Hackney and they would lead a blissful existence entertaining other car salesmen and making gin slings behind Tony's Bar. Tony would be happy. Tess would be happy without him. It was going to end in five days anyway. They had had a good temporary life together.

'I have to go,' she said, backing away and trying desperately not to look at the Rock of Gibraltar, glinting underneath the slivers of scallop.

'Well, bae, call me, let me know you're OK,' Tony said, looking slightly bewildered.

He was so nice. But this was necessary. She had obviously let him get too close. Well, she certainly wouldn't be making that mistake again.

'Bye, Tony,' she breathed.

Tess didn't wait a second longer. She made for the door and the humid, London air outside that smelled like freedom.

# Two

# McKenzie Falconer Media, London

It was almost 1.45 p.m. Running into the post room of McKenzie Falconer Media, Tess was already unscrewing the cap on one of the three plastic bottles in her hands.

And there was her best friend in the whole wide world, her rock, her anchor, the only person in London who knew *everything*: Sonya.

Sonya looked up from where she was laminating and binding and Tess immediately felt comforted. She had her best friend, right here, she had three bottles of full-fat Dr Pepper in her hands and Tony was six Tube stops away. She headed for the chair next to Sonya, currently occupied by a box of spiral binding coils. Before she had even reached the seat, Sonya had shifted the box and Tess plumped down, swigging at the first bottle like a liquid sugar junkie and dropping the other two on the desk.

'Three, Tess?'

She managed to only nod her head. Anything more than nodding would send the dark, brown liquid spilling down her chin.

'Really three?' Sonya repeated. 'Because last time you had three it was because your mum and dad were coming to visit. Together.' A horrified look crossed her face. 'Are your mum and dad coming to visit together again? Today? Sooner than today? I don't think I'm going to be able to get all the ingredients to cook the mackerel hotpot before today and—'

'Sonya,' Tess said, finally taking the bottle out of her mouth. 'My parents aren't coming.' She wasn't sure either of her parents were ever going to visit again after last time. And it had absolutely nothing to do with Sonya's skills in the kitchen. After The Day They Never Discussed, almost exactly twelve months ago, each sporadic visit was more awkward than the last. It was all eating, drinking tea and filling the silence with meaningless conversation until Tess took a call from 'work', made her excuses and her parents left. Why they even insisted on visiting *together* and putting on some weak pretence was beyond her. They had been divorced for years for God's sake!

'Oh. Oh, well then.' She looked confused. 'I don't understand.'

Neither did Tess, not fully. All she knew was her heart was working overtime and she was waiting for the sugar rush to kick in. 'Tony proposed to me.'

'Shoot!' Sonya exclaimed, clapping a hand to her mouth. She took her hand away again. 'When? How? Why?'

And that's how well Sonya knew her. Her friend understood what had happened was a disaster too. That's why she had asked three one-word questions and not asked if Tess had accepted.

'Just now, in Gianni's.' She took a breath. 'With a scallop.' She shook her head; this was sounding like a guess in Cluedo. 'I don't know.'

Tess slugged at the Dr Pepper again, trying to rid her mind of Tony's anxious face and her mystery relative giving birth or cutting off their little finger in a cheeseboard incident.

'Was he all right when you said no?'

'I didn't exactly say no,' Tess admitted.

'What?!'

'I didn't say yes.' She breathed. 'Of course I didn't say yes. It's been five weeks and two days and—'

Sonya held her hands up like barricades. 'Keep out! No commitment allowed here.'

She nodded, eager to move the conversation on. A few seconds longer and her mind would be filled with images from that fateful day when commitment had meant grand humiliation. The vicar with the regretful smile, the knowing look from the chauffeur who had spun around that church twelve times too many, and her mother's tearful expression as her daughter's happiness flew out of the stained-glass window taking the rainy-day nest egg and their Experian credit score with it.

'I ran away,' she said, guilt taking a stab at her too. 'I sort of ignored the ring bigger than Saturn and told him I had to get to the hospital.'

Sonya folded her arms across her chest. 'I hope you didn't use me again. Because one of these days your tall stories of me being rushed to A&E are going to give me bad karma. In fact, maybe that's it. Maybe that's why—'

'I didn't use you,' she said quickly. 'I didn't use any names, or any definite injuries or incidents. I just left.'

'So,' Sonya said. 'No one needs mackerel hotpot?'

Tess studied her friend a little more closely. There was something about her that wasn't quite right. What was it? Her gorgeous auburn hair was neatly French pleated as usual for work, her slight overuse of blusher was in place, smart yet comfortable yellow shrug over her favourite black and daisy-print dress ...

'Is everything OK with you?' Tess asked, screwing the lid back on her drink bottle.

'Yes,' Sonya answered. 'Of course. Apart from having to get fifty-eight more of these bound before three o'clock because the big machine that does them in batches is broken and Ian, my new assistant, is also broken – although in relation to him you could probably swap the word "broken" for "hungover".' She held up the report she was in the process of fixing together. 'And if anything else in my life turns to crap then I'm going to be very close to being broken too.'

And then it happened. Sonya let out a sob and put a hand to her chest, the region just below her neck that usually had a silver chain with a heart-shaped blue topaz stone set in it.

Tess didn't hesitate a second longer. She shoved the bottles of Dr Pepper on to the shelf and went to her best friend, putting her arms around her and holding her close, breathing in VO5 and the coconut oil Sonya had taken to coating herself in.

'What's happened? Where's your necklace?' Tess asked softly.

'I ... took it off,' Sonya forced out between sobs.

'What?' Something was wrong. Sonya never took the necklace off. This was a necklace that had almost half-strangled her that weekend in Brighton when it got caught in a safety chain on the waltzers. It was omnipresent. There in every picture Tess had of her.

'I took it off,' Sonya repeated, moving out of Tess's arms and wiping her eyes with the back of her hand.

'But why?' Tess asked. 'I know, in the past, I've suggested changing things up a bit when we've been in Accessorize but it's *the* necklace. The almost-engagement necklace.'

Sonya nodded sadly. 'I know.'

'Then ...'

'Joey,' Sonya stated through juddering lips. 'He's ...'

Now Tess felt sick. Joey was Sonya's boyfriend of at least a million years. They had been together since before Spotify took over the world. If something had happened to him then her worries about Tinder Tony would pale a shade lighter than Edward Cullen.

'He told me he wants us to go on a break.'

No. No, this could not be happening. Sonya and Joey may not be married or even properly engaged but they were the absolute epitome of the perfect couple. They were two halves of a beautiful, laughing, smiling, Pokémon Go-chasing whole. Tess might be determined that commitment was never going to be in her future but Sonya and Joey, they were the real deal. They were the beacon of hope in an ever-disposable world. They were nothing like Tess's sister Rachel and her ex-husband, Philandering Phil.

'He said he needed some space and when I said, what did that mean, he didn't really answer. I said, did he not want to do ballroom dancing with me any more, because that would be OK, one of the moves sets my tendonitis off anyway, and he said it was more than that.' She took a breath. 'So I said maybe we could do something a little bit out there – like not have lunch at Zizzi every Sunday – or we could, you know, try a couple of new positions ... in the bedroom ... or maybe even out of it and ...' Sonya swallowed. 'He wouldn't talk. At all. Not even when I mentioned the Summer Medieval Fayre to try to lighten the mood.'

Joey not talking about battle re-enactment was like David Walliams not acting camp. This was bad.

'So I said, what about Corfu?' Sonya carried on. 'When I booked it he was so excited. He told me all the different varieties of butterfly that live on the island and I told him all the Greek dishes ending in the letter "a" I wanted us to try. I've been so looking forward to quality time, just the two of us, relaxing, talking, not talking, trying ... new positions.'

'Sonya, what did he say?'

'He said ...' She breathed in hard. 'He said he didn't want to go.' Sonya sobbed again. 'It's next week, Tess. I'm not going to get my money back and I can't go on my own and ... forget all the incidental crap. My relationship! The *only* relationship I've ever had is ... could be ... over.' She sighed. 'Joey won't answer my calls or the thirty-five texts I've sent him since yesterday. Yes, I counted. I just don't know what to do,' Sonya admitted. 'For the first time ever, I don't know what to do.'

Tess took hold of her friend's hand and gave it a squeeze. 'It's OK.' She took a breath. 'Because it's all going to be all right.'

'It is?'

She couldn't vouch for Joey's next move but she could certainly help. 'I know exactly what to do.'

'You do?' Sonya asked, brown eyes wide. 'Are you going to call him? I just need to talk to him. He might listen to you.'

'No, Sonya,' Tess said. 'I'm not going to call him. And neither are you.'

A plan was forming. Her escape from the proposal disaster without any half-truths or fake relatives. She would call Tony – when she was far away – with a carefully prepared script. Greece, with her best friend. She was owed holiday. She had nothing to keep her here for a week. Maybe she could even find a little holiday romance. Not six weeks, just an easy seven nights of sun, sea and nothing serious. Exactly the way she liked it. The way it had to be.

Tess smiled. 'I've got thirty minutes before my next client. I'll bind as many of these as I can while you drink this.' She passed a bottle of Dr Pepper over. 'Then you can tell me where we're staying in Corfu.' She watched Sonya's expression lighten just a little. 'And most importantly, what I really need to know is does it have an infinity pool?'

# Three

# Kalami, Corfu, Greece

The sun was just coming up. Faint fingers of golden light beginning to appear on the horizon, that part between azure sea and the promise of cornflower-blue sky dappled pink, peach and violet.

Andras Georgiou hung from the beamed ceiling of his restaurant, hands, forearms, shoulders, core, all bearing his weight as he gazed out at the view that never failed to steal his breath. The pebbled shoreline of the bay of Kalami, the towering cypress trees either side of the beach scene and the village houses, scattered among the greenery.

He raised his body upwards slowly, focusing on the view and not the strain of the morning exercise – abs crunching, biceps tightening – and as he lowered his bare abdomen down he paused, his vision once more drawn to the beach.

'Straight lines! I need straight lines! Paulo! Do you even know what a straight line is?! One foot, in front of the other, not wishy-washy and all together! One, two, three, four.'

Andras listened to his mother Isadora's voice giving orders as he pulled his body up again, watching the group of people making their way across the pebbles in something resembling a conga line.

'Spiro! If *you* do not know what a straight line is I fear for your marriage!' There was a loaded pause that sounded close to menacing even from this far away. 'Remember what happened to Uncle Dimitri.'

Andras shook his dark head of hair and let go of the beam, dropping to the floor. He picked up his abandoned T-shirt, wiping the sweat from his body and moving through the restaurant. This wedding preparation was getting out of hand. Yesterday, his mother had moved a group of six diners from their table so she could stick her tape measure across it. When he had protested, suggesting that the tables for six were all of uniform size, she had glared at him like only she, or maybe she and Al Pacino, could.

'What is this?' It was his mother again, shrieking at the very top end of her vocal range. 'It is a monster! Where is my stick?'

'Mama, it is a tortoise, that is all.'

'It is the size of a small car!'

Andras baulked then, knowing exactly what they had stumbled upon. He dropped his T-shirt on to the counter and hurried down the steps, heading for the wooden boardwalk and the beach.

By the time he had jumped from platform to stones, his Nikes crunching as he jogged, his mother, his brother, Spiros and all the members of the family who had already arrived for the wedding, were bent over the 'monster'.

'It is dead!' his mother answered.

'No, it is still breathing,' Spiros replied.

'Where is my stick?'

'Mama, please, leave him.' Andras bustled into the group and put both arms around the bulky animal, lifting it off the stones and away from the harmful intentions of his family.

'It is prehistoric! A dinosaur! What is it doing here? Is it bad luck?' Isadora sucked in a breath. 'Antonia, look this up in wedding customs. What does a monster on the beach before a wedding mean?'

'The tortoise being here has nothing to do with bad luck, good luck, or any sign from the gods,' Andras informed her.

'And you know this, do you?' Isadora questioned, her eyes like glistening black olives.

'I know that he has been here a week already so ...' Andras started.

'*He*,' Isadora stated. 'I do not want to know how you know it is a *he*. It is hideous and it cannot be here for the wedding.' She paused, observing the giant tortoise as it retracted its head. 'Unless it can be cooked.'

Andras shielded the animal, taking a step back from the party of people. 'I will make sure it is nowhere near the restaurant for the wedding.'

'Nowhere near the restaurant?' Isadora queried. 'I don't want this monster anywhere near the *village*.'

That having been said, Andras was starting to wish he was a giant tortoise who could just retreat into his shell until the whole big, fat, clichéd Greek wedding of his brother and his bride-to-be Kira was over.

The tortoise seemed to agree, sticking out its tongue. The weight of the reptile challenged the core muscles he had just been working out as his mother's eyes zeroed in on him like a drone set to destroy.

'And what are you doing here anyway?' Isadora exclaimed. 'You said you were too busy for the procession this morning. You said you had a delivery.'

'And now I have a tortoise,' he quipped.

'Put down that horror and get in line,' Isadora ordered.

'Mama,' Andras protested.

'Andras,' Spiros began. 'I think I hear the delivery truck now.'

Andras took two steps back while the going was good, the tortoise still in his grip, and offered his brother a thankful glance. 'I think you are right, Spiro.'

'I do not hear a truck,' Isadora stated. 'And I have excellent ears.'

'I should go,' Andras told her, continuing to back away.

'Perhaps you need some help, yes?'

Spiros was raising his eyebrows higher than the island's tallest peak of Mount Pantokrator. Andras had immense sympathy for his brother, but Spiros had known what getting married the full-on traditional Greek way was going to entail. However, Andras also knew the reason their mother had only one traditional wedding to get excited about was on him.

'Do not even think about moving one step, Spiro,' Isadora said, threat coating her tone.

'Auntie Isadora,' a small voice spoke. 'I am hot.'

All eyes went to six-year-old Helena who was wearing traditional Corfiot dress complete with a hat covered in white lace, with colourful red, yellow and pink flowers woven into it.

'You cannot be hot,' Isadora stated. 'For the wedding it will be much, much warmer than this.'

Spiros whispered, his voice close to Andras. 'Help me.'

'Sorry,' Andras replied, hugging the tortoise to his bare skin. 'But I promise, I will keep the beer cold and the coffee hot. Whatever you need,' Andras stated.

'You know what I need,' Spiros said softly. 'I need you to find a buyer for my half of the restaurant.'

Andras moved his eyes to the tortoise who was now poking its head slowly out of its shell in curiosity. He knew his brother had been patient. He knew he was running out of time. He had asked almost everyone he thought might have the means to invest. His options left were either to try to get a loan himself or face up to the reality of running the restaurant with his mother as his partner.

'If there were any other way,' Spiros said, nudging his brother's arm.

'I know,' he answered. 'It is OK. You have a new life waiting, and a new wife.'

Andras watched Spiros's eyes go to his fiancée, Kira, just a few metres away down the beach, her bare feet in the edge of the sea, her thick dark hair moving in the breeze, smiling sweetly even while being berated by Isadora. Spiros adored Kira. They were going to live a joyful life together on the mainland where, in a year or maybe sooner, Kira would deliver the first of a couple of gorgeous children.

'I am a very lucky man,' Spiros agreed with a contented sigh.

'You should go,' Andras said as the tortoise began to kick its legs. 'Before Mama threatens you with what happened to Uncle Dimitri again.'

Spiros laughed, nodding.

'See you later,' Andras said, about to turn away.

'Andras,' Spiros called.

He stopped, faced his brother again. 'What?'

'She will kill me for telling you this,' Spiros said, taking a look over his shoulder as if to ensure Isadora wasn't in range.

'Telling me what?'

'Cousin Marietta,' Spiros said. 'Mama … she has plans for the two of you.'

Andras looked over to the wedding party, all the women frantically flapping their hands in front of the face of the perspiring, radish-faced Helena. Cousin Marietta seemed to sense his scrutiny and looked up, waving her hand.

'I'm sorry, Andras,' Spiros said, laying a hand on his brother's shoulder. 'But, it could be worse, yes?' He nodded. 'Uncle Vasilis has a building company and there are cows on her mother's side of the family.'

He couldn't bring himself to even try to reply.

'Windows for your house and meat for the menu, yes?' Spiros said cheerfully.

The tortoise made a noise – a cross between a cough and a laugh. Andras knew exactly how the animal felt. Suspended in mid-air, flailing and with a heavy weight on its back. The only difference was Andras didn't have a shell to hide in.

'I will see you later,' he said to his brother, hugging the reptile to his side.

Suddenly there was a chorus of screams from the wedding party and Andras looked up just in time to see Helena drop to the beach.

'Loosen the hat!' Isadora shouted. 'But be careful not to crush the flowers. Andras! Get some water!'

# Four

# En route to Kalami, Corfu

'According to the guidebook,' Sonya said, staring out of the coach window, 'there's a must-see church near here called Ipapanti.' She drew in a breath as if she was sucking the outside in. 'Whitewashed walls and a garden filled with palms, agave and cacti.' A sigh left her lips. 'Just saying those words makes you feel Greek, doesn't it?' She turned a little in her seat, eyes looking to Tess. 'Do you feel Greek?'

'No,' she answered shortly. 'I feel like the flight left far too early and you swallowed too much Aperol.' Tess looked back to her phone, gripping on to it as the coach bounced along the rutted roads at a pace to rival Lewis Hamilton.

*Damon Daniels. Thirty. Loves fine wine, good times and …*
*my abs.*

Tess had scrolled down already and there Damon was in his profile photo, most of his face missing, a taut abdomen glowing from the screen. An obsessed gym bod who liked fine wine. Most of the gym bods she'd dated in the past would look at her like she was a freak if she drank more than one glass of wine on a week night. It was all $H_2O$ and infuser water bottles stuffed with fat-burning citrus fruits. Not even a sniff of Dr Pepper.

She flipped back to the home screen of the new dating app she'd joined since Tinder Tony had started leaving her begging messages. Hooked Up, it was called. If she wasn't careful there would be no dating apps left to sign up to. And she *needed* a date. To get right back on the proverbial horse after the proposal nightmare. Something organised for when she got home. Who was next? She went to press—

'Aw, look, Tess! Look!' Sonya exclaimed, tugging at the sleeve of Tess's bright red, cardigan-cum-jacket. She had bought it because it looked a lot like one she'd seen in Harvey Nichols. 'Sheep in the road, being steered by a man with a stick. Doesn't that just warm your heart? Doesn't it make you glad you're here?' Sonya sighed again. 'It's so peaceful. So not London.'

Tess looked at her friend. Sonya's eyes might be transfixed with the scene outside the window, but her friend's right hand was at the bottom of her neck, fingers seeking out a necklace that wasn't there. Tess dropped her phone into her bag and joined Sonya in gazing out at their view as the coach slowed to a crawl to avoid the farm animals.

There was greenery to rival the Cornish moors here, inter-mixed with pockets of colour from budding flowers – yellows and lilacs – and, in the distance, as the land dropped steeply away from the road, was the sea. A sleek, almost still, wide ribbon of deep blue, sat at the bottom of this mountainous island. It was beautiful. It was nothing like Tess's last holiday with Rachel in full-on Philandering Phil meltdown mode again – Centre Parcs, climate-controlled, spa-perfect dome habitation. This was foreign. Hot. Exciting. Maybe that's what she was missing in her life. A *foreign* boyfriend. Olive-skinned perfection with a carefree attitude to match hers.

'Well, I think a week in that sea is going to do wonders for our skin,' Tess stated.

'It is, isn't it?' Sonya answered. 'And, apparently, if you smother the wet sand all over you like you're in the Dead Sea or something, it gets rid of all your impurities.'

'All of them?' Tess asked.

'I don't think we're talking soul-salvation and sin-cleansing,' Sonya admitted. 'But a little dermabrasion never hurt anyone.' She sighed. 'Joey liked to take care of his skin. In more of a Savlon way than a tea-tree-wipe way, but he had nice skin.'

'He *has* nice skin, not that I looked at his skin that closely.' Tess took Sonya's hand, drawing it down and away from its necklace-searching. 'What I mean is, he hasn't died, there's no need to refer to him in the past tense. Because he isn't in your past. He's just having a … man moment.'

'A man moment? What's a man moment?' Sonya asked, turning in her seat to face Tess.

She had no idea what a man moment was. It was just something that had come out of her mouth – possibly pinched from a *Cosmopolitan* article her sister had shown her one Kleenex-filled evening – that she hoped would make her friend feel better about this enforced break from her relationship. Now she had to deliver an explanation.

'It's just that stage they go through when they're caught between still being a bit of a boy and … growing up.'

'Joey's *twenty*-seven,' Sonya reminded her.

'I know. But he's still into *Robot Wars*, isn't he?'

'He does love *Robot Wars*.' Sonya's face fell. 'Is there something wrong with that?'

This wasn't going well. Tess shook her head. 'No, I was just thinking that maybe Joey's caught between wanting more *Robot Wars* and less …' She racked her brain for the right words. 'Dunelm Mill.'

'What does that mean?' Sonya asked. 'That I constantly drag him around furnishing shops ensuring he knows the difference between a pillowslip and a pillowsham?'

Tess swallowed. *She* didn't even know the difference between a pillowslip and a pillowsham.

'Have I got clingy? Is that what you're saying?' Sonya asked, face reddening. 'Maybe I've got controlling and planned out his life for him so he's feeling suffocated and stifled?'

'No,' Tess said, straightaway. 'I didn't mean that.'

'We had that ... odd conversation but ... we'd moved past that and things were good. Things were frothy-coffees-in-Costa good.'

'And they will be again.' Tess smiled. 'With chocolate curls on top.'

'He said he *liked* Dunelm Mill.' Sonya sniffed. 'And I *know* he likes the little craft shop we go in on a Saturday, the one that does hand-painted tea sets with cute puppies and kittens on and ... I didn't hear him moaning about haberdashery when the wool we found at the knitting expo got turned into a jumper all his friends said looked like a Ralph Lauren.'

Sonya was looking close to a teary meltdown and a couple of their travelling companions were peering across the aisle at them now the sheep issue outside seemed to have been resolved and they were back to being on their way.

'Sonya, this isn't the end,' Tess stated, softly. 'You and Joey are perfect for each other ... but perhaps he just needs a little time out to realise that.'

Sonya whispered. 'Is that what happened with Adam?' She lowered her voice even more. 'Did *you* have a break, you know, before the ... break-up?'

And there it was. That ache low down in the very depths of her stomach, no longer a sharp jab like a heavyweight boxing champion had sucker-punched her, more like a focused, steely fencing expert had foiled her with a precision riposte. She didn't talk about Adam. Back when she'd told Sonya about Adam it had been after three too many Margarita cocktails. She had rattled through the altar-jilting humiliation of a year ago, ridding herself of all the tears of loss and hurt and trying to ignore the first notes of Adele's 'Someone Like You'. The man she'd loved so hard, so deeply, had not only shattered her future and broken her heart, his actions had made her leave Buckinghamshire and permanently altered her relationship with both her parents.

She shook her head. 'No.'

But maybe, if they had, they would still be together. She pulled in a breath, her hand already reaching into her bag for her phone. Did she really believe that?

'I just … don't know what I'm going to do if he isn't going to be in my life any more,' Sonya admitted.

Tess wrapped her right hand around her phone and put her left hand on top of her friend's, delivering a comforting pat. 'Trust me, it won't come to that. I have experience, well, you know, with Rachel and—'

'Philandering Phil,' Sonya added.

'Quite.'

'Joey's quite the catch, you know,' Sonya said, eyes moving back to the window. 'When he's in his battle re-enactment costume you should see the heads that turn.' She sighed. 'And I don't want to think about his head being turned by some busty Cavalier damsel at the Tiverton show next month. What if we're not back together by next month?'

'Sonya, *you're* a catch,' Tess assured her. 'And you're the girl with the almost-engagement necklace that's going to turn into a definite-engagement ring as soon as Joey realises he can't live without you.' She smiled. 'I give it three days tops before he's calling.'

Tess pulled her phone out of her bag and tapped on Hooked Up.

'What are you doing?' Sonya inquired, holding on to the seat back as the coach took a sharp turn.

'Finding me a new man to come home to.' She grinned. 'After I've practised on a Greek one here, obviously.'

'What?' Sonya asked. 'Are you kidding with me?' She laughed, slapping her hands down on to her thighs. 'Now who's had too much Aperol?'

Tess looked at her friend, bemused. Had she said something funny? She knew Sonya would rather she found a man from 'more conventional' methods – like one of Joey's Roundhead-dressed friends – but with the relationship shelf life moving faster than a civil war sword, apps were easier and far less personal.

'I don't get it,' Tess stated, her voice tinged with some of the nervousness she felt about Sonya's reaction.

'We can look. Obviously we're going to look,' Sonya said. 'But no touching.' She grinned. 'Strictly girl time.'

'What?' She had barely managed to get the word out of her mouth.

'No men,' Sonya stated. 'We said so on the plane. Just you and me, swimming in the sea with dolphins and slathering ourselves with wet sand, drinking Greek wine and eating all the dishes ending in "a".' She sighed, her hand moving to the bottom of her neck again before she seemed to catch what she was doing and return it to her lap. 'Us time, Tess. Absolutely no men.' She giggled. 'Apart from the looking.'

Tess felt sick. She couldn't do it. The longest she had been without a date on her arm, since the Adam situation, was forty-eight hours. And that was because for twenty-four of those hours she had been head down in a project at work and for the other twenty-four the dating app she'd been using was undergoing website maintenance. She had to have someone. Anyone. A focus. A male distraction. Someone to post photos of on Facebook.

'I'm not sure I—' Tess started. She wasn't *not sure*, she was *quite sure* this was something she wasn't going to be able to do for a day, let alone a week.

'Hush,' Sonya interrupted. 'Now you have to make me a promise.' She pointed a finger, moving it up and down like she was training a dog. 'Promise me you'll stay completely and utterly single for this holiday. No waiters. No barmen. No tourists, even if they look like Jared Padalecki. No hooking up *at all*. Just girls enjoying being girls, without boys.'

Now Sonya sounded like a will.i.am song. She swallowed, wishing she had indulged in Italian aperitifs on the flight.

'Promise,' Sonya said again, blinking those warm, green, honest eyes.

She could do it for her best friend. Her best friend who was in relationship limbo and had paid for this holiday. She dropped her phone back into her bag and said the words. 'I promise.'

# Five

# Kalami Cove Apartments

There wasn't any Wi-Fi. Even if Tess held her arm out in front of her and shook her phone. There was no 3G either, let alone 4G. Right now, sitting under a cream parasol, with her suitcase at her feet because their room wasn't ready, her phone was as useful as a waterproof towel.

The Kalami Cove Apartments had been just tiny dots of terracotta and bright white on their approach down the side of the mountain. Nestled among the cypress trees were four blocks of buildings and a central area that comprised a reception and bar that faced out on to the patio. Out here on the terrace were a multitude of sunloungers, some occupied by guests with a lot less on than she had, and a large rectangular pool. It wasn't an infinity, but the water looked inviting and there were square inches of it without children with inflatables.

'Look at that view!'

Tess put her phone down on the table. Sonya had already peeled off her cardigan, T-shirt and trainers and was promenading towards the edge of the terrace in nothing but her three-quarter-length leggings and a cami.

It was stifling hot. Definitely in the thirties. More humid than Centre Parcs, even. But Tess wasn't considering which bikini to change into first, she was still thinking about what she'd signed herself up for on the coach. Staying single. For an entire holiday.

Of course, any normal person would be quite happy to get off the dating train after someone had proposed to them after five weeks and two days. But Tess's method was tried and tested. It worked for her. It had *always* worked for her. She got the male company, they got the female company and no one had to worry about what to buy each other for Christmas. It was reassuring. To not be on the shelf, but to also not be on the market either. It was a tactic she had suggested to Rachel when they'd last had lunch. She swallowed. How long ago had that been?

'Oh, Tess! Come and look!'

She scraped back her chair and got to her feet. Concentrate on Sonya. That's what was going to get her through No-Men-Ville. And it was true, between Sonya and Joey being inseparable until now, and Tess being constantly hooked up with one person or several others, their girl time had been restricted to snatched lunches in Sonya's post room cave at work.

She stood next to her friend, looking down and out over the scene.

Immediately below them were emerald-coloured bushes, copses of slender, towering trees, falling away with the mountain's terrain. Interspersed, like cubes of crumbly sponge cake, were houses – some concrete-roofed, others tiled, some seemingly held together by nothing more than washing lines and corrugated metal sheets. Then, at the very foot of the steep drop, was a strip of sand and pebble beach, the turquoise water softly rushing backwards and forwards. It was beautiful.

A sigh left Sonya. 'I wish Joey could see this.'

Tess linked her arm through her friend's. 'Stop that. He turned it down,' Tess reminded her. 'And you've got *me*.'

'I know,' Sonya said, squeezing Tess's arm. 'It's like our weekend in Brighton but with better weather and baklava instead of sticks of rock.'

Tess smiled before her attention was drawn to a rather delicious-looking meze being brought to a couple at one of the tables on the terrace. Bright, glossy rings of tomatoes, purple olives, creamy-looking taramasalata and succulent pieces of grilled meat. She hadn't eaten since the Fox's Glacier Mint she'd sucked on the plane to relieve her ear-popping during the descent.

'Oh my!' Sonya said, looking too. 'I didn't realise how hungry I was until I saw that.'

'Let's get one,' Tess agreed.

'To share?' Sonya asked.

'No.' She grinned. 'One each.'

'Bring on the girl time,' Sonya exclaimed, punching the air then rapidly retracting her arm. 'Ow, tendonitis, tendonitis.'

Andras had no idea how a restaurant could run out of bread. He had ordered the right amount every single day for the past five years but today, despite the eatery being at usual summer capacity *and* having considered all the bookings, it was almost all gone. As he powered up the steps to the Kalami Cove Apartments, white shirt clinging to his body with the heat, he wondered if he *had* made a mistake with the order this time. He didn't like mistakes. It was rare for him to make one, at least where the restaurant was concerned. But with the wedding stuff going on around him and the need for a new business partner on his mind, it was easy to get distracted. He only hoped that Alex would be able to bail him out.

Rushing up the final steps to the property Andras turned right, heading across the terrace and manoeuvring past the urns and ceramic pots spilling bright bougainvillea, towards the bar area where he was confident the hotelier would be found. Like himself, Alex owned this place, but with times tight, some owners had to be managers *and* workers rolled all into one.

A breath of relief left him as he saw his friend was behind the bar.

He hurried forwards, waving a hand. 'Alex.' Andras stopped at the bar, leaning his elbows on the countertop and relishing some time in the shade.

'*Yassou*, Andras,' Alex replied. '*Ti kanis?*'

'*Ime kala.*'

'Excuse me,' a woman's voice interrupted. 'I don't mean to be rude but I was here first.'

Andras turned his head, noticing for the first time that someone, a woman, was stood at the bar, just a little way away from him. She was maybe five foot nine, slim, with wavy blonde hair that just touched her shoulders and she was wearing designer-style jeans, a formal-looking top and a jacket.

He immediately held up his hands. 'I apologise. I did not realise.'

She shrugged. 'That's OK.'

'But if I could just—' Andras restarted. In Greek he asked Alex for a favour.

The woman swung around then, fully facing him. She had blue eyes. Aquamarine blue eyes. Andras offered her a smile.

'So you now *know* I was here first and you're still going to carry on with your lunch order anyway?' the woman stated.

He watched her place a hand on her hip.

'I do not want to order lunch,' he answered. He looked to Alex who was intently watching them, order pad and pen poised for action. 'I need some bread.'

The woman cleared her throat loudly then spoke. 'I would like to order two mezes please and a side of bread.'

Andras looked back to her. 'You want a side of bread with a meze?'

'You've ordered bread. Why can't I?'

'How much do you need, Andras?' Alex asked him.

'Whatever you can spare. I have three boats due in fifteen minutes.'

Alex smiled at the woman. 'One moment please.' He then headed off, out from behind the bar towards the kitchens.

'Stop! Wait! You can't just leave, I was first ...' the woman called to Alex's departing form. She looked hot and now a little flustered.

'You should take off your jacket,' Andras suggested to her.

'What?' the woman asked, her eyes on him again.

'It is hot today. Even for people who live here. You arrive here today, yes?'

The woman pulled a mobile phone out of her bag and began tapping the screen, then shaking it in the air. 'What's wrong with this place?' she asked. 'We're on the side of a mountain. A side of a mountain should be able to get some sort of mobile phone connection.'

'Maybe your phone is too hot too,' he suggested. 'Perhaps if you put it away, let it have a holiday, then when you are both cooler and more relaxed it will work again.'

She stopped shaking her phone, looked at it one more time then dropped it back into her bag with a sigh.

'Andras Georgiou,' he said.

She looked confused. 'What does that mean? My Greek isn't very good.'

He smiled. 'It is my name.' He offered out his hand as he watched her cheeks heat up.

Tess felt a roll of embarrassment flood over her, adding to her already sweltering temperature. She couldn't shake his hand. Her palms were dripping like a melting Cornetto and she didn't want to wipe them on her Burberry jeans. And, despite noticing he had that archetypal Greek jet-black hair – cropped short but not too short – olive complexion and rather nicely toned forearms, he was a queue jumper. Plus her man radar had been forcefully turned off. *Had* it been on though, he was definitely someone who would have got a second glance, maybe, if he hadn't usurped her.

'I'm here with my friend, Sonya,' she told him. She looked behind, seeking out Sonya and the sunlounger she'd left her on. She couldn't help but notice her friend was tying a bright yellow scarf around her head, probably to shield her red hair from the scorching sun.

'It is nice to meet you. I hope you enjoy your holiday. There are many sights to see here.' He smiled. 'Perhaps it will make a change from just looking at a piece of metal made by Apple.' He turned away from her.

She baulked. What had he said? Getting himself served before her and now insulting the fact she wanted to communicate with the rest of the world while she was here. Just who did he think he was?

The barman was coming back from the main building, a plastic tray of covered loaves of bread in his arms.

'I need my phone for work,' she stated, feeling compelled to explain herself. 'I have a very important job that requires me to be … here, checking for … things … because if something happens then—'

He looked at her again. 'An earthquake?'

'No. I—'

'A fire?'

'I don't think—'

'A flood then? You must build the arc like Noah? As soon as an email comes through?'

'I—'

'Bread,' Alex interrupted. 'I could spare one more tray but give me a call after three.'

'Perfect,' Andras answered, taking hold of the tray. 'See you tonight?'

'Your mother has not booked every table for wedding guests?' Alex asked him.

He smiled. 'Not yet.'

'Book me in,' Alex replied. 'When I finish here. Ten o'clock.'

Tess watched Andras balance the bread on one arm and wave a hand before turning away and heading off the terrace. What had just happened? This man – what had he said his name was? – had just got the upper hand with her. No one did that, personally or in business. She was always the one in control. She took a breath, looking for her drink that wasn't there.

'Now,' Alex said, picking up his notepad and pen again. 'Two mezes and some bread, yes?'

'And two large cocktails please,' Tess added. 'The stronger the better.' She swallowed. 'And do you have Wi-Fi here?'

'Yes, of course,' Alex smiled. 'When it is working.'

'It's not working?' Tess exclaimed.

'Not today,' Alex admitted. 'But maybe tomorrow.' He busied himself with the drink-making. 'You should try Georgiou's

Taverna for dinner tonight,' he suggested. 'I think you would like it. Dorothea makes a wonderful cuttlefish stew, and there is Wi-Fi.'

'That works?' Tess inquired.

Alex shrugged. 'There is only one way to find out.' He laughed, picking up the metal cocktail shaker. 'It is on the beach, just down the hill.'

# Six

# Taverna Georgiou, Kalami

Andras's mother, Isadora held her hand up in the air and clicked her fingers like she was summoning a Greek god down from the clouds. Then his cousin Marietta gave a little wave. A bottle of wine was in Andras's hands, the stubborn cork making him perspire even more. He turned away from his family's table and concentrated on the job in hand, literally.

'Andras!' Isadora called.

Cringing, his hand tugged at the corkscrew until finally the cork gave way with a satisfying pop. All the staff were fighting their way through a very busy lunchtime service and his mother wasn't helping with her constant need for attention.

'Andras! Come here!' Isadora squawked again.

He couldn't ignore her again. He turned around, offering a smile ... until he saw Papa Yiannis. The local priest was joining the table. In his long black robes, hat and beard almost reaching his midriff, Andras knew that there was going to be wedding talk. He didn't want to face wedding talk. Marietta turned to look at him again, her cheeks a little flushed. There was no escape. He would have to just make it quick.

Taking a deep breath, he moved towards them, with the hope of bringing the conversation to a swift resolution. He needed to focus on the restaurant ... and run some lettuce up to the tortoise he'd installed in his garden and named Hector.

'Mama,' he greeted, offering a smile.

'Did you not hear me calling for you?' Isadora asked him.

'I did hear you but I also heard the shout of Dorothea from the kitchen. We are very busy today,' Andras said. 'Business is good.' He looked at Papa Yiannis then did a double take. *Papa Yiannis*. He hadn't thought of asking a priest for an investment in the restaurant. Were men of the cloth allowed to own stakes in businesses? He could be the perfect candidate: quiet, obviously trustworthy, and in regular employment. He smiled at him. 'How are you, Papa Yiannis?'

'I am well, Andras. It is good to see the restaurant is thriving in these difficult times.'

'Thank you,' Andras said. 'I have plans to make it even more successful next season.'

'Sit down, Andras,' Isadora ordered.

'I cannot sit, Mama. I have customers to serve.' He held out his arms, indicating the full tables and the hubbub of lunchtime going on in their midst.

'Sit, Andras.'

Now the instruction wasn't a request but an order. Arguing would take longer than just doing as he was told. He pulled out the wood and rattan seat and sank down next to Marietta. His cousin hastily reached for a glass and filled it with water, setting it down in front of him.

'You would like some more food?' Andras asked his mother. 'Dessert perhaps? We have Dorothea's peach and vanilla cheesecake you like.'

'Papa Yiannis is here,' Isadora said, smiling at the priest as if they were all in the presence of God himself.

'I know that, Mama, I asked him how he was.' He picked up the water and took a swig.

'He would like to speak with you and Marietta,' Isadora stated.

Andras almost dropped the glass. A little water spilled from his lips. 'What?'

'Where are your manners, Andras? Wipe your mouth,' Isadora said, ripping a serviette from the wooden holder on the centre of the paper cloth-covered table.

He took the offered napkin and dabbed at his lips, mainly to stop himself from saying anything else. What did the local priest have to discuss with him and his cousin? Spiros's earlier comments started to come back to him.

'We are the chief members of the wedding party, Andras,' Marietta told him. 'It is our job to guide Spiros and Kira along their journey this week.'

Guide his brother and his soon-to-be-wife along a wedding journey? It sounded like something straight out of the kind of sickly romance novels that tourists read on the beach. And who was he to be some sort of a relationship guru? He had a failed marriage behind him. The only advice he was going to be able to offer was, *unless you want your heart broken, don't do it.*

'It is important,' Papa Yiannis began, 'that Spiros and Kira are fully supported by their family at this time. For them to understand how serious their vows of marriage will be and to prepare them for their upcoming lives together.'

Andras felt sick. He hadn't signed up for this. He might love his brother and want to be there, standing by his side at the ceremony, but this mentor business was a step too far. He was ill-equipped for it. Or maybe that was the point. Perhaps this was a kind of penance – from his mother and Papa Yiannis – a punishment for getting married in the town hall and not a church.

'Do not look so worried!' Isadora exclaimed, her face smiling. 'I have a list.'

'A list?' He tried to keep his voice even, but everything about this conversation was teasing each tender nerve.

'Cousin Antonia has all the wedding customs that must be performed and we need to help with this,' Marietta stated.

'Mama, of course I want Spiros and Kira's wedding to go smoothly but I run a restaurant and—' Andras began. He seemed to have to repeat himself several times before things actually sunk in. Or not.

'This is not for when you are running the restaurant,' Isadora assured him, her hand patting her tight bun of black hair pinned, like always, to the crown of her head. 'This is for when you *are not* running the restaurant.'

He blinked at his mother. 'But I am *always* running the restaurant.'

'Nonsense! There is down time,' she said, hands flapping. 'Things get quiet here around three or four o'clock, before the evening crowd come in.' She sniffed. 'Do you think I notice nothing?' She paused to swat at a mosquito. 'Then there is after dinner service, and your day off.'

He swallowed. He had one day out of seven away from the restaurant. It had been that way since his father had died. Most of his days off recently had been taken up with something that needed organising for the wedding. As much as he loved his family, he equally loved those few hours of peace. Lately he had been working on long-overdue renovations to his house.

'*One* day, Andras. For your brother's wedding … I cannot believe you would think of being so selfish and not straightaway say yes to this!'

He stayed quiet, knowing he was never going to win this argument.

'I can do most of it myself,' Marietta chipped in. 'But I thought perhaps we could talk about it more, over dinner tonight.'

A sinking feeling took hold of his gut and dived it down like a submarine hurtling towards the seabed. This wasn't just about wedding customs, this was, as his brother had forewarned him, about his mother wanting him paired off with someone she approved of.

'I cannot,' he said quickly. 'I will be running the restaurant.'

'Andras, you have staff,' Isadora interrupted. 'That is what staff are for. And this is an important week for our family.'

He didn't need to be reminded of that. 'I know.'

'Then what is the problem? After the service tonight you will leave your staff to run the restaurant and you will have dinner with Marietta,' Isadora directed.

Marietta topped up his glass of water. 'I will serve the *marithes* you like.'

He shook his head. He couldn't do this. It would be cruel. To go along with this to appease his mother. Agreeing now would give Marietta false hope. She needed to know that he wasn't in the market for a relationship.

'I am sorry, Marietta. We are fully booked for tonight and—'

'And after?' Isadora snapped. 'When you are closed?'

'I am …' What was going to end this conversation if running a restaurant, clearing it up for the next day, tackling the accounts and remembering to order the right amount of bread wasn't going to do it? Papa Yiannis was looking at him like he should start repenting now or end up in hell. 'I'm meeting someone.'

He picked up the water glass and concentrated on rehydrating as the sentence settled in the air.

'Meeting who?' Isadora snapped back.

And that's why he should have thought this through. How could he expect a simple, nondescript 'someone' to suffice when it came to his mother? He could pick one of his friends, perhaps Panos or Vasilis, but he had a feeling Isadora would just dismiss any friend like they were unimportant compared to this wedding of all weddings.

They were all looking at him now, his mother, Marietta, Papa Yiannis. He needed to say something.

'My girlfriend,' Andras rushed out.

The first thing he saw as he set his eyes to the paper table-covering was a water glass falling over and its contents spilling. Marietta quickly got to her feet, swiping up napkins and dabbing the mess.

'There is a lot of noise in here,' Isadora stated, leaning her body closer to him. 'I do not think I heard what you said.'

'Andras said he was to meet a girlfriend,' Papa Yiannis stated for half of the restaurant to hear.

He felt his cheeks heating up under the scrutiny of his mother and the priest. The one word – girlfriend – coming from the mouth of the man of the cloth sounded more like 'hoe'. What had he been thinking?

Isadora's eyes flew to Marietta. 'He does not have a girlfriend.'

'No?' Papa Yiannis asked.

'Of course not!' Isadora continued. 'He works all of the time. He has just said so. And if he had a girlfriend then I would know about it.'

Andras sat there, eyes moving back and forth between each person in turn, watching them react to his words almost as if he were no longer there. He was twenty-eight years old. He should not be treated like he was unable to manage his life on his own. He had started this train of conversation, he might as well get fully on board.

'She does not live here all the time. We have been speaking on the telephone and through email,' Andras spoke.

'What?' Isadora stated. And then her eyes narrowed, dark irises almost completely hidden as the shutters came down. 'She is not *Greek*?'

The words were spat out. He almost felt sorry for this imaginary non-Greek girlfriend he had made up. He shook his head. 'No, she is not Greek. She is ...' His mind somehow decided to go back to the Kalami Cove Apartments, the blonde-haired girl in a jacket, desperate to have a conversation with her iPhone. 'She is English.'

Isadora and Marietta both seemed to inhale like they were going to commence a free-dive. Papa Yiannis made the sign of the cross from left to right on his chest. This was madness. And their behaviour was only fuelling his fire.

'I am sure Marietta can deal with everything on your list, Mama. I really need to get back to work.' Andras stood up quickly.

'You will meet Marietta here, after evening dinner service. Ten o' clock,' Isadora said matter-of-factly.

He furrowed his brow. Had his mother not heard anything he'd said? 'Mama—'

'Do you think I was born in Byzantine times, Andras?' Isadora asked. 'You no more have a girlfriend than Papa Yiannis has a wife!'

The priest had the good grace to make another sign of the cross and pick up a glass of water. Andras stood his ground. 'I *do* have a girlfriend.'

'In England?' Isadora asked.

'Yes.'

'So how then can you be meeting with this woman tonight?'

He swallowed, not enjoying his mother's scrutiny. 'She arrives later.'

'Tonight?'

'Yes.' What was he doing?

'She is coming here,' Isadora continued. 'To the restaurant.'

He gave an uncomfortable nod.

'Good,' Isadora stated. 'Then we can all meet her for dinner. Do you have a photo?'

'A photo?'

'What does she look like?'

Why had he started this? Why hadn't he just agreed to have dinner with Marietta? He could have made it clear he wasn't in the market for a romance over the meal she had planned to make. Now he was having to invent people, make up a relationship that didn't exist and the only person coming to mind was the woman from Kalami Cove.

'She is blonde,' he answered. 'With eyes the colour of the sea.' He swallowed, unable to face Marietta.

Isadora sucked in a long, slow breath. 'Eyes the colour of the sea.'

He nodded. 'Yes.'

'Technology is amazing, isn't it, Papa Yiannis?' Isadora spoke, looking to the priest.

'Oh, yes,' he agreed readily.

'Being able to tell someone's eyes are the colour of the sea from just looking down the telephone.'

Andras smiled. 'Technology has moved on from Byzantine times, Mama. I have a camera on my computer.'

Isadora narrowed her eyes again. 'Well, let me tell you something else you will have if this carries on, Andras. You will have the prospect of your new silent business partner not remaining silent if you lie to me again.' She picked up a fork from the table and squeezed her hand around it. 'Remember what happened to Uncle Dimitri.'

'Andras!' Dorothea's voice calling across the restaurant was his saviour.

He smiled at his mother, nodded to the priest and looked finally to Marietta. 'I will see you tonight,' he said, backing away.

Heading towards the kitchen he started to realise he now had just a few hours to get himself a girlfriend and a handful of days to find a new business partner. Or death-by-Greek-wedding was going to be the only thing on his menu.

# Seven

# Kalami Cove Apartments

'I'm burning, aren't I? Do you think I'm burning? See, if I turn this way ... there's a line – ow – muscle spasm.'

Tess turned her head away from the view of the calming sea to the body of Sonya, now laying on her side, pulling away the skin on one thigh for inspection. Sonya hadn't been able to lie still for a second since they had changed into sunlounger wear. She had twisted and shifted in her new Bettylicious 1950s'-inspired bikini, talking about the heat, asking why the birds flitting to and from the paving around the pool didn't seem to suffer from the high temperatures, and wondering what the weather was doing where Joey was. Apparently battle re-enactment costumes had very little in the way of venting. If that's what he was actually doing. There had been conversation about how Sonya no longer actually knew what he was doing because they were on a break and Tess knew the break was all but breaking her friend's heart.

'Pop a bit more cream on,' Tess suggested. In between the heart-to-hearts she had been trying to find her Zen, except she was sure she would have a better chance of nailing it down if she could just check there were no emails from McKenzie Falconer. She had left the Blackberry Boudoir wine-bar chain portfolio still in limbo over their branding. At the last meeting it was down to a dancing berry as its avatar or a bottle peeping out from behind a sexy-looking curtain. Maybe it wasn't exactly a potential Act of God to avoid, like the annoying Greek guy had poked her with earlier, but it mattered. And in this day and age, there should be accessible Internet connection in all corners of Europe.

'Ooo, look, it's a lizard!'

Tess leapt up off the lounger in less time than it took a traffic warden to arrive when your parking ticket had run out. Sunglasses falling off her face, feet struggling to get into her shoes, she slipped sideways, bottom dropping then quickly connecting with an inflatable doughnut. She sunk down into the hole.

'Oh, Tess, are you all right? Goodness,' Sonya said, trying to get up. 'What happened?'

'That!' Tess exclaimed. 'That brown thing!' She kicked her legs, trying to get up and out of the rubber ring.

'What? Is there something in the pool?' Sonya asked, her eyes darting to the water. 'That child who's been pulling at her swim nappy for the last half an hour?' She tutted. 'I've never been convinced of the elasticity of swim nappies but not being a mother myself I've—'

'The lizard!' Tess interrupted. She eyed it. It was no longer than a Snickers, the width of a KitKat, but it had a bright blue head and it was looking back at her like it wanted to get intimate. God, was this what happened when you pledged to stay single for the summer? The local wildlife smelled a loner from thirty paces?

'It's so cute,' Sonya said. 'I'm going to take a photo of it.'

The lizard advanced, a scurry of six inches or so that had Tess clinging to the doughnut and holding her breath. 'Make it go away,' she breathed.

'Make it go away?' Sonya asked, easing herself off the lounger and picking up her phone. 'Don't be silly. People go out hiking, searching for days to find beautiful little lizards like this. It's one of the reasons Joey and I booked this holiday. Wildlife wherever you look!'

As Sonya's camera on her phone made a click, the lizard shot forward and Tess let out a scream that had everyone around the complex looking her way.

'Tess, you're not scared, are you?' Sonya asked.

'No! Of course not!' Tess answered. She let out another scream as the lizard darted back out from under the table. 'Help me! Get me out of this doughnut!'

'He won't hurt you,' Sonya said, taking another photo of the reptile as she slowly moved towards Tess.

'I'm pretty sure that's what my father said about the horse at pony club just seconds before it tried to savage my cheek.'

Tess swallowed back her fear, remembering her dad, holding her up to the dappled grey gelding. She was four, a novice rider, inquisitive enough to reach out over the stable door to try to pat the horse's nose. In a split second the horse had rounded, knocked her riding hat off her head and tried to bite a chunk out of her face. Only her dad's quick reactions in smacking the horse on the nose and pulling her away stopped the injury turning from bruising to open wound. There were tears over the drama that day but no permanent scars. Completely the opposite to her wedding day. If only her dad had just held her *that* day like he had after the incident with the horse. She took a breath. It had been almost six months since she had last had any contact with either of them. Every time her mum phoned she let it go to voicemail then listened to the 'checking-in' message she just couldn't face hearing live any more. Then, when she was certain her mum wouldn't be home, she left her own message on her answerphone. Still paying off the loans they had taken out to cover the cost and nothing to show for it. Tess knew they would never forgive her. And why should they? She couldn't forgive herself.

'Come on,' Sonya said, holding out her hand. 'Up you get.'

'Where is it? It's not nice when they creep up on you and invade your space,' Tess stated, straightening her sunglasses.

'Your space?' Sonya queried with a laugh. 'You're outside. Outside is *his* space.' She giggled. 'Fresh New Day isn't just an Ambi-Pur fragrance you know.'

Tess picked up her cocktail and put the straw in her mouth. She wasn't outdoorsy, some people just weren't, and there was nothing wrong with that. But if you *were* that way inclined you should really add it as a hobby to your online dating profile. She had wasted three one-night dates on secret outdoorsy men. There had even been one who felt the need to talk about the workings of a cow's stomachs during a steak dinner.

'So,' Sonya began, sitting back down on the sunlounger and putting her phone on the table. 'What are we going to do tonight?'

'Hopefully not hiking through the mountain looking for rare species of reptile.'

'Well, my thoughts were that we check out one of the cute little tavernas there's meant to be on the beach and spend the evening just sitting back, relaxing, taking it all in, you know, filling ourselves with something Greek.'

Tess swallowed. Yes, her immediate thoughts to the words 'filling ourselves with something Greek' meant she really did need to get back on the metaphorical horse – not the vicious grey from pony club. She needed to find some sort of companionship distraction despite this ridiculous all-girl rule. Alex at the bar said the restaurant the queue-jumper worked at had Wi-Fi. That would allow her to sift through potential mates ready for her return to London, and perhaps, if she was careful – when Sonya wasn't looking – there might be someone able to provide a little flirtation action. It had been over a week since the proposal. She needed to know her pheromones were still giving off 'no strings attached' rather than 'desperately seeking a husband'.

'There's a taverna called … something beginning with "G" that's supposed to be good,' Tess stated, sitting back down.

'Is there?' Sonya asked. 'Have you been reading my Marco Polo?'

Tess looked at her quizzically. 'The barman told me.'

Sonya laughed. 'Sorry, it's just Joey and me had this joke about guidebooks.' She sighed. 'He would hide them right before a trip and I'd call out "Marco" and he would say "Polo" until I got close and …' Sonya stopped, tears filling her eyes. 'Obviously, we didn't get to play that game this time.'

'Stop,' Tess said. 'Put your cocktail straw in your mouth and stop.' She picked up Sonya's drink and pushed it towards her. 'I propose we lay here a little bit longer, peacefully, letting the sun and that sea breeze gently rock us into maybe a little bit of a sleep …' She watched Sonya's eyelids drop slightly. 'Then we get showered and changed and head out for some Greek food and even more drink.'

Sonya sighed, putting down her cocktail glass. 'That's a good idea. I am a bit tired from the journey. Travelling does make you tired, doesn't it?' She yawned.

'You lie back and relax,' Tess said, her hand snaking down into her bag. If Sonya nodded off for half an hour she was almost sure she could shake some life out of a GPRS signal and peruse some potential mates on Hooked Up. Or she could find a site she hadn't tried before, maybe use a different name, like Patricia.

'If I drop off,' Sonya said, closing her eyes, her voice thick with tiredness, 'you have to promise me you won't fall in any more doughnuts.'

Tess smiled. 'I promise.'

'And no dating apps,' Sonya whispered, voice close to sleep.

*What?* Tess swallowed. Perhaps if she held off answering right away Sonya would slip into a snooze and she wouldn't have to say anything.

'Did you hear me?'

*Shit.* 'Mmm ... I heard you.'

'And no flirting with the barman either,' Sonya added. 'Although he does have a lovely smile.'

'Looking's allowed, I remember,' Tess answered.

She took her hand out of her bag and focused again on the beautiful view of the coastline. Two sail boats, their multi-coloured sails waving in the light breeze, moved across the ocean like a pair of elegant skaters on ice. Tess knew that keeping single shouldn't be this hard but she was the self-styled Queen of the Dating Scene. Without that OCD need to have someone on her arm, she wasn't sure who she was any more. And that was the biggest problem of all.

# Eight

# Taverna Georgiou

'I need a girlfriend,' Andras stated. 'And she has to have blue eyes.'

A bead of perspiration rolled across his forehead as he pulled off his shoes and settled himself down on the wooden dock next to his brother, feet hanging just above the sparkling water.

Spiros looked up. 'Am I supposed to laugh now, Andras?'

He shook his head. 'No. I am serious.' He pulled in a breath.

'You need a girlfriend,' Spiros said again. 'After eighteen months of showing no interest in anyone whenever we have been out, now you want someone?'

'Yes. No. Not really.' He was going to have to spell it out. 'You were right about Mama's plans with Marietta.' He dipped a toe into the water. 'They started talking about dinners and being together for things to do with the wedding and ...' He lowered his voice. 'Papa Yiannis was there.'

'Papa Yiannis was there?' Spiros stated. 'He was supposed to be meeting with me earlier and he did not come to the house.'

'I'm sorry?' Andras offered.

'You think you have problems?' Spiros said, shaking out the two large sheets of paper in his hands. 'Look at these.'

Andras observed the paper, eyes trying to scrutinise the text written on them, bright sunlight preventing their reading. 'What are they?'

'What are they? he says.' Spiros shook his head. 'I take it you did not have these for *your* wedding.'

Andras swallowed. 'You know that Mama did not want to acknowledge my wedding.'

'These are my rules,' Spiros continued. 'This list' – he shook his left hand – 'are all the things I have to do before the wedding.' He shook the paper in his right hand. 'This list, much longer, are all the things I must make sure I do *not* do before the wedding.'

'You would like me to look at them?' Andras offered. He no more had the time to look at this than he had the time to have dinner with Marietta but, for now, his staff were handling the late-afternoon crowd.

'No! *I* don't even want to look at them!' Spiros announced, his bare feet splashing in the water.

'OK,' Andras said. 'We can do one of two things here.'

'Go on.'

'We can either begin to go through these lists or we can find me a temporary girlfriend.'

Spiros looked at him. 'I don't understand. What do you need a temporary girlfriend for?' he asked. 'Just spend some time with Marietta this week, then when the wedding is over things will die down.'

'I can't do that now,' Andras told him.

'Why not?'

'Because …' He knew how stupid this was going to sound. He sunk his feet a little lower into the water. 'Because I told

Mama, and Marietta, and Papa Yiannis ... that I have a girlfriend.'

'What?!' Spiros exclaimed. 'Are you out of your mind?'

'It gets worse,' Andras added.

'How could it?'

'I said she was English.'

Spiros slapped his own forehead, one of the papers fluttering out of his grasp and floating down towards the sea. Andras reached out, grabbing it quickly and pressing it to his chest to flatten the creases.

'You are crazy. You lied to Mama, and to our priest!' Spiros exclaimed. 'Do you have a death wish?'

'Not at the moment. Because if I die now, I fear I would end up straight down past the Earth's core.'

'Well, you just have to tell the truth. Before it's too late.'

Andras shook his head. 'No. I just have to find someone English with blonde hair and blue eyes who can pretend to be my girlfriend for ... a short while.' His thoughts kept going to the woman he had met at Alex's apartments. The person he had somehow immediately thought of when he was creating this make-believe girlfriend. He didn't even know her name.

'Andras, it is almost my wedding,' Spiros began. 'I have these lists-to-do and lists-to-not-do, and you want me to find you a fake girlfriend with blonde hair.'

'And blue eyes,' Andras added. 'Who is English.'

'As I said: crazy!' Spiros threw his hands up in the air.

'Please, Spiros, anything you want.' He seemed to be saying that a lot lately and having nothing to back it up. 'Help me with this.'

Spiros shook his head.

'You know English people,' Andras continued. 'Kira knows English people from her work cooking with the villa company.'

'Andras ...' Spiros began.

'It's just for a week, until after the wedding.'

Spiros shook his head. 'You are talking about a holidaymaker. Someone who has come to Corfu to relax, to get away from it all.' Spiros kicked his toes at the water. 'Why would someone on holiday want to spend a portion of it pretending to be your girlfriend?'

He sighed. Spiros made an excellent point and he had no reply. This was, of course, a mad idea. He should know better. He *did* know better. And he was being selfish. Thinking about his own somehow-turned-ridiculous agenda and not his brother's wedding. He needed to just refocus, remember what was important, and keep pretending everything was all right. He looked out over the bay. Sunlight was dappling the aquamarine water; tiny silver fish darted about, just visible against the stones. He was still here. Almost still completely intact. That was the most important thing.

'You are OK?' Spiros asked him.

He nodded. 'Sure.'

Spiros let out a sigh. 'Well, Andras, your problem might be that you need a girlfriend, but according to this list, I need to find a donkey.'

'What?'

'One must be ridden to the ceremony and I must bond with it.'

'Are you serious?'

'Why would I joke about a donkey?!'

His brother was verging on sounding asylum-ready. He needed to take some of Spiros's burden away.

'I'll find one for you,' Andras said, patting his brother's shoulder. 'But, until then … it may not be big enough for anyone to ride, but you could definitely bond with it.' He smiled. 'I still have the tortoise.'

# Nine

# Kalami Cove Apartments

There was no air conditioning in their apartment. How Sonya and Joey could even have considered booking anywhere in Greece in July without air conditioning Tess didn't know. The furnishings were simple. Twin beds made with clean sheets and a light, contemporary biscuit-coloured cover, a wardrobe and a small dressing table with a stool that wobbled slightly when you sat on it. A small kitchenette area – two hob rings, a kettle, toaster and fridge – was at the other end, together with the shower room. The walls throughout were painted white and there was seemingly unnecessary double glazing with dark green shutters meant to keep it cooler. Despite having a tepid shower and dressing in a light gauze sundress, she was starting to perspire again.

It was so hot she had almost considered not wearing make-up. When was the last time she had done that? Watching Sonya touch up her cheeks with bronzing balls and a brush with more tufts than Donald Trump, she remembered exactly when the last time was. The day after the wedding. Her non-wedding. And the no-make-up-wearing had continued for a month afterwards. Not even a fingertip of BB cream. She shuddered. She was never going to let herself get like that ever again. That was why men were kept for nights at Nando's and nothing more permanent.

'By the end of this holiday I might not even need bronzer,' Sonya stated, turning her head left and right as she checked out her reflection in the mirror. 'I definitely think I'm looking less Draco Malfoy and more ... Quaker Oats with brown sugar mixed in.'

Tess smiled. It was so good to see Sonya looking a little happier.

'But, do I smell?' Sonya asked with a sniff. 'I think I smell. Can you smell me?' She lifted her arm and smelled her armpit. 'I've doused myself in a spritz with bergamot I picked up in Neal's Yard but ... well, what do you think?' Sonya offered her armpit towards Tess.

'I think I really don't want to smell your armpit.'

Sonya dropped her arm and pulled at the collar of her Grecian blue skater-style dress. 'It's warm, isn't it?'

'There's no air conditioning,' Tess pointed out.

'No, I know,' Sonya answered with a sigh. 'That's a Joey thing.'

'A Joey thing?' Tess queried.

'He's never been keen on artificial air,' Sonya stated, trying to unlatch the shutters that led to their small, ground-floor terraced area outside. They'd discovered earlier it had a view of the beautifully kept gardens and a sliver of sea in the distance.

'Artificial air?' Tess repeated. She was definitely getting to know Joey a whole lot more on this break without him even being here. He wasn't much of a talker on nights out, but a man who liked pizza and Ed Sheeran had to be OK, didn't he? And Sonya obviously thought so. Maybe she should have paid more attention.

'Not real air,' Sonya elaborated. 'You know, like fans, electric heaters, and air conditioning, obviously.' She sighed. 'I bought him one of those little masks for the flight, you know, the ones Japanese people wear on the Underground.'

All air, artificial or otherwise, was being sucked from the room and only hot, stifling waves of heat were left. Tess looked at Sonya struggling with the latch of the balcony door and she moved.

'It just won't open,' Sonya rasped. 'And I'm melting like that witch in *The Wizard of Oz*!'

'Me too,' Tess answered. 'Which one of us is going to turn to fizzing liquid first?' She tugged at the clasp until finally it moved, shooting up and out and allowing her to push the slatted wooden doors open. A blast of even hotter air, like someone had opened an oven in the Great British Bake Off tent, hit her. Determined not to be outdone, she made for the outside anyway, heading for the corner of the patio in shade.

'It's hot out here too,' Sonya remarked. 'It's hot, isn't it?'

'We need a fan,' Tess agreed. 'We should ask at reception.'

'Joey says that all fans do is blow stale air at you.'

'Right now I'm worried if we *don't* have stale air blown at us overnight we might not make the morning.'

'I'm dripping,' Sonya said. 'Under my arms, the backs of my knees ... higher up ...'

'Why don't you get us some bottled water out of the fridge,' Tess suggested. She hovered over one of the wooden chairs, wondering if sitting would make her cooler ... or worse. As her new heels were already pinching her toes she decided to sit as Sonya went back into the room destined for the kitchen area.

Tess gazed across the lawn to thick, lush grass so much tougher-looking than the light, skinny fronds of grass back home. Cream-coloured urns filled with reds, pinks and mauves were dotted around the lawns, all looking vibrant and showing no signs of wilting in the heat like her. Would this have been a little like Menorca? The colour and the sea she remembered from the brochures she had looked at with Adam, but he had made the final choice of hotel, said he'd wanted to surprise her. Something still niggled that perhaps, even then, six months before, he had been having doubts about the wedding, and their relationship. Had the honeymoon ever really been booked? And why was she thinking about this now? She blew out a breath. Obviously because of this ridiculous Internet starvation and the promise to Sonya to not hook up while she was here. And who knew what was going on at work. The whole Blackberry Boudoir empire could have been blown apart like a house of cards from a really strong sneeze. She should have got the branding signed off before she left. But they wouldn't make a decision without her, would they? Unless … Craig, the new guy, was super keen and he had been sniffing around her at the water cooler. She shivered in the heat. As soon as she had Internet connection she would call Russell and check in. Checking in didn't make you a work obsessive. It just made you conscientious, and everyone wanted 'conscientious' on their CV.

'I've got the water, and there was a bottle of wine in the fridge with a little note about it being a welcome gift.'

Sonya put both bottles on the table and retrieved two tumblers from underneath her armpit before plonking them down as well. Tess was reaching for the alcohol before she thought too much about where the glass had just been resting.

'So, here we are,' Sonya said, settling herself in a seat. 'In Corfu.' She sighed. 'In Greece.'

'Yes,' Tess answered. 'And is it everything you'd hoped for?'

She immediately regretted her words. Of course it wasn't what her best friend had hoped for. Sonya had been hoping for a break with Joey, getting into Roundhead positions too saucy for the re-enactment battlefield.

'Sorry,' Tess said quickly. 'That was a really stupid thing to say given the circumstances.' She went to carry on, to add that she wished she was Joey but then stopped herself. What would a life be without a little artificial air sometimes?

'That's OK,' Sonya said. 'I know what you meant.' She sighed. 'And it's been almost twenty-seven minutes since I reached up to my chest to find my almost-engagement necklace wasn't there.' Her fingers scrabbled towards her décolletage.

Tess grabbed her hand, steadying it down towards the wine glass on the table. 'I'm going to fill these glasses up and we're going to look out at that view and think about nothing else but the here and now.' She unscrewed the cap on the bottle and poured the wine. 'And *tomorrow*,' she added. 'We can plan for tomorrow.' She pushed a glass towards Sonya then picked hers up, swigging back the cool alcohol. It was good. It was sweet and soft with notes of pear and apple.

Sonya smiled, leaning an elbow on the table. 'Well, what me and Joey were—'

'Tch, tch, tch, tch,' Tess broke in like Judge Rinder. 'We don't need to mention his name every five seconds.'

'I wasn't. I was just saying that me and Joey—'

'Girl power?' Tess stated. 'Two singles for the summer?'

Sonya frowned. 'I can't even talk about Joey *at all*?'

'Not unless you let me go on my dating app.'

Sonya folded her arms across her chest. 'That's not fair.'

'No?'

'No, because you're not having a relationship crisis,' Sonya reminded her. 'You're not the one whose soulmate has asked for space.'

Tess swallowed. No, her soulmate just hadn't turned up. He'd left her in a wedding car, doing circuits of the ring road while the chauffeur hummed Richard Marx's 'Right Here Waiting'.

'Sorry!' Sonya exclaimed, hands going to her face, expression a mix of horror and exasperation. 'I didn't mean that.'

Tess smiled. 'Listen to us. What are either of us doing thinking about stuff back in England when there's a whole beach of possibility just down there.' She pointed towards the scene with her wine glass, liquid sloshing out and on to the table.

'We should find a man,' Sonya blurted out, slugging back some wine and shaking her head like the alcohol content had stung her.

'Um ... the boyfriend-who-must-not-be-named ... me not allowed to sneak a look at Hooked Up ... remember?'

'I meant a man to show us around. A *guide* man! Yes!' Sonya banged her hand on the table. 'Ouch, RSI ...' She cupped one hand with the other. 'So, in Barbados, where my mum and dad went, there were these lovely little men all in air conditioned Mercedes who would take you around the island for a good price. You know, the fish markets, the best dirty restaurants ...'

'Did you say "dirty"?'

'Dirty in a good way. Local and authentic,' Sonya added. 'Where the islanders eat.' She sipped her wine. 'And he told them all the stories, you know, who had an affair with which celebrity when they came to town ... how Rihanna was his third cousin ... who was murdered where ...'

'You want us to find someone to drive us around Corfu telling us where the killings happened?'

Sonya's eyes widened. 'Or we could do it by boat!' She clapped her hands together. 'Wouldn't that be lovely? Slipping into the little coves, looking for dolphins, eating ...'

'Where the dirty locals eat.'

Sonya laughed and flapped a hand. 'The way my perspiration is going I'm halfway to being a dirty local myself!'

Tess smiled. 'Me too.' She took a sip of her wine and sat back in her chair. 'OK. Let's do it. Let's find a guide man.'

'Ooo, it's so exciting!'

Tess held her wine glass up. 'To finding a guide man.'

Sonya chinked her glass and giggled. 'And getting dirty.'

'Sonya!'

'What?' She sipped at her drink. 'I meant eating goat intestines or whatever the Greek delicacies are, not seeking out a sex shop!'

'Amen, sister. Here's to Greek delicacies.'

# Ten

# Taverna Georgiou

It was a beautiful evening and, as Andras waited for his kitchen staff to be ready with the next dishes to serve, he took a moment to admire the view through the open frontage of his restaurant. Some small boats were tied up to the pontoon, bobbing gently with the tide, while half a dozen larger yachts – some white, some grey – had dropped anchor further out. The sky was still cloudless with only a breath of wind in the air. Despite everything, this place was still perfect.

'So, where is she?'

He snapped his attention back to the restaurant and the sharp whisper in his ear. Isadora was at his back.

'Mama—'

'Your girlfriend,' Isadora continued. 'The one with eyes the colour of the sea.'

There was mocking in her tone that pressed all his buttons. This was how she had been with Elissa. The woman he had fallen hard for, fought for, married. The woman who had broken his heart. Elissa was Greek, but despite that tick in the box with his mother, nothing else had endeared her to Isadora. Elissa spoke her mind. Isadora's old-fashioned views had clashed head on with his wife's, as he had always known they would, and he had not cared. He had admired her free spirit – it had been what had drawn him to her in the first place – but he hadn't counted on that being the thing that would eventually separate them.

'She is not here yet,' he found himself saying.

'So she is coming?' Isadora asked, the words a little breathy.

He nodded. 'Unless she is delayed for some reason. You know how flights are.' He saw movement from the kitchen out of the corner of his eye and took a step to the side. 'While we are waiting, perhaps concentrate on Kira's Uncle Timon,' he said. 'He is on his third glass of retsina already.'

He made to move off until his mother gripped his arm and drew him close.

'*You* should concentrate on Marietta,' Isadora told him. 'She will make the perfect wife.'

'I agree,' he responded, waiting for the look of delight to cross his mother's face. 'But not for me.' He smiled, regained control of his arm, and moved away.

# Eleven

# Kalami Beach

'Can we walk a little bit slower?' Tess asked.

She was out of breath already and her toes were being squashed like she was an Ugly Sister trying to force her foot into the petite glass slipper.

'If we walk a bit slower we'll just be standing,' Sonya answered with a laugh. 'Ah, look, we're here now. On the beach.' She took a big breath in. 'It soothes your soul, doesn't it?' She expelled the air. 'Can you feel it soothing your soul?'

No, she couldn't. The only thing Tess could feel was her feet on fire, the skin practically hissing and spitting as her Zanotti's pinched harder than a too-tight bra strap.

'I'm going to roll that sand and those stones under my feet,' Sonya announced.

Tess watched as her friend slipped off the flat sandals she was wearing, picked them up and proceeded to stamp her soles on to the stony beach. Why hadn't she worn flat shoes? The answer was because she didn't own any flat shoes, apart from a pair of cowboy boots, but even they had a Cuban heel. Still, there was nothing stopping her from unlatching her buckles, releasing her feet from the designer traps and setting her bare toes into the sand right here and now. Except that it was one thing she never did. She *always* wore shoes. The only places she didn't have something on her feet were the shower – her own shower at least – and bed. She felt unsettled without shoes, like the Earth was going to suddenly spin the other way if she kicked them off. She swallowed as she watched Sonya padding down towards the water. Her friend was carefree, despite what was going on with her relationship back home. She was living completely in the moment. Tess gingerly put one foot to the beach. Never mind barefoot, she could do this *in* shoes.

'Oh! This water!' Sonya exclaimed. 'It's like liquid paradise!' She turned her head. 'Come on in, Tess!'

She waved a hand and trod forward, teetering on to a large white pebble, heel sinking into the ground. It was like trying to navigate jelly with rock-hard pieces of Daim bar in it. She tried again, lifting her foot up and out of the grainy floor then pitching it back down in a location she deemed almost flat. She felt secure for a mere second before a tiny white crab scuttled over her toes.

She let out a scream, stamping her other foot and only succeeding in getting a collection of small stones that felt like glass into her strappy shoes. She hated stones almost as much as she hated small animals that crawled.

'Shall I come and get you?' Sonya called.

Tess shook her head, eyes darting among the sand and shingle for any sign of the crab, or its mother. 'No, I'm OK here.' She wasn't OK. She was unbalanced, spiky slivers of rock under her soles, and the tops of her exposed shoulders were being seared like a steak on the grill at a Beefeater. Suddenly she longed for London. London with its actual pavements and restaurants you didn't have to walk down hills to get to.

'Look at the view!' Sonya said. 'It's just so … perfect.'

Her friend's enthusiasm stirred something in her. She was being desperately closed to this new situation she found herself in instead of embracing it. In a few minutes, she was going to be sitting in a lovely taverna, some sweet white wine topping up the half bottle she had drunk at the apartment, there would be fresh, delicious Greek food on the menu and ... Wi-Fi.

She looked out at the sea, the sun turning it different shades of blue – turquoise in some places, a deeper, richer, navy in others. This holiday was going to be what *she* made it. And her primary reason for being here was to spend time with Sonya and help her friend manage the fallout from Joey's sudden need not to be part of a couple. This could be good for Sonya. It could be good for her too. She closed her eyes, letting the sun heat up her cheeks, its strength restoring a little courage. She opened her eyes again and called to her friend.

'Come on! Let's go and eat something ending in "a".'

# Twelve

# Taverna Georgiou

'Oh, look, Tess,' Sonya exclaimed. 'Look at the gorgeous flowers, and the cute little wooden tables, and the little itty-bitty matching chairs, and the adorable little shells pushed into the walls!' Sonya drew in an excited breath as they approached the restaurants along the beach. 'I want to touch them. Don't you just want to touch them? They're like little—'

'Greek dolls' houses?' Tess offered.

She looked up at the olive-wood-carved sign hanging from the entrance stating 'Georgiou'. It was simple, very Greek. All it needed to perfect the rustic charm was some checked table-cloths and dancers in costume shouting, '*Opa!*' There were candles glowing in the centre of the tables and Tess could see that wine was being served in rose-gold coloured flagons. She'd never had wine from a flagon before.

Sonya inhaled loudly through both nostrils. 'I can smell everything.' She turned back to Tess. 'I want to *try* everything! All at once!'

Tess wobbled on her shoes as she hurried towards the small strip of concrete outside the restaurant just in front of three steps leading to the entrance. She needed one of the little itty-bitty chairs to rest up on and stop her toes from disintegrating.

'*Kalispera.*'

'Hello,' Sonya greeted.

Tess looked up. It was the dark-haired man she had met earlier, looking even better than she remembered. He was wearing a black shirt, the sleeves rolled up past his elbows, exposing a rather fine length of just the right type of forearm – strong, firm, showing definition in motion. Dark, well-fitting trousers covered the rest of him. She suddenly remembered his name.

'Sonya, this is Mandras,' she introduced.

'The one who needed bread and delayed my meze,' Sonya said, shaking a finger in mock annoyance. '*Yassou*, Mandras, it's lovely to meet you. I'm Sonya.' She held out her hand.

He shook Sonya's hand then looked to Tess with a smile. 'It is nice to meet you, Sonya. And my name … it is *A*ndras. No "M", like the character in Captain Corelli.'

Tess's shoes pinched a little more as she shuffled forward, following her friend's lead.

'Do you have a table for two? Gosh, you're very busy,' Sonya remarked, surveying the inside of the restaurant as she moved up the first step.

'Most of these people are my family,' Andras informed her. 'There is a wedding here soon.' He smiled. 'Come, Victor will find you one of our best tables with a view of the sea.' He held his arm out to direct them to a nearby waiter clutching a pair of menus.

Tess stepped forward and, as she did so, Andras moved to block her way, ducking his face close, his mouth near to her ear, so near her skin responded by breaking out in goosebumps. This was obviously some sort of Tinder-withdrawal cold turkey.

'What is your name?'

She turned her head, just enough to increase her personal space, and meet his eyes with hers. She smiled, holding his gaze before replying, 'I'll tell you my name, if you tell me your Wi-Fi code.'

His wide, thick lips, ludicrously heavy on the Cupid's bow, moved wider into a smile as his head nodded. 'You still have not found out if you must save the UK from a plague of locusts or other disaster.'

Tess smiled. 'The code.'

'Georgiou123.'

She snorted. 'I could probably have guessed that.'

'No one said it was a secret,' he replied. 'Wi-Fi is free for all restaurant guests.' He pointed to a large chalkboard on the traditional stone wall. 'The code is on the board up there.'

'Thank you,' she answered, preparing to move past him.

He reached out, his hand touching the bare skin of her arm and drawing her back towards him. He was so close now their bodies were almost touching. She realised she was enjoying that a little too much. If only Sonya hadn't imposed this stupid rule she could be getting busy with Mr Greek Adonis for a few nights of no strings fun. He *was* hot.

'And your name?' he asked. 'Is that to remain a secret?'

His hand lingered on her arm, his fingers brushing down her skin until her fine blonde hairs had no choice but to react, sending shivers right the way through her. She was losing control to him again. This simply didn't happen.

She leant forward, bringing her mouth close to his ear and whispered. 'It's Patricia.' She drew back and winked. 'But you can call me Trix.'

He smiled. 'I like it,' he said softly.

And then he drew her towards him, kissing her on the cheek. Except this was no faint air kiss you might reserve for a client you had been helping for the past couple of years or a distant relative you only saw at family funerals – this was full contact. Both lips meeting a cheek with absolute intention. And, as he finally drew back, extending his arm to point out Sonya and the waiter moving into a table overlooking the water, Tess was hot. *Very* hot. And slightly giddy. On the plus side, she could no longer feel the pain in her toes.

She moved her feet forward and pins and needles took hold, distracting her from the head-rush that was threatening to take over her whole body. This was pure lust. The last time she had experienced that so quickly was with Erik the scaffolder when, for her pleasure, he'd hung by one arm from a red-brick semi-detached.

Now Sonya was looking at her. She walked towards her friend, stealing one last glance over her shoulder at Andras. He was chatting to a group of people at a table with what looked like a whole octopus at its centre. Those trousers were cut to perfection over glutes she would definitely be dreaming about tonight. She faced Sonya again. Her friend's hand was already navigating around the bottom of her neck seeking that pendant. She hurried forward to join her.

'So, Mama, she is here,' Andras stated, leaning over his mother's shoulder and replenishing her glass of wine.

Isadora put down the lobster claw she was working on and sucked at her fingers. 'Who is here?'

'My girlfriend,' Andras said. 'Patricia.'

'Where? Show me.' Isadora was up and out of her chair quicker than a superyacht overtaking a Minoan ferry. He should have accounted for that. He was being too ambitious here.

He quickly took hold of his mother's arm. 'You can't go over there.'

Isadora remained standing, folding her arms across her chest. 'Why not?' Her black eyes held his until he had to look away. Victor was presenting Sonya and Patricia with menus. He needed to think on his feet.

'She has brought someone with her.'

'Her mother?' Isadora questioned.

He shook his head. 'A client. A very important client from her business in the UK.'

'Where?' Isadora asked.

His mother then turned her attention to every single diner in the restaurant, scanning each one as if she could learn their inner workings and secrets just with one glance.

'Table nine,' Andras answered with a swallow.

He watched his mother focus in on Sonya and Patricia.

'After dinner,' he began. 'When they have finished talking business I am sure—'

'You will be meeting with Marietta,' Isadora ended, plumping back down into her seat. 'And you will send this Patricia to me.'

His throat dried up and he countered the anxiety by adjusting the flagon of wine on the table. 'Of course.' He smiled. 'She can't wait to meet you.'

Isadora clapped her hands together. 'Wake up, Timon!' she shouted at Kira's uncle whose eyes were closing. 'We have much to get through.'

He needed to think of something and quickly. He only had two options now. Get Patricia out of the restaurant straight after her meal and beg her never to come back, or ask for her help. Spiros caught his eye and his brother held up the two lists like scrolls brought down from Mount Olympus. Right now he wasn't sure whose shoes he would rather be in.

# Thirteen

The view was spectacular: candy-pink bougainvillea trailing from the whitewood latticework that framed the window, the golden sand and stone beach, the bobbing boats tethered to the jetty and that forget-me-not-coloured sea barely moving, the tide a gentle back and forth, trickling over the shoreline.

Tess looked back to her phone, the pinwheel still going round and round searching for a connection to 'Georgiou Taverna Free'. Why did technology seem to be so difficult here? It was fine on the coach. Did they just happen to be booked into the Internet blackspot of the island?

'Oh! I'm going to have saganaki to start with,' Sonya announced. 'No, no wait … I'm going to have *dolmades*, that's vine leaves and rice and herbs and—'

Tess pushed her phone to one side. 'But neither of those end with the letter "a",' she teased.

'Oh my! You're right! So, I'd better have … taramasalata.'

Tess looked at the menu hoping there were no scallops. As much as she adored them, she still couldn't face anything involving a shell just yet.

'So, you didn't mention the guy you had a spat with at the apartments was hotter than peri-peri sauce.' Sonya leant over the table, hitching her red head to the right as Andras moved through the restaurant.

'Sonya Culkin!' Tess exclaimed.

'Just looking, that's all,' Sonya stated, reaching for the water jug and pouring herself a glass. 'I'm not silly enough to think that Joey doesn't—'

'Tch tch tch tch!' Tess interrupted, finger to her lips.

'Sorry, but there was actually this one woman dressed as Maid Marion at the Robin Hood Day last month he looked at for quite a long time.' She sighed again. 'And I'm not talking about her wimple here.'

Tess's eyes went to Andras, balancing plates up those impressive forearms, moving his athletic limbs effortlessly between tables. How much wine was she going to have to get Sonya to drink before she reneged on the single thing?

'OK, we should order some wine,' Sonya said as if reading Tess's mind. 'Where did our little waiter go?' She elongated her body upwards, eyes seeking. 'He had nice eyes too, if I was looking.'

Tess looked back to her phone and pressed the screen. Still nothing was happening on the Wi-Fi front. She turned the Wi-Fi button to off. She was just going to have to phone the office tomorrow. Make up some excuse as to why she needed to speak to Russell. Then, when she knew Blackberry Boudoir was sorted, she could relax a little bit more.

'Here he comes,' Sonya announced, waving her hand in the air as Victor approached. She smiled as the waiter stopped and took out his notepad. 'Could we order some white wine?'

Tess watched her friend's cheeks flood with colour and her heavy mascaraed eyes begin a dance like two horny butterflies preparing to mate. Just how precarious *was* her relationship with Joey? Maybe there was more to this break business than met the eye.

'White wine in one of those gorgeous flagons,' Sonya continued.

'Dragons?' Victor questioned, looking confused.

Sonya laughed, her cheeks reddening further, a finger curled around a loose tendril of her auburn hair. 'One of those jugs. The gold-coloured ones.'

Victor laughed and nodded. '*Karáfa.*'

'Oh! Like carafe! Silly me!'

'No,' Victor answered. 'Not silly.' He smiled. 'Very beautiful. *Ómorfi.*'

Before Sonya could start to melt from the attention, Tess interjected. 'Do you have Dr Pepper?' She swallowed. 'To go with the wine?'

'You are not well?' Victor asked, looking slightly alarmed.

Sonya laughed. 'It's a drink.'

'I do not think we have this here,' Victor answered.

Tess sighed. This was Greece, not some tiny uninhabited island cut off from the rest of civilisation. She should be able to get a well-known brand of soft drink and an Internet connection.

'I will ask the boss if he knows of this,' Victor said.

'Thank you.'

He left the table.

'Do you really need Dr Pepper?' Sonya asked.

'I'd quite like one.'

'But we're having wine,' Sonya said.

'I know. I just could do with a sugar rush.'

'Then have a Coke,' Sonya said. 'Coke is on the drinks menu.'

'Why are you cross? Because I made Victor leave while you were flirting with him?'

'I wasn't!'

'Eyelashes batting like a hovering hawk.'

'We're allowed to look,' Sonya reminded her. 'We said we were allowed to look.'

Tess made a grab for Sonya's hands and held them tightly in hers. 'Something isn't right,' she began. 'I think this is way, way more than too many visits to Dunelm Mill, Son, isn't it?'

'No,' Sonya breathed out, shoulders shaking.

'You're keeping something back about Joey.'

'Tch, tch, tch, tch,' Sonya mimicked, averting her eyes and dropping them to the tablecloth.

'You have to tell me everything,' Tess stated. 'Please, Sonya. I want to know what you're worrying so much about.'

Sonya shook her head, emotion looking like it was about to brim over. 'Joey promised me, when I asked him, that it had nothing to do with it but ... I've been churning it all over since we got here and ... I don't think I believe him.' A tear snaked out of her eye. 'I mean, I know it was quite a while ago but ...' She sniffed. 'He just came right on out with it and I didn't know what to say. Well, I did know what to say – I practically recited the whole Collins English dictionary rather than talk about the subject he'd just dropped in there, completely unannounced.'

'Came right on out with what?' Tess asked, still holding Sonya's hands.

'There was no build up. No gentle questioning. It just happened, one day, when we were halfway through a spicy cheese-feast stuffed crust, you know, the new ones that burst with the little jalapenos and scotch bonnets—'

'Sonya, what did he say?' Tess demanded.

There was a sharp intake of breath and then: 'He said ... he said he'd changed his mind. He said how nice it might be to have a baby.'

Tess just stared at her friend, unblinking, almost waiting for the punchline.

'Say something,' Sonya whispered, squeezing Tess's hands this time.

Tess swallowed. 'Are you sure he said "baby"?'

'Yes.'

'Not "Jay-Z"?'

'No.'

'Or "pup-py"?'

'Why would he say Jay-Z or puppy?'

Tess shrugged. 'I don't know. I'm just thinking you misheard. That he didn't say—' She didn't really want to say it again.

'Baby,' Sonya stated. 'You can say "baby".'

'I don't want to say it,' Tess said.

'*I* should have said it though, shouldn't I?' Sonya spoke. 'I should have said it a long time ago, at the very beginning, but he said from the start that he didn't *want* a family and so I thought I didn't *have* to say it, and now he's changed his mind and we're on this break and I *still* haven't said it.' She sighed. 'And I need to. Don't I need to now? So he can make a proper decision about us ... about me.'

'Sonya ...'

'Because that's got to be it, hasn't it? Not Dunelm Mill. And if it is then we're never getting back together.'

'Sonya ...'

'Because a baby is the one thing I can never give anyone.'

Tess swallowed the lump in her throat and gave her friend's hand another squeeze. 'Oh, Sonya.'

'I'm stupid,' she sniffed. 'I've been stupid to think I could carry on pretending—'

'Not pretending,' Tess stated. 'Just not wearing a badge telling the world you can't have children.'

'But Joey isn't a stranger on the Tube. Joey's my boyfriend. My long-term boyfriend.' She sighed. 'I should have known this was going to happen.' She threw her arms up in the air.

'I *did* know it was going to happen. I mean, that's what people do, isn't it? They fall in love, they get married, they have children ...'

'He told you he didn't want children. And anyway, you know there are other options to having children rather than the traditional method.'

'No one wants that!'

'That's not true,' Tess said straightaway. 'I mean, look at ... look at Elton John.'

'And you tell me how he and David Furnish were ever going to be able to go down the traditional route!'

She swallowed. She was making a complete mess out of this when she should be doing so much better. Sonya had confessed her inability to have children to draw out Tess's jilted-at-the-altar past over those margaritas. A secret for a secret. Two sad stories that had bonded them even closer. And they'd both agreed. Once. They talked about their life-changing moments for that one time and then it was all put back in the box to never be cried over again. Except this summer seemed to be unlocking that box, spilling out the parts of their lives both women preferred to keep hidden away.

'We can sort this out,' Tess offered. 'Honestly, we can have some wine and even though we said we wouldn't, we can talk about it if that's what it takes to make you feel better.' She patted Sonya's hand.

'He updated his Facebook page today,' Sonya informed her. 'An old photo when he was with two Cavaliers and a wench I could tell was fertile just from her rosy cheeks.'

Tess's jaw dropped. 'When the fuck did you get signal?'

'Excuse me.'

Tess turned her head. It was Andras, standing at their table. Just how long had he been there?

'Please,' he said, addressing Tess. 'I am sorry, we do not have Dr Pepper here.'

'Oh.' It hardly seemed important now. 'That's OK.'

'Perhaps I can get you something else?' he offered.

'You are the boss?' Tess asked him.

'I am the boss.'

Of course he was. Tess looked to Sonya. Her friend had released her hands and was searching the contents of her bag, as if trying to hide her tear-stained face. She turned back to Andras. 'I'll have full-fat Coke with three sugars, please.'

'Three sugars?' he queried, raising an eyebrow. 'This is a lot of sugar, no?'

'Is there a sugar shortage as well as a distinct lack of Internet connection?' She wasn't sure she liked her quirks being scrutinised.

'No, I have sugar,' he answered, smiling and taking a step back.

'A couple more things,' Tess called.

He stopped moving and she smiled.

'Taramasalata for my friend, please.'

'And for you?' he asked her.

'For me?' She drew in a breath. 'Well, Andras, seeing as your Wi-Fi isn't working ... you tell me the best place to stand in this village to get 4G and I might just tell you my *real* name.'

# Fourteen

Her name wasn't Patricia and he had told his *mother*. Andras shook his head as he headed back into the kitchen. It was OK. It was OK because unless he asked Patri – whatever-her-name was – for help, the two didn't have to meet at all. She just had to exist. At the other side of the restaurant.

There was a tapping on his shoulder and he spun around, greeting Spiros.

'Andras, what is going on?'

'I have dishes to bring out,' he answered, stepping on into the other room. The heat from the range of ovens hit him and Babis and Eryx were already there passing him orders – kleftiko and souvlaki for table eighteen. Dorothea had her scarf-covered head stuck in a pan of frying garlic and onion.

'Mama says your girlfriend is here,' Spiros stated bluntly.

'Spiro, I am very busy,' he replied, rushing back into the restaurant.

'You ignored my advice and found someone to pretend to be your girlfriend instead of telling the truth?' Spiros continued, tracking Andras.

'And I am already regretting it,' Andras responded. 'You were right. I am an idiot and now I am in an even worse situation.' He smiled at the occupants of the table for two. 'Kleftiko and souvlaki. Enjoy.'

'Marietta is nice,' Spiros continued, following Andras again as he made for the kitchen a second time.

He looked over his shoulder at his brother. What was that supposed to mean? 'I know Marietta is nice. She is my second cousin. You also told me about the benefits of building works and free meat.'

'So, perhaps the best thing to do is to give her a chance,' Spiros suggested.

Andras stopped walking and Spiros almost bowled into him. 'Do you really mean that?'

Spiros shrugged. 'Why not? You tried marriage your way before. Perhaps it is time to try Mama's way.'

Andras felt the anger begin to bubble inside him. 'Did Mama send you over here?'

'No,' Spiros answered.

'Really?' He eyed his brother with suspicion.

'I am only thinking of you, Andras. I am leaving soon, and ... I just want you to be happy.'

Andras tried to swallow down his frustration but it didn't seem to be working. The animated chatter from his customers, the banging of pots and plates from the kitchen, were all making his hackles immediately raise up. Why was he always painted as the loose sheep who needed guidance?

'You want me to be happy but you think I should marry someone not of my choosing?' he asked Spiros firmly.

'Andras—'

'*You* chose Kira. *You* fell in love with Kira. Mama didn't arrange *your* marriage.'

'I know, but—'

'I am divorced. It did not work out. It does not mean any relationship I might have in the future will end up the same way.' He tried to stop his mouth forming a hard line. 'And if it does, so what? It will be *my* choice and I will own it no matter what happens.'

Spiros put a hand on his arm. 'You are angry.'

He drew his arm out of reach. 'Elissa was not a mistake. We had good times together.'

'But she left you,' Spiros said.

'And how do you know that the same won't happen to you? People change. Circumstances change. Time changes.'

As soon as the sentence was in the air between them Andras regretted it. It had been cruel and unnecessary and he thought no such thing. Kira and Spiros were perfect for each other.

'I am sorry, Spiro.'

Spiros shook his head. 'No. It is OK.'

'It is all this wedding stuff and Mama and Papa Yiannis, the restaurant being so busy and thinking about finding a new business partner.' He undid the top button of his shirt. 'I cannot focus on anything.' He sighed. He didn't *want* to focus on anything except living his life the way he wanted to live it, without all the suffocating trappings of his Greek family.

His eyes went to the table Isadora was sat at. His mother was getting to her feet, observing the room, looking ... looking at ... Not-Patricia.

'Quick!' Andras said to Spiros. 'Get Babis to play the *bouzouki*.'

'What?' Spiros answered, looking bemused.

'Greek dancing. Now!' Andras walked into the centre of the room, moving in a diagonal direction to head off his mother. He clapped his hands loudly and called at the top of his voice. 'Everybody! Tonight ... right now ... we will all perform the *sirtaki* dance. So please, everybody, stand up and join with us!'

He grasped hold of his mother's arm. 'Mama, you will dance with me.'

'What is going on, Andras?' she asked, eyes like sharp pins. 'Greek night is not tonight.'

'Why not?' Andras said. He held up Isadora's arm and span underneath it. 'We are in Greece, no? Every night is Greek night.'

'What's happening?' Sonya asked, turning her head away from the beach view as music began to play.

Tess looked as all the diners, some a little reluctant, rose from their seats, joining hands and shifting away from the table to find space. 'I think we might be about to experience our first taste of Greek dancing.'

'Ooo!' Sonya said, excitement brewing. 'Shall we join in?'

Tess's eyes went to her phone. Vodafone GR was all it was managing. Not a flicker of anything World Wide Web related. She needed to look after Sonya, take her mind off the Joey situation, and now the potential baby aspect of the enforced break. It would be a whole lot easier to manage if she had sunk a large rose-coloured flagon of wine though.

'Yes, let's dance,' Tess agreed, holding her hand out to Sonya.

But when skin met skin it wasn't Sonya's hand that found hers, it was bigger, stronger … and male. Before Tess knew it, she was being pulled away from the table by Andras.

# Fifteen

'What are you doing?' Tess exclaimed as she was ushered through the gathering crowds, feet burning with every step.

'Come, please,' Andras stated, his gaze moving from her to the other side of the room and back again. He seemed uneasy.

'But my friend is back there,' Tess protested again.

He stopped walking and turned to face her. Eyes the colour of a deep, dark, chocolate gateaux. She swallowed in anticipation of … something.

'I need …' He stopped talking, eyes moving from her to the middle distance where people were beginning to sway in time to the finger-picking of the *bouzouki*. Whatever was going on here wasn't coming easy.

'I need your help,' he stated.

Confusion furrowed her brow. 'My help?'

He nodded. 'Yes.'

She tilted her head a little. 'We have to get our own starters?'

He squeezed her hand tightly, refocused his gaze on her again. 'My mother is on her way.'

'Your mother,' Tess repeated.

'Yes,' he replied.

'That's … nice?' she offered.

'No,' he said quickly. 'It is not nice. It is very … difficult.' He sighed. 'Please, just … join in with the dancing and I will try to keep her away.'

'What?'

'But if I cannot, just agree with everything I say.' He went to leave, then swung back, taking hold of her hand again. 'And your name. It has to be Patricia.'

With those words said, he joined her hand with a woman just moving into the circle of dancers. Tess turned back, ready to interject but he was already gone, clapping his hands and paying attention to an older woman with her dark hair in a tight bun.

'What happened there?' Sonya asked, muscling in next to Tess and taking hold of her hand. 'That was almost a Mills and Boon moment.' She grinned. 'Kidnapped by the Gorgeous Greek.'

'Something's happening,' Tess stated, her eyes still fixed on Andras and the woman he was encouraging to dance despite her reluctance. 'And apparently, I'm at the centre of it.'

'What?' Sonya asked, stepping left then right as one of the waiters started shouting movement instructions.

'Apparently, the boss needs me to agree with everything he says and pretend my name is Patricia.'

'You *did* tell him your name was Patricia,' Sonya reminded as she swung her right leg across her left leg.

'I know but—'

'You're not thinking of hooking up with him, are you?' Sonya asked.

'*Opa!*' one of the waiters exclaimed as they drew the wobbly circle first in and then out across the flagstone floor.

'No,' Tess replied. 'Of course not.' Although it had been too many days without a male partner on her Facebook page, and his eyes were delicious. 'Single all the way.'

'This way,' Andras called, arm around Isadora on his right and a customer on his left. 'And that.'

He felt his mother move her arm, shrugging and attempting to work her way out from the circle.

'Let me go, Andras,' she said. 'I want to meet with your girlfriend.'

'She is dancing,' Andras said, realigning his mother's arm. 'Like *we* are dancing.'

'When people should still be eating,' Isadora stated. 'It is not even nine o' clock and it is not Greek night.'

With one quick twist, Isadora slipped her arm from his and spun from the circle, making quick stick-aided strides across the room towards Patricia-who-wasn't-Patricia.

He backed out of the dancing too and headed after her. 'Mama!'

'What is the matter, Andras?' Isadora said. 'This girlfriend of yours has travelled from the UK to see you and you do not seem to want to introduce her to me.'

'I … it isn't that …'

'No?' Isadora asked, stopping now she was only a metre or so away from the girl with the blonde hair.

'No.'

'Then introduce me,' she said with relish.

His eyes found 'Patricia'. She was going through the motions of Greek dancing, the sheer fabric of her dress shimmering as she moved, but she was looking directly back at him. There was only one thing he could do.

'Fine,' he answered, ushering his mother forward. 'I will introduce you.'

'They're coming,' Tess said through gritted teeth.

'Who?'

'Andras and, I presume, his mother.'

'What do they want?'

'I have no idea.' She smiled at the advancing pair.

'Patricia,' Andras greeted, stepping forward. 'I would like you to meet my mother.'

'Hel-lo,' Tess responded tentatively as the very tall older woman towered over her. She wore a grey knit dress and low, sensible shoes that looked at least a size ten. Tess felt compelled to roll her shoulders back and tighten her core under the woman's scrutiny. Andras's mother seemed to lean in a little as if she were inspecting every single visible inch of her. The already humid air thickened at the same moment the *bouzouki* player took the music into a minor key.

'Patricia, this is my mother, Isadora,' Andras stated.

What did she do? Put out her hand? Air kiss? The presence of the woman was making her think she should really feel inclined to bow. Why was she even worrying? She didn't even know what any of this was about?

'It's nice to meet you,' Tess said quickly, eyes flitting over to Andras. 'You have a very lovely restaurant.'

The woman's dark eyes seemed to go from glistening olive to murky oil well. '*Andras's* restaurant.'

Tess nodded. 'Yes.'

'I'm Sonya,' Sonya chipped in, holding her hand out to Isadora.

'Sonya is Patricia's business client,' Andras jumped in. 'From England, too.'

'I am?' Sonya answered. Tess nudged her with her elbow. 'Ow, funny bone, not so funny.' She cleared her throat. 'I *am*.'

Isadora swung her attention to her son. 'I am not stupid! You tell me this already.' She looked back to Tess. 'How long have you been in a relationship with my son via the interweb or whatever it is you have been doing in long distances?'

Sonya gasped. 'Oh my!'

Tess watched Andras. He was the epitome of tense. His shoulders raised, his well-built chest moving in and out like the process of breathing was a skill he was yet to master. This was not the self-assured individual she had encountered at Kalami Cove this afternoon.

She looked back at Isadora, meeting the woman's hostile glare.

'It's been—' Tess began.

'A few months,' Andras interjected. 'Since we met on the other side of the island, at Paleokastritsa.'

Tess nodded. 'Mmm, the—'

'Clear water where we snorkelled,' Andras continued, his eyes finding hers.

'The restaurant—'

'On the beach,' Andras added. 'We ate scallops, remember?'

*Scallops!* Did it have to be scallops? She regrouped, wetting her lips. 'It was lovely weather.'

Her cheeks were heating up and she could feel Sonya's eyes boring into the side of her face without having to check and look.

'It is funny,' Isadora spoke, clasping one of her giant hands with the other. 'Andras tells me the restaurant is so busy this season he does not have the time to leave it.' She sighed. 'How much time did you spend together in Paleokastritsa?'

'A week,' Tess and Andras answered simultaneously.

Isadora eyed them both.

'We met on my day off,' Andras elaborated. 'After that we would meet halfway or Patricia would come here.'

'That's right,' Tess added. Why was she so desperate for this woman to believe this mad story? She knew nothing about this man. He had annoyed her at first meeting. Why would she want to do him a favour? It was then a thought occurred to her: she could definitely play this to her and Sonya's advantage. Perhaps a few free meals ... and access to a computer that worked.

'Patricia has talked about you all the time,' Sonya jumped in. 'It's been Andras this and Andras that and how much she misses your Greek ... your—'

'You,' Tess interjected. 'How much I miss you.' She moved forward and reached a hand out, bringing it up to Andras's face and caressing his cheek.

Andras felt the softness of her fingertips as he looked into those ocean-coloured eyes. As every millisecond went by he could feel his shoulders lose a little tension.

'Dance,' Isadora stated suddenly.

Andras looked at his mother. 'What?'

'You say this woman is your girlfriend, then you will dance for her.'

'Mama, I have a restaurant to run,' he protested.

Tess smiled. 'I would really love to see you dance, Andras.'

He saw the playful look in her eyes now. She was good. She had helped him out but now she wanted a little something in return. And what choice did he have?

'Do we get to smash plates?' Sonya asked.

'Yes, Andras,' Tess said. 'We must smash some plates.'

He was well and truly caught.

# Sixteen

'Babis!' Andras called, beckoning the *bouzouki* player towards him.

Tess felt the heaviness of Isadora's eyes fall on her. Perhaps this hadn't been such a good idea. She had no idea what this situation was and this woman looked capable of snapping her in two with just one of those glances.

'What are you going to do?' Sonya whispered in her ear.

'I don't know,' Tess answered.

'Maybe you should come clean.'

'I can't,' she replied.

'Why not?'

Why couldn't she? Apart from the fact she would look a complete idiot if she told the truth now. No, it wasn't that. It was Andras's whole demeanour when he'd asked for her help. *Troubled. Desperate.* Something within her had twanged with empathy.

'Because I'm going to ask him if he knows a guide man for us.'

'That's a good idea,' Sonya answered.

'Patricia.'

She would just play this out tonight, she would ask him if he knew someone with a boat to take them around the island and they wouldn't come here again.

Sonya dug an elbow in her side. 'Patricia, Andras is talking to you.'

She'd momentarily forgotten her name was Patricia. 'Oh, sorry.'

He held out his hand to her and she looked at it, unmoving.

'We will dance,' he stated.

Had he said *we*? Shit. She was sure the talked-about dancing had been in the singular.

'Oh, I don't dance,' Tess answered with a light laugh she reserved to get herself out of work projects she had no interest in.

'You do not dance with your boyfriend?' Isadora snapped straightaway.

Tess looked to Sonya who mouthed the words 'guide man' through half hand-covered lips. Her friend was right. She was complicit in this now. And it had the possibility of being a means to a tour guide end.

She smiled at Andras. 'You'll have to teach me,' she said, slipping her hand into his. Her feet were already swollen and hurting like she'd walked on cobbles in stilts. Just how much worse could it be?

Andras drew her away from his mother and Sonya, leading them to the centre of the room where Babis was preparing to play again.

'I am so sorry for this,' he whispered to her. 'I did not think this through.'

'Clearly,' she said, through gritted teeth. 'Or you might not have picked someone whose only dance move is the occasional dab when she's drunk.'

'What?'

'Just hold me up.'

Andras nodded towards Babis and the gentle sound of strings being softly strummed drifted around them, circling the restaurant and echoing off the beamed ceiling. He squeezed her hand. 'Tell me your real name.'

'It's Tess,' she answered.

He nodded. 'We will tell my mother that it is short for Patricia.'

'Hang on ... just wait ... this is only for tonight, right? I mean—' Tess began.

'Shh,' he said, placing a forefinger over her lips.

Her stomach rolled in response to the contact. She really should have slipped in a singles night before she came away. Her body seemed to be telling her she was in desperate need of a fix of male attention right now.

'Just listen to the music,' he purred.

She closed her eyes, trying to loosen her shoulders and remember that she was in Greece. Here no one knew who she was. What she did for a living. Or that she was single again at twenty-nine and had been left at the altar by the only man she had ever loved.

Suddenly her hand was being lifted up and she opened her eyes to Andras, as he manoeuvred her arm, turning her until she was alongside him. He positioned her hand to rest at the base of his neck and held it there, his eyes connecting with hers. God, this was erotic. Their fingers, on top of each other and the heat from the nape of his neck seeping into her was causing volcanic bubbling in her insides.

Then his free hand snaked around her waist and, in time to the *bouzouki*, she was pulled into him, until their bodies fell next to each other, connected at the hip.

Why had Babis chosen this song? Andras hadn't danced to this since he had danced with Elissa after their wedding in Corfu Town. It had been a half-empty bar, no one there they knew, just the band and strangers clapping their hands in time. But it had meant everything. It had been a celebration of their love, their unity, starting their lives *their* way … but it hadn't lasted. And now, here he was, dancing in his restaurant with someone he didn't even know, with his mother and half the Georgiou family watching.

'Sorry,' Tess whispered as her foot stepped on his.

He smiled at her. Despite the situation he was in with this charade, he couldn't fault her. A stranger, coming to his aid, joining in with this farce, after he had been so judgemental to her earlier that day. He knew why he had criticised her need for connection with the outside world and her work, but his feelings about it weren't her fault. And here she was now, dancing with him in front of his family, just because he had asked her to.

He spun her around then caught her with one arm, lowering her slowly backwards and leaning along with her. 'Thank you,' he whispered. 'For doing this.'

She smiled. 'Just for tonight.'

He brought her up again, faces close, noses almost touching. 'A week,' he stated so only she could hear.

'What?' she gasped out loud.

He acted on instinct, covering her mouth with his and holding her close as he muffled her voice with a kiss.

# Seventeen

It took Tess a millisecond to realise what was happening and then her first reaction was to hit Andras. He was taking advantage again. Leading things. Dictating. *She* was the decision-maker. In everything. But then something else began to happen. Andras's tongue started practically *having sex* with hers. What was he doing? Whatever it was, she had *never* been kissed like this before. It was as if she had erogenous zones on her taste buds and they were all exploding like kernels in a popcorn-maker. She didn't want him to stop. She wanted him to carry on, possibly for the whole holiday.

Then he broke away, letting her go and stamping his feet, raising his arms in a move not dissimilar to a Spanish bullfighter. She felt a bit dizzy, her mouth still reacting to his, even though the lips were back with their owner and she was standing like newborn Bambi. And then she caught sight of Sonya. Her best friend was staring at her, eyes wide, a look somewhere between alarm and shock, her hand on her chest, fingers searching for the almost-engagement necklace.

What was she doing? Dancing with this man? Kissing this man? On the very first night, when she'd sworn off men for the whole holiday. Despite the crazy circumstances, she had gone along with it and now she had broken her promise to Sonya. She needed to put a stop to it.

She began to stamp her feet, fingers lifting her dress a little, like she'd seen the one who copped off with Ben Cohen do in a *Strictly* Paso routine, wafting the material from side to side. Andras had stopped dancing now and was watching her, as were the rest of the diners at the restaurant, some of them clapping their hands together in time to the *bouzouki*. She had no idea what she was doing but it was her intention to shimmy – if that's what this movement was – to the other side of this makeshift dance floor and propel herself out of this scenario and back to what she should be doing: pepping up Sonya.

Stamping again, she attempted to pass Andras, shaking her dress and trying to look professional.

'What are you doing?' he asked, amusement on those thick, beautiful lips that had rocked hers.

'Leaving you,' she said just loud enough for him to hear. 'Escaping while I can. And don't worry: Patricia won't be patronising your restaurant for the rest of our holiday.' She stamped again, this one hard and sending shockwaves up her calf. 'Just tell your mother I had important business to do and—'

He caught hold of her arm. 'You don't understand.'

'You said a week,' Tess replied, entwining her hands, her arms either side of her face as she waved her head like she was a Bollywood dancer. 'I can't do this for a week. I'm here with my friend and I don't have time for games like this.'

'You think this is a game?' Andras answered, taking her hand in his and pulling her into him again.

'Whatever this is it has nothing to do with me,' she reminded him, leaning against him as if it were the most natural move in the world.

'I will give you anything you want,' Andras whispered in her ear.

Had he made his tone deliberately suggestive or was that her libido and his Greek accent filling in the gaps? She swallowed. 'Like what?' She turned a full circle, still performing.

'Unlimited Internet access,' he said, clasping hold of her hand.

'I'm not sure that exists on Corfu,' she responded dismissively. 'And your free Wi-Fi is free because it doesn't actually work!'

'I will make it happen.'

She was itching to check in with work and to update her social media with some photos of the sea view she'd taken from the terrace earlier, but it wasn't enough.

'I need a guide man,' she stated, copying his moves as he hopped from one foot to the other.

'A what?' he asked.

'Sonya wants someone to show us around the island, by boat. All the pretty little coves, all the flora and fauna and cute creatures.' She shivered. She'd look at creatures from a safe distance. 'This has to be a great holiday for her. Doing things. Not thinking about things at home.'

He put an arm around her waist and drew her in close, dipping his mouth down to her ear. 'I cannot do this. With my brother's wedding and the restaurant—'

She pulled him closer. 'Is now the time to re-mention that I am dancing in the middle of a restaurant, on my very first night in Greece, pretending to be your girlfriend with no idea why?'

He moved their hands so they were palm to palm and swayed her backwards and forwards, hips gyrating in time to the hypnotic song she was probably going to be humming for days. Why wasn't he immediately answering? She needed to be clear. Just like she was in business.

'That's my final offer,' she said, meeting his eyes with hers. 'Unlimited Internet access and a guide man for the whole holiday.' She swallowed. 'Take it, or I'm leaving.'

He looked at her, still moving her to his rhythm. Why was she nervous about his reply? She didn't want to be this pretend girlfriend and have to lie to his ferocious-looking mother. And she was sure they could find someone else to show them around Corfu if they had to.

'OK,' he replied.

'OK?' she said a little too keenly.

'Come here tomorrow morning, at eight. I will get the boat ready.'

'Eight?'

'I have a restaurant to run,' he reminded her.

She circled under his arm as directed. 'And the Internet access?'

He smiled as she turned towards him again. 'You will have to trust me, Patricia.'

*Trust a man?* She didn't trust any of them. 'It's Tess,' she reminded, pulling him to a halt. 'Now end this dance so I can go and eat my food.'

'*Opa!*' he shouted, raising their arms in the air.

The *bouzouki* player strummed a final chord and everyone in the restaurant began to applaud.

'Take a bow,' Andras instructed. 'For someone who has not danced before, you are a natural.'

With her cheeks suddenly flaming from the exertion of the moves and the humidity in the air, Tess dropped her torso into a swift bow before heading off on pins-and-needles feet she was certain would never be the same again. Casting a glance back at Andras, shaking hands with diners, his dark hair a little ruffled from their dance, she wondered just what she had let herself in for.

'So, despite everything we've been saying since we flew from Luton, you've got a new boyfriend,' Sonya stated as Tess dropped into the chair opposite her. 'I did see what I thought I saw, didn't I? You and the supposed fake boyfriend performing a very convincing tongue-on-tongue role play over there.'

Tess sighed and reached across the table, taking Sonya's hand in hers. 'That kiss,' she began, 'was as fake as you could get.'

'Really?' Sonya exclaimed.

'Really,' Tess answered. 'If he does it again I'm going to have to insist on breath mints. It must be all that garlic they put in their cooking here.' Her stomach knotted up with the lie. His taste had been nothing but man perfection.

'Ew!' Sonya replied.

'But the good news is ... I've got ourselves a guide man!'

'Who smells like garlic?'

'That's some of the bad news,' Tess stated, sipping from her Coke with three sugars.

'*Some* of the bad news?' Sonya said. 'I'm not sure I like the sound of that.'

She just had to say it quickly. Get it out there. 'I have to be the fake girlfriend for a week.' She picked up the rose-gold-coloured carafe and began filling Sonya's glass. 'Here, have some more wine.'

# Eighteen

Andras watched the swallows dip and swerve across the morning skyline, their wing tips sometimes brushing the ocean, other times frisking the cypress trees either side of his view. How did it feel to be free like that? Just flying with the breeze, changing your direction in an instant with no consequence?

He had tossed and turned all night, a dozen things fighting for space in his already cluttered mind. His lack of a new business partner. His role in the wedding with Marietta. His new girlfriend from England. What had he been thinking, kissing her? Granted, at first it had been on impulse, to stop her blowing their cover, but he hadn't needed to commit to it quite as much as he had. Maybe it had something to do with not having had a woman in six months. At first, after Elissa left, he thought he could just throw himself into the tourist crowd. There were plenty of women looking for a Greek Romeo to while away the hot summer nights, but it had all felt so ... wrong. He was using and *being* used and he wasn't sure which party got the rawer deal. He may not want to be burned again but it seemed fickle sex wasn't for him either. Perhaps he and Papa Yiannis had more in common than he thought.

He leapt upwards from the chair he was standing on, bare torso straining, as he caught hold of the ceiling beam. He was going to have to do a few things he didn't want to do today. One was finding Spiros a donkey, and the other was leaving someone else in charge of the restaurant.

He pulled his body up, forearms biting. He had hoped to persuade Victor to take Tess and Sonya out on the boat, but his head waiter had reminded him it was his day off and, whereas ordinarily he would be only too happy to cancel, he was visiting his mother in the hospital. The only choice left was to take the women out himself and put Mathias in charge. He hated leaving anyone else in charge. Not because he thought the restaurant wouldn't survive without him, but because he knew the restaurant *could* survive without him. Now, the main concern was getting out on to the water before his mother involved him in wedding planning he had sworn he didn't have time for.

'Oh my!'

Sonya reached out a hand that landed hard on Tess's arm and she stopped walking, eyes following her friend's line of vision.

They had come down the road way to the restaurant, entering through the back. And now there was Andras, wearing nothing but a pair of jeans that moulded around him like a second skin, back stretched and showing every perfectly positioned muscle working beautifully as he rose up and down from one of the beams in the restaurant ceiling.

Tess liked male backs almost as much as she liked a strong forearm. There was something about a set of muscular shoulder blades and that shaped curve that ran down to the coccyx. She swallowed, unable to keep her eyes from roving over his form – tight biceps pumped from the workout.

'We should say something,' Sonya whispered. 'Announce we're here.'

'Uh-huh,' Tess said, focus still on the semi-naked demigod.

Sonya cleared her throat and the sound reverberated like the thunderous roar of an advancing storm. Andras dropped down onto the chair then jumped down onto the tiled floor, reaching for his T-shirt.

'*Kalimera*,' he greeted, using the clothing item to wipe the perspiration from his torso as he advanced towards them. 'You are early.'

Tess looked at her watch. It was exactly eight o' clock. She looked back to him. 'You said eight o' clock.'

He smiled. 'A Greek eight o' clock,' he answered. 'Somewhere between eight and nine.'

'Oh. Shall we come back?' Sonya offered. 'We could have another coffee and—'

He shook his head. 'No, it is fine.' He pulled out two chairs. 'Please, sit down. I will get you some coffee. Then I will wash.'

*Wash?* Tess still couldn't drag her eyes away from that smooth, ripped chest; the thought of that *and* water …

'Coffee would be lovely,' Sonya stated. 'Wouldn't coffee be lovely, Tess?' She nudged Tess with her elbow.

'Yes,' Tess replied quickly. 'And this unlimited Internet you promised?'

He nodded and held out his hand. 'Please give me your phone.'

Tess hesitated for a moment, like he had asked for her to cut off her arm and pass that over.

'The code for my business Wi-Fi is in Greek and is sixteen letters long,' he explained.

'Gosh!' Sonya exclaimed. 'No name of your first pet and the year you were born here.'

Tess dipped her hand into her Michael Kors handbag, pulling out her iPhone and dropping it into Andras's palm.

In minutes, hopefully she would be connected to London life, work and dating apps of opportunity. She could focus on potential no-strings mates who didn't come with a Greek family attached. Perhaps she would have a quick scan in the toilets where Sonya couldn't see.

'It's a beautiful day,' Sonya remarked, looking across the restaurant at the view.

It *was* a beautiful day. Even though Tess had been tired from the journey it had been lovely to wake up to the sunshine in a cloudless sky, the sun's first rays filtering through the terrace shutters.

Andras passed the mobile back. 'You are online.'

'Really?' Tess said, like someone had announced she'd won the Euromillions.

He nodded. 'I pray for no great flood.' He looked to Sonya. 'Coffee with cream, am I right?'

Tess watched Sonya flush.

'Didn't I spoon up all your cream last night?' Sonya asked with a giggle.

'I have milked another goat this morning,' he replied.

'You have?' Sonya asked.

'He was joking,' Tess stated. Then she looked up, needing confirmation. 'You were joking, weren't you?'

He smiled. 'One moment, yes?'

Tess watched him head off to the kitchen, taut perfection gliding past tables. Shaking her head, she concentrated on her phone that really did now have three bars of Wi-Fi.

'So, I looked at the map last night and there are some lovely little places not far from here,' Sonya stated.

'Mmm.' The first thing she was going to do was check her email.

'There's Kouloura just around the corner, well, not the corner, the coast.' Sonya laughed. 'The coast is more a boaty term. Then there's Agios Stefanos where all the celebrities go.'

Tess watched the roll of emails come flooding in. She tried to catch them as they flashed by. Harrods. Admiral Insurance. Music Magpie. *McKenzie Falconer.*

It was an email from Russell entitled Blackberry Boudoir Final and there was an attachment. Her heart was racing. Why was there an attachment with the word 'final' in the subject line? *She* was the head of that project. Only *she* should be using words like 'final'. She tapped on the email.

'Of course, our guide man is bound to know other places off the beaten track, isn't he?'

Tess skim-read the contents of the text. Phrases like 'not the vision they had in mind', 'new direction' and 'swift turna-round' all merged into one until she wasn't really taking in anything.

'Have you brought some flat shoes?' Sonya asked.

Tess clicked on the attachment and waited for it to load.

'Tess?'

'Just a second.'

Slowly, little by little, piece by piece, the image started to appear. Gone was the cheeky blackberry behind the curtain, nowhere to be seen was the animated wine bottle or any of the other images she had put forward for approval. In front of her eyes was nothing that resembled a blackberry at all. In front of her were two indistinguishable fruits and foliage that resembled a penis.

'Fuck!'

Sonya jumped, knocking an ashtray off the table and on to the floor.

'Fuck it!' Tess got to her feet, her whole body flooding with heat. This couldn't be happening. It just couldn't. What were the clients thinking? What was Russell thinking? Did no one see that this didn't look like the avatar of an exclusive wine bar-cum-brasserie establishment but a lap-dancing club? Was it just *her* who saw a penis and a pair of balls, not shrubbery and fruit?

'What's wrong?' Sonya asked. 'Is it Rachel? Or your parents?'

Tess put the screen towards her friend. 'Tell me what you see here!'

Sonya squinted, looking at the graphic. 'I see some … are they grapes?'

'Allegedly blackberries,' Tess stated.

'And is that a banana?' Sonya added, looking closer.

'See! I knew it!' Tess exclaimed, almost triumphant.

'What is it?' Sonya asked.

'A disaster! That's what it is!' She looked to her friend. 'What do I do?'

'Is this the new client?' Sonya asked. 'The chain of wine bars?'

'Yes! Currently being represented by bits of a man's anatomy.'

'I take it that wasn't the look they were going for.'

'I need to call Russell.' Tess started to pace backwards and forwards over the flagstone floor before tapping the screen of her phone.

'Tess, it's six o'clock in the morning in England.'

Was it? Instinctively she checked her watch. Sonya was right. There would be no one there and Russell had never answered his mobile before eight on the occasions she had had to avert near-crisis before.

'Coffee.'

Andras was back. He placed a wooden tray on the table and took off two rather nice contemporary white mugs, setting one in front of Sonya and the other in the space where Tess wasn't yet sitting. She watched him pour the coffee and push the jug of cream towards her friend. She couldn't concentrate. All she could see were blackberries that weren't bloody blackberries.

'Thank you,' Sonya said.

What was she going to do? What the fuck was she going to do?

'You would prefer Coke with three sugars?'

Tess looked up at Andras then. A Dr Pepper substitute was exactly what she needed and somehow her fake boyfriend knew it. She nodded her head and sank down onto the chair. 'Yes, please.'

'*Parakalo*,' he replied, backing away.

Sonya put a hand over Tess's and inched her iPhone out of her grip. 'Wi-Fi is overrated.'

Tess stretched out her pinkie, determined to reconnect with the device.

'Uh-uh,' Sonya said, taking a firm hold of the phone. 'Drinks and a boat tour with our guide man.' She waggled a finger. 'No worrying about blackberries. Say, "Yes, Sonya."'

Tess swallowed. 'Yes.' She breathed out, hard and heavy. She felt sick to the stomach but, right now, at 8 a.m. in Greece, there was absolutely nothing she could do about it.

# Nineteen

'Take off your shoes!'

Tess stopped walking. She had picked her way across the stones and sand, but thankfully the wedges she was wearing weren't grinding her feet as much as last night's choice of footwear. She looked across at the boat – a small cream and navy-blue affair that looked like something out of a Bond movie. It was bobbing gently on the water with Sonya already aboard, her friend sitting down on one of the cream-cushioned seating areas and applying suncream. Andras, meanwhile, was standing barefoot on the bow, jeans and a chest-hugging white T-shirt over the rest of him. Earlier, over a coffee and a well-sugared Coke, Tess and Sonya had watched him strip down to trunks smaller than those worn by an Olympic swimmer and dive into the ocean, soaking his olive-skinned body in the surf, before towelling himself dry. It had been like a manly version of burlesque, if there was such a thing.

'What are you doing?' Andras called again. 'Come into the water! Take off your shoes!'

Tess eyed up the shelving beach ahead of her. It wasn't far, just ten metres or so. She put one foot forward, arms outstretched like a tightrope walker. Why couldn't he have just tied the boat to the pontoon-thingy instead of dropping the anchor and expecting them to wade to the vessel?

'Tess! Take off your shoes, *parakalo*!'

She looked down at her feet, encased in the gold leather straps, safe from the earth she was standing on, untouched by anything. She couldn't remove them.

There was a crunching sound and she raised her head to see Andras powering up the beach towards her. She struggled forward, one foot then the other, wobbling quickly like she was strutting on a catwalk of hot coals.

'There is no time for this,' he stated as he reached her.

'I'm coming. I just need to—'

The rest of her sentence was lost in the air as Andras swept her up into his arms, again turning to the sea and making his way across the beach, taking her with him.

'Put me down!' Tess squealed, kicking her legs.

'I will,' he answered. 'On the boat.'

'I can walk!'

'At the speed of a tortoise.' That reminded him of Hector. He really needed to find a permanent home for the animal. Somewhere that didn't consider his presence a curse and wasn't going to make him the prime ingredient of a stew.

'I'm on holiday,' Tess remarked. 'People shouldn't be rushed on holiday.' She continued to fight in his arms. 'Greek time, like you said.'

He had to give her that comment. They reached the boat and he lifted her up until she finally wriggled free from his arms and clambered aboard. He watched her step from seat to floor, her hands brushing down her expensive-looking dress, handbag swinging from her shoulder.

'You are OK?' he asked her.

'Somehow I'm covered in sand,' she replied.

He smiled. 'Life is a beach.' He set about pulling up the anchor.

'I hope you remember I'm doing you a favour here,' Tess stated, plumping down next to Sonya.

'And I am returning this by being your ... what did you call this?'

'A guide man,' Sonya stated. 'Like they have in Barbados.'

He watched Tess fold her arms across her chest. 'This had better be good.'

He started the engine of the boat. 'This is Corfu,' he declared over the noise. 'Everything is good.' Apart from his life, which was beginning to resemble a Greek tragedy. Still, perhaps a day out on the water would give him some perspective.

Sonya and her Marco Polo map had made suggestions of where to go before they set sail until Andras talked about tides. Apparently, it would be better to head south towards Nissaki and Barbati now, then take a slower cruise back up the coast for the other stops Sonya wanted. And now, as they planed over the ocean, Tess couldn't keep her eyes off the landscape.

Corfu wasn't just good like Andras had said, it was beautiful, from each and every angle. From the sparkling ocean they were speeding across, to the rugged, shrubbery-infused rocks that towered up towards the cloudless sky. There was a new view every second. Villas poked their brick-and-glass frontages out of rocky crevices hanging over the sea and small cottages sat dotted amid lush olive groves. Why had she never considered visiting Greece before? She swallowed. Because ever since Adam she hadn't considered anything except doing exactly what *he* had done – running away – from everything in her life except work. And work was not her happy place at the moment. She closed her eyes and breathed in the sunny, salty air.

'Mmm, these crisps are good,' Sonya announced over the roar of the engine, spray splashing over the sides of the motor-boat and hitting the bag of snacks she was holding on to. 'Oregano. Who would have thought of oregano crisps?' Sonya shook the bag at Tess. 'Have some. Try them.'

'I'm fine,' Tess answered. She raised her voice a notch. 'How far is it?' she called to Andras.

'How far is what?' he called back over his shoulder.

She sighed. It wasn't just the external scenery she had been admiring. Skippering the boat had meant Andras was stood in front of them at the helm, those tight glutes beneath the denim, not to mention the muscular forearms directing the wheel. She didn't want to be his fake girlfriend for a week, she wanted to *have* him – literally – not just a snog when his mother was looking. If it hadn't been for Sonya's stupid single pledge she could be moulding her hands to that sweet ass and posting their picture on Insta. How ironic was this situation?

'How long until we stop?' she called again.

The engine noise lessened slightly and the boat came down from riding the crest of the waves and fell into a more sedate pace across the water.

'We do not have to go so fast,' Andras told them. 'We will soon be there.'

Sonya stared at her map. 'Are we anywhere near the Rothschild mansion?'

Andras smiled. 'You English. You are always interested in the people with lots of money.'

'Prince Charles stays there,' Sonya said, looking at Tess.

'If you'd said Shia LaBeouf I might have been more interested.'

'The Rothschild house is near Agios Stefanos,' Andras stated. 'The other way from here.'

'Oh,' Sonya said, disappointment in her voice.

'I will point out this and all the other places of interest on the way back down the coast.'

'Any good bars soon?' Tess asked, stretching her arms out behind her.

Andras pointed. 'Nissaki is just coming up.'

Tess sat up in her seat, following the direction of Andras's finger. Ahead of them, to the right of the boat, was a large biscuit- and terracotta-coloured hotel springing out of the green mountainside and dominating the immediate landscape. Set just below this was a long stretch of beach, a handful of what looked like tavernas skirting the land side. As their captain slowed the boat and they started a gentle cruise towards shore, the colour of the water began to change. Deep dark blue quickly transformed into bright light greens and turquoise. Tess edged her way across her seat to the side of the boat and looked over into the sea.

'Can you see the fish?' Andras called.

'You can see the fish?!' Sonya exclaimed, leaping up from her seat and rushing to the side of the boat too.

'Whoa!' Andras exclaimed as the boat rocked right. 'Come back please or you will tip us right over!'

'Sonya!' Tess exclaimed.

'Sorry!' Sonya said, quickly scrabbling back into the middle of the vessel. 'Going to the other side.' She sat down and leaned over on the left, looking into the ocean. 'Oh my! I can see them! Can you see them, Tess? Fish! There's tiny little silver ones and ones with stripes and, oh, quite big black ones …'

'Let me know if you find Dory,' Tess said, focusing her gaze into the water again.

'I've never seen water this clear! Look how clear it is!'

Tess watched a small shoal of grey fish with blue trims swirl through the water in front of her and she felt Sonya's excitement. Seeing them so easily, moving right around them, it was something special.

'Wait until you *swim* with the fish,' Andras stated, driving the boat in closer to land where a man was beckoning them in.

'Swim with them?' Tess answered. Seeing them from the boat was one thing, getting up close and personal was quite another.

'Of course,' Andras answered. 'That is why visitors come to Corfu.' He smiled. 'For man, or woman, to be at one with nature.'

'I can't wait!' Sonya exclaimed, stripping off her top and adjusting the straps of her tankini.

Tess swallowed. She'd been thinking more of having a cooling cocktail and soaking up some sun rather than puckering up to a vertebrate. She had never seen the attraction of a fish spa.

'But for this you really will have to take off your shoes,' Andras told her.

She looked up at him, her toes clenching automatically. Sarcastic bastard. Suddenly his attractiveness was losing its shine.

# Twenty

# Nissaki Beach

Andras stood outside Mikalis's Taverna taking it all in. With Tess and Sonya settled on sunloungers on the beach, he was going to try to make the most of his day. The taverna looked good, recently refurbished, just like he wanted to do with Georgiou's. Everything had been painted a bright white – from the wooden ceiling to the struts of the frontage – and there were small pots of lavender everywhere you turned: on each table, hanging from hooks on the roof, by the entranceway. Plus the restaurant was busy, bustling with customers even now, mid-morning.

He stepped up into the building and had gone no more than a couple of paces before ...

'Andras Georgiou!'

He smiled as short, bald, rotund Yiannis Mikalis practically skipped across the tiled floor towards him, hands outstretched.

'Yiannis.' He greeted them with a smile as the man embraced him, slapping his back with two meaty hands.

Yiannis drew away, clasping Andras's hands and squeezing hard, but with affection. 'What brings you here? Spying on my restaurant?' He let go of Andras and looked proudly at the interior. 'It looks a little different from last summer, no?'

He nodded. 'It looks wonderful, Yiannis.'

The owner nodded. 'Sometimes you have to forget about what is going on with the finances of Europe and just carry on being Greek.' Yiannis laughed. 'This place had not had a facelift since 1990. It was time.'

Andras swallowed. His restaurant was long overdue an upgrade too. He didn't want to go all sleek and ultra-modern like some of the other restaurants in the area had done, but perhaps a coat of paint and some new furnishings, maybe some cushions for the chairs and then, after that, there might be a chance to dream bigger.

'So, how are the wedding plans coming along?' Yiannis asked, beckoning him further into the restaurant and pulling up a chair. 'Your brother has not been suffocated yet?'

'You know about the wedding,' Andras stated, sitting down.

'Come on! Everyone knows everything on Corfu,' Yiannis said, sitting opposite.

'He is completing tasks on a list like he is searching for treasure.'

Yiannis clapped his hands together. 'We have all been there, my friend.'

He nodded then cleared his throat. 'Yiannis … I was wondering …'

'Let me get you a drink. Ouzo?' He clapped his hands in the air and a waiter headed straight towards them.

He was nervous but he wasn't sure the alcohol was going to help. He was running out of options for the restaurant. He didn't want his mother as his partner. He thrived on his independence and he didn't want to have to compromise.

'Yiannis, I'm looking for a business partner,' he stated without prelude.

The other man began to cough. 'I'm sorry. What did you say?'

'Spiros is moving away with his new wife. He needs to free up his investment,' Andras elaborated.

'Well, I ...'

'I'm asking you, Yiannis, as I know what an astute businessman you are.' He swallowed. He did respect the man but he was also thin on options closer to home. 'And I also know you have an eye for potential.'

Yiannis went to speak but Andras continued quickly.

'The restaurant is doing well, really well, I don't really have the time to be away from it today but ...' Why had he said that? What was supposed to come next? He had to be here today because someone was pretending to be his girlfriend and in exchange he had taken them out on the boat? That didn't sound professional at all. 'It was necessary to ... come to see you.' A little flattery never hurt.

'Andras—' Yiannis began.

'Think about it. You would not have to do a thing more than you are doing here, unless you wanted to, of course. My brother left the running of the restaurant to me and I am happy to continue that way, but I am also happy to change things, if that's what you would like.' He stopped talking, his mouth dry. Where was that ouzo, or water?

'Andras,' Yiannis started. 'I am sure your restaurant, as always, is doing well. I just—'

'I have plans for refurbishment and maybe some marketing. I just need a cash injection and I am certain I can increase profit.'

'Andras.' Yiannis placed a hand on his forearm as if to still him. He took a breath, sensing what was coming.

'Just think of it,' Andras said. 'It would be such a great investment.'

'Andras,' Yiannis said again. 'I have nothing to invest.'

He swallowed. He should have known this before he even came here. Greece was still under incredible financial pressures.

'Everything I had I invested here.' Yiannis spread out his arms like the restaurant was a choir of performers he was introducing. 'This season I hope to make a small profit but there is no money for anything else.'

Andras nodded. 'I understand.'

'I am sorry, Andras. If there was a way I could help then I would.'

A waiter arrived with a bottle of ouzo, two small tumblers and a carafe of water.

'There is one other thing,' Andras stated as the waiter poured them each a drink.

'Anything,' Yiannis responded.

'Do you know where I can get a donkey?'

# Twenty-one

Tess's stomach was filled with a rather rustic white wine and a Greek-style pizza – Kalamata olives, hunks of creamy feta cheese, red onion and tomatoes – that had been as big as an olden-day stagecoach wheel. Now, laying on a lounger on the fine, white stone beach, she was considering a snooze. No amount of prodding at her phone was getting Wi-Fi and Vodafone had texted (how it had got through was anyone's guess) to tell her her data allowance had been reached and no more would be available until tomorrow unless she wanted to ring a number she was sure was going to cost a month's wages.

'Come in the water!' Sonya called.

Tess opened one eye and looked at her friend some hundred metres away, shoulder deep in azure sea. The outlook was spectacular, ocean still and sparkling, sun high in the sky, small boats coming in and out, the faint sound of Greek music from the beachside tavernas. The recognition of the music reminded her of the previous night. Dancing. In front of a whole restaurant. And that kiss …

'In a minute,' she called back to Sonya. And it would be a very long, Greek minute if she got her way.

'Perhaps a cocktail? Compliments of my friend Yiannis's taverna.'

At the sound of Andras's voice, Tess sat up and opened both eyes. There was their boat captain, holding a tray with three delicious-looking drinks filled with ice, straws and neon plastic monkeys clinging to the rims.

She grabbed one and sucked greedily, only pausing to say, 'We need to talk.'

'I agree,' he answered, putting the tray on the small table and dropping on to a vacant lounger. 'I have a restaurant to run. I cannot be your guide man for the whole of the day.'

'What?' Tess said, turning her head. 'No. *You* need to tell *me* exactly why I have to be your fake girlfriend.'

'Ah.'

'And, I'm afraid, if the reason isn't good enough then I'll have to—'

'My mother wants me to marry my cousin.'

She put the cocktail glass down quickly, eyes moving back to Andras. He was prostrate, eyes hidden behind aviator sunglasses, arms behind his head, that skin-skimming T-shirt taut across his body and revealing just a hint of the waistband of his jeans.

'Oh.' It was all she could manage.

'It is a good enough reason?' he asked, turning his head to face her.

'Well ... I didn't know the Greeks were into arranged marriages.'

A long, low sigh left him. 'It is not to do with religion. It is mainly to do with my mother.'

'And you couldn't just tell her no?'

'Not unless I want to suffer the same fate as Uncle Dimitri.'

She immediately imagined a stoning or one of those medieval torture racks, with Andras strapped to the wood, squirming under tight rope bindings ... naked. She swallowed. No, that wasn't torture, that was Christian Grey-esque. And she needed to stop this right now. The fact he was right here, practically her boyfriend – so close and yet so far – wasn't making anything easier.

'So, you couldn't have found a nice, easy-to-please Greek girl to … fill the position.' She cleared her throat as a flush spread up her body.

'No,' he answered. 'My mother knows all the Greek girls and I think that might please her almost as much as marrying my cousin. Plus …' He stopped and she found herself leaning a little towards him, eager to hear what was coming next.

'Yes?' she asked.

'For some reason, when I invented the girlfriend … she was English.'

Tess felt her lips form into a smile. 'Ah ha.'

'With blonde hair,' he continued, turning his face towards her.

She couldn't see his eyes through those mirrored sunglasses. She didn't like not seeing his eyes, particularly when her heart had started palpitating, reminding her that she hadn't had sex in a few weeks, which was basically for ever.

'And blue eyes,' he finished.

She wet her lips and cleared her throat before making any attempt to reply. 'And there I was.'

'Yes,' he answered. 'There you were. In my restaurant.' He smiled. 'And I knew you were perfect.'

'Perfect?' she queried.

'Yes.' He nodded. 'We had already argued. You are wrapped up into your work with the Internet. You would not think this could be anything but a business transaction. A favour for a favour.'

'Ah, I see,' Tess said, sitting up a little and elongating her body. 'You couldn't pick someone who was going to fall in love with you.'

'Yes,' he answered. 'How did you know?'

'Well, let me see ...' She tapped her left index finger with her right as she started to count. 'You're a Greek waiter ...'

'Restaurant owner,' he interrupted.

'Sorry – *restaurant owner*. This means you're basically on show to holidaymakers for four months of the year—'

'It is really about seven months,' he said. 'We start at the beginning of April and finish at the end of October.'

'What I'm trying to say is you must have your fair share of swoony singles trying to get a piece of your meze.'

She watched the corners of his mouth twitch upwards in amusement.

'Do they tell you they love you?' Tess carried on. 'Do they whisper it over the candles, with dewy eyes as you serve up one of those apricot and vanilla cheesecakes? Are there tears at the steps of the transfer bus?'

'I don't date—' he started.

'Purlease! Don't give me the "I don't date customers" line. You're dating one right now. Me. Your best fake date ever.'

'I don't date at all,' Andras finished.

The short sentence almost made Tess catch her breath. He didn't date. What did that mean? He wasn't in a relationship if he needed her, so what else was there apart from dating? Being happily on his own? She shuddered like a keen wind had shattered the wave of heat.

'What do you mean you don't date? Are you ... a monk?' Tess asked.

He laughed and shook his head. 'No.'

She would probably get it more if he had said yes. She swallowed. 'I don't understand.' She blinked, still looking at him. 'Are you secretly gay?'

He lifted up his sunglasses, revealing those dark eyes. 'What would that have to do with not dating?'

She didn't know really. She was clutching at straws. 'Well, I thought, with your mother keen for you to marry, and you asking me to ...'

'And me not saying the cousin she wanted me to marry was female ...'

She nodded. 'That's true. Although I'm not sure how that would fit with her Greek traditions.'

He laughed then, loud and hard. 'No,' he agreed. 'And I am not gay, Trix.' He pulled in a long breath. 'I just do not date. It is as simple as that.'

*Simple*? Not dating wasn't simple. It was crazy. Mad. Unthinkable. And he'd called her Trix. Why had she invented that stupid nickname?

'But ...' She couldn't help herself. She had to know. Perhaps this was going to be an insight into how she could stop people from proposing to her after weeks. 'What about sex?'

Long seconds seemed to pass by and Tess could feel the sun on her skin, each centimetre sizzling as she waited for his response. This time he took the aviators off and put them down on the table. He shifted his body weight, turning onto his side and looking directly at her.

'I have sex,' he stated.

The three words all seemed to roll over Tess like a deep tissue massage. She found herself holding her breath.

'But that is all,' he answered shortly. 'Sometimes good sex, other times really, really great sex – you know ...'

She was actually considering if she *did* know, because he was making this no-dating-at-all sex sound like the Big Mac of All Sex. Perhaps this was where she had been going wrong.

Thinking that casual dating was casual enough. Andras just had sex. No Italian meal as a prelude. Just sex.

'There is no confusion. We have sex. We say goodbye. There is no breakfast in the morning or holding hands. Everyone knows where they stand, no?'

He was staring at her and she couldn't look away. She wanted to have sex with him. In fact, she didn't think she had ever wanted to have sex with anyone more.

'Tess,' he whispered.

'Uh huh,' she replied, her stomach revolving with longing.

'Keep very still.'

She instantly tightened her core, her whole body aching for another one of those kisses …

Then, suddenly, he waved a hand and she screamed as something fat and black took flight from around her midriff area, buzzing its way past her face. She leapt from the sunlounger, hands flapping, feet stamping into the fine stones. She hurriedly shoved them into her shoes.

'What was it?! What was it?!'

He laughed. 'It was just a bee.'

'Oh no,' Tess began. 'Bees are yellow and black, small, should be in hives. That *thing* was black like a … flying beetle.'

'It is a carpenter bee. They can be a little aggressive.'

'Really? Well, so can I if it comes near me again.'

He laughed at her again, shaking his head. 'Please, tonight, you must wear repellent for the insects.'

'Ah,' Tess said, brushing sand off her lounger before dropping down onto it again. 'Well, thank you but Sonya and I are eating at the Durrells' house tonight, the White House restaurant.'

'I'm sorry,' Andras stated. 'I had a text from Spiro. There is a family dinner. You must come with me.'

'What? I can't,' she exclaimed. 'I have Sonya to—'

'She can come too,' Andras answered.

'But—'

'You do not need the Wi-Fi any longer?' he asked. 'Or someone to point out the house of the Rothschild family as we sail back?'

He knew she needed Internet connection as much as she needed air to breathe. And she needed this holiday to be perfect for Sonya.

'And if I come ...' All she could think about was sex. Sex with him. Theoretically, if this sex was as casual as he was implying, she wouldn't be breaking Sonya's single rule if she had it, would she? She shook her head, refocused. 'I want you to take us somewhere tomorrow too. Anywhere Sonya wants to go.'

'I—' he began.

'That's the deal,' she said firmly.

'Then we will find a way,' he agreed.

'Tess!' Sonya called. 'Come into the water! It's just so cleansing!'

'In a minute,' she called back. She picked up her cocktail and took another sip.

'She is right,' Andras said. 'The water *is* beautiful.'

Eyes moving right, she watched him strip off his T-shirt then unfasten the buttons of his jeans. Why did the guy talk about sex all the time *and* have a body to die for? Now, wearing nothing but those small trunks, he stood in front of her.

'Are you coming?' he asked.

There went her G-spot.

She rushed out an answer. 'Soon.'

He nodded. 'OK. Well, remember: do not forget to take off your shoes.'

Tess looked down the sunlounger to her feet. They were still clad in the gold strappies she had felt the need to slip on when soles met sand to ward off the bee. Dating. Casual sex. Whatever she did, nothing had really changed since that summer day in July last year.

'I'll catch you up,' she replied, sitting back with a sigh.

## Twenty-two

# The beach near the Rothschild Mansion

Andras cut the engine and moved to the rear of the boat to drop the anchor. They had left Nissaki and taken a slow cruise back up along the coast, passing Kouloura and Kalami and stopping, much to Sonya's delight, at the beach right underneath the Rothschild family mansion.

'There are signs,' Sonya called. Stripped to her tankini, she was hovering above the gap where a small metal ladder dropped into the ocean. 'Private property and … is that a hazard sign?' She put her hand up, shielding her eyes from the sun and looked closer.

Tess's eyes went from where she was applying more suncream on her shoulders to Andras, who had just ripped his T-shirt over his head. She swallowed. On board a boat, bobbing in the azure sea off a gorgeous Greek island with a hot Adonis she could kiss the face off – well, apparently only in role-playing terms.

'The beach cannot be private,' Andras informed them, his hands on the waistband of his jeans.

The way he said 'private' was almost perverted.

'No?' Sonya asked.

'No,' Andras said. 'No beach in Greece can belong to someone.'

'Great,' Sonya said, turning around and shuffling backwards towards the ladder. 'Come on, Tess! Swimming around below the Rothschild mansion. In the same water as Charles and Camilla.'

'I'm not sure that's selling the experience.' Tess watched Andras unbuttoning his jeans. Someone this hot getting his kit off was definitely selling it to her.

There was a noise from her bag, immediately recognisable as emails arriving. Out here, in the middle of the sea, there was Internet. She put down the suncream, wiped her hands on her towel and grabbed for her bag.

'Ooo, a little cold on the toes!' Sonya exclaimed, lowering herself in.

'You should let go,' Andras called to her. 'Just do it, quickly.'

Tess found her email hoping there would be one from work, telling her they had realised what a literal cock-up they had made of the Blackberry Boudoir branding and they were reverting back to her designs. She scanned through. *John Lewis. Travel Republic. Vistaprint.* Nothing new from McKenzie Falconer. She was going to have to make that call.

Suddenly the phone was taken from her hands.

'Come in the water,' Andras said.

She got to her feet quickly, swiping for her mobile and just hitting air as he held the item out of reach. 'Give that back. I need to make a call.'

'Going in!' Sonya called.

'Relax,' Andras urged, his hand with the phone still at full stretch. 'Have fun with your friend.'

Just as Tess's eyes moved to the back of the boat there was an almighty splash and Sonya disappeared, quickly re-emerging with a gasp of delight.

'Cold but … amazing!' she breathed, arms performing a quick breaststroke as she began to tread water.

'I'll come in,' Tess said, eyes back on Andras.

'You will?' Andras stated. He couldn't have sounded more unconvinced if he had tried.

'If you give me my phone.'

He held his arm firm, the phone still too high and too far.

'We should take a photo,' she said. 'Of the two of us.' She swallowed. 'Being a couple.' She smiled. 'To show your family on Facebook.'

He smiled. 'I am not on Facebook.'

'What?' He couldn't be serious. Who wasn't on Facebook?! 'But how do you … connect with people?' The moment the words were out she felt like an idiot. She started to blush. Just how social-media needy did she sound right now?

'We talk, Trix,' he answered. 'Using our voices not our fingers.'

She swallowed, eyes going to those long, lean, olive-skinned fingers curled around her phone. The things they could do …

'I'm swimming to the beach!' Sonya shouted, appearing over the side of the boat, hair now slick from the water, arms moving as she propelled herself along.

Andras finally lowered his arm. 'But we can take a photo,' he agreed. 'Show my mother we have been out today.' He handed her phone over, then slipped an arm around her shoulders, ready to pose.

That torso was so close, almost touching hers. She held her breath, fingers seeming to find it difficult to open the camera app. Finally, she had it open and selected selfie mode.

'Ready?' she asked him, eyes directed at the camera.

'*Etsy*,' he replied.

She snapped the photo then quickly tapped to see the result.

'It is OK,' Andras said, looking at the picture.

Tess swallowed. It was more than OK. It was brilliant. Blue sky and perfect sea behind them, boaty stuff just visible and Andras looking like David Gandy's younger brother. She couldn't wait to load that up to all her social-media accounts.

'So, now we put this down,' Andras said, taking the phone from her again and dropping it onto the seating without care for its delicate disposition. 'And we jump into the water.' He took hold of her hand.

'Jump?' Tess queried. 'But Sonya went down the ladder.'

'It is better to jump,' Andras encouraged her, pulling her over to the back of the boat.

Tess swallowed, immediately looking down at her feet. There was no way she wanted to lose the shoes to the bottom of the sea like the Heart of the Ocean necklace in *Titanic* but the alternative … She was keeping them on. Andras still gripping her fingers, she stepped up alongside him looking down into the water, strips of turquoise combining with deep, inky areas.

'After three,' he said, squeezing her hand.

She didn't reply, just felt the need to close her eyes.

'*Ena, dyo, tria!*'

She jumped up and out, Andras's motion taking her forward faster, and within split seconds she felt the sea pull her in, her body shooting downwards, cold water enveloping her and momentarily stealing her breath. She kicked for the surface, lungs bursting, until she emerged, sunlight on her face. Her shoes were still on her feet.

'Oh! It's cold! Cold!' Tess shrieked.

'It is good, no?' Andras responded.

He was right next to her, far more adept at keeping himself afloat than she was. He was calmly swaying in the water, while her moves were more warding-off-potential-attacker. It was then that the cramp hit. Her calf suddenly tightened, delivering a hideous straining pain that had her gasping.

'What is wrong?' Andras asked, moving closer to her.

'My leg,' she breathed, shaking it out and trying to stretch against the weight of the water. 'It's cramp.'

'Hold on to me,' he urged.

She didn't hesitate. She put her arms around his neck and focused all her effort on making the ache stop hurting. His arm went around her waist, drawing her into his body as his legs worked at keeping them above the water.

'You are OK?' he asked.

Finally, the pain began to subside and she nodded, taking a deep breath. It was only then she realised the intimacy of their position. Her arms around his neck, his torso fixed to hers. His hair was wet, slicked back from his face, those heavenly ebony eyes framed by deep, dark, long, wet eyelashes. Tinder Tess would have taken advantage of his perfect tableau of gorgeousness and occupied those lips with hers. Could she? Should she? While Sonya was busy on the other side of the boat swimming to the beach?

'Let us see who can make it first!' Andras said, relinquishing his grip.

Before she could do anything else he had kicked his body backwards into the water and was disappearing beneath the sea.

# Twenty-three

'This place makes you feel happy to be alive, doesn't it?'

Tess opened her eyes, finger swirling through the aqua-coloured water, legs gently kicking to keep her body afloat. The cooling sea was giving her a relaxing, all-over-body balm of relaxation. The knots she permanently carried across her back seemed to be dissipating ever so slightly.

'Doesn't it made you feel happy to be alive?' Sonya repeated.

'It does,' Tess admitted, eyes moving to the pebble beach where Andras was emerging from the water like a sexy sea god, stepping across the stones like he was walking on luxurious shagpile. How did he do that? Go barefoot over those rocks just ready to spear your soles? Actually, just going barefoot without thinking about it was enough to make her a little envious.

Sonya sighed. 'So, Joey's at a fancy restaurant.'

Tess moved her body around in a circle until she was facing her friend. 'What?'

'He posted on Facebook just after we left Nissaki.'

'Well, what restaurant? With who?'

Sonya's shake of her head answered all the questions in one go.

'Sonya, where's the restaurant?' Tess asked.

'Margate.'

Tess almost breathed a sigh of relief. She had only been to Margate once. When she was a child. It had been a social-club outing with Rachel and her parents. One of the last trips before her mum and dad had split up, although she was sure it wasn't the seaside resort that had done for their marriage. Margate was traditional – fish and chips, jellied eels, not as upmarket as Brighton – not somewhere you first thought of for a romantic destination, unless it had changed. Lots of seaside towns were using phrases like 'café culture', 'vintage chic' and 'traditional charm' to invigorate business. She should know. She had helped rebrand a chain of boutique hotels.

'A re-enactment lunch he forgot to tell you about?' Tess suggested.

'Meeting someone who can give him a baby?'

'No,' Tess said strongly. 'Don't be silly, Sonya.'

'Maybe this has been coming since that conversation and I just pushed it under the carpet. Maybe he's been seeing someone more fertile for weeks …' Sonya gasped. She put one hand to her mouth, seeming to forget she was swimming and her head started to submerge. She recovered with a cough then spluttered. 'Maybe she's already ferti*lised*.'

'That's ridiculous,' Tess said. 'This is Joey. Lovely Joey. He's not a …' She struggled to think of a softer word than 'bastard'. 'He's not … mean or cruel.'

'Actually, he did a very convincing performance as an executioner at the Re-enactment Spring Ball.'

'It's just a restaurant, lunch with a friend. You could phone him,' Tess suggested. She watched a mix of emotions cross her friend's face and then, finally, Sonya shook her head.

'No. He said he needed a break.'

'And did you discuss the terms of this break?' Tess asked. 'Is it the type of break where you can … see other people?'

'What?' Sonya exclaimed, her hand on her chest. 'Is that what people do on breaks?' Her voice started to rise to panic level. 'I thought it just meant ... not seeing each other for a bit. Watching Sky box sets and maybe he would order too much of that pad Thai he likes that I don't like and—'

'It probably does mean that,' Tess said quickly. 'But if you're worried, maybe you should ...'

'Turn into a controlling, stalking, needy, almost-fiancée?' Sonya sighed. 'No. I don't want to do that either.' She breathed. 'I have to trust him.'

'Well ... like his post!' Tess announced, one hand out of the water and pointing. 'No ... no, don't *like* his post, *love* his post.'

Sonya giggled. 'That sounds a bit rude.'

'You go on Facebook and you *love* that restaurant post and anything else he puts up.' She coughed. 'No commenting. Just the love button. And then you and I are going to make some posts of our own. If we can establish connection for more than five seconds.'

'At the White House tonight? Because Joey really wanted to eat there.'

Tess swallowed. 'Ah. About that ...'

'What?'

'We might have to change our reservation.' Her gaze went over to Andras. He was sitting on the beach now, those long, athletic legs stretched right out in front of him. 'If we want to keep our guide man we need to go to a big, fat, Greek wedding-planning dinner tonight.'

Sonya smiled. 'That actually sounds kind of fun.'

'Hmm,' she answered. 'Just don't forget to call me Patricia.'

# Twenty-four

# En route to Kalami

Andras was watching Tess. She was laying across the front of the boat, body relaxed, face turned up to the sun. Her shoes were still on her feet but there was no phone in her hand and there was definitely less tension in her expression. Why that seemed to please him so much he didn't really know. Although perhaps, if she was more chilled, enjoyed all the island had to offer, then acting his girlfriend might not feel such a trial. He shook his head as he held the wheel of the boat. What was he doing? Blackmailing someone to play a part for him just to appease his mother? And just why did he always fall back into the trap of trying to live up to his mother's high Greek expectations?

'We are almost there,' he called out to the women.

'Oh! Already?' Sonya said, turning her body away from the seascape. 'And we didn't see a dolphin.'

Tess sat up, smoothing her hair with a hand. 'Oh, there's always tomorrow.' She was looking directly at him now. 'Isn't that right, Andras?'

He smiled back. 'Maybe not for the whole of the day but after six courses of food tonight and pretending to be in love with me, I think you will have earned another boat trip.'

Tess laughed. 'I never said I would pretend to be in love with you.'

'I think this is exactly what we have already agreed.'

He watched her stand, towelling her body down. She did have a body she obviously took care of. Long legs, a waist that curved like an hourglass ... He looked back to the sea.

'Oh no, Andras. You simply said I had to pretend to be your girlfriend.'

He looked back to her then. 'And there is no love with this?' He was intrigued now.

'Of course not,' she answered. 'Dating is casual ... we talked about casual.'

He remembered. Except how he chose to live his life when it came to relationships was not ordinarily in tune with anyone else.

'Tess is a somewhat of a serial dater,' Sonya blurted out.

'A what?' Andras asked.

'Tess likes to date,' Sonya continued.

'What Sonya is trying to say is, I'm not like your starry-eyed holidaymakers falling for your heavy accent and your hot lamb shanks.' She smiled. 'There's no danger of me wanting a proposal of marriage before the last plate has been smashed.'

'Or before the last scallop has been opened,' Sonya added.

Was it his imagination or had Tess's stance just altered at her friend's words?

She smiled quickly. 'I'm off arthropods at the moment.' She patted her midriff. 'A couple of bad experiences.'

Her humour was restored and Andras gave his attention back to their journey across the waves, the afternoon wind making the sea a little choppier than the journey that morning.

'Tonight I expect there will be lamb shanks,' Andras stated. 'Just like you said.'

'I do like lamb,' Sonya announced, hands to her hat as the keen breeze whipped the rim.

'Where is this dinner tonight?' Tess asked him.

'At my mother's house,' he answered.

'Which is?'

'In Kalami.'

'Near your restaurant?'

He shook his head. 'No.' Then he pointed a finger as they rounded the headland and began to sail towards the mountain scene ahead of them. 'Up there.'

'Right up there?' Sonya queried. 'On the very top of the mountain!'

'*Ne*,' he answered.

'I hope you're not expecting us to walk,' Tess told him.

'No, of course not.' He smiled at her. 'I have a moped.'

'With some sort of sidecar for me?' Her hands went to her hips, riled again. 'Sonya's coming with us, or had you forgotten?'

'I think *I* would prefer the sidecar option,' Sonya stated. 'I've never been very good at getting my leg over …' She paused. 'Over things, you know, like walls and horses and … shopping trolleys.'

'We won't be getting on a moped,' Tess stated firmly. 'Either of us.'

He smiled then. 'You are never relaxed, Trix.'

'Because, funnily enough, my holiday has so far consisted of acting a part for you!'

'And wine,' Sonya chipped in. 'We've had quite a lot of wine.'

He smiled again at Tess, slowing the boat further as they started to travel into the bay. 'You should not worry,' he said. 'I have a car.'

Out of the corner of his eye he saw something move and instinctively he ducked. The small missile still caught him on the chest then fell to the decking.

'No wonder you don't have a real girlfriend!' Tess screeched. 'You're so annoying.'

He glanced to the floor for a second then concentrated on navigating towards Mathias who was beckoning the boat in from the wooden jetty. 'And I guess you will not be needing your honeycomb and caramel lipstick anymore.'

'What?'

'It was a gift for me, yes?'

'Oh my,' Sonya said, stifling a laugh. 'Is that what you threw at him?'

'Give it back,' Tess said, standing up and looking annoyed.

'Sit down please, I cannot see the dock.'

'Here,' Sonya said, handing a plastic tube to Tess. 'Try my apricot and cream one.'

Folding her arms across her chest, Tess sat back down as the boat gently swayed towards the shore and the solid, if a little rickety, pontoon. Why did he have to be so irritating as well as being the sexiest man she had encountered since the ex-TV-Gladiator who played rugby? Actually, Dougie – had that been his name? – had been a little too preoccupied with his teammates and she had started to question his sexuality after date number four – watching and singing along with every single word of *Legally Blonde the Musical*. He hadn't made the whole six weeks.

'My mother is coming.'

At Andras's statement Tess immediately felt the need to sit up straight and move her shoulders back. This was crazy. She had nothing to lose here. If Andras's mother worked out all this was a sham then ... so what? Her eyes went to the helm of the boat then and she watched Andras in deep concentration as he prepared to dock. What made someone give up on anything romantic except sex? At least with her dating lifestyle she actually had conversation as well as fun between the sheets. Who did he talk to? Share things with? Grr, she didn't care!

'She has my cousin with her,' Andras added. 'And my brother's fiancée.'

'Ooo, the lucky lady getting married? Is that her? With the long, dark hair all down her back?' Sonya asked. 'I always wanted hair that long but my hair just goes to fluff – newborn Easter chick fluff – when it gets too far past my shoulders.'

'The cousin your mother wants you to marry?' Tess asked.

'She does?' Sonya exclaimed. 'That's the reason you're fake-dating Tess?'

'Yes,' Tess answered. 'I haven't had a chance to catch you up with that.' She looked back to Andras. 'What are their names?'

'My cousin is Marietta. Spiro's wife-to-be is Kira.'

'And your mother's name?'

'You have forgotten this?'

'The way she looked at me last night, I thought I might have to call her Mrs Georgiou ... or ma'am.'

'It is Isadora,' Andras answered. '*Yassou*, Mathias!' He moved to grab the rope and with one giant swing, threw it over to his colleague who caught it and began to tie the vessel up.

'I am so sorry about this,' Tess whispered to Sonya. 'I know this wasn't what you had planned for our trip and it wasn't what I had planned either and actually, if you want me to put a stop to this farce right now then I will.' She swallowed, her insides pumping mixed signals.

Sonya smiled. 'I had the best day today. Swimming in that sea, enjoying lunch and cocktails at Nissaki Beach, Andras telling us all the stories about when the Albanians tried to invade. It really helped to take my mind off ...'

Tess saw the emotion invade her friend's expression and she reached for her hand, slipping their fingers together and uniting them with a squeeze.

Sonya tried again. 'It helped take my mind off England.'

'You must come! Come now!' It was Isadora's voice, loud and unrelenting. Tess's attention was taken from her friend.

'What has happened?' Andras called, his tone a little anxious.

'Get off the boat, Andras!' Isadora yelled, arms flapping.

# Twenty-five

# Kalami Beach

He was looking for signs of smoke, or worse, flames, as he leapt from the bow. Leaving the restaurant for the day had been a mistake. Now, when he made it up the pontoon and the beach to his business premises – make that his whole life – what was he going to find?

'I knew I could not trust you,' Isadora said. 'I knew this would happen.'

'Mama,' Andras stated. 'What has happened? Please, tell me.'

'It is horrific!' Isadora continued. 'I do not know any other words to describe it!'

His heart was thumping furiously, his eyes looking past his mother to the restaurant. The bright sunshine was preventing him from seeing into the building. Was that … were there … people still dining? If people were still dining then whatever had happened could not be the apocalypse his mother was describing. But the kitchen being destroyed in the middle of the season, before the wedding … that could destroy *him*.

'The tortoise was in the kitchen,' Kira informed him. 'Almost inside the refrigerator.'

'The tortoise,' he stated soberly. This hand-waving and stress was about Hector? He wanted to shout at his mother, tell her she had almost given him a heart attack.

'I think it is quite cute,' Marietta stated.

'It is disgusting!' Isadora screeched. 'A dirty, unholy creature gorging itself on what we will be feeding the customers.'

Anger was still bubbling. Since when had it become *we* will be feeding the customers? They were still *his* customers.

'Go!' Isadora directed. 'Your brother is trying to contain it.'

Only then did he look behind at the boat, realising he had all but abandoned Tess and Sonya. He watched as Mathias held his hand out to Tess to aid her disembarkation.

'Mama—' he began.

'Go with Kira,' Isadora interrupted. 'Marietta and I will see to your friends.'

He was blindsided. Tess was about to ambushed, before the family dinner. He wouldn't blame her if she just gave in and told the truth. She didn't deserve to be caught up in this.

'What are you waiting for? The animal could be starting to gnaw on your brother's vital parts at any second, right before his wedding night!'

'In that case,' Kira began with a smile. 'Please run, Andras.'

He took one last look at Tess and Sonya, now on the pontoon, eyes directed his way, before taking off up the jetty with Kira.

'Predators can smell fear you know,' Tess whispered to Sonya as she made baby steps towards the two Greek women on the wooden bridge.

'In *Planet Earth II* it was more about the predators' team-work than about any of them smelling fear.'

'Case closed then,' Tess stated, swallowing. 'Here's the team. The head matriarch of the pack and the lone female who's desperate to mate with the eldest offspring.'

Sonya gripped Tess's arm. 'Oh, I see … you think we're about to be surrounded and mauled.'

'Greek style,' Tess responded through gritted teeth.

'So, what was my job again?' Sonya asked. 'Was I your boss?'

'No,' Tess said. 'Absolutely not.'

'*Kalispera*, Patricia and Susan,' Isadora greeted, pounding up to them, Marietta a little behind.

Just what size were her feet? Tess swallowed. 'It's Sonya,' she answered on instinct. 'Not Susan. You must have misheard last night.'

'What?' Isadora asked, black eyes homing in on her.

'You can call me Susan,' Sonya bleated quickly. 'I quite like that.'

'You must both be very tired.'

This came from Marietta. Tess surveyed the woman Andras's mother wanted him to marry. She had the dark, glossy Greek hair that looked like it had been conditioned by something salon and more expensive than Tresemmé and she was pretty, in a non-make-up, natural way – the look Tess seemed to need a gallon of foundation to achieve. Why had she wanted her to be ugly? This wasn't some sort of competition. This was just a means to an end. Wi-Fi and a tour guide.

'Tired?' Sonya asked. 'Oh no, quite the opposite.' She stretched her arms up to the sky. 'I feel completely invigorated. Don't you feel invigorated, Patricia? It's all that sea air and warming sun on our skin. It—'

'Will make you turn red like a *fráoula*,' Isadora stated.

'What?' Tess asked.

'A strawberry,' Marietta translated. 'You English must be careful of your delicate skin.'

Was it Tess's imagination or did a beam of sunlight just hit Marietta's cheeks and make her complexion look even more smooth and absolutely-no-need-for-concealer-here ready? Her own cheeks seemed to crease on instinct. She forced a smile, perhaps a facial muscle exercise would reduce lines. 'What would you like us to bring to the meal tonight?'

'Bring?'

Isadora said the innocent word with such volume and ferocity she made it sound like a deep insult.

'Yes,' Sonya verbally stepped in. 'We're very much looking forward to it. We could bring some wine and some nibbles. We had the most lovely oregano crisps—'

'Nibbles?'

Now the picking random words out of their sentences was getting a little annoying. If she *really* was Andras's girlfriend, and Sonya *was* an important client she was entertaining for business, she would feel put out by this woman's lack of manners. For all Isadora knew, she could be becoming Tess's mother-in-law one day. She swallowed. It was time to start fully embracing this role.

Tess reached forward and patted Isadora on the arm. 'We'll bring red and white wine and the crisps.' She directed a smile at Marietta. 'Andras loves crisps.' She batted her eyelashes at Isadora. 'What time would you like us to arrive?'

'This is why we came to meet you here,' Marietta stated. 'Tonight, it is for the family. There is no need for you to come along.' She smiled. 'It is very Greek and we will all be talking in Greek, and you will find this very boring.'

Ah! They were here to try to brush her off! Conflicting feelings were invading her gut like a stand-off at the Battle of Waterloo. She and Sonya could spend the night at the White House as planned, not pretending to be called by any other name, just eating and drinking and being on holiday. But she was Andras's girlfriend to them, and what would backing out say about their relationship? They were supposed to be going out, having had an intimate time together earlier this year. A romantic glass-bottomed boat trip at a difficult-to-pronounce place beginning with 'P'. She had flown here to spend time with him. If this were real, she would not just shrug her shoulders and say OK. Not if he really meant something to her, and that was the story. And, if she didn't go, what would Andras's fate be? Forcibly suctioned to his cousin for the evening? *His* marriage being planned out between courses?

'Oh, I don't think so,' Tess answered. She'd almost sounded menacing. She cleared her throat. 'Andras is so looking forward to introducing me to the whole family before the wedding.'

'There is not enough food for additional guests,' Marietta countered.

'Please!' Tess stated with a laugh. 'I may not speak the language – yet – but if there's one thing I know about your lovely country, it's that no one ever goes hungry.'

'All those gorgeous dishes ending in "a",' Sonya added, with a lick of her lips.

Tess focused her gaze on Isadora, almost daring her to uninvite them. Eye to eye, strong will to strong will. She wasn't going to give up. She always won now. It had taken time, but once she'd learnt to unshackle success and triumph from the ball and chain of emotions, and see them simply in terms of results, there was nothing to get in her way.

Isadora still had her eyes on her but Tess held on, her expression, she hoped, giving nothing away. Finally, the Greek woman opened her mouth to speak.

'We will eat *kleftiko*.' The 'o' was emphasised so much the sound could have started an earthquake.

Tess smiled. 'It sounds delicious, doesn't it, Sonya?'

'Absolutely,' Sonya replied, nodding quickly. 'Utterly delicious.'

'Seven?' Tess asked, this time looking to Marietta.

'As you wish,' Andras's cousin replied.

'Right,' Tess said. 'We had better head back to our apartment and start getting ready.' She smiled again at Marietta. 'I have a new dress I think Andras is going to just love.'

With those words said, Tess sashayed past the two women, hoping to God she was going to make it along the pontoon in her wedges without turning her ankle over.

'That was a bit scary,' Sonya whispered, arriving at her shoulder. 'Isadora had that same look in her eyes Kathy Bates has in *Misery*.' Sonya shuddered. 'That poor lamb for the *kleftiko*. I wonder how long it was shackled before it met its maker?'

'Probably not as long as Andras will be if he marries Marietta.'

'You're right,' Sonya agreed.

'So, you're still OK with this?' Tess asked, looking to her friend as they stopped, preparing to step down onto the beach.

'Being Susan?' Sonya said with a smile.

Tess sighed. 'Yes.'

Sonya linked her arm through Tess's and guided her down on to the stones. 'I think by the time we get to the pudding tonight, Andras will be offering to take us out on the boat again.' She drew in a breath. 'And I did love the boat.'

'Me too,' Tess admitted.

'And you hardly touched your phone all day,' Sonya added.

She swallowed. She still had an avatar of a penis to sort out. Bloody Blackberry Boudoir!

'Who needs dating apps when you have a fake boyfriend,' Sonya whispered, nudging her with her elbow.

Her stomach pinged at that comment, Sonya's words reminding her. She was single. Still single. Going on three weeks now. It was the longest spell she had been without someone since she'd made the pledge. If she didn't do something soon, she might have to get a cat.

# Twenty-six

# Andras Georgiou's home, Kalami

'Why do you do this, Hector? I feed you. I have given you plenty of space.' Andras sighed, observing the large wooden pen he had constructed in the early hours of the morning. 'How do you get out?'

The tortoise seemed to grin as it munched on a cabbage he had given it. What was he doing talking to the animal? Did he think it might actually reply? Perhaps he was losing his mind here.

One hand on the fence surround, he leapt up and out over the solid wall of the enclosure. Resting his back against the panels, he looked out at his view. It was as striking as the day he had first come up here to see the land. Then it had been nothing but scrub – a tangled web of spiky plants all fighting against each other – but *he* had seen its potential at once. Clear the undergrowth, work around and together *with* the terrain, keeping the staggering sea views at its heart. *His* heart had sung the moment he had arrived here, his arms grazed by thorns, scrambling through the thickets of gorse until he had got to the very edge of the precipice and the uninterrupted scene of azure water and the beach below. He swallowed, remembering how differently Elissa had reacted to the plot.

He turned around, facing the house he had started to build for them. She had not seen what he had seen. She had seen too much work. She had seen time spent in the bare bones of a shack that had stood at one edge of the site, not as the beginnings of something very special and worth waiting for, but as a chaotic mess that would never be finished. A fantasy home that would never be realised.

Looking up at the glass-frontage of his large, open living space, he knew buying the land and starting this project had been the right thing to do. It still might not be finished, but it would be, in time. For him it had never been about the end product; the journey itself had been, and still was, ultimately satisfying. Even if there was no longer anyone to share it with.

He checked his watch. He had an hour to get showered and changed before he needed to be back at the restaurant. Before the dinner at his mother's, he wanted to make sure his staff were going to manage tonight without him. He turned back to Hector and eyed the seemingly content tortoise. 'Please, stay here tonight. Just until I am certain my mother is not going to put you on the wedding menu.'

The tortoise elongated its tongue and made a groan.

Andras nodded. 'Yes, Hector, that is exactly how I feel.'

## Twenty-seven

# Kalami Cove Apartments

'Russell, it looks like a penis.'

Tess ground her teeth together and simultaneously pressed the telephone to her ear a little tighter. She didn't think she had ever said the word 'penis' so many times in such a short space of time. She even suspected a career porn actress had said the word 'penis' less.

'And just what sort of fruit are the two genitalia accompanying it meant to be? Because they don't look like blackberries,' she continued.

From her position overlooking the apartment gardens Sonya let out a snigger.

'No, what I want to know, Russell, is when did my clients start wanting their branding to contain pornographic cartoonesque fruits as opposed to my classy, sophisticated icons they all but signed off on before I went on holiday!'

She hadn't meant to raise her voice but Russell didn't seem to be seeing the issue here. Surely someone else in McKenzie Falconer could see that this signage looked like the most private part of a man's anatomy!

She baulked at his answer and then swallowed. He couldn't be serious.

'I'm sorry, Russell, what did you say?' she checked. 'They're meant to be *mangoes*?' What did she do with that? She settled for clearing her throat. 'So, are they changing the company name now? Because I was under the impression our clients' business was called "*Blackberry* Boudoir" not "Mango Magic" or "Club Tropicana".'

Sonya rasped out another laughy gasp and Tess turned away, trying to concentrate on the phone conversation alone. She didn't blame her friend for finding this amusing; she would too, if it wasn't her professional mess to sort out.

'So, have they signed off on these new designs yet?' she asked. She waited for the answer before carrying on. 'So, have they even *seen* these designs yet?' Now she was praying. She didn't care if the company had decided blackberries were too quintessentially English and the avatar needed to have a more worldwide appeal, she was damn sure they wouldn't want the universal sign of the willy. 'They haven't.' She breathed out, the tension in her shoulders reminding her it was still there and no amount of blue sky and sunshine was going to rid her of it completely.

'Then this can be fixed, Russell. You go with *my* designs. Like we planned.' He was trying to interrupt her now. She hated it when he did that. 'You tell them what will work best for their business,' Tess carried on. 'Tell them that to have other fruits – rude-looking or not – on their branding would be confusing. It would be like having Budweiser with little wine bottles and apples on the label – wait, what did you just say?' She'd tried not to be put off by his interruptions but ... 'Did you say you wanted me to produce new images?' Now she felt sick. 'I can't do that, Russell, I'm on holiday, in Greece, and if you think the Internet is bad in that Midsomer village you live in, you want to try coming over here. Russell, I can't. I have no laptop, no design software, no ...' God she needed some wine ... or some ouzo. 'You want me to draw them. With a pencil and paper.'

Sonya wasn't laughing now *or* looking at the outside space. She was staring right at her, open-mouthed.

'Russell, that's a really big ask. You know ordinarily I would.' She shook her head, the contents of her stomach rising rapidly. 'Drafts in three days?' She blew out a breath, shoulder blades contracting together.

Sonya was shaking her head and rapidly moving towards her, a worried look on her face.

'I can't promise it will be my best work but ...' She looked at Sonya. 'But I can promise you it won't look like a dick, or make you look like one when you present it to the clients.' She turned her back on Sonya. 'OK. I'll see what I can do. OK. Bye.'

She ended the call and closed her eyes, knowing what was to come.

'Please tell me you didn't just do that,' Sonya began. 'You didn't just do that, did you?'

'Do what?' Tess asked, turning back and opening one eyelid at a time.

'You're going to work! Do designs! On holiday!'

'You only said I had to stay single. You didn't say I couldn't work,' Tess countered.

'Tess, it's supposed to be a holiday. You're meant to be relaxing,' Sonya reminded her.

'How could I? Knowing that Russell and whatever other dipshit drew a cock for branding were trying to wreck my portfolio? I bet it was Craig. He's just way too keen about everything.'

'So, when are you going to fit this designing in? Over dinner with your fake boyfriend's family? Or tomorrow when we're meant to be sightseeing?'

Sonya did have a point. She would probably be sick if she had to work on a speedboat. 'It's not for you to worry. I'll still be there looking for dolphins with you.'

Sonya sighed. 'It isn't me I'm worried about. It's you.'

'I'm fine,' Tess stated. 'A little lacking in the *real* boyfriend department but I made a promise to you and this could actually help.'

'Using work as a dating distraction?'

'Well ...' She was, wasn't she? She'd momentarily panicked when Russell had suggested she draw something but then sweet relief had walked in. McKenzie Falconer needed her. She was necessary. She was saving the day. There was more to life than having a partner on her arm. God, she *really* did need sex though.

'They take you for granted,' Sonya continued. 'They take everyone for granted.' She sighed. 'I know I may only work in the post room but I see it filter from the top downwards. The CEO passes his stress down to the board, the board passes it down to the managers ... before anyone has realised it they're all behaving like nasty, evil robots who have sold their souls and moved to No-Weekends-Off-Ever-Town, and their health suffers and their family lives suffer and ... the poor, poor babies.'

As Sonya hit the 'b' word she burst into tears and Tess hurried to help her sit down on one of the terrace chairs before she collapsed. Her friend started waving her hand in front of her face. 'I'm fine. I'm totally fine.'

Tess sat down opposite her, squeezing her hands in hers. 'Any update on Joey in Margate?'

Sonya shook her head, tears escaping.

'And you *loved* the post?'

'Y-yes,' Sonya stated.

'Well, that's good. No news is good news.' She smiled. 'And we'll take a selfie halfway up the mountain later, get the best views in focus and us looking all tanned and gorgeous and we'll post that.'

Sonya nodded.

'Then, once we've eaten all this lamb and ensured Andras doesn't end up chained to a bed by his cousin in a non-*Fifty-Shades-Misery*-ankle-breaking-way, you can help me brainstorm ideas for Blackberry Boudoir that don't involve erotic plums.'

'No erotic plums,' Sonya repeated, nodding.

'Unless it's the name of a cocktail,' Tess said. 'Then we might have a lot more than just a pair.'

'I see what you did there.'

'So, do we have a deal? Tanned, gorgeous Facebook photos, no rude fruits and as much fun as we can manage at a big, fat, Greek wedding dinner.'

'Deal, Patricia,' Sonya agreed.

Tess smiled. 'We're in this together, Susan. Sister suffragettes.'

'Without the hunger strikes, unless they really don't have much food tonight.'

'Trust me,' Tess stated. 'We are going to eat like queens.' She smiled. 'Come on, Andras will be here soon.' She stood up and brushed her hands down the front of the new lemon-coloured peplum dress she was wearing. An updated profile picture on Hooked Up might not go amiss if she could sneak a peek on there later and this was definitely the dress to do it in.

'He does have a car, doesn't he?' Sonya asked. 'Because I'm still worried about the whole leg-over thing.'

'He said he had a car.'

There was a loud beep of a horn that sounded like it was coming from somewhere near the front of the main building. Tess looked at Sonya.

'Are you thinking what I'm thinking?' Sonya asked.

'That he's here already and you haven't sprayed us with insect repellent yet?'

'No.' Sonya shook her head. 'That that horn didn't sound like it belonged to a car.'

# Twenty-eight

Of all the times for his car not to start this was the worst. Ordinarily, Andras did not have to transport anyone anywhere. Usually it would be just him and perhaps some boxes of items for the restaurant. It was never two women dressed for a dinner party. He swallowed as he saw Tess and Sonya appear at the archway at the front of Kalami Cove Apartments. This was his fault, making a joke about his moped. He looked over his shoulder to Babis on the moped behind him. Babis should be cooking right now, not playing taxi. But there was nothing he could do. He just needed to get on with this.

He waved a hand at the pair, smiling and turning the throttle a little. He already knew what reaction he was going to get from Tess. If she could not stand to get her bare feet dirty, she was not going to be the kind of girl to relish a ride on a moped.

'You are ready?' he asked when they were close enough to hear him.

'That depends,' Tess answered. Her eyes were going from him to the body of the vehicle he was sitting astride. 'Where's your car?'

'About that ...'

'There isn't one, is there?' Sonya said, looking nervous.

'You said you had a car,' Tess followed it up.

'I do have a car,' he answered.

'Then ...'

'I am afraid that today my car decides to behave like the Wi-Fi. It is not working.'

He looked to Tess, waiting for her to digest that information.

'Then we'll call a taxi,' she stated.

He shook his head. 'There are no taxis in Kalami.'

'What?'

'Taxis are for the main towns only. If we call a taxi it will come from Acharavi. It will take perhaps half an hour, maybe more.'

'Look at me,' Tess stated.

He watched her stand tall. The stunning dress that hugged her figure and stopped mid-thigh was not lost on him.

'This dress, this *designer* dress, was not made for moped-riding.'

'No?' He couldn't resist teasing her a little. She was strung so tightly. 'What was it designed for?'

He saw her hesitate, not prepared for his reply.

'For ... going out for dinner ... and for business ...'

'And standing still,' he offered. 'Like that craze on the Internet. The mannequin challenge.'

'Oh!' Sonya gasped. 'Joey and his friends did that in full battle costume. It was so good. One of them had to stand with his axe poised over an enemy's throat. I always thought one ill-placed sneeze and it might have all gone horribly wrong.' She smiled. 'But it didn't.'

'I will walk,' Tess stated firmly.

'Walk,' he replied.

'Yes, you know, one foot in front of the other. I've been doing it since I was thirteen months old, I'm quite accomplished at it.'

His gaze slipped down her long, slim legs knowing instinctively what he was going to find on the dusty tarmac. And there they were: high-heeled pale shoes, thin straps he knew were not going to withstand a two-mile walk to his mother's home.

'It is up a mountain,' Andras stated.

'Point us in the right direction,' Tess ordered.

'Wait, what?' Sonya chipped in. 'Did you say "us"? Because I have a metatarsal issue that hasn't ever been fully resolved and as much as the "leg-over" thing is worrying me, I'm not sure mountain-climbing is going to do my pre-existing condition any good.'

'You cannot walk,' Andras told Tess bluntly.

'Watch me.' She turned away and began strutting out onto the road heading for the way out of the village.

Andras drove the moped forward, keeping her pace, the engine struggling to idle.

She turned to him, still strutting in those high shoes, her face already reddening in response to the hot evening. 'What are you doing?'

'What are *you* doing?' he responded.

'I am going to find your mother's house to eat a Greek god's bodyweight in lamb.'

'Tess, it is too far for you to walk.' He shifted the moped further forward to keep in line with her. 'Please, get on the bike.'

She stopped abruptly then and turned to face him. A bead of perspiration was starting to weave its way down from her brow. She was hot. And she was doing him this huge favour. He should have borrowed a car.

'You do not have to come,' he stated, killing the engine. 'I will say you are not feeling very well … or, I will tell the truth.'

'No,' she said immediately and with force.

He looked at her a little quizzically.

She shook her head, blonde hair shifting across her back. 'No, don't do that.' She took a breath. 'I want to come.'

'You *want* to come?' he repeated, with a swallow.

'Because earlier, they told me *not* to come,' she stated, her blue eyes looking directly into his.

'They did?'

'And no one does that to me and … Sonya is going through a … difficult time.'

He watched her look over her shoulder at her friend. He turned then too, saw Babis aiding Sonya's mount on to the pillion.

'Sonya loves the boat.' Tess sniffed. 'I need you to take us out on the boat and—'

He turned back to her. 'And?'

'And I'm going to need a computer.'

'A computer.'

'Do you have one?'

'There is something wrong with your phone?'

She shook her head. 'I'm going to need something bigger.'

He felt the need to wet his lips. 'Bigger?'

'More substantial,' she answered. Now he was starting to perspire a little himself.

'For work,' she said. 'I have to do a bit of work while I'm here.'

He nodded. 'Of course. Work.'

'So do you have one?' Tess asked.

'Yes.'

'That works?' she asked.

He smiled. 'Yes.'

'Good,' she answered. He watched her breathe out, smoothing her hair back and away from her face. 'Why is it still so hot?'

'This is Corfu in the summer,' he reminded her. 'Perhaps the breeze from the ride up the mountain would help.'

Right on cue there was an ear-splitting shriek and Babis's moped roared into life. Sonya was clinging on to the Greek man, red hair flying out from underneath the helmet. The woman waved a hand and then was gone, hammering up the incline on two wheels and leaving a trail of dust.

'Turn away and close your eyes,' Tess stated with a resigned sigh.

He carried on looking at her, wondering what his gaze had to be diverted from.

'Close your eyes,' she demanded. 'Because me getting on that thing' – she pointed at the bike like it was a sworn enemy – 'is going to be more overexposure than on the Playboy channel.'

Still, his eyelids didn't seem to want to commit.

'Andras!' she shouted.

His eyes shut then. But, as he heard her shoes move on the gravelly road, then felt her hand on his shoulder, her body slowly slipping in close to his, every part of him was remembering the joy of female contact and rapidly starting to forget his current desire for absolute abstinence.

'Well, what are you waiting for?' Tess asked, her arms clasped tight around him like a rock climber clinging to a life-saving precipice. 'Just, make it quick and promise me wine when we get there.'

'*Kanena provlima*,' he replied, restarting the engine. 'No problem.'

# Twenty-nine

# Isadora Georgiou's house

'I thought ... I thought my heart was going to burst right out of my chest!' Sonya pulled the helmet from her head.

Tess shivered, her eyes on Andras as he parked their vehicle. She had just had the ride of her life. Her arms wrapped around a gorgeous Greek, winding around and up the mountainous terrain, spectacular scenery around each and every curve of the road – the sparkling sea, copses of olive trees, grazing goats and sheep, ancient ruins – a sliver of excitement had coiled right the way through her. She had never been anywhere quite like this before, and with her new dress barely covering her Brazilian, sat astride a throbbing engine, an easy, relaxed smile had spread right across her face.

'I think I got arthritis on my arthritis,' Sonya announced, crunching over the stones, legs wobbling.

'Did you?' Tess asked, still watching Andras. His shirtsleeves were rolled up to each elbow exposing those delicious forearms. She watched him get off the moped with a lot more ease than *she* had a few moments earlier. Black jeans just fitted enough to hint at what was beneath and that plain, pale blue cotton shirt covering those delectable abs.

'Yes,' Sonya said. 'But, apart from the aching all over and the feeling like we might fly right over the ravine any second

... oh my, I loved it!' She giggled. 'I've never been on a moped before. I almost can't wait for the ride back.'

Tess watched Andras as he spoke to Babis. Their journey had been equally as fast and thrilling as Sonya's description, but along with the air of reckless abandon on terrifying not-even-B-roads, Andras had also been considerate. Perhaps it was because her fingernails had been digging into his flesh when he'd powered around a particularly tight turn, but nevertheless he had slowed down, calling over his shoulder to check she was all right the moment she tensed.

'So, here we are,' Sonya said, looking ahead at the very traditional one-storey building in front of them.

'Here we are,' Tess repeated. Despite its one level, the house was an imposing structure that seemed to sink back a long way, further than the eye could see from their current vantage point. Just in front of the property, bordering the rounded parking area-cum-garden were abundant flowering clematis bushes, followed by gunmetal grey urns each side of the door, filled with heady-scented lavender plants. It seemed that every space on this island was filled with gorgeous plant-life – expertly nurtured – unlike Tess's patch of garden at home.

'*Spiti* Georgiou,' Sonya stated, breathing in deep.

Tess looked at her friend. 'What?' she queried.

'*Spiti* is the Greek word for "house".'

The engine of Babis's bike started up again and then the chef sped from the driveway, waving a hand at them both.

'So,' Tess said. 'What's the Greek for "I wonder if the mother and the cousin are going to poison our dinner"?'

'Perhaps we should forget the translation and try to guess which one will try to do it first,' Sonya remarked as Andras moved towards them. She flapped a mosquito away with her hand. 'No, deep breaths, we mustn't think like that.' She closed her eyes and sucked in her lungs. 'Because after all that sea air ...' She opened her eyes and grinned at Tess. 'I'm really, really hungry.'

Andras moistened his lips as he looked at the women. That dress. Totally inappropriate for riding in. The eye-averting Tess had made him do when she'd got on the moped hadn't done anything to stop the fact her thighs had been closed around his hips on the drive. And his body had reacted to it without hesitation. Looking at her now, as he walked over the stones towards them, well, he was starting to realise that overcomplicating things had been a bad idea. His libido was in need, and there was no denying she was an attractive woman. Perhaps, after the dinner, despite his pledge to himself about meaningless sex, he would head into Corfu Town and find someone anonymous to lose himself in. That would scratch the itch for a while.

He smiled at Tess and Sonya. 'You are ready for dinner?'

'Oh yes!' Sonya stated at once. 'I can smell ...' She sniffed hard, nose in the air. 'Spiced meats and ... rosemary.'

'Really?' Tess answered, stepping forward. 'All I can smell is Andras's family's disapproval of his non-Greek girlfriend.' She smiled at him. 'I've heard she's a terribly bad influence from England who is going to commit him to a life of debauchery and all things unholy.'

His eyes began to stray to the low-cut neckline of her dress and he quickly put the brakes on. He looked directly at her. 'All things unholy?'

He watched her swallow, the bravado melting a little.

She nodded her head, confidence restoring. 'Things like ... not saying grace before we eat. Not marrying people we are related to.' She batted her eyelashes. 'Lots and lots of s—'

'Souvlaki!' Sonya announced. 'I can definitely smell souvlaki.'

Andras smiled and held his arm out, indicating the front door. 'Shall we go in?'

'Yes,' Tess said. 'Bring on the arsenic.'

Stepping through the old wooden door, unsteady on its hinges, Tess opened her eyes as wide as they could go to try to find some light. This was not the typical house she had seen on *A Place in the Sun* – all white walls, multiple aspects letting in the natural light; the walls here were a muddy mushroom and she could barely see where she was stepping.

'Is there no electricity?' Tess asked, hands reaching forward, worried that if she lost Andras she would be twisting and turning through these narrow corridors for ever.

'Ooo, cobwebs,' Sonya said from behind Tess. 'I do know from Marco Polo there are a few big species of spider in Corfu.'

'I wish you hadn't said that,' Tess answered. 'Andras, why is it so dark?'

'I do not know,' he responded. 'A power cut perhaps?'

'A power cut?' Tess exclaimed. 'No light at all when it gets dark?' *No plug to charge her phone* was what she had really wanted to say.

'No heat to cook the dinner,' Sonya said, tone dismayed.

'Is anyone even here?' Tess asked.

Suddenly the door opened and Tess was blinded by light. She stooped behind Andras, shielding her eyes as several shrieks pierced the air. Dots floating in her vision, she reached out sideways hoping for a nice, solid wall to cling to. Instead she felt ... fur. She screamed, retracting her hand and falling sideways.

'It's a rat!' Tess exclaimed, lips shaking with the words.

'It's not! It's my hair! Ow!' Sonya exclaimed, hand to her head.

One of the shapes in front of them said something in Greek. Bright sunshine carried on stinging her retinas. Something else was spoken, and this time the urgency in the woman's voice was enough to make Tess's stomach fall a little. Something was wrong.

Andras moved, leaving her and rushing past the group of women – she could just make them out now – into the deep bowels of this unconventional house.

'What's going on?' Sonya asked as the women followed Andras.

'I don't know,' Tess replied. 'But I need to get out of this creepy corridor.'

'Traditional,' Sonya stated. 'Not creepy.'

'What about the pitch-black to bright light combination?' Tess asked. 'That was creepy. It was like some sort of SAS tactic to throw us off balance.'

'Do you think so?' Sonya asked.

'I know so,' Tess answered. 'But we are not going to succumb.'

'No,' Sonya said, a little hesitant. 'Unless they withhold food. Then I might just do anything for a *gyros*.'

'Come on,' Tess said, linking an arm with her friend. 'I think my fake boyfriend might need us.'

# Thirty

His cousins had told Andras it was an emergency and his first thought was for his mother. She might look as strong as an ox and have the demeanour of an angry, stubborn goat but she was close to seventy and she had been working furiously on this wedding for months. Then they had said it was Spiros. There had been no relief, just a further stomach-dropping motion as he ran through the house, heart pummelling his chest wall, fear gripping his every part. Spiros was hurt. But how hurt? And would the ambulance make it up here in time?

Barrelling out of the door and on to the lawn he could see, across the grass, someone laying on their back. He looked nowhere else, just to the unmoving form of his brother.

'Have you called the ambulance?' he shouted. 'Done anything for him?'

He skidded as he dropped to his knees, arriving at his brother's side and immediately reaching to loosen the top button of Spiros's shirt. Why had no one done that already?

'What happened here?' he asked, looking to his relatives who all seemed remarkably calm.

He looked back to his brother's lifeless form. 'Spiro!' he said, voice tight. 'Can you hear me?'

There was no reply. His brother's eyes were tight shut, his skin a little flushed. What did that mean? Pale, grey skin was worse than coloured cheeks, wasn't it? Unless, like his father, it was a stroke.

'Spiro,' he said again, this time more urgently. He put a hand to his neck, hoping to feel the thump of a heartbeat.

'He had a fall,' Marietta stated.

'What sort of fall?' Andras asked. He pressed the back of his hand a little harder to his brother's neck.

Suddenly Spiros's eyes snapped open and he grinned from ear to ear. 'A fall from a donkey!' He laughed loud. 'Hee haw! Hee haw!'

Confusion flooded Andras as, all at once, there were cheers, laughter and hands clapping together. He sat back on his haunches as his brother rolled up, still laughing. Then, in his periphery, came the donkey being led by Helena in Corfiot dress again, cheeks as pink as a radish.

'Smile, Andras,' Marietta said, her hands on his shoulders. 'Spiros has completed another task on his list thanks to you.'

Spiros smiled at him. 'The donkey you organised arrived half an hour ago.' He laughed. 'It seemed like too good an opportunity to miss.'

He still had no idea what was going on except that his heart was still somewhat in crisis, not knowing whether it was safe to feel relieved. He swallowed, unable to comment.

'Opportunity for …' he said.

'To make a joke with the best man,' Marietta answered.

Spiros slapped his shoulder. 'It was on my list.'

Those scrolls! To make a joke with him? From where he was sitting it was more a case of them making a joke *of* him. He got to his feet feeling nothing but humiliated and angry.

'Come, Andras.'

He turned around at his mother's voice. How could she be in on this? To let him be convinced something terrible had happened to his brother?

'This …' He loosened the top button of his shirt. 'This is not funny.'

'Andras,' Isadora said. 'It was a simple joke. A joke that has been played in our family for years. You remember when Mikalis got married?'

He didn't remember his cousin Mikalis's wedding. The only memories he had right now were of finding his father's car at the side of the road and him unconscious inside it. He had pulled him out of the vehicle, got down on his knees in the dirt and tried to find some response, just like he had with Spiros.

Spiros laughed. 'Mikalis made his whole body look like he had the most terrible disease and his best man had no idea what to do.' He laughed again. 'They actually got all the way to Corfu Town, to the hospital, asking for the doctor in charge of special diseases, before Mikalis had to admit it was just paint!'

Andras looked back to the house. Tess and Sonya were out on the lawn, their eyes on the scene. Had they witnessed this hoax? This deliberate attempt to make him look stupid? He gritted his teeth together, seething. 'Excuse me, I should get a drink for my girlfriend.' He looked directly at his mother then. 'It seems no one is attending to our guests.'

He heard Isadora inhale deeply before she replied. 'There is wine in jugs on the table. Or does "your girlfriend from England" usually need someone to serve her like in *Downton Abbey*?'

'I will see to the drinks, Isadora,' Marietta said, getting ready to move.

'No,' Andras snapped. 'You have done enough.' He tried to calm down, adrenalin still rushing through him. 'I will do it.'

'Andras, I did not think …' Spiros began tentatively. Was his brother finally realising just what memories his prank had evoked? 'I did not think that …'

Waving a hand, Andras cut him off. He couldn't talk to him any more. He needed to move away from the family group before he said something he might later regret.

'Do we help ourselves, do you think?' Sonya asked, eyeing the earthenware flagons of liquid sitting on the long, rustic trestle table covered in a pretty white lace tablecloth.

Tess's attention was with Andras as he made his way over. Something had happened down there in the middle of the garden. She had seen the urgency in his movements as he'd left the house, the way he had dropped to his knees on the grass and tended to his brother. Then a donkey had come onto the scene and people had started clapping. Andras's eyes had darkened and the tension in his torso, when he'd stood up, had told her he was furious about something.

'I don't know whether I should but I'm quite thirsty and …' Sonya deliberated.

'Have wine,' Andras stated as he finally reached them, his breathing ragged.

'Oh, are you sure?' Sonya asked. 'I didn't like to—'

'Have it,' he said. 'Have all of it. Drink from the flagon. I am going to.' He picked up one of the jugs and poured some into his mouth, a little drizzling down his chin.

Tess swallowed, watching as he wiped long fingers over his stubble, removing the liquid.

'Well … I'll get a glass,' Sonya said, picking one up from the table.

'What happened over there?' Tess asked softly.

He shook his head. 'My family and other animals. Just like the book.'

'Shall I fill up wine glasses for you two?' Sonya suggested.

'What was wrong with your brother?' Tess asked.

He scoffed. 'Nothing. My family thought it would be funny to trick me into thinking he was half-dead for the sake of a list of wedding traditions.'

Tess looked over to Isadora and Marietta, heads close together as they walked up the garden. What were they plotting next?

'I do not know why I am surprised,' Andras said. 'It does not matter what I do, it will never be right.'

Tess turned back to Andras. 'Right for who?'

'Right for my family. My mother.'

'Well,' Tess stated. 'Her name on the birth certificate doesn't give her the right to tell you how to live your life.' She sniffed. 'You worry too much about what she thinks. So much so you created a fake girlfriend, for God's sake.'

Sonya nodded. 'Tess does have a point.'

'And you?' Andras said, his eyes on Tess. 'You do not worry about the thoughts of your family? Do things that you do not want to do for them?'

The question had Tess wishing Sonya would hurry up with that wine she was taking ages to pour. Her family. Her mum and dad who had sunk every penny they owned into Rachel's wedding that had ended in divorce and then hers that never even got out of the church. No, she didn't do anything for them. She'd run away and packed her guilt with her. And she was still not even halfway close to saving up the money to repay them both. Until she had done that, there was always going to be an awkwardness between them. Perhaps it was of her making, but she knew she had let them down and it still felt so utterly horrible. So she kept her distance. Out of sight. Out of mind. She had no real idea what they were doing with their lives right now. Was her mum still doing pottery? Was her dad still dating that Canadian woman? And what about her sister? They hadn't spoken since Rachel had gone through the stage of following Phil when he left work again because someone had told her he had another new girlfriend. When was that? Was it really months?

'Let's have some wine, yes?' Sonya said, arms breaking into the space, a wine glass in each.

Tess took the glass and knocked back a large mouthful. She smiled at Andras, the alcohol hit restoring a little confidence. 'One thing I do know is, my family would never involve national dress, or a mule, in any of their dramas.' Right on cue there was a bray from the donkey who seemed to have its head stuck in a bush of bougainvillea.

He leaned forward, face only inches away from hers and she instinctively held her breath. 'But costumes,' he breathed, 'and an ass ...' He wet his lips. 'Might make things a little more interesting, no?'

She quivered. She actually quivered, as her brain conjured up all manner of kinky right there on the lawn. It was not the Corfiot sun making its slow-burning descent that was heating her up, it was Andras, so incredibly close ...

'Pass them the babies!'

Before Tess had time to wonder where she could find something leather and tight on a Greek island, a large, bald six-month-old was thrust into her arms. It grinned, gums, a few teeth and drool sliding from its mouth. She couldn't tell immediately if it was a boy or a girl but it had an air of Vladimir Putin about it.

'Ooo, I'm not sure I ... hold on! I'll have to put the wine down. Oh, hello little one,' Sonya said, as the baby was pushed at her.

Tess looked at her friend, arms around the small child who was immediately trying to rip her earrings from her lobes.

This was the last thing Sonya needed. Getting up close and personal with someone in nappies when her relationship was faltering due to unresolved baby issues ... She shook her head.

'Ba!' the baby in her arms declared, thumping its fist on her chest.

'I'm not really a ... that is, I don't really ...' Tess began. All Greek eyes were on her as the baby decided to try out a full drum solo on her boobs. 'Which one of you is the lucky mother?' She swallowed. 'Such a lovely ... boy.'

'It is a girl!' Isadora exclaimed. 'You do not know the difference between a boy and a girl.'

'Usually, unless it's Eurovision.'

Andras scooped the child out of her arms, raising it up to the sky and causing it to chuckle excitedly. 'This is Athena.'

'Lovely,' Tess stated, picking up her glass of wine and having another gulp.

'Ow! Sorry,' Sonya said. 'This little one seems to like my hair and my earrings.' She tried to gently tease the baby's fingers from her earrings and where it was attempting to pull out fistfuls of her hair.

'Come!' Isadora announced. 'We will roll them on the bed!'

Tess almost spat out her wine. 'What?' She looked to Andras as Sonya was finally relieved of her baby. 'What did she say?'

'It is another Greek tradition,' he answered, Athena tugging at the collar of his shirt. 'Babies are rolled around the bed of couples who are to be married. It is believed to promote fertility.'

Tess laughed. 'Are you serious?'

'Yes, we are serious,' Isadora said, appearing at close quarters and snatching Athena from Andras's arms. 'Perhaps, when the time comes, I will roll a baby around your bed too.'

Tess swallowed. How could the woman make something involving a baby sound like a threat?

Andras spoke to his mother in Greek, then slipped an arm around Tess's shoulders, drawing her into his body a little. Tess watched as Isadora's expression immediately darkened.

'Dinner will be ready soon,' Isadora stated, launching Athena against her shoulder and turning for the house.

Tess looked up at him. 'What did you say to her?'

He smiled. 'I simply said that she was welcome to roll the babies around our bed any time she liked.'

Her stomach squirmed just thinking about Andras's bed – him between the sheets, her on top of him. This scenario was starting to get a lot harder now she was banned from seeking any other male attention while she was here.

'They were lovely babies, lovely,' Sonya said, and her comment made Tess pull herself together. She held her glass out to Andras. 'Could you get us something a little stronger than wine?'

He nodded, taking the glass. 'I know just the thing.'

Tess smiled, then as soon as he left the table she made a move back to Sonya, putting an arm around her shoulders. 'I'm so sorry about the babies.'

Sonya shook her head. 'Don't be silly. Babies are everywhere.'

'But not usually forced on you like that.'

Sonya sighed. 'Little chubby cheeks … little eeny weeny fingers and toes …'

'Covered in drool,' Tess reminded her quickly. 'Covering everything you own, including your body, in drool. And, if they're ill, you'll be wishing for *just* drool.'

'They can be nice, though. All those smiles and giggles,' Sonya mused. 'You know, a little person you've made with the man you love.'

Tess gave her friend's shoulder a squeeze. 'Let's focus on *us* smiling and giggling as we stuff ourselves with Greek food tonight.'

'And drink,' Sonya added. 'If we have enough drink we might end up being the ones drooling over everything.'

'Cheers to that,' Tess replied.

# Thirty-one

Tess sat back in her chair, hands on her stomach as it started to feel like it was trying to burst out of her designer dress. They had eaten five courses and it was rumoured a sixth was on its way. So much for there not being very much food! First there was creamy taramasalata and nutty houmous, together with every variety of olive known to man; next was *dolmades* and *spanakopita* – the stuffed vine leaves Sonya loved so much the night before and a Greek cheese and spinach pie. Then there was lamb *kleftiko*. The tender hunks of beef in a sauce called *sofrito* had practically melted in Tess's mouth and it had been accompanied by a delicate, fragrant rice dish, the like of which she had never experienced before. If it hadn't been for the sly digs from Isadora every third sentence, the meal would have been almost perfect: sweet white wine, the liqueur Andras had apparently found in the depths of the house, Sonya smiling and happy talking to Kira and making up a rather elaborate backstory for her role as a business aficionado. Not to mention the gorgeous man next to her, and in the background the sun slowly sinking into the horizon.

'What do you do?'

Tess jumped in her seat at Isadora's question yelled down the table in her direction. As she steadied herself all Andras's relatives looked to her. There were fourteen of them – she'd counted – plus the babies and Helena, the girl with flowers in her hair.

'What do I do?' she repeated, gaining some time.

'In UK. For work,' Isadora elaborated. 'Susan is a customer, am I right? What is she a customer for?'

'Mama, I do not think—' Andras began.

'No,' Tess stated. 'It's fine.' She smiled at Andras's mother. 'I work in branding.'

'Branding?' Isadora stated. 'What is this?'

'Something my father does to cows?' Marietta asked. The comment earned her a light laugh from other members of the family. Athena, on the lap of her mother, banged an olive-wood rattle down hard on the table. Tess continued to smile. She wasn't going to let these women make her feel inadequate. She was also going to think up lots of extra ways Andras was going to pay her back for this torture. If it hadn't been for the lush food she might have just spilled the giant Greek beans about the reality of the situation.

'I design logos and banners for companies to help pep up their websites and social-media accounts, or I create a whole new business identity from scratch.'

'You draw pictures,' Isadora stated. 'Like Athena and Leto with crayons.' This prompted another laugh from the family and Athena was tossed from one relative to the next, bouncing on knees along the table.

'Yes,' Tess stated. 'I suppose it is a bit like that.'

'Patricia is very good at what she does,' Sonya piped up. 'The best, actually, otherwise she wouldn't have my business.' She took a sip of her wine. 'Owning an international haberdashery, jewellery and unique porcelain conglomerate, I haven't got time to waste on anyone who isn't dedicated, professional and an expert in their field.'

'So, it is all work for you,' Isadora stated. 'That is why you don't like the babies.'

There was a collective gasp from around the table and Tess felt her mouth drop open.

'No ... I mean ... yes ... I don't like ... I mean ... I *do* like the babies, of course I like the babies.' She was floundering. How could she be floundering? She ate people like Isadora for breakfast in business circumstances. She stood up, chair rocking backwards, and held her arms out across the table. 'Give me Athena.'

'Trix,' Andras said, putting a hand on her arm.

'Trix? Ah ha!' Isadora exclaimed. 'You tell me her name is Patricia.'

'It is!' Sonya jumped in. 'Trix is short for Patricia.'

'Come on, Athena,' Tess said, shaking her outstretched arms and widening her eyes and smile to endear herself to the little girl.

'Whatever is going on between you is pointless, I hope you know that,' Isadora said.

Andras got to his feet and instinctively Tess dropped her arms.

Andras had had enough of this. All the way through what was meant to be a family celebration and a chance to discuss Spiros and Kira's wedding, Isadora had looked at Tess as if she were a Kalamata olive that needed pitting. She had already done so much for him over this crazy situation, it was time to take action.

'Mama, Trix and Susan – Sonya,' he corrected, 'are my guests here tonight.'

'I am well aware of that,' Isadora snapped.

'Then please, I know it is your home, but you taught me that guests should always be treated with respect.'

His mother made no reply.

'Helping businesses is a good job to have.'

'In a city,' Isadora said. 'Just like the job Elissa had.'

There was another gasp from the family. He gritted his teeth. His mother seemed hell-bent on trying to belittle him at every turn. Even in front of his own family.

He put the flat of his hands on the table, hoping to garner a little strength from the stance. 'Yes,' he replied. 'And there are times, like right now, when perhaps I wonder if I should have worked in the city with her.'

He swallowed as silence descended. Fourteen people, two babies and an eight-year-old seemed to freeze, and the only sound came from the cicadas in the bushes.

His eyes stayed with his mother. Why was she doing this? Was this what he was going to be forced to put up with when Spiros left and Isadora took over his brother's share of the restaurant? His idyll here, the life he'd chosen, was starting to feel like a very small room where the walls were quickly closing in.

'I can smell ... honey and walnuts!' Sonya announced loudly, her voice breaking the silence. 'I'm right, aren't I? Can you all smell honey and walnuts?'

Andras watched Sonya, eyes and hand gestures encouraging the guests to re-engage with the conversation.

Isadora got to her feet, body language still defiant. 'It is *kataifi*.' She shot a look at Sonya. 'Syrup. Not honey.'

Lowering himself back down to the chair, Andras picked up his glass of wine and took a swig of the pale-coloured liquid.

'Are you OK?' Tess asked him.

He turned to look at her. 'I should be the one asking you that question.' He sighed. 'My mother and Marietta, they have ...'

'Picked at me all night? Glared at me like I single-handedly killed all the celebrities in 2016?' She nodded. 'I did tell you they didn't want me here.'

'And I didn't listen.'

'You did,' she answered. 'And I told you I could handle it. And I have.' She swallowed. 'I am.'

'This is all my fault. Involving you in my family drama and all these ...' He lowered his voice. 'Lies.'

She nodded and picked up her wine glass. 'Believe me, if I was any ordinary holidaymaker here to relax and soak up the Greek ambience then I wouldn't be doing any of this.'

'But you want a guide man for Sonya.' His eyes went to where Sonya was repinning the flowers in Helena's hair a little way away.

'It's more than that,' Tess admitted. 'It's a really great distraction.'

'From?' he asked, leaning in a little closer to her.

A sigh left her then. A deep, shoulder-hunching, whole-body-shivering exhalation he almost felt inside himself.

'From thinking about my own life, and all the things I've done wrong.' She smiled but the expression caught a little. 'Maybe wishing that my family cared enough to interfere.' She shook her head. 'Or rather, that *I* cared enough to let them interfere.'

'Tess ...' Andras began, his hand moving, wanting to make contact.

She shifted her chair back. 'God, what am I saying?' She looked at her wine glass like it might contain truth serum. 'What is in this stuff?' She got to her feet. 'Excuse me just for a second while I head into the gloom and find the loo.'

'Tess ...' he began again, making to stand up. But she was gone, tottering across the grass and making for the house.

# Thirty-two

'I rolled a baby over a bed!' Sonya slurred as she strapped the motorbike helmet over her head, tucking in the stray bits of hair Baby Leto had pulled out earlier. 'I really rolled a baby over a bed.'

Babis had been called back up and they were outside Isadora's house getting ready to leave the dinner party. The sky was pitch-black, the lack of light pollution making the stars shine out like a million fairy lights strung across an ebony canvas.

'Who knew that could be a tongue twister,' Tess responded.

'What?' Sonya asked.

She shook her head and looked back at the rustic door, willing Andras to walk through it. 'Nothing.' She was longing for her hard, single bed in the humid, stale air of their room at Kalami Cove. Just a bit of quiet – aside from Sonya's snoring – no one making her feel unwelcome or uncomfortable, or making her remember her life prior to being Miss Six-Weeks-And-Completely-Self-Reliant.

Babis started up the moped and Sonya let out a shriek. 'Whoa! Sorry! I just didn't want you to take off before I was ready.'

'It is not an aeroplane,' Babis called, grinning.

Tess looked to the door again then back to Sonya. 'Have you got the key?'

'Yes,' Sonya answered.

'You should go on,' Tess stated. 'I'll be right behind you as soon as my moped driver turns up.'

'Are you sure?' Sonya hiccupped. 'Sorry.'

'Yes, go and put the kettle on or open some more wine.'

'Ooo, I bought some baklava bits in the supermarket, we could have those with it.'

Tess nodded. 'Good idea.'

'We are ready?' Babis asked Sonya.

'We are ready,' Sonya replied, putting her hands on his hips.

Throttling up the bike, Babis span the moped around the circular drive, showering the surrounding vegetation with pebbles as he zoomed out of the property, Sonya's squeals breaking through the warm air.

Tess let out a sigh. What was she supposed to do now? Andras had said he was ready to leave, she and Sonya had made their way to the front of the house, and now she was just waiting, on her own in the dark, the only sound the bugs in the trees and some faint barking of dogs. Her skin prickled in response to something – perhaps the balmy air – or the fact she was alone here, in the quiet, black night on the side of a Greek mountain. There were no street lights here or the hum of traffic, just perfect, calming tranquillity. She wasn't used to it. She wasn't sure how to *be* in it. What did you do when there was nothing to do? Even just for a minute?

She quickly reached into her bag and took out her phone. There was signal: 4G *and* phone signal allegedly. Looking at her access to the world, she wondered what app she should look at first. *Dating? Facebook? Work email?* Instead she found her finger hovering over the photos icon. She pressed and up came the selfie she had taken earlier with Sonya. After the so-sweet dessert they had walked across Isadora's grass to the very edge of the land. Stopping at the tiny fence meant to prevent a fall down the cliff side, they had carefully positioned themselves so the rapidly disappearing sun was visible behind them, together with the shimmering sea, and the beautiful flora and fauna of the mountain, then adopted their best poses. Tess smiled at the picture now. Sonya looked happy, almost worry-free. She knew that wasn't truly the case, but perhaps this mad, ridiculous dinner party had been a tonic for her friend.

Tess swiped left and her breath caught in her throat. There was the photo she had snapped with Andras on the boat earlier that day. Those eyes! That smile! He was utterly divine to look at. And she didn't look too shabby either. Ideally she would have reapplied some lipstick or lipgloss at the very least before the picture but she looked OK. She flicked her vision to the top of the phone. It was still showing 4G. Maybe now was the time to post this photo of her new squeeze. It had been far too long since she'd posted coupledom on Facebook. She pressed the icon to share … and then stopped. She took a deep breath, thumb still hovering. What was she waiting for? She hadn't posted a couple's picture since Tony at the Radisson. He'd positioned two croissants over her robe-clad chest and made a comment about them being moist and buttery. She'd edited the photo so it was just a headshot. Her hair had looked nice and Tony's tan looked more teak than mahogany.

'Tess, I am sorry.'

Andras's voice made her jolt for the home button. She stabbed at it and dropped the phone into her bag in one motion. She turned to face him, shoes crunching the stones a little.

'I was trying to get away and then Spiros, he is drunk, he is trying to talk to the donkey and my mother is warning him he will go the way of Uncle Dimitri and …'

Tess smiled. 'It's fine.'

'No,' he said, stepping closer to her. 'No, it is not fine.' He sighed. 'Nothing about tonight was fine.'

'Well,' Tess began, 'I thought the food was very nice.'

'I am ruining your holiday,' he stated softly. 'You came here to Greece to see Greece, not to get involved with a complicated family and spend your break being insulted.'

'If I'd wanted that I could have auditioned for *Coach Trip*.'

'What?'

'Sorry,' she smiled. 'You did promise another day out and a large device.'

'A what?' he asked.

'A laptop,' she replied.

'After tonight, somehow it does not seem enough,' he stated, those dark eyes fixed on her.

Her stomach revolved, the flirtatious answer already on her lips. 'That depends how many inches it is.'

She watched him react to her reply. He was unmoving, just holding her gaze, his chest rising and falling underneath his shirt, torso still. Sonya was halfway down the mountain. Andras didn't do dating. This would be just physical connection pure and simple. She tilted forward slightly, her shoes scuffing the stones. And then Andras took a step back.

'I should get you back to your apartment.'

She quickly reached for the strap of her handbag in a weak show of play-acting. 'Yes. Babis rode off with Sonya a good five minutes ago.'

He passed Tess her helmet. 'Then shall we?'

# Thirty-three

# En-route to Kalami Cove Apartments

This time, Tess was relishing the moped experience. Her dress was still way up over her thighs, but in the dark, with Corfu taking on a whole different look as they meandered around the tight twists and turns of the mountain road, she felt more relaxed. She held on to Andras, trying to lean into the corners like he'd instructed her to and mould herself to the machine. So, it wasn't exactly a throbbing Harley Davidson underneath her, but the hot engine vibration, the wind whipping her hair and Andras's body beneath her hands were all sensations she could get used to. Except she wasn't sure a moped in London – in the rain, next to a double-decker bus pumping out exhaust fumes – would be quite as exciting.

She closed her eyes and let the warm air caressing her cheeks connect her with the moment. She was in Greece, on holiday, she was going to sort out Blackberry Boudoir, she was going to get Sonya and Joey back on an even keel, she was going to …

Before another thought could make its way into her mind the moped began stuttering, and it was all Tess could do to prevent herself from falling off. Her eyes snapped open, she clung on to Andras as finally, with a skid and a squeak of the brakes, they came to a halt.

'What happened?' Tess gasped, her hands moving to her helmet as if to expect it not to be there. 'Is there something wrong with the moped?'

'I do not know what to do with him!' Andras exclaimed, dismounting. 'Everything I do is never enough!'

Tess clung on to the moped as it rocked side to side until Andras kicked the stand down. She watched him then, moving into the dark alongside a rather craggy-looking verge.

'Andras,' she hissed. 'Don't leave me on my own here.' There was no light nearby, just a few pinpricks of gold and yellow over the side of the ravine, deep beneath the trees. Trees that could house plenty of Greek critters, or worse. Didn't Sonya say something about a large spider inhabiting Corfu? 'Andras!'

There was only one thing for it. She eased herself off the moped and tentatively made steps into the night after him.

'Andras!' she said again. 'What are you doing?' Her foot twisted as it came into contact with something slightly stick-like. She hoped it was a stick.

'We will have to walk,' Andras called.

'Walk?' Tess exclaimed. 'Down the rest of the mountain?'

'No,' he answered. 'Just a few metres.' He appeared then, out of the shadows, something in his arms. What the hell was it? Suddenly there was a groan like the Earth's core was being uprooted and Tess let out a scream, jumping back.

'What is that?' she questioned, tentatively. 'In your arms there?'

'This is Hector,' he stated, holding the tortoise up and out.

'Don't bring it any closer!'

'This is the tortoise who was trying to eat the contents of the restaurant fridge this afternoon.'

'You mean, that was really a thing?' Tess said. 'I presumed it was an excuse your mother made up to get you to leave Sonya and me on the dock.'

He smiled, shaking his head. 'No, not that time.' He held Hector out again. 'He is real. See.'

'I can see quite well from here, thanks.' She eased herself back a little more. 'What are you going to do with it?'

'Him.'

'What are you going to do with *him*?' Tess corrected.

'Take him back to my house and think of a way to make him stay in his pen.' He smiled at her. 'It is not far. Come.'

'How can you see where you're going?'

Andras grinned into the darkness as he made the final turn to the driveway of his home. Hector was a weight in his arms but he did not envy Tess walking any distance in those shoes she was wearing. 'In Corfu we are used to village life. Not city streets lit up all of the time. You become accustomed.'

'Like with the lack of Wi-Fi.'

'*Ne*,' he agreed. 'It is just up here.'

He heard her sigh. 'You've been saying that since we left the moped.'

'I will let you see my fifteen inches,' he called, another smile forming on his mouth. What he wouldn't give to see the expression on her face right now.

'Promises, promises,' came the reply.

He pushed opened the gate, trying to keep a firm grip on Hector whose legs were wiggling in resistance. 'We are here.'

'Oh, really?' Tess responded, catching up to him. 'That wasn't too far.'

'Now there are just fifty-nine steps up that way.' He pointed skywards.

'Fifty-nine?' Tess breathed.

'Yes.'

'It's a good job I've got abs like Joe Wicks.'

Andras began to mount the steps, Hector planted against his hip. He was sure this animal was getting bigger by the hour.

'Wait!' Tess called. 'Not quite so fast.'

'My laptop is at your service in only fifty-nine steps.' He smiled to himself as he heard her footsteps quicken ever so slightly.

'I'm sure the views are incredible but who seriously builds a house on the side of a mountain like this?' Tess panted.

'Actually, I did,' Andras answered.

'You built a house.'

'Yes.'

'With your actual hands and bricks and wood.'

'And glass,' he answered. 'There is quite a lot of glass.' He readjusted Hector in his arms and took the final steps two at a time.

'You must have had help though? I mean, you run the restaurant ... when would you have time to build a house?'

He felt his core tighten up at her question. What could he say?

'When I was not working.'

'Late at night? During the winter?'

He moistened his lips. 'I did not sleep.'

Work was all he had done after Elissa left. Running Georgiou's and building the house. Anything to stop himself from thinking too hard.

He moved forwards across the grass and his motion activated the exterior lights, flooding the area with a golden glow. He hastened to put Hector back in his pen, ensuring the lock was latched up.

'Wow!' Tess exclaimed, moving on to the rough expanse of lawn and turning her head left and right as she took it all in.

He didn't respond, just watched her, first looking out over the mountain below them – the clear view of a dark sky and a moonlit sea – then to his part-finished home. He watched her take steps towards the house.

'You built this!' she exclaimed.

'*Ne,*' he answered. 'Yes.'

'By yourself?'

'Yes.'

'It's amazing,' she said, looking over her shoulder at him. 'It's like something out of *Fantasy Homes by the Sea.*' She drew in a breath. 'It's all wood and old stone but sleek and ... look at the view. Even in the dark, it's spectacular.'

He swallowed. No one had called his house 'spectacular' before. His mother hated it. She thought when Elissa left he would either move back home or live in the apartment above the restaurant. But he was never going to do either of those things. Moving back home would have been saying not only was his marriage a failure, but his life too. Things might not have worked out with his wife, but giving up on everything and letting his mother think he regretted any of the decisions he'd made would have been a terrible idea. He would have been entrapped – he might have ended up having to create a fictitious girlfriend to get out of a family arrangement. He shook his head. At least here he had some space, far enough away to seek solitude when he needed it. And, in the back of his mind, there was always the thought that if things got tough with the business, or with his family, this house could be his nest egg.

'Can I see inside?' Tess asked.

'Yes,' he said quickly, his mind returning to the moment. 'Of course. I will get you the computer.'

# Thirty-four

# Andras Georgiou's house

'This part of it … it is not finished,' Andras remarked.

Tess was now standing in a shell of a building, nothing like she had seen from the outside. There was a makeshift kitchen and a tired-looking wooden table and nothing else but grey cement and dust. It was a little reminiscent of Isadora's dark home they had visited earlier.

'I have not had a great deal of time to work on this section yet.'

'So I see,' Tess remarked. 'What are your plans for it?'

'Well,' he began, moving into the room and motioning with his hands. 'My idea is that everything in the house makes the most of the situation, the views. The most sensible place to put the kitchen sink would be against this wall.' He walked forward, placing his hands on the rough bricks.

'But there wouldn't be a sea view when you're washing up.'

'It will have a dishwasher, of course, but no … so I have to work out a way to integrate a central island and a table where every seat has a view.'

'You're expecting a lot of guests?' she asked, looking at him.

He shrugged. 'You know I have a big family.'

'What's through this way?' Tess asked, walking forward.

Just like outside, lights began to automatically come on as she moved through the building. Hardwood flooring met her shoes and she was immediately overwhelmed by how different this room was to the bare walls she had just left behind.

There were two cream sofas with patterned orange, green and yellow throws over the back of them, matching cushions and a large olive-wood coffee table supporting an open file of paperwork, a laptop and two half-finished mugs of something. To the right was a wood-burning stove, a light-leafed tree in a white urn that almost reached the ceiling, and a wicker chair suspended from the beams by a chain, a comfy-looking cushion at its centre. But Tess was immediately drawn to the windows, the lights outside now turned off. It wasn't the pitch-black view she had expected. Slowly, as her eyes grew accustomed to the lack of light, she could clearly see the cypress tree outlines, falling away down the mountain and finishing at the sea, the sky, and the mountains of Albania across the water. She could only imagine what this looked like during the day.

'You like the room?' Andras asked, moving next to her.

'It's amazing,' Tess admitted, looking up at him. 'I've never seen anything quite like it before.'

'No?' he asked. 'Not even in London?'

'London is a city,' she reminded him.

'But it has great views, no?' he asked. 'Big Ben. Buckingham Palace?'

'My apartment has a balcony with a view of a takeaway pizza place and a taxi rank.'

She watched him smile. There was something she had been itching to ask him all night but every time it crossed her mind her heart started to palpitate like a warning shot. It wasn't any of her business really but …

'Who is Elissa?' It was out this time before she could check herself.

A long breath left him and he folded his arms across his chest as if he was having to protect himself from something. She waited, just watching, wondering if he was going to answer.

'She was my wife,' he replied.

'You were married.' She didn't know why she had felt the need to clarify it. Wife was quite clear enough.

He nodded. 'Yes.'

'What happened?'

'We are not married any more.'

It was a straightforward answer but his unwillingness to elaborate spoke volumes. Should she push him further? What was the protocol for a fake girlfriend when talking about previous real relationships?

'It was a long time ago.'

A slightly awkward silence descended into the beautiful open-plan space. And then he stepped away from her, moving to the coffee table and picking up the laptop. He held it out to her. 'Here.'

'I can take it back to my apartment?'

'After tonight, it is the very least I can do.'

# Thirty-five

# Kalami Cove Apartments

Isadora bringing up Elissa tonight had thrown him, but standing in the house he had built for the both of them, and telling Tess about her had felt even more awkward, and he didn't really know why. Perhaps it had been Tess's reaction to his hard work, the appreciation she had shown for what he had achieved, that had set him a little off balance. Tess had stood in the hollow would-be-kitchen and seen potential; all Elissa had seen was a disaster zone.

He stopped the moped outside Kalami Cove, turned off the engine and dismounted quickly.

'Take the laptop a second?' Tess said, holding out the computer she had cradled to her body with one hand all the way down the mountain.

He took the computer then held his free hand out to her. 'Take my hand.'

'It's OK,' she breathed. 'I have done this several times tonight. I can almost do it without looking like I should be performing in a strip club.'

He couldn't stop himself from looking as the hem of her dress rose up and she manoeuvred herself off the pillion. At the last second, her heel caught and she fell forward. He caught her quickly, steadying her as she regained balance.

'You are OK?' he asked. The weight of her body was pressed against his, the laptop the only thing separating them.

She nodded and gave a small smile, indicating the computer. 'Please don't drop that now. Not after I've carried it the entire journey.'

He passed it over to her then reached forward, his fingers at the fastening of her helmet.

'Be gentle,' Tess said. 'Last time I caught my hair in it.'

'I will be gentle,' he whispered. Why wouldn't his fingers work to undo this? He could feel her warm breath on his skin and his insides were rolling like the waves on the shoreline. What was happening here? Finally, the clasp came loose and he removed the helmet, Tess's hair falling out of the confines of the plastic and framing her beautiful face. He swallowed, just drinking her in. It would be so easy to just put his fingers back to her hair, tease it gently away from her neckline and ...

'Thank you,' Tess said, taking a step back from him. 'For the laptop, and for showing me your house.'

He smiled. 'You are welcome.'

'We'll see you tomorrow. Did Sonya decide on three o'clock?'

He nodded. 'Three o'clock.'

'A Greek three o'clock or an English one?'

'If you wish to see Paleokastritsa we should make it an English one.'

'Goodnight, Andras,' Tess said, waving a hand.

'*Kali nichta.*'

Tess wasn't going to turn around. She was going to keep walking through the entrance archway and down the path to their apartment without looking back. Her heart was hammering in her chest. When Andras had taken off that moped helmet, his fingers brushing her jaw, his face so close, she thought her insides were going to explode. She had wanted him to kiss her again. She had willed him to kiss her again, which proved she totally sucked at mind-influencing. And then her own mind had been infiltrated by thoughts of Sonya, on her own in their room with baklava bits, and she had moved, quickly, before she did something she was surely going to regret in the morning. What was wrong with her? When had she grown a conscience?

Hearing the moped start back up, she hugged the laptop to her chest and raised a hand, knocking on the door of the apartment.

Within a few seconds the lock turned and Sonya appeared.

'I am so sorry I was so long. This giant tortoise escaped and Andras insisted on taking it to his house and—' She stopped talking, observing her friend closer in the orange glow coming from the wall lamp above the door. 'Sonya, what's the matter?'

Her friend shook her head. 'I'm OK. It's nothing. It has to be nothing, doesn't it? Because … because he's almost engaged to me.'

'Sonya, tell me what's happened,' Tess begged.

'He's checked in again.'

'Checked in? In Margate?'

Sonya shook her head, tears spilling from her eyes. 'On Facebook.'

'Oh, Sonya, I do that all the time. Especially at nice restaurants. I would have done it at Georgiou's if I'd actually managed to get signal.'

'It isn't another restaurant,' Sonya blubbed. 'It's a hotel. Four stars.'

'Well, you knew he was in Margate and—'

'And this time he's tagged someone.'

'O-K.'

'Someone called Ceri.'

# Thirty-six

# Taverna Georgiou

Andras smoothed down a tablecloth and gently pushed the condiments on table five closer together. It was almost 8 a.m., and soon holidaymakers would be making their way into the restaurant for breakfast. It was another hot day and, as he looked out over the shore, his boat gently swaying with the motion of the ocean, he half-wished he was escaping out on the water again. Yesterday had been good, more than good; he had really relaxed for the first time in a long time. Perhaps he had needed it far more than he realised.

He took out the specials card, wafted it in the air and then replaced it again. Why had he done that? It was fine. He was just being overcritical. The restaurant hadn't been a state when he had arrived at 5 a.m. to collect in the bread order. His staff had managed well, and Dorothea would be sure to give him a full rundown of events when she got here. Perhaps this was proof that he needed to let go a little. Nothing was perfect and, if he managed to secure a new business partner, he had to be prepared to be adaptable. He might need to compromise, accept change, perhaps change that wasn't driven by him. He swallowed. The same theory ought to apply to relationships, except with Elissa he had offered every compromise he could think of and it still hadn't been enough.

'There is a mark!'

He looked up at his mother's voice. What was she doing here this early? What was she doing here at all? He stepped quickly towards her.

'Good morning, Mama.'

'This is not good enough, Andras,' Isadora continued.

'Mama, what are you doing here?' Andras asked, watching her as she moved on to another table, eyes scrutinising the settings. 'Last night you said you had wedding plans with Kira today.'

'I do,' she stated. 'Later.' She sucked in a long, slow breath, looking around the room. 'I have come to view things.'

'What do you mean?' he asked lightly. 'You come to the restaurant almost every day.'

'Yes,' Isadora agreed, swinging around to face him. 'But when I have come here before I have come here to see you or to eat – most of the time, both – and this week I have visited to plan the wedding celebration.'

'And now?'

'And now I am here with the eyes of an investor,' she made clear.

'Mama, I know that Spiro has talked to you about the restaurant but I—' Andras started.

'You have found another business partner?' Isadora asked bluntly.

What did he say? He hadn't. But he wanted to. Needed to. To retain his independence. But he didn't want to lie. He was already deceiving her with Tess, albeit because he had been backed into an impossible corner.

'Not quite,' he responded.

'Not quite,' Isadora repeated. 'That means no.'

'No, it means …'

She waved a hand, as if to dismiss him and headed off to another table, lifting the edges of the tablecloths and blowing away what he hoped was imaginary dust. 'You are tied up with the woman from England.'

He felt immediately defensive. 'You mean Tess.'

'This is what you call her now? Not Trix?' She huffed. 'So, is that what *I* am to call her?'

'I am sure she would like that.'

'And her last name. It is Parks?'

Andras baulked. He had no idea what Tess's last name was. He could neither confirm nor deny and now he was perspiring.

'There is nothing on the Interweb about someone who brands called Patricia Parks.'

'What?' Andras exclaimed. 'You've looked Patricia up on the Internet?'

'Not me. I do not know how these things work.'

Then he understood. 'Marietta.'

'I know what her plan is,' Isadora said, beginning to move table mats from table twelve.

'What her plan is?' Andras asked, not following the conversation.

'Patricia is not her real name, it is obvious,' Isadora said. 'She is duping you.'

His first instinct was to laugh. His second was to wonder where on Earth this was going. 'What?'

'Crumbs, Andras,' Isadora said. She ripped off the tablecloth like a magician doing a trick where all the crockery remained in place. 'There are crumbs on this tablecloth. It needs to be washed.'

'I'd rather go back to talking about how I am being tricked by Tess.'

Isadora let out a long, low, almost sad sigh. 'Andras, I know how you have been since Elissa left you.'

Did she? He felt the need to stand a little taller, straighten his back, pull in his feelings.

'You have been looking for a replacement – many replacements – quite often, if the village gossip is to be believed.' She pointed a finger. 'But I am telling you, this replacement cannot be found in a tourist.' Isadora sighed again. 'A woman on holiday is looking only for one thing.'

Now he wanted the conversation to stop altogether. He turned his attention to the beach scene. Milo was just coming along, setting up the loungers and parasols for the day. The sun was high in the hyacinth sky and within an hour or so the small strip of beach would be filled with another day's sun-worshippers. Boats would be docking as soon as lunchtime came around.

'Andras! You are not listening to me!'

He turned back. 'I am not being tricked by Tess.'

'Pa!' Isadora exclaimed. 'You are a man! A man is easily led by his ego being massaged, like in some of those places in Kavos.'

'Mama—'

'She wants your money,' Isadora continued. 'She has been grooming you over the Interweb. I have read about it.' She sniffed, nose going down to a candle. 'She knows you have this place, the house, you're a single man who is vulnerable. She has given you a fake name so she can work her way into your affections and then take away everything. Well, I will not stand by and let that happen again.'

A seed of discontent was growing quickly in his gut.

'She is the same as Elissa,' Isadora continued. 'Elissa comes here with her fancy clothes and her fancy ways and her *career*.' She scoffed. 'She is Greek on the outside but not Greek on the inside. And that is what you need, Andras. You need someone like you.'

'Someone like me,' he repeated.

'Yes.'

'Who is it that you think I am?'

'What sort of a question is that?'

'One I am expecting an answer to.'

'You are a Greek man who needs a wife who will support him.'

'Is that it?' Andras asked. 'Is that all you think I am?'

Isadora picked up the candle she had sniffed and passed it over to him. 'This one needs to be replaced. No scent.'

He took the candle, moulding his fingers around it. 'I cannot run a business with you, Mama.'

'Don't be ridiculous! If you have not found another partner then you *have* to run the business with me!'

He shook his head. 'No.'

'No? What does that mean, no?'

He pushed the candle back to her. 'You want to run the business? Have it for the day.'

'What?'

'You are in charge,' he stated, passing her a batch of menus. 'I am going out with Tess.'

'Wait. Andras, you can't just walk out on your responsibilities. I have wedding planning to do and—'

With anger and frustration fuelling his every step, he left the restaurant.

# Thirty-seven

# Kalami Cove Apartments

BB.

*BB.*

Blackberry Boudoir.

Tess squinted at the screen on Andras's laptop, the sunlight making it almost impossible to see. Not that seeing mattered when she just about had no idea where to start with this rebrand. She felt it wasn't now just a case of getting rid of the ill-shaped fruits, she wanted to rip up everything that had gone before and start afresh. She needed to be the one to make this right. Because at work, if not in her personal life, that's what she did. She put things right.

She glanced away from the computer, turning slightly in her terrace seat, to look into the apartment. Sonya was still asleep and it was no wonder seeing as they didn't get into bed until gone 3 a.m. There had been so many tears and a Facebook stalk of the woman named Ceri, who Sonya had turned into the Antichrist by 1 a.m. She hated Joey right now. Whether this friend was platonic or not, you didn't check into four-star hotels with another woman when your almost-fiancée was feeling particularly insecure. Especially when habitually you were a Premier Inn kind of guy.

Sonya stirred, her red hair shifting on the pillow. Her friend had eaten all the baklava bites by herself and drank their whole supply of wine, but Tess had successfully talked her down from sending Ceri a message threatening to hollow out her insides with a crochet hook. Aware of Sonya's intimate knowledge of all things Hobbycraft, even *she* was a bit afraid.

She clicked out of the McKenzie Falconer system she had eventually managed to log on to at a geriatric, handicapped snail's pace and looked at her online banking. And there it was: eleven thousand eight hundred and fifteen pounds. She should feel some sense of achievement. With her apartment to pay for, she had forgone literally everything else to stash away that cash. The designer wear she'd needed to fit in in London was all second-hand from eBay and she had sold her car when she'd moved to the city. She was the career woman faking it on a shoestring, and it was no more than she deserved. But the pot was still thirteen thousand one hundred and eighty-five pounds short. She swallowed the guilty lump that immediately sprang up in her throat. She had thought about paying her parents back in instalments. She had even gone so far as to work out a repayment schedule, but that involved contact, talking about what had happened with Adam, not just leaving a catch-up message on a voicemail. No, it needed to be over in one go. Once she had every penny she would pay it back and hope for a full and final absolution.

She flicked over to Facebook and there was Rachel, her mouth being forced apart by some sort of plastic contraption. A quick scan of the comments told her it was a game called Speak Out. There seemed to be wine involved and four others were tagged in the post including someone called Pete 'Mudda-Fudda' Ames. Her sister looked well. Drunk, but well. Perhaps she was finally turning a corner regarding the Phil situation. She hovered over the comments box. Should she say something? Maybe just a smiley face? Or was that stupid?

She sighed. Her sister didn't need her. She was having fun with someone whose nickname was Mudda-Fudda. She clicked back to the fonts she was working on. Still nothing looked right. Maybe she should really take Russell's advice and do this the old-fashioned way with pencil and paper.

'Ow! It hurts!'

Tess turned back to Sonya who was moving, barely, one arm emerging from the sheets like a robot with severe battery drain.

'What hurts?' Tess asked.

'Everything.'

'Your little toe?'

'What?'

'Does your little toe hurt?'

There was a hesitation. 'I don't think so.'

'See, things are looking up already.'

There was more groaning as Sonya finally raised her body up from the bed, hands sweeping away a bad case of bed hair. 'It's hot again.'

'Yes, we really need to ask about a fan, regardless of anyone's feelings about artificial air.' She swallowed. Perhaps she shouldn't have made reference to Joey.

'I don't expect there's any artificial air in the rooms at the four-star hotel in Margate.'

'Listen, Sonya, I really think you should call him now,' Tess said.

'What?' Sonya said, gathering up the sheets around her body and walking out onto the terrace, swaying a little and needing to catch hold of the shutters. 'But that means you think something is going on with this Ceri.'

'No, it doesn't mean I think that.'

'I looked her up again, you know.'

'What? When?' Tess asked as Sonya lowered herself down on to the chair, wrapping the sheets around her like she was fastening a toga.

'I know you thought I was asleep but … I couldn't. So I waited for *you* to fall asleep and then I went through her Facebook profile.' Sonya drew in a breath. 'She makes quite a number of her posts public. If I was a concerned friend I would be suggesting she tightens up her security.'

'But you're not her friend,' Tess reminded her. 'You're someone who wants to gut her with knitting implements.'

'She's a member of the Weston Re-enactment Society.'

'That's great!' Tess exclaimed. 'That means this is something to do with battles and bludgeoning and not gimp masks or paddles.'

Sonya shook her head vigorously. 'No, you don't understand.' She took a breath. 'Weston are Greenwich's arch-rivals.'

'Re-enactment Societies have rivalries?' She didn't know whether to laugh or cry.

'Not all of them, but Weston, they're known for being so showy-offy. They have a massive budget and they put on these outlandish events, you know … If we have musicians playing the traditional penny whistle, they'll have a guy playing some ancient, only-one-in-the-whole-world Neolithic instrument.'

'I see.' She didn't see. She didn't get the whole re-enactment thing at all.

'So the fact that he's spending time with another woman, and a woman who is part of the *Weston* Society is just … well, he may as well be wearing a jumper stating his allegiance to Nazism.'

'Sonya,' Tess said softly.

'Yes.'

'I think you're losing focus here.'

'He hates Weston,' Sonya continued. 'He calls them the Weston Wan—'

'OK, listen, stop,' Tess urged quickly. 'Let's just look at the evidence here.' She wasn't sure she really wanted to look at the evidence but for some reason she really didn't want to hear Sonya say the word 'wankers'.

'He's in a four-star hotel in Margate with someone with much nicer hair than me who's a member of a re-enactment society he loathes. It doesn't get better, no matter how many different ways you try to look at it,' Sonya sobbed.

'We don't know he spent the night at the hotel,' Tess stated. She was a genius! And if she found out that Joey *had* spent the night in that hotel she was going to use more than craft supplies to disembowel him. 'He's just met someone at one. For a drink or something.'

'W-what?'

'Well, what time did he post?'

'Eleven fifty-nine p.m.'

'Greek time or English time?' Was she clutching at straws?

'I don't know. Does Facebook change things to your own time zone?' She was already starting to look more hopeful.

'I think it does.' She didn't have a clue. 'So that would mean it was only nine fifty-nine p.m. in England.'

'I don't understand what you're saying,' Sonya said, playing with the skin on her chest where her necklace should hang.

'I'm saying this hotel might have a really cool wine bar or something and Joey is there – with other people too, not just Ceri – who aren't his friends on Facebook so he couldn't tag them. And it could be something perfectly innocent, like a truce between the two societies. Yes, a picking up of the gauntlet rather than a throwing down. And then he's gone back home, or to his room, completely alone.'

Had that sounded plausible? She just felt she needed to nurse Sonya along. There wasn't anything much either of them could do while they were in Greece unless Sonya made a direct effort to contact Joey and have it out with him. Despite what she'd said earlier, she wasn't sure confrontation on the phone or via WhatsApp was the right course of action now, not when things were so up in the air and the baby factor was weighing on her friend's mind.

'Good morning.'

Sonya jumped in the chair, almost losing the sheets. 'Oh my!'

And there was Andras in the gardens, just outside their terrace, dressed in the black trousers and white shirt that was his restaurant day 'uniform', dark hair perfectly tousled.

'What are you doing here?' Tess asked. 'Don't tell me you need your laptop back already.'

'No.' He shook his head.

'We were going to meet this afternoon, weren't we?' Sonya added.

'We were,' he agreed. 'But, if you would like, we can spend the whole day in Paleokastritsa.'

Tess observed his stance. He looked agitated, his hands by his sides but as if not knowing what to do with them. 'I thought you had the restaurant to take care of.'

He nodded. 'I decided to take a day off.'

'A day off,' Tess stated bluntly. 'Just like that.'

'Yes.'

'But you don't take days off,' she said. 'You told me you haven't had a day off since—'

'Tess,' Andras interrupted. 'I am offering my services as a guide man for the day to thank you for putting up with my family last night. If you do not want this then …'

'Oh no!' Sonya exclaimed, standing up and catching the sheets under her armpits. 'Oh no, we do want it, don't we, Tess?'

Tess turned in her seat to look at Sonya trying to stop herself revealing too much skin as she waddled towards the apartment doors. 'Are you sure, Sonya? Because if you want to just hang out here and, you know, relax and think about things, then ...'

'No,' Sonya said with a determined shake of her head. 'I don't want to think about things.' She sighed. 'I spent all night thinking about things. Today I want to do things. I want to see things. Lots of Greek things.'

'OK then,' Tess answered.

'I'll just get dressed. I'll be two ticks,' Sonya said, moving into the apartment and closing the shutters behind her.

Tess looked back to Andras, still behind the metal fence. 'I think you'd better come over here and tell me what happened with your mother this morning.'

He shook his head. 'It is that obvious?'

'Mmm.'

'Well, to talk about that will require more than the coffee you are drinking.'

'Sonya drank all our wine.'

'And I will be driving us.' He reached into his trouser pocket and pulled out a set of keys, shaking them at Tess.

'Your car is working again?'

'No,' he answered. 'I have Spiro's.'

'It is a car, isn't it? Not a moped,' Tess checked.

He grinned. 'Yes, it is a car.' Putting two hands on the fence, he vaulted himself over and landed next to Tess's chair like he was Louis Smith dismounting from a pommel horse. Snatching up her coffee mug he took a sip of it, then quickly put it down. 'You have far too much sugar.'

'I'm going to be needing much more if you and I are going to last until this wedding.'

He smiled, sitting down on the chair next to her. 'It is a trial, isn't it? All this being nice to one another, swimming from boats, visiting beaches and holding hands, dancing close.'

Was it her imagination or had he inched his body slightly closer to hers? Damn, he was hot. And he was making her hot. But Sonya was a couple of very flimsy shutters away …

'And now my mother thinks you are someone trying to get your hands on my money.'

That was a passion-killer. 'What?'

He smiled. 'I will tell you all about it when we get to the other side of the island.'

'I can't wait.'

# Thirty-eight

# Paleokastritsa

'It says in my guidebook that the monastery is called Theotokos.'

Sonya's words were almost whipped away by the breeze as Andras motored around tight turns up the side of another mountain en route to their destination. The open-top Jeep had been fine when they had left Kalami and taken a slow, steady saunter along bamboo-lined roads, staggering views from every vantage point, but now the almost hairpin bends were back and Andras had ramped up the pace.

'And apparently there are six beaches,' Sonya continued. 'I thought it was a little place. It looks little on the map.'

'Yes,' Andras called over the engine and the wind. 'It is small but it has many beautiful coves and beaches.'

'Which one did we meet on?' Tess teased, looking across at him.

'Maybe we can decide today,' he suggested. 'So we are prepared should there be any more questions.'

'Ooo, we could make up your whole story!' Sonya announced. 'And take photos, like evidence.'

Tess now wished she hadn't mentioned the backstory Andras had created on that first night. And Sonya was becoming way to obsessed with the word 'evidence' since Joey's hotel check-in on Facebook.

'We are here,' Andras said, pulling the Jeep to a stop.

'This is the monastery already?' Sonya asked, already opening the car, eyes ahead of them as if she was taking it all in.

'Yes,' Andras answered.

'So do monks actually really live here or is it just some kind of museum?' Tess inquired.

'There are real monks,' Andras answered, getting out of the car and putting on his sunglasses. 'And I should have thought ...'

'Thought what?' She got out of the car and shut the door behind her.

'You will not be able to go in dressed like that.'

Tess looked down at the cream cotton sundress she was wearing. It was a bargain ASOS purchase with a plaited belt with gold bits on the end, simple but stylish. What was wrong with it?

'You cannot show too much ... skin ... in front of the monks,' Andras stated.

Sonya let out a giggle. 'Will I be OK?' She twerked her Capri-pants clad bottom.

'I'm wearing a perfectly acceptable dress,' Tess said, following Andras towards the entrance.

'It is too short,' Andras said.

'Says who?'

'Says the monks,' Andras replied. 'I don't make the rules.'

'Well,' Tess said. 'Should I take it off then?'

'No,' he answered quickly. 'They will give you something.'

'Oh, Tess, look at these views. Take a photo of me. The trees are so green and the sea is so ...'

'Blue?' Tess offered.

'Well, I know it's cheesy but yes it really is. It's so special.' Sonya swallowed.

Sonya was melting, on the inside, churning over the things she had previously said she didn't want to think about. Tess put an arm around her friend's shoulders. 'Andras can take a photo of us.'

'Of course,' he answered readily.

Andras couldn't help but smile at Tess. She was wearing a grey and neon-green, elephant-patterned pleated skirt that touched her ankles and a bright orange cardigan. The monks had taken exception to her dress and made a good job of finding her the most ill-fitting cover-ups they had. He had watched her looking at the gatekeepers, clearly wondering whether to object or not. She had chosen not and had pulled on the skirt with as much grace as she could manage.

'You're looking at my skirt, aren't you?' Tess hissed as they walked across the beautifully paved terrace, small manicured trees growing at the bases of triangular-turreted white walls, beneath the sand-coloured brickwork of the ornate bell tower.

'It is very nice,' he said with a smirk.

'It's the ugliest thing I have ever had to wear.'

Andras smiled. 'It is not about fashion here. It is about respect.'

'I know,' Tess answered. 'And that's why I put it on.' She sighed. 'Not that it isn't crazy itchy. No one should have to wear something this long in this heat.'

'I'm just going over there to take some more photos!' Sonya called back to them, waving a hand and heading further away.

'So have you been here loads of times before?' Tess asked him.

He nodded. 'Yes, but not for a long time.'

'Did you come here with your wife?'

He hesitated, Tess's question jarring for a moment. No one really brought Elissa up, apart from his mother when she wanted to prove that he was incapable of managing his life.

He shook his head. 'No.'

'Sorry, I didn't mean to pry, I just …' She fanned her hand in front of her face. 'Can we find some shade?'

'Sure,' he answered, leading the way forward.

He stepped into the whitewashed brick tunnel, bright red-and-pink plants in pots, gnarly vines criss-crossing overhead and creating a perfect canopy to escape the intense heat. He stopped at a wooden bench. 'You would like to sit?'

'Yes,' Tess said. 'I think I would.'

He dropped down on to the seat with a sigh, bringing his hands up through his hair.

'So your mother came to see you this morning,' she guessed.

'Yes, she was at the restaurant early, when I was setting up.'

'And was that why you left? To spend the day here?'

'I just got so mad and I don't like to be mad.' He sighed. 'But … she does this to me. I feel like I can't even breathe.' He turned to her. 'Do you understand that?'

She moved her head half in a nod and half in a shake. 'I don't, not really, because … I don't have any sort of relationship with my family.'

'You are lucky. You are free,' Andras stated.

Tess shook her head with determination. 'No, I don't think so.' She sighed. 'I used to think that, but lately … I don't know, maybe it's what Sonya's going through or work being so incredibly frustrating or … I don't know … being here with your Greek time and your boats.' She smiled and he knew she was about to tighten up. 'Cut to the bit about her thinking I'm a gold-digger.'

'She thinks you have found me on the Internet, because of course a restaurant owner from Kalami is very high profile, and you are going to get me to marry you and then you will take the restaurant and my house that she doesn't even like and my life will be over.'

'I did love your house,' Tess reminded him with a small smile.

'And I don't even own the whole restaurant,' he admitted sadly.

'No? Well, I may as well pack my bags and get on the first plane home.' She brushed her hair off her face, then scrunched up the skirt in both fists, playing with the nylon material.

'The restaurant was left to Spiro and me in equal shares when my father died. My mother got the house and everything else, which wasn't much. Now Spiro needs the money for his new life with Kira.' He sighed. 'I cannot blame him for that. And he has given me plenty of time, I just cannot find anyone to come into the business with me.' He adjusted his sunglasses on his face as a few tourists sauntered by, eyes on their guide-books. 'I have so many plans for the restaurant. I want to update things. I want to think about doing more events, like with Spiro's wedding. I want to market to a wider audience. I get great business from rich people in their super-yachts. But if I expand, and there *is* room to expand, I can book more large groups, offer party nights, something a little different.'

'You would have to be careful, though,' Tess stated.

'Careful?'

'Part of what makes your restaurant so popular is its charm and it's Greekness.' She looked at him. 'Don't get me wrong, I think it's a great idea to think about expansion and something different, but you need to make sure you don't alienate your current clientele.'

'I'm not afraid of change,' Andras said. 'That is what holds back my family.'

'I know, but take it from someone who has managed the branding and marketing for a lot of businesses: don't ever lose the core of what's working.'

He nodded. It was good advice. 'It does not matter. I have not been able to find anyone, so my mother will be my new business partner.'

'Have you approached the bank?' Tess asked.

He shook his head. 'The way things are in Greece at the moment, the bank will not lend me the money.'

'Why not?'

'Because—'

'You have a thriving business. You have a house that must be worth a fortune just for its location, and this is not the money-grabbing girlfriend speaking. Why would they not lend you the money?'

He had thought about the bank but he had dismissed it almost instantly. Perhaps he had done that too quickly. If he got a loan from the bank, gave Spiros the money for his share of the restaurant, he wouldn't have to have any business partner. He could run things his way. As long as he could manage the loan repayments. Finding out had to be worth it, didn't it?

'If you like, I could help you put together all the details the bank might need,' Tess said.

'I can't ask you to do that, Trix,' he replied. 'You are already doing so much for me and—'

'See that girl over there?' Tess said, indicating through the tunnel to where Sonya was half-leaning over the rustic wall trying to get the best photo opportunity. 'You bringing us to all these places, telling her the history of things, it's really helping to make this holiday special. I'm sure I can manage to put together some documents in between holding your hand and …' She swallowed. 'Dancing close.'

He felt the need to take his sunglasses off then, and pushed them up on to his head. Looking at her, soft blonde hair resting on that bright cardigan, it was all he could do to stop himself from reaching out and touching it. He slipped his hand across the space between them and placed it on top of hers, heart picking up in pace. What was he doing? There was no one here to watch them. No one making notes about their relationship. No family. But he wanted to reach out to her.

His hand was on hers, his fingers gently caressing the skin and her stomach was revolving like the London Eye but several times quicker. What was happening? Why was he holding her hand? And why was it making her feel like she was being turned inside out? It felt sexy and comforting all at the same time and she didn't know what to do! Apart from break the moment. Quickly.

She withdrew her hand and pointed a finger at him. 'Plus, I have your laptop.'

'You do,' he agreed with a smile, pulling his hand away. 'And how is that going?'

'It works,' Tess answered. 'Nothing wrong with the machine. Just my ability to put anything together at the moment.'

'You are working on a branding project?'

'Yes,' she said, smiling. 'Have you got any ideas for a chain of boutique wine bars called Blackberry Boudoir?'

'Perhaps a change of name?' he suggested.

'Oh, I think that's pretty much set in stone,' she answered.

'Really? Just because it has always been that way?' he asked. 'If I make changes to my restaurant I was considering a different name. Georgiou's does not really say "relax", "escape" or "unwind".'

She sat up a little straighter on the bench, a wave of excitement running through her. She had thought earlier she'd like to rip things up and start again, she just assumed she had to stick to the name of the company. But this *was* a rebrand. Just because the clients hadn't asked for a name change didn't mean they wouldn't be open to the suggestion if she came up with a great one and presented it well.

'You are OK?' Andras asked.

'Yes,' Tess said, leaping up from the bench. 'Yes, I'm fine.' She looked over at Sonya, still snapping photos, then back to Andras. 'I need to find some paper and a pencil.'

# Thirty-nine

'This place is so beautiful,' Sonya exclaimed with a loaded sigh.

They were sitting outside on the balcony of a taverna-cum-tea room that overlooked the whole bay of Paleokastritsa. Craggy, green-speckled stone surrounded coves of turquoise water that shimmered in the sunlight. They could see everything from their high vantage point: the beaches, the boats bobbing close to shore, others further out sailing into the distance, and the imposing Angelokastro – Castle of Angels – that Andras had told them about while they waited for the lemon drizzle cake to arrive.

'It is beautiful,' Tess agreed, sipping at her Coke with three sugars.

'So's he,' Sonya stated, her eyes moving to Andras, who was leant against the balcony railing.

Despite what he had said about leaving his mother in charge for the day, he had felt the need to check in with the restaurant. After all his comments when they had first met about her being addicted to her iPhone and business, now he was the one making a call.

'I mean, he is gorgeous, anyone can see that, and you're getting on so well,' Sonya continued.

'What?' Tess stated, coming to the conversation.

'Andras and you. You're getting on so well,' Sonya repeated.

'I have no idea what you're talking about,' Tess answered. 'Firstly, if you remember, I'm his made-up girlfriend. Don't start believing the fiction we invented. Our eyes didn't really meet on the glass-bottomed boat earlier in the season.'

'I know.'

'And secondly, you said I had to remain single for the entire holiday.'

'I know,' Sonya stated. 'I know I did say that, but I meant single as in, not doing your usual thing.'

'My usual thing?' Tess asked.

'The thing. The six-week thing,' Sonya whispered.

'Why are you whispering?' Tess asked.

'Well, I know I told him that you like to date but that was before, and we don't need him to know about the six-week thing, do we?'

Tess bristled and pushed her glass of Coke away. 'I don't know what you're trying to say here, Sonya.'

'Well,' Sonya began, sitting forward in her chair. 'I just feel that, you know, perhaps this is all fate.'

'Perhaps what's fate?'

'Everything,' Sonya replied. 'Maybe me and Joey going through this almost-break was meant to be … to help you.'

'What?'

'Joey can't come to Greece. You have holiday due. Then, when we get here, we walk into Georgiou's at the exact time when Andras has to find an English girlfriend with blonde hair and blue eyes.'

Tess looked at Sonya. 'That description wasn't a decree sent down from Mount Olympus, you know. He made that up without thinking it through properly, probably because we had a row over bread at Kalami Cove.'

'Like I said. Fate.'

'I don't believe in fate.'

Sonya clutched her chest, fingers where the necklace should be. 'You don't? Not at all? Not even those little red fortune-telling fish you get in Christmas crackers.'

'Sonya, they respond to the heat on your hand.'

'No!'

Tess's eyes went to Andras. That arse in those trousers and that white shirt. She just found him attractive. That was all. Exactly like Sonya first said. He was the poster boy for a holiday Romeo. She swallowed. She didn't really want to think of him like that. And then that thought caught. Why not? Why didn't she want to think of him as a quick fix? She had been wishing he'd just take her – literally – practically since they had met. And he hadn't. Maybe that's what was getting to her. Perhaps Sonya was right. The fate she didn't really believe in was showing her she couldn't get her own way any more. It was karma for breaking Tony's heart in Gianni's.

'What I'm saying is … I give you permission,' Sonya said, forking up some lemon cake.

'Permission for what?' Tess asked.

'To break the single promise.' Sonya sighed. 'I think, maybe, if you gave it a chance, you could find yourself feeling something for Andras.'

Tess pulled the drink back towards her, needing to clasp her hands around something. She didn't want to hear what Sonya was saying. She didn't feel. And her best friend knew that. 'Feeling' had been packed up with Adam's CDs, photos of them as a couple and a T-shirt of his she had sniffed while crying for the first month a long time ago.

She shook her head. 'I don't do that,' she said, as if Sonya needed reminding.

'I know,' Sonya replied. 'But … I don't know … I just hate to see you doing the six-week thing and not really ever getting anything out of it.'

'Sonya, I am having the time of my life,' Tess said, shifting in her seat and picking up a napkin she began to shred with her fingers. 'I get meals out at some really great restaurants. I saw three West End shows last year. I've done a Ferrari driving experience and … I've been in a Zorb!'

'And danced a very convincing Zor*ba* with that Greek god over there,' Sonya said.

'I don't need anything else,' Tess said, the words catching a little as she tried to remain calm. 'I have my work. I have …' She racked her brain for something else to say. 'I … have my work.'

'But there could be so much more,' Sonya said. 'There could be real passion and a depth of feeling that you've never known.'

She had known it. She had thought she had known it with Adam. And he had thrown what they had away. She swallowed, nausea crawling up her insides.

And then Sonya breathed out, a lip-trembling breath that made Tess know she was thinking of Joey. Despite everything, Sonya still had faith in true love. But Tess knew better. Tess knew that true love was a fantasy. Because men lied. All of them. Her father had lied to her mother. Phil the Philanderer had lied to Rachel. And Adam had lied to her. That's why she was so determined to break the cycle. And the only way to do that was to stay on top, stay in control, and not give any of herself. Ever.

She smiled at Sonya, game face restored. 'You think I can't stay single for this holiday, don't you? That's what this is really about.'

'No, don't be silly. Of course it's not.'

'Well, I can, you know. I've not been on any dating sites for days.'

'That's great!'

'And I can totally be single for the rest of this holiday.'

'Apart from the fake Greek boyfriend.'

Tess's eyes went to Andras again. 'Yes, well, he's practically given me his laptop for the duration and he's taking us to all the best places.'

'He *is* doing that,' Sonya agreed.

'Right,' Tess said, picking up her handbag and pulling out a pen. 'Pass me all those napkins and let's start thinking of new names for Blackberry Boudoir that make it sound less bordello and more upmarket chic.'

'Less Margate and more Brighton?' Sonya suggested with a sigh.

'Exactly.'

Then, just as she was about to put pen to napkin, her mobile erupted into life. A glance down at the screen told her it was her mother. She sat back, just hearing the ringtone and watching the screen, the phone moving slightly as it vibrated.

'Who is it?' Sonya asked. 'Work?' She made like she was going to move forward in her seat and look at the phone.

Tess snatched it up and quickly pressed the button to cancel the call. 'Yes, work. I couldn't answer; I haven't done enough on the project yet.' She set the phone back down and picked up her Coke. 'Now, where were we? New names.' She smiled. 'Let's brainstorm.'

Andras strode over to their table, his phone in his hand and a look of concern on his face. 'We have to go.'

'Go?' Sonya asked. 'Before we've finished our cake?'

'What's wrong?' Tess asked.

'It's the restaurant,' he began. 'It's my mother … and Spiro's donkey.'

'Hurry up and eat that cake,' Tess urged Sonya.

'I am sorry,' Andras stated with a sigh.

'It's OK,' Tess replied. 'You have a business to look after and we have rebranding to do.'

'One more … mouthful … mmm,' Sonya said, shovelling in the last of the cake.

'I will make it up to you,' Andras said, touching Tess's arm.

She swallowed, the contact jarring her. She got to her feet, hurrying to scoop up the napkins. 'Superfast broadband?'

'I think I may struggle with that,' he admitted.

'Can I take the cake with me?' Sonya asked.

# Forty

# Taverna Georgiou

'I will take you to the apartments,' Andras stated when they had reached Kalami again, about to swing the Jeep left.

'No,' Tess said. 'We'll come with you to the restaurant. I could do with a coffee and I want to see this crisis your mother called you back for.'

He looked over at her. 'You think there *is* no crisis?'

'I just think, perhaps, the crisis might have been exaggerated in order for you to come back and be away from your English girlfriend.'

'It was Dorothea on the phone,' Andras said.

'And you couldn't possibly imagine your mother forcing her to make that phone call?'

Tess had a point. The restaurant noises he had heard in the background of the phone conversation hadn't been panicked. It had just sounded like a normal busy lunchtime. But Dorothea had sounded a little out of sorts. Perhaps his mother had been towering over the little Greek woman, her hand on a heavy skillet … Perhaps he should have stood his ground. He had abandoned the restaurant this morning, knowing it would be his staff left in charge, not his mother, and that they could cope with whatever might happen. So why had he immediately run back? Had he let his mother play him again?

'OK,' Andras said, continuing along the road towards the restaurant.

He stopped Spiro's car at the side of the road, got out, then walked around the front to open the door for Tess, then Sonya.

'Ooo, thank you,' Sonya said, sandals hitting the ground, sun hat going on her head. 'Wait,' she said as Andras and Tess prepared to cross over the road and head towards the restaurant back entrance. 'You two should hold hands.'

'What?' Tess said.

'You should hold hands,' Sonya repeated. 'Mrs Georgiou needs to believe you're a couple so you need to walk in holding hands.'

Andras looked at Tess, gauging her reaction. He didn't want to make her feel uncomfortable. This scenario was so unfair on her.

'Fine,' Tess said, holding her hand out to him.

'Coffees with cream, on me,' he said. 'As soon as I get rid of the donkey.' He slipped his fingers between hers and their eyes met. 'If there is a donkey.'

'There won't be,' Tess stated. 'I can almost guarantee it.'

Despite Tess's confidence he found himself taking a deep breath as they crossed the road and walked into the back of the restaurant. What was he going to find? What outcome was better – the donkey crisis or his mother having lied to get him back here? The one thing he really hadn't expected were priests, about ten of them, some shaking sheaves of lavender, others sprinkling water and the rest waving censers of incense, all while his customers tried to enjoy lunch.

'Oh my!' Sonya exclaimed, hands to her mouth.

'What the—?!' Tess stated.

Andras gripped Tess's hand tighter, moving through the restaurant quickly, taking her with him and focusing his vision on the woman in front of the team of priests, seemingly orchestrating.

'Mama,' he began. 'What is going on?!'

Isadora span around, eyes going to where his hand was tethered to Tess's, clutching her chest like angina was taking over. 'Oh my God! Thank the Lord you are here!' Her eyes seemed to narrow as they looked to Tess. 'But you, you cannot be here.'

He squeezed Tess's hand instantaneously. 'Mama, Tess is my girlfriend, and just why the hell is Papa Yiannis and every priest on the island in my restaurant?'

'The restaurant,' Isadora said, speaking in hushed tones. 'It is cursed.'

Andras snorted, shaking his head.

'What's going on?' Tess asked. 'Non-Greek speaker here. Although I am quite good at translating body language.'

Andras looked to Tess. 'My mother says my restaurant is cursed.'

'All of a sudden?' Tess asked. 'By what?'

'By you!' Isadora blasted out in English.

'Mama, you will not talk to Tess that way,' Andras warned.

'We look you up again on the Interweb this morning,' Isadora stated. 'Not Patricia Parks, *Tess* Parks.' She pointed a finger. 'We find you on the Book of Faces and Titter. You are with men, always with men, a different man almost every day. You have come here to spread your poisonous ways in Corfu. Well …' She finally paused for breath. 'You have come to the wrong resort for that and you have chosen the wrong family to try to steal from!'

He felt Tess's hand lose grip in his and he immediately tightened his hold. He was not going to let her be pulled apart in public when this whole set-up was a charade of his making.

'Enough!' he ordered. The volume of his voice stopped every conversation and silenced the dining noises. Even the chanting from the priests had lessened.

'Andras—' Tess began.

'No,' Andras said, looking at her. 'This has gone on long enough.' He sighed. 'Too long.'

He was going to tell the truth. Here, holding the hand of his made-up girlfriend, he was going to tell his mother that her outdated ways and matchmaking had made him invent a relationship. That he had felt backed into a corner he could not escape from and he was not going to let it happen any more. She needed to back away from his personal life and, as far as the business was concerned, he wasn't prepared to give up hope of another investor yet. Or perhaps a loan from the bank, as Tess had suggested.

'Don't do it,' Tess said through gritted teeth.

He turned his full attention to her then. 'What?'

'Don't do it,' she said again. 'Please, don't do it.'

'This is not fair to you,' Andras almost whispered. 'And it has to stop.'

'Not on account of me,' Tess answered. 'And because … what your mother just said … it's all true.'

He felt her let go of his hand.

'I knew it!' Isadora exclaimed in nothing less than triumph as a thick, grey plume of smoke from the priests almost hid her form.

'Tess,' Andras said, taking a step towards her departing form. He didn't want her to leave. He wanted her to be here while he faced off with his mother and put an end to this situation he had put them in.

'I'll talk to her,' Sonya said, backing away, her expression a little sad.

His emotions high, as if this really was some sort of break-up, he turned back to his mother. Holy water spattered him on the cheek and he furiously wiped it off.

'Mama, you need to leave,' he stated. 'And you need to take the priests with you.' He indicated the customers, some of them getting up to go. Patrons were coughing, others wiping at their eyes.

'I knew it!' Isadora repeated. 'I knew the moment I set eyes on her that there was something wrong and you did not believe me!'

He drew in a breath, considering what to say. 'There is nothing wrong.'

'Nothing wrong? That woman has had more men friends than you have served bowls of olives.'

'So what?' he blasted. 'She is with me now!' Another lie all too quickly came.

'She wants you for your money! For the restaurant!'

'I don't have any money.' He paused. 'And why is it so impossible to believe that she might want to be with me for me? Just that! Only that!' Why he was defending a fictitious relationship, he didn't know.

Isadora took a step forward towards him. 'Because she is like Elissa. The she-wolf in Greek clothing.' Her voice weakened a little. 'And she broke your heart.'

He looked closely at his mother then. Was there a tremble to her lips? Was there a little glaze to her eyes? Her bravado was definitely impaired.

'Mama …'

'No!' she said, raising a hand. 'Enough talking now! I am very busy. I have to meet Spiro and the donkey and hope that the vet can find some antidote for the ingestion of lupins. The restaurant must be cleansed before the wedding. There are bad spirits here, I can feel them all over me.' She shuddered.

He went to move forward, to reach out to her but she turned away, heading for Papa Yiannis who was toying with the string of worry beads in his hands.

Tess powered up the steep incline towards Kalami Cove at workout speed. She just had to get away from the restaurant and the crazy Greek stalker who had googled her.

'Tess, stop! Please stop! My old hamstring injury is aching and I'm getting boob chafe!'

She listened to Sonya puffing and panting and slowed a little. But the lessening of pace just made her mind whir again. Why was she feeling this way? Andras's mother had simply given a very good outsider's account of her social-media activity. Her life, filled with men. Why had it made her feel so … shameful?

'The woman is insane,' Sonya began, reaching Tess and doubling over, hands on her thighs as she tried to draw out her breaths. 'You know that, right? I mean, there were more holy men in that restaurant than there were up at the monastery.'

'I know,' Tess answered. Why was her voice so small? She was not Andras's girlfriend. She was playing a role. She didn't need to feel hurt by his mother's opinion of her. What she really needed to do was look into her Facebook privacy settings. She swallowed. Was this hurt she was feeling?

'You did a nice thing back there,' Sonya said, standing up and wiping her brow with the back of her hand.

'What?'

'Andras was going to tell his mother that your relationship wasn't real.'

'I know,' Tess said with a sigh.

'And you wouldn't let him,' Sonya said, grinning a little bit too much.

Why hadn't she let him? Why had her stomach dropped to the flagstone floor at the thought of him confessing? She swallowed, her mouth dry.

'I need his laptop,' she answered confidently. 'That's why I rushed out of there really.' She pushed her shoulders back. 'I need to do a bit of work before we go out for dinner tonight.'

'Oh,' Sonya said, disappointment in her tone. 'I thought that maybe—'

'And, of course, you know, what she said about my boyfriends.' She sniffed. 'I had to make it realistic. If I was dating Andras and his mother had said what she said, I would have been upset about my track record with men being exposed.'

'You would?' Sonya asked.

Crap. She hadn't meant Sonya to interpret it that way. She needed to turn that around.

'Well, you know, a slightly weaker individual.'

'But not you,' Sonya said.

'Of course not.' Tess laughed but it sounded hollow even to her.

'OK, well, the good news is you're still with Andras ...'

'Faking it,' Tess reminded her.

'So we still have our guide man.'

'And his laptop and Internet connection.'

'And we've got dinner at the White House tonight.'

Tess breathed in then slowly exhaled. 'Yes, I can't wait.' She smiled at Sonya. 'Just girl time. You, me, wine and food at the Durrell's house, and no Greek family dramas.'

'*Yammas* to that,' Sonya said. A shaky sigh left her.

'No update on Facebook from Joey?' Tess asked, linking their arms and starting to walk again.

Sonya shook her head. 'Nothing since the hotel last night.'

'Think of it as a good sign,' Tess said.

Sonya nodded. 'There's nothing else I can do, is there? And I promised him space. If a woman from his most detested re-enactment society is able to turn his head then perhaps what we have isn't strong enough.' She smiled. 'And I want to believe that it is.' The smile faltered a little. 'I really want to believe that.'

Tess drew her friend closer and whispered softly. 'I want to believe that too.'

# Forty-one

As he set the tables for evening service, Andras watched his brother and Kira on the beach. They were alone, save for Milo packing up the sunloungers. They were holding hands, bodies close, barefoot on the stones, looking like a billboard advertisement for a happy-ever-after. The sea lapped their feet as they moved across the shoreline and Andras watched as Kira tickled Spiros, then left him, running into the water with a squeal of excited delight. It was simple. Pure and simple, everyday, beautiful love.

He immediately thought of Tess and his first reaction to that thought was to start polishing the glasses a little more vigorously. Why was he thinking of her? Because his mother had shared personal information and that was all his fault. He had been going to come clean, for her, not for him, but she had stopped it. Why? Obviously for Sonya. And for connection to the Internet. What else could there be?

'Andras.'

His back was slapped and there was his grinning brother, sand and weed on his feet from the beach.

'If you want a table for dinner you need to wash off your toes,' Andras said, replacing a wine glass. 'How is the donkey?'

'Nil by mouth for two days until the danger has passed.'

Andras shook his head. 'It really *was* in my restaurant?'

'Our restaurant,' Spiros reminded him.

Andras let out a sigh. 'Spiro ... about the money ...'

'I know what you are going to say.'

'I am going to ask the bank to lend me the money.'

Spiros shook his head. 'Andras, you know how the banks are at the moment. This is not something that can be done.'

'I think it could be,' he replied. 'Tess, she is knowledgeable in this area and she thinks, with the business doing well and with my house as security, there is every chance that they will give this to me.'

Again Spiros shook his head. 'I am not sure I believe I am hearing this. You are taking financial advice from Patricia.'

Andras swallowed. 'You can call her Tess.'

'Andras, she isn't your real girlfriend.'

'Shh,' he said, looking around the restaurant to see if anyone was listening. 'I know that. But she knows about business.'

'She is a holidaymaker. Why would she give you good advice? What is in it for her?'

Andras stopped polishing the cutlery in his hands. 'Spiro, you sound like Mama.'

'Mama has a point.'

Andras sighed. 'She told you too, didn't she?' He thumped down the knife and fork. 'She told you that she and Marietta had been looking Tess up on the Internet.'

'And with good cause,' Spiros answered.

'What? Spiro, you know that Tess is doing me a favour.'

'And it is just getting you into more and more trouble with Mama.'

'Spiro, getting into trouble with Mama was something we did when we were kids. It should not be something that happens in our twenties.'

'Do you wish not to be Greek?' Spiros asked, shaking his head. 'You know how things are.'

'I know that I do not wish to have my life chosen for me.'

'But you have to be sensible about it.'

'What does that mean?'

'Well, I think Mama is concerned that you will choose someone else like Elissa.'

'You mean someone I actually care about instead of someone I am already related to?'

'Someone like Tess,' Spiros added.

He opened his mouth to say once again that Tess was not his real girlfriend, but the anger he felt about his brother's attitude won out. 'What is so wrong with Tess?'

'Brother, the fancy clothes and the perfect make-up are nice to look at, but it is superficial and in time that will all fade.'

Andras watched his brother's eyes go to the bar area where Kira was sitting, skirt drenched, long dark hair speckled with sand and sea salt. It was nice to know that his brother's affections were not skin-deep but not so nice to know that that's what Spiros thought drove *him*.

'Is that all you see?' Andras asked him.

'Andras, girls like that, they are from a different world to us,' Spiros said. 'It is nice to visit this world, like for a holiday, but at the end of the day ...'

He didn't want to hear any more. He had always known his brother gave in to their mother far more than he ever had, but until now, he had never once thought that Spiros held the same outdated attitude.

'I will get you your money, Spiro,' he stated.

'Mama is putting pressure on me to sign my share over to her.'

'I will get you your money,' he repeated.

# Forty-two

# The White House, Kalami

'Thank you,' Sonya said as a waiter showed them to their seats. Tess made her way around the cloth-covered table to the rattan chair. It was amazing how good she was getting at negotiating rocks, stones and the Corfiot roads in heels. She sat down and took in the view.

The White House was the former residence of British authors Lawrence and Gerald Durrell and recently the family had been brought back into the spotlight because of the ITV series inspired by the book, *My Family and Other Animals*. The building was now a restaurant and apartments, set at one end of the bay of Kalami. Whitewashed with green shutters, an open extension from the main building made up the taverna area and beneath, on the natural rocks, as close to the water as you could be, were the tables Tess and Sonya were sitting at.

Tess breathed in, eyes on the rippling water. There was hardly a breeze tonight, but the July humidity had dropped slightly. Tonight it was more warm and comforting than oppressive. And oppressive wasn't required when you had a missed call from your mother on your phone and a voicemail you didn't want to listen to.

'So,' Sonya said, exhaling. 'Have you spoken to Andras since earlier?'

'Sonya, you've been with me all afternoon. We wrote dozens of potential new names for Blackberry Boudoir in an Excel spreadsheet.'

'I know,' Sonya said. 'I just thought he might have called to arrange our next outing ... or something.'

The list of company names wasn't the only Excel spreadsheet Tess had looked into. She had found Andras's accounts for the restaurant. For a brief second she had considered opening it and pulling together some information for him to present to the bank but it felt like a breach of trust. It was unlikely he'd want her to know the precise nature of his finances. He might only want her guidance in telling him what the bank would be looking for. She focused back on Sonya.

'If he calls about "or something", I will let you know.' She scanned the other tables, looking for a waiter. She really needed some wine.

'Smooth As Silk!' Sonya blurted out like she had branding Tourette's.

'Sounds like a body lotion,' Tess stated.

'Sweet Harmony?'

'A hairspray,' Tess said.

Sonya sighed. 'And that's why I work in the post room and not as a marketeer.'

'Sorry,' Tess apologised. 'I think it's going to be one of those jobs where the right name is either going to take a long time coming or it's just going to pop up out of nowhere.'

'Plum Nights!'

'I think if I go with that I would be able to use those old graphics,' Tess stated.

'You would like some wine?'

A smiling waiter was by their table.

'Yes, yes please, we would,' Tess replied.

'It feels better, doesn't it?' Dorothea grinned, fingers pulling down her red headscarf, as Andras collected two plates of *spanakopita* from the serving hatch by the kitchen.

'What feels better?' Andras asked.

'The restaurant,' Dorothea replied. 'Without the evil spirits clouding everything.'

He stopped in the doorway, the plates steady in his hands. 'You do not believe my mother, do you, Dorothea? Because the only thing I could see clouding my restaurant today was smoke from the priests.'

'It feels cleaner now,' Dorothea continued. 'Bad vibes have been removed, light and love return for the wedding of Spiros and Kira, no?'

He was done with this superstitious nonsense. If there was one part of his Greek life he wanted to eradicate, then this was definitely it. And since the parochial cleansing and the things his mother had said, he hadn't been able to stop thinking about one person: Tess. How must she be feeling knowing she had done him this huge favour and his family had been stalking her private life on the Internet?

He kept remembering the look on her face, tears in her eyes she had seemed determined not to let fall. He knew already, from spending time with her, that there was more to her than her beautiful hair and the way her nose twitched when she was concentrating on something. And now he was concerned. Because of that immediate, intense reaction. Because there was something she was afraid of. He needed to know what it was. He *wanted* to know.

He looked at the food in his hands, quickly becoming cold. Mathias swerved by, heading for the wine racks. Andras held the plates out to him. 'Mathias, could you take care of table nine for me? I have to go out.'

The food was absolutely divine, as good as Georgiou's. Tess's taste buds were on full alert and dancing like a frenzied Ed Balls on *Strictly*. She slicked a slab of feta cheese through the spiced olive oil and put it into her mouth, letting the hot, creamy, salty sour sensation work its magic on her tongue …

'Joey's at a nightclub.'

Sonya's statement had the food climax fizzing out. She looked across at Sonya who was clutching her mobile phone in her hand.

'Sonya, why are you looking on your phone?' Tess asked. 'Didn't you say you were going to have a little faith?'

'I know,' Sonya said, voice wobbling. 'But I set an alert … to tell me when Joey posts and …'

Tess shook her head. This wasn't good.

'He doesn't like nightclubs,' Sonya said. 'They have too much—'

'Stale air?' Tess offered.

'Loud music,' Sonya finished off. 'Joey likes to talk. He says if you're going *out* out then you need to be able to have a proper conversation. Not have everything drowned out by … technotronics.'

Tess wasn't even sure technotronics was a real word. But that wasn't the issue here. The issue here was Joey *wasn't* here and he had told the world he was in Margate with a woman, in a hotel, and now he was doing something else that would usually be out of his comfort zone, leaving Sonya back in panic mode.

'OK,' Tess said, taking a calming breath. 'There are two things we can do.' She made sure she had Sonya's full attention. 'We can do exactly like we've been doing, loving his posts, putting up some fabulous ones of our own, or …'

'Or?' Sonya said, elbows on the table, looking across at Tess as if she held all the answers.

'I've said it before. You can phone him,' Tess said bluntly.

Sonya didn't move. Not one eyelash. She just carried on looking at Tess as if she hadn't spoken. Perhaps she needed to rephrase the suggestion.

'Phone him, Sonya.' She sighed. 'Please, phone him.'

She watched her friend swallow, her fingers seeking reassurance from the necklace that wasn't there. 'Well, what would I say?'

'Just check in,' Tess said. 'Keep it casual. Tell him you're having a great time here and tell him about all the things we've seen and done.' She moved her eyes over to the scenery again. Aquamarine sea, the lush, green cypress trees, the golden strip of beach, all against a backdrop of the blue sky turning pink as the sun descended. 'Tell him he would love Kalami.' *She* loved Kalami. A shiver rolled over her shoulders.

'He *would* really love Kalami,' Sonya said, circling the rim of her wine glass with a finger.

Another thought struck Tess. 'Did you say he was at a nightclub?'

'Yes,' Sonya said. 'Somewhere called "Maxim's".'

Tess checked her watch. 'Sonya, it's only six o'clock in England. What nightclub is open at six o'clock?' Now she had a theory. 'I think I know what Joey's doing.'

'What?' Sonya asked.

'Just go and call him,' Tess ordered.

'What, now?' Sonya said. 'Before my chocolate soufflé in baklava parcels?'

'Yes, now,' Tess said, flapping away a mosquito.

She saw a mixture of emotions in her friend's expression. Instant elation at the thought of contacting the man she adored, but then something else, more contemplative, something slightly wistful, verging on anxious. She so wanted this relationship issue to be resolved. For Sonya. And for that tiny bit of her that was warmed by the thought of a strong, enduring relationship. As that feeling hit she felt the need to bring her glass of wine to her lips.

'OK,' Sonya said, shifting in her seat and picking her handbag off the rock floor, mobile phone still in her hand. 'OK.' She looked like someone had just told her she had to slip into the anchor chair on BBC News.

Tess smiled. 'Go get him.'

Sonya nodded and crossed her fingers in the air.

Tess watched Sonya begin to negotiate the uneven rock and head towards the main building for a little privacy. And that's when reality bit. She was alone, completely alone. Surrounded by tables filled with couples, families and groups, all connecting with each other and enjoying the simple, warm, candlelit ambience. There was no one to connect with now Sonya was off reconnecting with Joey. There would be no one to eat at Gianni's with when she got home. No stories about someone else's day – Tony and his car showroom clients or Daniel and his hair-and-nail salon. Her fingers itched for the phone in her hand. The scrolling, attention-sucking draw of the dating app. She made a move, lowering her hand towards her bag until she remembered the voicemail her mother had left. She couldn't look at that red dot and ignore it. And she definitely didn't want to listen it. She let out a breath. She was being ridiculous. She could do this. She could be dateless in Corfu. She was just going to sit back, absorb the setting sun, the Albanian mountains in the distance, and that cerulean water so close she could almost touch it.

'Tess,'

The soft, warm, Greek lilt immediately had her turning away from the shoreline towards the sound and its owner. Andras.

# Forty-three

'I … Sonya is just inside and … we're waiting for baklava and chocolate soufflé.'

Why was she stuttering and stammering like a nerd? It wasn't as if he could see inside her mind and know she was thinking about all those other guys his mother had thrown at them like man-confetti earlier. And it was hot again. Could the humidity rise rapidly like that?

'The baklava here is very good,' he answered. He looked at the vacant seat opposite her. 'May I sit down?'

She nodded before picking up her napkin and pulling at the very corner with her thumb and forefinger.

He poured himself a glass of water and sipped at it. 'It is hot tonight,' he remarked.

'A little,' Tess replied.

'Tess, I would like to apologise—' Andras began.

'Oh no,' Tess interrupted. 'There's no need for any apology.'

'I believe there is.' His tone was insistent. 'My mother and Marietta … they should not have been looking on the Internet for information about you.'

'It doesn't matter,' Tess said, eyes trying to seek out anything other than his gorgeous ebony ones.

'It matters to me,' he carried on. 'You have come here seeking rest and relaxation and I have been selfish, putting you in the middle of this crazy family and …' He paused. 'I still do not know why you would not let me tell her the truth.'

Now her stomach started to sizzle, like it was a grill pan cooking spitting sausages. Why hadn't she let him tell the truth? She moved her fingers from the napkin to the base of her wine glass, gently smoothing the fat pad of glass in a circular motion.

'Expectation.'

She shocked herself by saying the word out loud. It had been right there on her lips, coming out before she could pull it back. Why was all this truth-telling slipping forth whenever she was with him? And when it tumbled into the space between them, why was she desperate for his opinion on it? She looked at him, caught between wanting him to say something, anything. Ask her what she meant or make light of it. Nothing was forthcoming.

'I ...' she started. She didn't quite know what she wanted to say. 'I don't like ... expectation.'

'You don't,' he said soberly, his eyes finding hers despite her efforts.

'No.' She shook her head. 'I'm not saying that if you told the truth about me, about us, that you would be destined to have a life you don't want, because I don't think you're weak.' She swallowed again. 'But I do think your mother would think she had won. Beaten you into submission over something. And you would still be left with that expectation hanging over you.' She sighed. 'I don't like the thought of that.'

She couldn't believe she had said that. She put her glass to her lips only to find all the wine had been drunk. She put it down again.

'You sound a little like you are speaking from experience of your own,' he said softly.

'Maybe,' she admitted.

'From your family?' he asked.

'Once,' she replied, a half-smile on her lips. 'Until ...' She closed her lips together. She had to stop. If the setting sun, the alcohol content of the chilled retsina and Andras's exposed forearms combined any more, she was in danger of letting everything go ... and she never let *everything* go.

'You created a fake Greek boyfriend?'

Andras could see she was struggling. It was as if there was something she wanted to tell him, but sharing it was going to cause her pain. He could not imagine what it was. But, as much as he wanted to know, he was not prepared to push her now. And, really, it was not his business.

She smiled at him. 'Now, Andras, that was *your* idea, not mine.'

'I know,' he said, holding his hands up and smiling back.

'I'm sorry I wasn't a more appropriate match,' she told him.

'What do you mean?'

'Well,' Tess said, picking up the bottle of wine and pouring some into her glass, then a little in a spare glass for him. 'Imagine if your mother's Internet search had discovered I was a virginal, Greek-cooking enthusiast who spends her weekends tending her garden.'

Andras shook his head. 'If she found out that she would know this was not real.'

'No?' Tess said, looking at him quizzically.

'No,' he replied, leaning forward a little. 'That is not the sort of woman I have an interest in, and Mama knows that.'

'So, what sort of woman do you have an interest in?' Tess asked.

She took a sip of her wine but her eyes didn't leave his and he felt something stir inside him. In truth, Tess was exactly his type in every single way and that was just starting to scare him more than the thought of being set up with Marietta.

'My mother is a strong woman,' he began.

'You're looking for someone just like your mother!' Tess exclaimed.

'No,' he said quickly. 'No, that is not what I meant.'

'Then ...'

'My mother thinks that to be strong you must be in charge,' he elaborated. 'But to me, strength does not mean forcing or bullying. Strength is something that comes from the soul.' He watched her expression. She was watching him intently, those sapphire-coloured eyes studying his.

'Is that right?' she asked.

He nodded. 'I think so. I think some people are born with inner strength but for others ... well, I think it comes from surviving. From going through times where you did not feel you were strong but something made you hold on and regrow, and then you knew you would make sure you did not feel that way again.'

'No expectation on your shoulders,' Tess added.

'Well, I think there will always be some kind of expectation from somewhere,' he answered. 'Because you cannot change other people, especially people like my mother.'

'But if there's no one *in* your life then you can't let anyone down,' Tess blurted out.

He baulked. 'What?'

What had she just said? Tess shifted on her seat. This was again tiptoeing ever closer to a truth she didn't visit. She had to regroup.

'Nothing. I just mean, you know, you not dating, not getting involved ... there's no handholding, breakfast-making expectations to live up to.' She topped up her wine glass again, even though there was no need. 'Anyway, we are digressing. You were telling me what you look for in a woman.'

'I think the conversation began because you were apologising for not being a virginal gardener.' He smiled. Those thick, luscious lips widening to show pristine teeth.

'I make no apologies for that.'

'Good,' Andras answered. 'I am glad.' He reached across the table, taking her hand in his. It took half a second before she realised what had happened and she was stuck between shifting her hand away and holding on tight.

He let her go and her hand was left there, looking awkward between the salt and pepper cellars. She drew it back.

'Let me take you out,' Andras said.

'I am out,' Tess replied, fingers going to her hair.

'After dinner. Late. When my restaurant is closed.'

Her insides squeezed together involuntarily. 'You don't need to do that.'

'I want to,' he replied. 'I know this great club. I haven't been there for so long. We can dance. We can just forget all this wedding and family stuff.' He smiled. 'Let me show you how much fun Greece can be.'

Tess opened her mouth not really knowing what was going to come out of it. The more she looked at him the more she was thinking about all the sorts of fun they could have minus their clothes. Cheap thrills and no expectation other than total physical satisfaction.

'What's this about fun?'

Sonya's reappearance at the table stopped Tess saying anything at all. Now she concentrated on trying to read her friend's expression. What had happened with Joey? Had there been tears? Was that a smile?

'To apologise, for the behaviour of my mother, I would like to take you out tonight,' Andras said, standing up and moving the chair for Sonya to retake her seat.

'We don't have to go,' Tess said immediately. 'I told Andras there was no need for an apology.'

'Why wouldn't we want to go?' Sonya asked, sitting down and picking up her wine. 'I haven't been dancing in ages and, what's good enough for Joey at Maxim's – despite him telling me for years he doesn't like nightclubs ...' There was a bit of a lip wobble.

'Well, I don't know. I just thought ...' What had she thought? That the more time she spent with this man, the more she craved the entire male catalogue of Hooked Up? She shook her head as if trying to eradicate the feeling. 'We can go if you want to.'

'Great,' Andras said. 'My friend Fotis will drive us in his truck. Meet me at the restaurant at midnight.'

He had made it sound like an assignation with a secret agent. A dirty, sexy secret agent. Where was the wine waiter? Her glass had been empty for what felt like hours.

'A truck,' Sonya said. 'Another something to get my leg over.'

'I must get back,' Andras said, making to leave. 'Oh.' He turned back to the table, looking directly at Tess. 'You are still thinking of a company name for the clients with wine bars?'

She nodded. 'Absolutely.'

He smiled then. 'It is probably not the right kind of thing, but I was thinking ... Black Velvet.'

It was like time had stopped and tumbleweed was about to come rolling across the floor. It was simple. It was smooth and suave, dark and enticing. She was already imagining a swirl of ribbon writing and an elegant glass in the branding.

How had he done that? She was supposed to be the marketing guru!

'That's it!' Sonya exclaimed. 'That's the name!'

Tess swallowed, a little overawed but in absolutely no doubt that Sonya was right.

# Forty-four

# Passion Nightclub, Kassiopi

'No one mentioned anything about it being a foam party!' Sonya shrieked over the thumping beat of a Calvin Harris track.

Tess laughed. Her friend's red hair and half her face were coated with surf-like bubbles as they danced in the very middle of this compact sweatbox of a nightclub. It was good though. Like Andras had promised.

They had clambered into Fotis's truck just after midnight and it really had been a proper truck. Squeezed into the cab, a line of truck-driving trophies fixed to the dashboard, the very crazy, somewhere-near-twenty-stone Fotis had bounced them over the mountain to the village of Kassiopi. Even in the dark it was picturesque. Fishing boats and larger tourist vessels bobbed on the water in the harbour, glowing lamps lit the whole area and above them, on the hillside, were the ruins of a fortress, Greek flag still flying from its crumbling walls. Only the pumping disco sounds from Passion Nightclub stirred the darkness. It was just set back from the harbour and, as it was the only nightclub here, it was packed.

And now she was in the thick of the crowd, caught up in the group euphoria that came from hot, sunshine days, the holiday spirit and the accompanying ouzo served in shot glasses. This was better than any club she had been to in London.

The vibe was so relaxed, everyone carefree and just enjoying the music. However, Andras, his dark hair damp, tendrils licking over his forehead, his shirt wet and slightly see-through where the froth had soaked it, was *not* adding to the chilled theme. His moves were melting her like a Magnum ice cream left out in the sun. She knew he was a good dancer from his Greek display the very first night they met but there it was for a crowd, here it was just him having fun and letting go. And if there was one thing Greek men seemed to do, it was let go. This was no conservative-side-stepping-back-and-forth-wondering-who-was-judging-you-dancing. This was every-single-sinew-working-like-Beyoncé-dancing. And it was hot!

'So, Sonya!' Tess called, turning away from Andras, stepping closer to her gyrating friend and dipping her head to her ear. 'Are you going to try calling Joey again?'

Sonya shook her head. 'Not tonight.'

She supposed that was the best idea. After twenty-three attempts to get him to pick up before dessert at the White House, maybe a little time-distance and sleeping on it was the best idea.

'Sonya! You dance with me!' Fotis had appeared in their circle, a big grin on his face, perspiration slicking his hair. He was so tall and so round, it was like dancing next to a circus strongman.

'I won't leave you,' Tess murmured.

'You will,' Sonya said. 'I'll have another one of those Path Shooters.'

'Alley Shooters,' Tess corrected.

'Yes! Ow, tennis elbow!' Sonya said, as Fotis took her hand and shot her arm up into the air as the strobes started to flash.

Tess shimmied her way through the dancing throng to the bar area, positioning herself to wait for attention. The amount of wine she had consumed with dinner, plus aperitifs before they left Georgiou's and now two shots down, she was starting to feel a little buzzed.

'Hi.'

The Eastern-European accent made her turn her head and she smiled at the twenty-something, blond-haired guy on her right. 'Hi.'

'My name is Stefan,' he greeted.

'Hello,' Tess answered, waving in an attempt to attract a member of the bar staff.

'What is your name?'

'I'm sorry,' Tess answered. 'The music is very loud. I can't hear you.'

He put a meaty hand on her arm. 'What is your name?' he repeated, leaning in close. He smelled of sweat, beer and *gyros*. It wasn't a good mix.

'Patricia,' she said. That had tripped off the tongue.

'Patricia,' he breathed, more fumes heading her way.

'Yes.'

'I am Stefan.'

'I know.'

'You would like to dance close to me.'

It was worrying he hadn't ended the sentence with a question mark. She shook her head.

'I think you would like this,' Stefan said. The thick fingers were back on her arm, this time spidering their way up towards her shoulder. She shrugged off the advance and took a step away, waving a twenty-euro note at anyone behind the bar who was going to deliver alcohol.

'Come on,' Stefan said. 'Come and dance with me.'

This time there was nothing subtle about his moves. He lunged forward, body blocking her, hands primed to rove.

Tess stood her ground. 'You touch me again and the only thing you will be dancing with is a medical professional.'

He stayed where he was, so close his perspiring body was almost touching hers. She needed him to back off now. She wasn't sure she remembered whether you went for the balls or the windpipe first in self-defence.

And then, suddenly, Stefan was tipping back, moving away from her like he was being forklifted. A few people gasped, drinks spilled and it took a second for Tess to catch up with what was going on. Andras had Stefan by the shirt and was manhandling him towards the exit, just as one of her favourite Zara Larsson tracks came on.

She muttered apologies to clubbers as she hurried through the writhing bodies in a bid to catch up. Then, as she got closer to the entrance she fell out of the revelling crowd just in time to see Andras pushing Stefan towards the doormen, yelling something unintelligible. Was that Greek? English? She couldn't tell. But when he turned around she was shocked by just how furious Andras looked. Hair a little displaced, shoulders wide, he moved towards her.

'Are you OK?' he asked. 'Did he hurt you?'

His voice was thick with anxiety. It took a second to respond. 'No,' she answered, swallowing as his tone affected her. Then fight mode kicked in. 'What the hell did you think you were doing?'

'What do you mean?' he questioned loudly. 'That guy, he was bothering you. If I hadn't come over he—'

'If you hadn't come over!' Tess snorted. 'I'm quite capable of looking after myself!'

'It did not seem that way.'

Suddenly she was overcome by just how hot she was. The club atmosphere began to close in on her skin, a wave of humidity rolling over her. She eyed the doors and took a step forward. 'I'm going to get some fresh air.'

'You can't,' Andras said, grabbing her hand.

'I can do whatever I want,' Tess stated.

'The guy has just been thrown out of the club. He will be out there. He will be waiting for a taxi ...'

She tutted and brushed past him, heading for the doors.

# Forty-five

Andras's whole body was racing as he followed Tess to the door. When he had seen that man touching her, leaning in so close, looking like he wanted to … well, he had felt enraged. Completely and utterly furious and unable to do anything to control his immediate, base reaction. Those feelings were persisting and, for some reason, he couldn't ignore them.

'Tess,' he called, going through the door behind her as she pushed her way outside.

'I'm fine,' she answered, stepping out onto the road and making for the paved path that led to the harbour. 'Just a bit hot and needing five minutes.' She stopped walking once she had reached the very edge and stood, looking out over the boats, the lights from Limani bar across the water casting a rainbow reflection on the surface of the sea. He wanted to touch her hair. He wanted to smooth his hands down her arms and wipe every trace of that man from her. Instead he put his hands into the pockets of his jeans and stood along-side her.

'The things your mother and Marietta found out about me on the Internet, they're all true,' Tess suddenly spoke.

He didn't answer straightaway. He had come to know that sometimes, to get more from Tess, you needed to wait a little, let her settle with her own words.

'The longest I ever stay with anyone is six weeks.'

He watched her shoulders roll, as if letting that information go had lightened her whole being. She sighed, her head turning slightly towards him. Still he remained quiet.

'Aren't you going to say anything?' Tess asked, turning a little more.

'What do you want me to say?' Andras whispered.

'I don't know,' she admitted. 'Something. Anything.' She threw her arms up in the air. 'I suppose ... I want you to know what sort of person I am.' She nodded then. 'Yes, I want you to know that my life is my work. I love my work. And I date lots of men because I can and ... I don't care what anyone thinks about that.' She sniffed as if it was a final conclusion.

'But you wish me to comment on this?' he asked.

'Well, seeing as you seemed to feel the need to attack a man for talking to me, I just thought you needed a sharp reminder that we are not a real love-struck couple who met on a sun-drenched beach back in the spring.'

She was right, of course. He had overstepped the mark, crossed the boundaries and what was worst of all, he didn't want to acknowledge exactly why.

'I do not need any reminder,' he answered.

'No?' Tess shot back.

'No,' he replied.

She was looking at him now, those cobalt eyes latched onto his, her chin showing defiance, her button nose giving off cute, her lips set to sexy ...

He caught her mouth up in his, feeling that same sweet, erotic taste he had first experienced in his own restaurant in front of everyone he knew. He should stop. He should pull back. He should not have his hands in her hair, smoothing her jawline as he brushed the strands away from her face. Her hands were on him too now, one smoothing over his shoulder, slipping beneath the wet material of his shirt, the other tracing a fingertip path down the back of his neck. His whole body was on fire, craving to get closer to her …

'You have to have sex with me, Andras,' Tess whispered. 'That's what we have to do.' She kissed his lips again. 'That's all we have to do.'

Just the thought of very slowly sliding down the zip at the back of that figure-hugging dress she was wearing was making him hard. She was beautiful. She was strong and opinionated. She was full of attitude, and life.

'Touch me,' she begged. The need in her voice was pushing all his buttons. He snaked a hand over her breast, then began sliding over the flat of her stomach reaching lower.

'We just need to do this,' Tess whispered. 'And then … we can both move on.'

It was like someone had turned on a searchlight. The dark, soft-lit harbour night, jasmine on the breeze, had suddenly turned into Interrogation Room 101 for him. He let her go, slipping out of her embrace, and putting his hands firmly back in his pockets.

'What's wrong?' Tess asked, her lips shaping into a pout.

'This isn't right,' he answered.

'It was feeling more than right from where I was standing.' She folded her arms across her chest.

As much as his body was telling him he *really* needed this sexual workout, something else was telling him this was not the path to travel.

'Why are you looking like that?' Tess inquired.

What did he say? Did he lie? Did he tell the truth? Which one would scare her more? Which one scared him less?

'I had to react to the man in the club,' he said. 'What if there was someone from my village in there? We are supposed to be dating.' He looked at her then, to gauge her reaction.

'And that was all it was?'

Her reply almost sounded disappointed. What was he trying to achieve? He nodded his head.

'So, here … outside.' Her gaze went to the harbour. 'It was just for authenticity too?' she asked. 'In case your mother has a long-range telescope set up or spies tracking us?'

'You say that as if it cannot be a consideration.' He gave her a half-smile.

'Having sex would surely help cement the validity of this relationship though.' She smiled, reaching out a hand and running her fingertip over his pectoral.

He wished she would stop saying the word 'sex', it was practically killing him. He needed to be clear. While clear thoughts were with him.

'I won't have sex with you, Tess.'

He could feel the beat of his heart in his neck and he hated every frantic throb of it. He didn't want to hurt her. He wanted to protect her. And himself. This was a dilemma of his own making.

'But you told me that's all you do …' she said. 'No holding hands or awkward morning-after-the-night-befores. Just something simple.'

He remembered the conversation. He knew what he did. What he *used* to do. But this was different. It wasn't simple. It was about as complicated as it could get.

He nodded. 'I know.' He wanted to reach out to her right now.

'Then …'

'We should go back inside.' He looked towards the doors of Passion. 'Fotis loves to dance. Sonya, she will need saving from dehydration.'

'Andras,' Tess said.

The way she said his name hammered at him. He closed his eyes for a second. He needed to say more.

'Tess, I am so grateful for all your help.' He let a sigh leave him. 'So grateful.' He shook his head. 'But the truth is … I do not want to be like one of your men from England.'

He waited for his statement to really reach her before continuing. 'We are friends now, yes? Friends who happen to be single. Friends who are helping each other and tonight have just had a little too much to drink.'

'I think you'll find that "friends with benefits" is a bit of a 2017 watchword.' She smiled. 'All the cool kids are doing it.'

He nodded soberly. 'Then I think that … perhaps the cool kids are doing it because, like us, they are not really ready for anything else.'

# Forty-six

# Kalami Cove Apartments

Tess was sober. She was actually completely and totally sober. She didn't know how she could be sober after spending the night drinking shots she had never heard of *and* something Fotis had insisted on that was poured into boiling hot black coffee to create a potion that bubbled like witch's brew. Well, she did know actually. She knew that after she had clambered out of the cab of the truck, after Sonya had moulded herself to the wall of the apartment pretending to be a gecko then fallen into a snorty sleep, she had put the kettle on and non-creepy-alcoholic coffee-d up her insides.

She hadn't wanted to sleep, even if tiredness had willed her to. There was too much swimming inside her mind. For a moment, she had looked at the voicemail icon on her phone and thought about calling her mother. It wasn't that she didn't ever think about it when she was at home. Usually late at night. Usually under the influence. But back in London, she always thought better of it. And the same had happened last night.

She also hadn't been able to stop thinking about Andras. Even now, sitting on the veranda, breathing in the scent of bougainvillea and wisteria, she still couldn't stop thinking about him. She had wanted to be infuriated by his need to act all Neanderthal over Stefan's wandering hands, and she had acted out a pretty competent performance, but, in truth, what she had actually felt was protected. And that had terrified her. Which was why she had told him about the six-week rule. As if she needed to be punished for feeling that way, the way she had often felt with Adam. To know, or at least to think that you knew, that someone had your back, that someone was there, if you needed them. But then he had kissed her, robbing her of every sensible thought and making her body twang with longing, before throwing her libido to the ground like a WWF wrestler.

Last night she had been cross and frustrated – so frustrated in every single way – that she had opened Andras's laptop and gone into the restaurant accounts without a second thought to his privacy. And what she had found there had been pleasing. The business wasn't just doing well, it was thriving. Turnover was up already this year from last and, despite a lean spell when the Greek economy had been at its most fragile, the figures were sound. Certainly sound enough for a sensible bank to give him a business loan.

And that's what she was doing right now. She wasn't creating branding for Blackberry Boudoir/Black Velvet, she was coming up with a draft business plan for Taverna Georgiou, for Andras to take to the bank. Why?

She sighed, stretching up her arms, enjoying the warmth of the sun on her skin. She was picking up a bit of colour now and there did seem to be something almost magical about waking up to the sound of the sea and the scent of the salt-water and sand on the breeze. She closed her eyes, just letting the morning sun settle her mind and her soul.

A deep, throaty moan invaded her consciousness and she snapped her eyes open. What the hell was that?

'Sonya?' she said tentatively, looking back into the apartment at her friend's form on the bed. There was no sign of movement or indication of moaning there.

The growl hit her ears again, followed by two sharp coughs. She knew there was a new couple next door to them now. They had been sat on their veranda at three o'clock that morning lighting incense and chanting. For a second she thought the priests might be back.

Head leaning slightly over to their neighbours' terrace, Tess couldn't hear anything further. But then she saw it. Just off the terrace, behind a white flowering bush, something moved. Standing up, she walked to the metal fence and narrowed her eyes, shading them with her hand. Another groan, a slow move forward and the noise-maker was revealed.

A tortoise.

Hector.

# Forty-seven

# Taverna Georgiou

Andras watched his mother from where he was clipping the breakfast/lunchtime paper tablecloths to the tables in the restaurant. Isadora was standing in the centre of the room, a measuring tape in one hand, the end of which was sticking out like it might be used as a weapon, should the need arise. He had never known a wedding to need so much measuring. He secured another clip to the table he was working on and saw his mother's lips were moving, as if she were talking to herself.

'Isadora,' Kira said, coming up behind the older woman and resting a gentle hand on her shoulder. 'Please, come and sit down.'

Isadora shook her head. 'I cannot. There is still much to arrange. I need to make sure Andras does not keep moving these tables around. For three days I have had to move them back into position. It is only days until the wedding.'

'I know,' Kira answered. 'But the tables are fine, really.'

'They are not fine,' Isadora snapped. 'There are too many inches here ...' She indicated the tables to her left. 'And not enough inches here.' She sniffed. 'When you and Spiros come into the room, every pair of eyes should be on you two.' She turned, taking in the tables. 'Everyone is going to see how happy you both are. Starting your new life together. As God always intended for you, right back when you were both so young.'

Andras watched his mother reach into her blouse pocket for a tissue. He had never seen her this emotional before. Shouting orders, directing everyone's lives, yes, but not upset. His mother never showed any weakness. This was a little like she had been yesterday, after she had shouted at Tess, when she had mentioned Elissa.

Kira put her arm around Isadora, patting her back. 'We are going to have the perfect wedding, because everyone has worked so hard, *you* have worked so hard.' She rubbed Isadora's shoulder. 'Come, let's have some coffee and think about making some small adjustments to Helena's dress.'

Isadora shook her head. 'No!' She straightened up, seeming to come out of whatever funk she had slipped into. 'No adjustments can be made. It is traditional Corfiot dress!'

'But, Isadora, she keeps fainting,' Kira stated.

'Pah! The girl will get over it. Now,' she said, putting her hands on the nearest table. 'Help me move this one.'

Andras shook his head. It was absolutely no good telling his mother the tables could all just be moved to her specification the night before the wedding. This was much more than Greek Feng Shui. He had a feeling it also had a lot to do with the past.

'Can you help me?!'

Andras turned to the back entrance of the restaurant and there was Tess, hair loose and wild, thin sundress covering not much of her body ... and next to her was a sack truck, Hector tied to it with what looked like a hosepipe. Andras hurried across the room.

'*Theé mou!*' Isadora exclaimed. 'This creature! This monster! It is a curse! It will be the death of me!'

'Are you talking about me or the tortoise?' Tess answered with a smile.

'Why do you do this?' Isadora continued. 'The restaurant was blessed yesterday. It was cleaned and purified, inside and out, and now you have brought this ... this demon back into the sanctified space.'

'Ah, so you *were* talking about the tortoise and not me,' Tess replied.

'I will deal with it,' Andras said, untying Hector from his transport as his head began to emerge from his shell.

Tess took a deep breath in. 'It does smell of something in here today.' She sucked in another breath. 'I just can't put my finger on what it is.'

'It is fresh air!' Isadora stated. 'The Greek sea air and nothing else!'

'No,' Tess stated with a shake of her head. 'No I don't think it's that.'

'Dorothea is making courgette balls,' Kira offered.

'Maybe it's that ... yes. I'm sure it's that,' Tess said. 'I think.'

Andras picked Hector up and placed him on the restaurant floor. 'You would like some breakfast?' He wanted her to stay.

Tess shook her head. 'No. I've left Sonya – Susan – making omelettes.'

'Andras, that animal cannot be on the floor of the restaurant,' Isadora shrieked.

He swiftly picked Hector up in his arms and turned to Tess. He wanted to say something, anything to get over the awkwardness of last night. Kissing her like that, wanting to touch her just about everywhere, then backing out as fast as he could ...

'I can take you out later,' he said. 'This afternoon, maybe, when the restaurant is quieter. Perhaps to Kalamaki Beach?'

'You will be busy,' Isadora said immediately. 'You and Marietta are needed at the church to run through things before the wedding day. We leave here at three o'clock.'

He turned to his mother. 'That is today?' He was sure Spiros had said it was tomorrow.

'Yes, that is today. You have a copy of the schedule. I do not know why I bother with these if nobody reads them.' She tutted. 'And there is the dinner tonight, with Kira's family, on the beach. Or have you forgotten that too?'

He hadn't forgotten. He just hadn't read the schedule. Although, if his restaurant was providing the food, he ought to have had his eye on the ball a bit better.

'Isadora, come, let's go and have that coffee,' Kira suggested, slipping her arm through her soon-to-be-mother-in-law's.

'Not until that creature has been removed!'

'I'm just going,' Tess replied as Kira managed to extract Isadora from the conversation, shepherding her to a table by the sea view.

'I'm sorry,' Andras began. 'I thought the wedding things were tomorrow.'

'You don't have to apologise to your not-real girlfriend,' Tess said.

'But I do have to keep up my guide-man end of the bargain.' He had a thought. 'Why don't you come with me?'

'Where?'

'To the church.'

'That sounds like a whole lot of fun.'

'It is in the village Kira comes from, Agios Spyridon. About twenty minutes from here. It is very pretty. We can take the boat. There is a beach, and a couple of bars, if you do not want to come into the church.'

'I don't know,' Tess said with a sigh.

'Tess …'

'I'll ask Sonya,' she answered. 'It's her holiday really.'

'OK,' he said.

'OK,' she answered, taking a step away from him.

'Tess,' he said again, wanting her to stop.

She turned back. There was something different about her. It wasn't just the clothes or the flat shoes or her hair being untamed. It was something he couldn't put his finger on.

'You didn't say where you found Hector,' he said.

'He was in the gardens of Kalami Cove, eating the plants.'

He shook his head. 'For a tortoise, he moves fast.'

She nodded. 'I think you might need a taller fence. Despite his appearance, I'm pretty sure he's a climber.'

# Forty-eight

# Agios Spyridon

'Oh my! This is beautiful!'

Sonya's observation was in no way exaggerated. Tess leaned out over the bow of Andras's boat, taking in the bay of Agios Spyridon as they approached over the waves. A long, golden stretch of sand beckoned. There were loungers on the shore, together with a couple of pedalos and two small speedboats, but the beach wasn't busy. Slim eucalyptus trees swayed behind it, then beyond were more of Corfu's undulating fields and hills, the peak of Mount Pantokrator clearly visible on this blue-sky, thirty-degree day.

'There is the church,' Andras called over the boat's engine. He pointed at a tiny lemon-painted stone building sitting just off the sand. It was like someone had placed a Mr Kipling's Fondant Fancy on the rocks.

'Really?' Sonya said in awe. 'That's really the little church? Oh, Tess, look at it! It's like a cute doll chapel covered in marzipan.'

'Mmm,' Tess answered. She couldn't deny it was beautiful but the whole church thing had been pinching at her since Andras had mentioned it that morning.

'How many people does it hold?' Sonya asked.

Andras slowed down the boat as they neared the shore, letting the engine just tick over as they eased towards land. 'I do not know. It is not very big.'

'I thought there were almost a hundred people coming to the wedding,' Tess piped up.

'And that is how many the church will hold if my mother has her way,' he answered.

'A hundred people!' Sonya exclaimed. 'A hundred people in that little chapel?'

'I am joking,' Andras said, smiling. 'The church service, it is for just family. The reception and second ceremony on the beach at Kalami is for everyone.'

'Second ceremony,' Tess said, shaking her head.

'You think this is … how do you say? … Over the top?' Andras asked.

'Oh, just a little,' Tess answered.

'We are Greek, remember.' He smiled, as if that explained everything.

'Well, I think it's lovely,' Sonya said softly.

Of course she did. Because, despite only being almost-engaged, this was what Sonya had been dreaming of since she had started getting serious with Joey. Sonya was the big white wedding, dove-releasing, chimney-sweep-needing, jazz-band-in-a-marquee type. Tess knew her friend had a scrapbook of ideas for her wedding. Sonya had never shown her, because of Adam, but Tess had found it when she was searching for the karaoke CDs during a girls' night. Tulle and lace scraps were there, the business card and leaflet of a company that hired out wigwams in the New Forest, her wedding song list with some scratched out and others added as time progressed. Tess had slammed the book shut after three pages and never opened that drawer in Sonya's place ever again.

'It is not so bad,' Andras said, waving at the man on the beach who looked ready to help them with the boat. 'At least it is someone else's wedding, no?'

He wasn't wrong there. Tess focused on getting nearer to dry land and then she realised what was missing …

'Where's the dock?' she asked.

'There is no dock here,' Andras answered. 'I will let down the anchor when we get closer. We may tie up to the other boats.'

'But … I'll have to get out in the sea.' She swallowed. She hated this. Her Zanotti's were starting to show signs of salt-water damage already.

'We can swim,' Sonya said. 'You have your bikini on under your dress. Like we did near the Rothschild house. The water here looks even clearer.'

'It is OK,' Andras answered. 'If you cannot take off your shoes I can carry you.'

She closed her eyes. What was going to be worse? Removing her shoes and feeling the earth touch her soles or letting Andras carry her up the beach again like a scene from some lame romance film? She wasn't sure, but now, as they chugged forwards, Andras looking like he was concentrating, she could see a group gathering on the sand. And in the middle of the pack was Isadora, her imposing figure standing out above even the men of the party. She would be watching and waiting for Tess to mess up and, whether she understood the reasons why or not, she didn't want to make a fool of herself. Her fingers went to the buckle on her left foot. She could do this. She could totally do this. After all this time, being scared of going barefoot had to stop.

'Ooo look! There's a little crab!' Sonya announced, head hanging over the boat, hair almost touching the surface.

She swallowed. Great. The earth *and* crabs. It was like the entire universe was plotting against her. Everything she hated under her feet and a Greek matriarch waiting to watch her every move.

Andras greeted the man from the beach who was wading out to meet them.

'I'm so hot,' Sonya remarked, flapping her hand in front of her face. 'I can't wait to get into that water.'

Tess could wait. She could wait a billion years, or until the Georgiou family stopped looking, whichever scenario came first.

'We can get out now?' Sonya asked, looking to Andras.

'Yes, of course,' he answered.

'Here I go!' Sonya exclaimed.

Tess watched her friend deftly step up on to the side of the boat, fingers pinching her nose, and launch herself into the sea. Sonya resurfaced with a smile on her face, wading towards the shoreline.

Right, that was it, there was no more hesitating to be done. If she didn't do something then Andras was going to stop being busy with ropes and anchors and he would probably throw her over his shoulder like a fireman. That thought made her shiver but also spurred her into action. She had to do this. She *had* to do this. It was just taking off her shoes, getting into the sea, walking up the sand and putting them straight back on again. Her heart began to palpitate. She could do this. It was just walking ... it was sand, not cold flagstone. There were no violet and cream flowers anywhere, no father by her side, no organ music ... just the faint thrum of euro-pop coming from somewhere and the sun on her back. It was nothing like the same. Nothing like it ...

'You are OK?' Andras asked.

That was it. She couldn't stop now. She wrenched at the straps, tugging the leather upwards until the buckle came loose enough to negotiate with.

'Fine,' she answered. Was that her voice? All squeaky and uncontrolled?

'I could—' he began.

She leapt up off her seat at the side of the vessel. 'No! I'm fine.' She looked down at her feet, still inside the sandals. It should be as easy as a tube of Pringles: one firm rip, the foil top comes off, then no stopping to think about anything else. She closed her eyes then quickly, one by one, took off her shoes. An overwhelming feeling immediately surrounded her, just like it did every time she took off her shoes. Memories, sadness, anger, hurt, pain. She gritted her teeth, sandals hanging from her fingers, and stepped up onto the ridge of the boat, trying to maintain her balance.

'Tess,' Andras said.

She couldn't have him saying anything else. She just had to jump. A little bunny hop into the thigh-deep water, trying not to think of crabs, a quick fifty-metre shuffle, then straight on to the sand and back into her shoes. She gritted her teeth together, then … jumped. Splashing down, her feet were moving before they had even made contact with the surface. There would not be crabs, or little fish, or weed. She was going to hold on to her game face, she was going to swagger through the water like a model on a photoshoot and then, as soon as she was on dry land, the sandals were going back on.

She was almost there. She could see sunbathers, children making sandcastles, running with buckets full of water, parasols gently rippling with the light breeze … she just needed to relax, pretend her feet weren't bare, convince her mind that they were covered by gossamer, or at least New Look's lightest nylon-Lycra mix.

She didn't see the dog coming. One minute she was competently facing her fears, the next one of her Zanotti's was wrenched from her hand and a large, scruffy, taupe-coloured dog was running up the sand, the wedged shoe hanging from its slathering mouth.

Sheer terror gripped her as the other shoe in her hand dropped to the ground. She stopped walking until she realised her feet were on the sand and it felt like they were burning. She lifted them up, jogging on the spot, her eyes seeking out the sprinting dog.

'Help!' It wasn't a shriek, it was a faint, yet desperate plea to no one in particular and yet everyone all at once. What was she going to do? It had one of her shoes. She had no wearable shoes. Her eyes went to Andras's family. They were mere metres away, all looking at her as she continued to perform some sort of Navaho Indian circular dance routine on the beach. They already thought she was evil. Now they would think she was evil *and* deranged.

'Tess!' Sonya called.

And there was her friend, towelling her damp skin down with her sundress, perfectly able to be calm and relaxed with bare feet. Tess felt sick. Where was the dog? She squinted her eyes, focusing her gaze down the beach, looking for the back end of a sandy mongrel.

'It is OK.'

Andras's voice flooded her ears and her senses. She turned her head, looking for him, waiting to snap back a reply that she was fine. That he should just leave her alone. Instead, the expression of sympathy on his face made her insides crumble like an OXO cube. She would not cry. She *would not* cry.

'My … sh-shoe,' she attempted.

'I know,' he answered softly.

And then he was lifting her, gathering her up in his arms before making gigantic strides up the sand like she was no weight at all. Tears were forming before she registered it, her head pressed against Andras's bare shoulder and chest, determined not to look at the Georgious or Sonya, just willing herself away from this situation, blocking everything else out.

Andras had seen the dog snatch Tess's shoe and he instinctively knew what he had to do. Carrying her now, he wasn't heading for his family, or the church, or even the dog, he was going to solve this, quickly.

'You are OK?' he asked, stepping between large rocks up the incline to the small road that ran parallel to the beach.

He knew she was close to crying. She had clung to him, hiding her face away from the prying eyes of his family.

She didn't reply, just carried on sniffing, her face pressed against his torso, waves of hair and her tanned legs over his arms the only things visible.

He gave a quick look for traffic, then headed across the road. Tarmac turned to tiles and he stopped outside, underneath the blue and white canopy of the St Spyridon mini-market.

'Tess,' he said. 'You need to choose.'

She shook her head.

'Tess,' he whispered. 'There are shoes.'

He felt her move slightly then, shifting a little in his arms until eventually her head was lifting slowly, the blonde waves falling back and the tip of her nose appearing first, followed by those blue eyes.

'Look,' he encouraged. 'They may not be designer but they are good for the beach.'

He watched her strained face scanning over the selection of flip-flops on the rack. Her breathing was beginning to even out. She removed one arm from around his neck and reached out for a plain pair of white flip flops with a small Greek flag on the side of the rubber thongs.

'These ones?' he asked.

She nodded.

He plucked the sandals from the rack, removed the cardboard sleeve from the toe peg and reaching down, slipped one on to each foot. Then, he gently lowered her to the ground, steadying her as he did so, until she stood upright, facing him, her eyes a little reddened, her lips still showing signs of tremor.

'OK?' he asked.

She gave an unconfident nod.

'I'm just going to pay for the shoes,' he told her. 'Wait here.' He made to move off before stopping again. 'Do not approach my crazy family without me, or any crazy dogs.'

Her mouth moved into a half-smile, and only then did he leave her.

# Forty-nine

'I am so sorry.'

Andras had bought her a 500ml bottle of full-sugar Pepsi in the mini-market and she was halfway down it already. She was only just starting to feel mildly better. They were walking back down to the beach, hands entwined together and she was mentally trying to recover *and* ready herself for a confrontation with Isadora that was bound to come.

'You do not need to apologise.'

'I need to pay you for the shoes.'

He shook his head. 'It is not needed.'

'Well ... I can give you something else then.' She took a breath. 'I've had a look at your accounts.'

'You have?' he asked, turning his head to look at her.

'Yes. I mean, perhaps I shouldn't have looked without asking, but I needed to get an understanding of how the business was doing and the laptop was right there and ...'

'Tess, I have nothing to hide,' he told her. 'I accepted your offer of help.'

'OK, good.'

'So?' Andras asked.

'So what?'

'How are my accounts?'

He was smiling at her now and he squeezed her hand. The contact was comforting, even though it was for the benefit of the family. They were now heading to the church, making their way along the quiet road, crunching over fallen leaves, pockets of sand and small pieces of bamboo driftwood.

'The taverna is doing brilliantly,' she admitted. 'I see no reason why a bank wouldn't give you a loan, depending on how much you wanted to borrow, of course.'

'You really think so?' he asked.

His voice was upbeat and just the sound of that had a strange effect on her too. She swallowed, loosening her grip on his hand a little. 'I do think so.' She cleared her throat. 'I wrote some notes, and the beginnings of a proposal, for you to take to the bank ... if you decide to do that.'

Her cheeks were flushing. She released her hand from his, unscrewed the bottle of Pepsi and took a swig of it.

'Thank you, Tess.'

He caught her hand up in his again, interlocking their fingers.

'No, thank you,' she answered. 'For the flip-flops, and the Pepsi ... and for Black Velvet.'

He looked at her again, tendrils of his jet-black hair falling over his forehead. 'You are going to use the name?'

'Yes,' she answered. 'I am.'

'What is going on?!'

It was Isadora's voice bellowing as they drew closer to the group who were now outside the church door.

'Will you come in with me?' Andras asked, stopping and turning to face her.

'Oh, I don't know if I should. I thought Sonya and I would just sit at this bar here and—'

'I ask too much of you already,' he interrupted.

'No, I just ...' She swallowed, not really knowing how to continue. He hadn't asked a thing about the reason behind her need for shoes, just like the last time. He had just ultimately been so understanding and strong and ... there.

'You see Marietta?' Andras asked.

Tess scanned the crowd of relatives for Andras's cousin. It took only a second to pinpoint her. She was gazing over at them, eyes mainly on Andras, looking like a starving wolf.

'If you are not there it is likely I will be savaged,' Andras said, as if reading her mind.

'I think you are overestimating your manly allure.'

'My what?' he asked, leaning into her a little.

'Your attractiveness to women,' Tess added.

'I am?'

No, he really wasn't. And why had she started this thread of conversation? All she could now think about was the kiss they had shared on Kassiopi's harbourside last night.

'Andras!' Isadora yelled, banging her stick on the ground. 'We are waiting for you.'

'Come with me,' Andras said again, squeezing her hand.

Tess's eyes went to the cupcake-looking church, its yellow walls brushed by wispy tree branches, sun glinting through the boughs. It was nothing like the church she had stood in with Adam and ... she had shoes on her feet now.

'OK,' she replied. 'Sonya and I will sit at the back.'

'*Poli kalo*,' he answered with a smile.


'It's a beautiful church, isn't it?' Sonya said with a sigh.

Tess didn't need to move her head to know that her friend's fingers would be tracing her neckline. She was right though, it was a beautiful church. Small but beautiful. The walls at the side were painted plain white, arched windows letting in a little light, then at the front of the building was a wall in deep blue and green hues, illustrated with religious icons. Men *and* women with beards, some winged cherubs, all wearing colourful togas, halos surrounding their abundant hair. It was nothing like the Norman walls of her local church with its plain pillar candles and a cassocked Reverend Heather, who looked a lot like Brian Blessed. The Greek priest's beard reached his waist and he was handling a holy book *and* an incense censer. But despite it being foreign to her, it was still two people, rehearsing pledging their life to each other and promising for ever.

'I don't understand a word they're saying but,' Sonya started, 'you can see how much they love each other.' She sighed. 'The way Kira looks at Spiros … it's just like the way Pelagia looked at Captain Corelli when he was playing his mandolin.' She sighed again. 'It's so beautiful.'

'I know,' Tess said, sarcasm coating her tone. 'With Isadora breathing down her neck and the rest of their families making sure she can't run.'

Sonya turned in her seat and Tess immediately regretted being so blasé. She should backtrack. She was just a spectator here. This wedding had no connection to any other wedding. Not hers and not any wedding Sonya might have planned to the nth degree in a scrapbook of confetti dreams.

'Is that what you see?' Sonya asked.

She shook her head quickly. 'No. I was being stupid.' She sniffed. 'It's nice. Of course it's nice. It's a wedding.'

'What happened on the beach?' Sonya whispered, ducking her head a little as, at the front, the bride and groom now seemed to be wearing crowns made from olive branches and white flowers.

Tess swallowed. 'Nothing. I just … the sand was burning my feet and the dog ran off with my shoe.'

Sonya nodded. 'And Andras carried you across the beach.'

'A total overreaction, but you know how the Greeks love a display.' Tess indicated the performance at the altar.

'And he didn't look at you like he was Captain Corelli?' Sonya asked.

'What is it with the Captain Corelli references? You do know that film was set on Kefalonia, not Corfu.'

'And now you're changing the subject,' Sonya said, a wisp of a smile on her lips.

'Speaking of changing the subject, have you tried calling Joey again?'

Sonya shook her head a little too quickly.

'Sonya ...' Tess left the end of the sentence open until Sonya cracked.

'I called him before we left Kalami. Seven times.'

'And he still didn't pick up?' Tess asked. 'How does he know you're not ill or something?'

Sonya shrugged. 'I guess he doesn't care.'

'I don't believe that.'

'He's probably too busy with Ceri.'

Sonya's voice came out a little loud and Isadora's beady focus was directed their way. Tess watched her friend mouth a 'sorry' as the priest continued to chant.

'Do you want to know what I think?' Tess whispered.

'What?'

'I really think Joey's at home. One of the things Rachel used to do when she wanted to get Philandering Phil's attention was sit at home with a bucket of KFC and check herself into places on Facebook.'

'But it's dishonest, and Joey isn't dishonest, *wasn't* dishonest ...' She sighed. 'Really hoping he hasn't turned dishonest.' Sonya shook her head until some of her red hair escaped a Kirby grip.

'I'd be looking at it as a positive,' Tess said. 'If that's what Joey's doing then he isn't in Margate and he isn't with Ceri.'

The words seemed to take a few seconds to sink into Sonya's consciousness. 'Oh!' Her hands went to her mouth in a I've-Just-Discovered-Ben-and-Jerry's-Phish-Food-At-The-Back-Of-The-Freezer kind of way. 'Oh, I see!'

'So, perhaps the reason he isn't answering his phone is because if he does, you're going to either hear the Tube announcer at Pimlico or the sound of him watching *Robot Wars,*' Tess suggested. 'He's probably driving somewhere right now that has appropriate seagull and arcade machine noises.'

'Do you really think so?' Sonya asked, wide-eyed with hope.

Did she really think so? She didn't *really* know, but almost anything was better than the alternative. She reached over and patted Sonya's hand. 'I think Joey always looks at you like Spiros looks at Kira.'

'He used to,' Sonya answered with a forlorn tilt of the head, taking in the couple at the altar. 'But now I wonder if he needs more than me. Someone to give him something else to make him completely fulfilled.' She turned her gaze to Tess. 'Something that looks cute and screams.'

'Bjork?' Tess answered. 'Sorry, that wasn't funny.' She squeezed Sonya's hand again. 'You need to have that discussion with him. A proper, truth-telling discussion with all cards on the table.' She looked over at the wedding party. 'You tell him exactly how you feel. You listen while he tells you exactly how he feels. And then you talk ... and you don't stop talking until everything is all right again.' She swallowed, a memory bubbling up in her mind. That's what she had wanted to do with Adam. She'd needed answers and he'd just given her total silence. She turned to Sonya. 'I've seen enough marriage practice.' She stood up. 'Let's go and check out that bar across the road. I saw some giant cocktails coming out earlier.'

'But what about Andras?' Sonya asked. 'Won't Isadora be suspicious if you leave the church for a bar.'

Tess looked at Andras, standing gorgeously tall, Marietta close, watching his brother.

'He's a big boy,' Tess said. 'He can look after himself.'

# Fifty

# Finikas Bar, Agios Spyridon

'What was that last one called?'

Tess's eyes were just starting to get a little hazy around the edges. It was so relaxing here, sitting out under the shade of a palm tree, a plastic bottle of sugary drink hanging from the fronds to keep the flying critters away from the tables, the sea rolling softly up the sand, the sun warming her shoulders, her best friend by her side, well, across the table.

'Sultan's Kiss,' Sonya said, her words a little slurry.

'It was nice,' Tess stated. 'Creamy and rich and sultanery.'

'I don't think it's called Sul*tana's* Kiss,' Sonya said. 'It's sul*tan*, as in a ruler in Arab lands.'

'And it goes very well with this meze of olives and cheese.' Tess dipped her finger into the terracotta dish on the table, fingers picking up Kalamata olives and chunks of saganaki. The salt and sour hit licked up her tongue.

'We are naughty,' Sonya said, giggling. 'We're supposed to be at the wedding rehearsal.'

Tess cleared her throat. 'Actually, we're meant to be on holiday having fun. The wedding rehearsal is linked to that ridiculous dating farce I got myself into on the very first night. We don't really owe anyone anything.'

'But it would be awful if Andras had to marry that Marietta, wouldn't it?'

'Sonya, no one has to marry anyone. It isn't the Dark Ages
– no matter how much Isadora's house was giving off that vibe
– and, as I said back in the church, he can look after himself.'

'Ooo!'

'Honestly, Sonya, perhaps I made things too easy for him
caving into the fake dating thing. Maybe we should have
found alternative Wi-Fi and man-guiding. It might have been
better for him all round if he had a final big, fat, Greek
showdown with his mother.'

'I'm going to have to go and chase him!' Sonya jumped out
of her chair, swiping up her camera from the tabletop.

'What?' Tess blinked, confused. 'Andras?'

'No! There's a sling-tailed agama right over there!'

'Is that the name of our next cocktail?' Tess asked,
grinning.

'No, silly, it's a lizard.'

Tess's flip-flopped feet came off the ground and up on to
her chair. 'Where?'

'It's run off over there. I need to get a photo,' Sonya said.
She turned, pounding over the dry grass in pursuit of the
animal.

Tess reached for her cocktail glass and watched her friend
creeping up on the unsuspecting reptile. Actually, from what
she could see, it had quite interesting patterns. Maybe she
could incorporate a little lizard print into her Black Velvet
branding.

It was then that her mobile phone erupted. A chill ran down
her as her mind quickly produced two names: McKenzie
Falconer or her mother. Checking the screen, she saw it was
Rachel. Rachel was OK at the moment, she was playing crazy
games and posting on Facebook and, as Tess was mildly pissed
right now, she'd pick up for once.

'Hello.'

'You're still alive then.'

Rachel's harsh tone and the comment had Tess closing her eyes and wishing she hadn't answered.

'Mum's been trying to ring you.'

Did she say anything yet? Or just let her sister continue? She eyed the Sultan's Kiss as if it could provide the answer.

'She wanted to talk to you before you found out from someone else.'

That sentence propelled Tess into a response. 'Found out what? Is Mum all right? And Dad?'

'Dad's in Canada, beaver watching. Yes, I thought the same as you're thinking, but it's not a lap-dancing bar, it's the actual animals, you know, fat tail, big teeth.'

'Then what is it I need to know?' Tess asked.

'It's Adam,' Rachel stated.

Tess sat up a little straighter, adopting the age-old position of someone who was not going to let the next words have any impact on her at all. She was boardroom, tax-office-under-investigation, I'm-sorry-you-have-a-venereal-disease ready.

'He's getting married again.'

The words hit her like a shot from a sniper. One hard, full velocity pump to the heart. But she was not going to let it penetrate. She was going to zip up her virtual Kevlar and regroup. No emotion would be shown here.

'Rachel, someone can't get married "again" when they haven't been married at all.' Had that sounded appropriately cool and detached?

'That's splitting hairs, Tess. You know what I mean.'

No, she didn't. And she really didn't want to continue the conversation any further.

'That's lovely,' she breathed. 'How wonderful. Another wedding in the village. Reverend Heather will be so … loudly pleased.'

'He's not getting married in the village.'

She wanted her sister to shut up right now. She wanted her to moan on about Philandering Phil or tell her about her new Mudda-Fudda Facebook friend, anything but this.

'He's getting married in New York. Some fancy-pants hotel in Manhattan to, get this, an heiress to a diamond-mining company.'

Did heiresses to diamond-mining companies really exist in things other than James Bond films? She didn't know. She didn't care. She didn't *want* to care.

'Mum bumped into his mum in a charity shop. I mean, he's marrying some bint who's an heiress to the Mexican equivalent of De Beers, and his mother's in a charity shop, and she's all la-di-da with our mum. Fucking cheek after what he did to you.'

Her mum was in a charity shop. Just like *she* was, seeking out the best of a bad lot, hoping that no one would guess where it came from. Both scrimping and saving, all because she had believed in true love and happy endings. The guilt invaded her every sense.

'So she hates me even more now. That's what you're saying.'

That Sultan's Kiss had a lot to answer for.

'What?' Rachel asked.

'Mum. She hates me even more than she did already. Because Adam and the Queen of Diamonds are having an expensive wedding and her nose is being rubbed in it.' Tess picked up one of the shots of ouzo they had been given with the bowl of Greek delights and downed it in one. 'She's listening to all this, amid the Laura Ashley seconds, and she's remembering how she's maxed out on loans and all her rainy-day money got spent on morning suits and the vintage car I didn't even want, and that bloody Madness tribute band I didn't want either but Adam insisted ...' She picked up Sonya's ouzo shot and downed that too. 'D'you know what? I think that was all it ever was to him, a mad, crazy, expensive party to show off to his friends, but I'll never really know, because he never actually talked to me!'

'Tess—' Rachel tried to interrupt.

'But, I was the great white hope, wasn't I? And I joined in with that. I was so sure of myself. This was the man for me. He wanted to marry me and it was going to be forever. Not like Mum and Dad. Not like you and Phil. I was going to be the one who got the happy ever after and held on to it. And all I did was fuck everything up. I left Dad with no money. I left Mum with no money and ... I left Aunty Gladys without any of the cheese and red onion flans she had been going on about for weeks ... and for what?'

What was happening? Tears were building up in her eyes for the second time that day. The alcohol, the potential for sunstroke sat out here, only her legs shaded from the Corfiot heat, the shock of the dog stealing her shoe, the church and the upcoming wedding, the fact she had been single on Facebook for over a week ... it was all doing its best to eat away at her resolve.

'Actually, Aunty Gladys said the food was all paid for anyway so she filled the boot of her car with the flans,' Rachel responded.

'Well,' Tess breathed. 'Good for her.'

'Tess, Mum doesn't hate you. Why would you think that?'

'Why would I think that?' She puffed an irritated sigh down the phone. 'I can see it written all over her face.'

'When?' Rachel asked.

'When what?'

'When was the last time you've seen her face? Because I think it's been almost six months.'

'It hasn't been that long,' Tess protested. She really had no idea how long it had been.

'You never come home.'

'Because everyone hates me.'

'Tess, that's mad. No one hates you, except maybe Reverend Heather, because the word is he had a very special sermon planned for your wedding including dance moves that would have put Little Mix to shame.'

She didn't raise a smile. Couldn't. 'Mum and Dad sunk everything they had into my wedding.'

'I know, and they did the same for me and Phil and look what happened there.'

'At least you actually made it through the wedding day.'

'I really don't know if that was better or worse, and that wasn't meant to be a joke.'

'I know Mum struggles to make ends meet … and Dad lives out of a suitcase because he doesn't have a down payment for a house.'

'Is that what you think? Dad lives out of a suitcase because he wants to. He's always had a nomadic vibe going on. Hopping from place to place means he can hop from woman to woman. I'm pretty sure there is another beaver connection to that Canada trip he's not admitting to … but Tess, him travelling has nothing to do with not being able to afford a house. He just likes spending his money and crashing with friends.'

'Mum has nothing though ... they took out loans ... and she's shopping at charity shops, you said so.'

'Mum's shopped at those since she divorced Dad. She loves a bargain, you know that. She's fine. She's even started doing a salsa class with someone called Ashley. I'm thinking male.'

'But she can't go to New Zealand any more and she really wanted to go to New Zealand. She had posters up around the house and a map with pins in.'

'That was years ago!' Rachel exclaimed.

Yes, she knew it was ages ago but it had been her mother's divorcée dream, escaping to the other side of the world on a trip she had wanted to go on since she left university and could never afford to. She'd talked about it, endlessly, making New Zealand seem like the epicentre of the universe. Tess had always wondered how someone could talk so authoritatively and passionately about somewhere they had never even been.

'It was what got her through the split with Dad,' Tess added. 'It was her focus, her goal.'

'Goals change, Tess.'

'Because I made them change. Because my wedding wasted her hard-earned savings! Everything she'd worked for her whole life! All gone! Just like that! Spent on vol-au-vents and prosecco and ... a Suggs lookalike!'

'Is that what you think?' Rachel said.

'It's what I know. It's why she hates me. And I don't blame her. I hate me too.'

'Tess!'

'What?' She needed another drink. Never mind the Sultan's Kiss, she fancied going all the way with him.

'Mum does not hate you. She loves you. She misses you. She wonders what she's done to make you stop coming home to visit.'

'What she's done?' Tess scoffed. 'She hasn't done anything apart from coat everything with a layer of disappointment whenever we're in touch, but I get that, because I'm disappointed in me too.'

'But it wasn't your fault,' Rachel stated. 'Adam was the one—'

'I don't want to talk about it any more.'

Tess scanned the table for something, anything else, she could drink. She plumped for picking up a handful of olives and dropping them into her mouth in one go. She didn't want to relive the moment.

'It wasn't your fault, and even if it was, Mum and Dad would do it all over again. For both of us.' She sighed. 'Because it was never the money they were upset about, it was the fact we were both let down so badly.' Rachel sniffed. 'That our hearts were broken.'

As her sister's emotions began to get the better of her, Tess realised she was in danger of choking on olive stones. She hurriedly looked for a napkin to spit into.

'Tess, Mum is always asking me how you are and all I can give her is a rundown on what you've been up to on Facebook. Although I've had a bit of trouble pinpointing the latest guy to tell her about, as there seems to be quite a succession of them.'

'I date,' Tess stated, on the defensive. 'It's allowed in 2017.'

'I wasn't having a go, I just … I think Mum would really appreciate a catch-up.'

'I can't do that yet,' Tess said, swallowing down the last of the olives in her mouth.

'Why not?'

'Because the next time I see her, I want to be handing her a cheque for every single penny of the money she wasted on my wedding.' She sat up taller as she saw Andras leading the Georgiou family, the donkey, a goat and six chickens out of the church across the road. 'I'm going to pay off the loans and get her to New Zealand if it's the last thing I do.'

# Fifty-one

# Kalami Beach

'We don't have to eat here tonight at this family dinner thing if you don't want to,' Tess whispered to Sonya as they walked along the wooden pontoon back at Kalami. Andras had driven the boat back from Agios Spyridon and he was now walking just a little behind them, having tied and secured the vessel. Tess could already see the throng of the Georgiou family ahead, arriving back at the restaurant.

'The thing I don't get,' Sonya began. 'And it might be because I've had quite a few kisses from the Sultan ...' She giggled. 'Is how the goats and chickens can be taken into the church yet the poor tortoise is herded out whenever it appears.'

'Hector,' Tess said. 'His name is Hector.'

'But what's the donkey called?' Sonya asked with a hiccup.

'I have no idea.' She linked arms with her friend. 'So, shall we eat somewhere else tonight? Escape this madness for a bit?' After her phone call with Rachel, she needed to unwind a little. Work out if she believed what her sister had said. That perhaps, maybe, her mother didn't still wake up every day reliving the time she threw away her life savings.

'Patricia!'

Tess's shoulders prickled at the sound of her fake name being bellowed down the beach. It was Isadora and her first instinct was to turn around and look for Andras.

'Do not look to Andras! You look to me!' Isadora yelled again.

'This doesn't sound good,' Sonya stated.

'I am sorry,' Andras said.

Tess shivered as Andras stepped up alongside her, slipping his hand into hers so naturally. She swallowed. 'What does she want?'

'The dinner for Kira's family, tonight, on the beach.'

'She *really* wants me to go,' Tess exclaimed.

He let out a sigh. 'At the church, she says that it is unlucky if you do not go. Kira's Aunt Melissa is a little sick.'

'And what does that have to do with me?'

He sighed. 'Everything has to be odd numbers. So you and Sonya—'

'What? Another Greek custom?' Tess suggested with a raise of her eyebrow.

'Dinner on the beach. I think it sounds heavenly, and romantic,' Sonya said.

'With my family and Kira's family?' Andras asked.

'It sounds ... cosy and homely,' Sonya offered as alternatives.

'I really, *really* have to go?' Tess asked.

Andras ducked his head a little, his mouth close to her ear as they continued to walk, all the time nearing the restaurant and Isadora's watchful eye. 'You do not have to,' he said. 'Say the word and I will—'

'No,' Tess shook her head. 'I need your laptop to finish the Black Velvet designs tomorrow.'

'This isn't about the laptop any more.'

'Well, Sonya wants to go to Corfu Town sometime.'

'We could get a bus,' Sonya suggested.

'Have you even seen a bus since we got here?' Tess asked.

'Well, a coach trip then.'

'It is OK. Like we agreed on, I can take you,' Andras said. 'Perhaps I can fit it around a visit to the bank.'

'And this dinner on the beach will be free of charge, won't it? Because we're practically family,' Tess continued.

'Of course.'

'Well then, let's go and see what we have to do.'

Andras had a job to keep hold of her hand as Tess made bold strides up the jetty, pausing before seeming to realise she was wearing flip-flops, then pushing on over the stones of the beach until they reached the waiting Greek matriarch.

'You will be here tonight,' Isadora said, as an order rather than a question. 'For the dinner on the beach.'

'I'm looking forward to meeting more of Kira's family,' Tess said, breezily. 'I do hope her Aunt Melissa feels better for the wedding.'

'You both will sit with other women,' Isadora continued.

'Other women?' Tess queried.

'At this meal, the women will all sit together and the men will all sit together.' Isadora smiled widely. 'Apart from Andras and Marietta. As the *koumbaro* and *koumbara* they will sit together, as a couple, alone ...' She exhaled. 'Completely on themselves.'

Andras couldn't tell if the last phrase was due to his mother's broken English or deliberate.

'Mama,' he stated. 'This is not necessary and it is not anything to do with Greek custom.'

'It is Georgiou custom,' Isadora snapped back. 'When I was married to your father this happened. When your father's father was married to your grandmother this happened. When your grandfather's father was—'

'OK,' Tess said. 'Getting the idea now.' She smiled. 'And it's fine.' She slipped an arm around his waist. 'Absence, after all, makes the heart grow fonder.'

'Abscess? We cannot have infection here. We have a hundred people coming to a wedding in two days' time. We cannot have quarantine.'

Tess tightened her grip on his waist, pulling him a little closer. God, her fingers were so close to touching skin where his shirt was a little free from his waistband. Why did he want that connection so much? Why was he equally terrified of it?

'I simply meant,' Tess began, 'that gazing at Andras from across the beach, the sweet smell of lavender in the air, the candlelight, the Greek music and Dorothea's heavenly food, it's going to make me realise just how lucky I am to be here.' She let out a light breath, eyes locking with his. 'To have him.'

The air seemed to still, along with his heart. He needed to wise up to what was going on here: that Tess played a good game and that she was his mother's equal.

'That's so lovely, isn't it?' Sonya jumped in. 'Isn't it lovely?'

'We will meet here at seven,' Isadora decreed, banging her stick on the stones. 'Do not be late.'

'Oh, we won't,' Tess said, her eyes still connected to his. 'I've got a new dress I've been dying to show you.'

'You have?' he answered quickly. 'I cannot wait to see it.'

Tess smiled, bringing her face closer to his. 'If I'm honest, there isn't really much of it to see.'

Her lips met his then, and that almost familiar taste of lipgloss coupled with raisins and a sweet cream filled his senses.

'Andras has much work to do now,' Isadora stated with another bang of her stick.

Tess withdrew. 'See you at seven.'

'*Ta leme sindoma.*'

He watched them walk up through the restaurant, acknowledging Spiros and Kira and the other members of the family they had met before, until his mother drew his attention back to her with another hearty thump of her stick.

'Tonight your focus will be with Marietta,' Isadora said sternly. 'She has worked so hard for this wedding. She deserves better treatment from you. More respect.'

'Mama, we have talked about this.'

'You need to give things a chance, Andras. Perhaps spending a little more time with someone who is going to be here forever rather than just for a few weeks will make you see.'

'Make me see?'

'The right path.' Isadora sniffed. 'I have been speaking to Papa Yiannis. He thinks it would be good for you to sit down with him and talk about the future.'

He couldn't do this again. He *wouldn't* go through this again.

'I have to go,' he said, already moving away from his mother. 'I need to prepare for tonight.'

'Andras!'

'I will be the *koumbaro* Spiros deserves,' he said. 'But, Mama, as I have told you before, with regard to Marietta, that is all.'

# Fifty-two

The beach looked beautiful. The subtle glow of candles on the long trestle tables, coupled with strings of fairy lights interwoven around plants and potted trees outside Taverna Georgiou and glass lanterns set up along the jetty, all created a relaxed, warm, inviting atmosphere as Tess and Sonya made their way down on to the pebbles and sand.

'I could cry,' Sonya remarked, an obvious lump in her throat as she spoke. 'It's so picture-perfect-holiday-brochure-of-dreams.' She sighed. 'The cicadas' song, the soft, gentle lull of the water, the glowing sun low in the sky, the intense heat dulling to a spicy humidity that promises cold white wine, succulent Greek meze and a night of music and dance.'

Right now, Sonya sounded like an audio travel guide set to make anyone rush online and book with Thomson. And her words were working their magic on Tess too. This place, the little bay on this gorgeous island, was charming her day by day. The relaxed pace, the wall-to-wall sunshine, the amazing vistas … it was a little piece of heaven on Earth. And, unlike any other break from work before, she was enjoying it with a vigour she'd never known. It was then it hit her. Apart from the phone call with her sister, she hadn't checked her mobile once today. She hadn't looked for emails. She hadn't even thought about Facebook. She hadn't Instagrammed since a bikini selfie at the apartments and she hadn't Tweeted or even Snapchatted since she arrived in Greece. Her fingers moved to the clasp of the clutch bag she was holding. Did she need to make contact? Did she need to do all these things right now? She took a deep breath and withdrew her hand.

'Is that Spiros with a plate on his face?' Sonya queried as they drew nearer to the tables.

'I think it is,' Tess agreed.

'These Greek customs are a little bit out there, aren't they?' Sonya said. Then she grinned. 'But I like it.'

'Even the all women eating together, all men eating together thing?' Tess asked.

'I suppose it's a bit like a combined hen and stag party. Food, drink, dancing ...'

'I can't see any tequila shots or L-plates on the bride.'

'But the groom is balancing a plate on his face,' Sonya reminded her.

Andras turned from where he was bringing baskets of thick slices of bread down to the tables on the beach the moment he heard Tess laugh. She didn't laugh often, he'd realised, but when she did, it was a sound like no other. Such a release of energy and enthusiasm, a sweet, relaxing, full-hearted babble he'd recognise anywhere now.

Tess and Sonya, arms linked, were crunching over the pebbled shore towards the tables he'd helped lay earlier and, as he looked at them, he saw that Tess had been right. The dress she was wearing left little to the imagination, his imagination, and, as he looked to his male relatives, drinking, smoking and shooting the breeze as Spiros span around with a plate on his face, all eyes were turning to the woman dressed in virginal white but looking anything but.

He watched Nikos nudge Vasilis and Vasilis then nudge Panos and a gut-churning feeling of jealousy began to mix like ouzo and water. All that was once clear was now becoming cloudy. He put down the bread and made his way towards the women before his relatives could undress Tess with their eyes any further.

'You are here,' he breathed. He didn't hesitate. He stepped straight forward and kissed Tess full on the lips then hurriedly moved back, kissing Sonya first on one cheek and then the other.

'It's two minutes past seven now,' Tess remarked. 'I'm surprised your mother hasn't sent a goat to fetch us.'

'Hector ended up here again,' Andras informed her. 'She had to call Fotis to put him in his truck and take him back to my house.'

'That tortoise is remarkable,' Sonya said. 'I really need to take some photos of him before we leave.'

*Leave.* Yes, they were leaving. He didn't even know when. It didn't even matter. After the wedding he would be caught up with the restaurant, hopefully with Spiros paid off and a small cash injection to make some improvements. He wouldn't have time for anything else; he didn't need time for anything else.

'Come,' he said, offering out an arm in the direction of the long table at which some of the women were already sat.

'Oh, there's some of that gorgeous bread already.' Sonya smiled at him. 'I could basically just eat that all day long, if I didn't have a slight coeliac thing going on.' She stepped ahead.

'So,' Tess said softly. 'Where's your lovers' table with Marietta?'

'Don't say that,' Andras said.

'Why not? That's what your mother thinks it is.' Tess grinned. 'She will have laced your food with some Greek-style aphrodisiac.'

'And there are scallops to start.'

He watched as Tess's face visibly paled before his eyes, her bright expression dimming like a candle on the verge of running out of wax.

'Tess,' he whispered. 'Is something wrong?'

And then she recovered, oh so quickly, too quickly, and smiled. 'No scallops for me, thank you. I find them a bit gritty.'

He took her hand in his. 'I have a meeting with the bank tomorrow.'

'You do? That's great.'

'Maybe later we can talk about the best things to say.'

'Yes.' She nodded.

'So, I'll be sitting just over there tonight, but I also must work, so I will come and rescue you from my crazy family any time you need me to.'

He watched Tess's eyes go to the intimate table his mother had had set up yards away from anyone else, next to the jetty, almost in the water, fresh stems of bougainvillea in a vase next to the lit candle. The whole scenario was ridiculous but it was all about keeping the family peace now it was so close to the wedding. Once the nuptials were done then things could go back to normal.

'It looks lovely,' she commented somewhat wistfully.

'It is just for show,' Andras said. 'I am doing this only for Spiros and Kira.'

'It doesn't matter really, does it?' Tess said. 'I mean, it's a little sad in a way that your mother is doing this to break us up, and in reality we're not together.'

He swallowed then nodded. 'I know. But—'

'So, I guess I'm sitting over here, yes?' Tess said, striding forward in pursuit of Sonya.

He watched her go, the eyes of his cousins still admiring her form, those long, tanned legs, moving with ease over the beach in the shoes he had bought for her.

'Nikos!' he called across to his fisherman cousin. 'Some things tonight are not on the menu!'

Nikos laughed, waving a hand at him. 'Relax, Andras, tonight is about welcoming the joining of our two families, no? We will all be celebrating our getting closer a little later.'

Andras watched Tess smooth her hands down the short, fluted skirt that stopped mid-thigh and settle herself into a chair opposite Kira. He didn't want to be spending the evening with Marietta. He wanted to be … with Tess. He swallowed that realisation down. What was he thinking? Was his mother right? Was he continually to be attracted to strong, independent women who were only interested in him for the length of their holiday … or the length of a marriage until they got bored?

'She looks beautiful, doesn't she?'

It was his mother's voice in his ear but his eyes were firmly fixed on Tess, the way the candlelight brought out the gold and bronze in her hair, how the dress – a different, softer style to what he had seen her in before – complemented her body. 'Yes,' he whispered. 'She does.'

The bang of a stick broke the moment and he turned to his mother then.

'I am talking about Marietta! Look!'

He had no choice but to turn his head and there was his cousin, dressed in a ground-sweeping pale blue dress, her dark hair wrapped and coiled into plaits that sat on top of her head. She was undeniably pretty. But he felt nothing apart from platonic affection. They were cousins. That was all they were going to be.

'Beautiful,' Isadora repeated, both hands clasping the top of her stick.

'I need to get back to the restaurant,' Andras said.

'But ...'

'I need to work, Mama. I will be with Marietta as soon as I can.'

# Fifty-three

'Patricia!' Kira called across the table. 'You need to sign these!'

'Please,' Tess said, leaning forward in her chair a little. 'Call me Tess.'

'Tess!' Kira shouted again. 'You need to sign these!' All the women around them began to laugh out loud as a pair of shoes were launched across the table towards her.

Like an England goalkeeper, Tess blocked one shoe from hitting a bottle of white wine and the other fell down into her lap. She looked at Sonya in the hope of some explanation, then picked up both the delicate silver beaded shoes and examined them. 'I don't understand.'

'In Greek weddings, we have many traditions,' a lady who had been introduced earlier as Juno said.

'We are getting accustomed to that,' Sonya replied with a giggle. 'See what I did there? Customs … *ac*customed.'

'You must sign the sole of the shoe,' Juno ordered. She took one shoe from Tess, turned it over and pointed at the bottom of it. On the plain, taupe-coloured underbelly of the decorative footwear there were signatures in pen.

'It is for good luck,' Kira elaborated. 'If the unmarried women at my wedding do not sign my wedding shoes, then my love for Spiro might die.' She clutched at her chest, her elbow almost upsetting a jug of water she might have benefitted from drinking. 'You do not want my love for Spiro to die, do you?' She batted her eyelids at Tess and adopted a sad face that was quite amusing. She hadn't yet seen Kira look anything but completely placid and in control. After copious amounts of alcohol, the bride was loosening up, even her usually immaculate hair was looking a little banshee.

'Your love won't die,' Sonya said, hand rising up to her chest.

Tess caught her friend's hand before it could reach the place where her necklace should be.

'True love never dies,' Sonya continued.

'You are married?' Kira asked Sonya.

Sonya shook her head. 'No.'

'Not yet,' Tess added. 'But she's going to be.'

'And then there will be babies,' Juno stated, drawing on her cigarette. 'Lots and lots of babies.'

'Well,' Tess jumped in. 'Not everyone wants babies.'

The gasp that went up from the table almost blew out all the candles. At any second Tess expected someone to come and eject her from the party. Why didn't she ever learn to just not say anything? It wasn't her job to change the Greeks' views on family matters, just because she might not be zen with marriage and babies and till death us do part.

'I love babies!' Sonya declared. 'I would love nothing more than to have lots and lots of babies but—'

'Sonya lives in a very small house,' Tess leapt in. She could sense her friend's fragility. Now was not the time for sharing her secret. On a Greek beach with lots of goddesses of fertility sat around them.

'A small house?' Kira queried. 'You are not allowed to have babies if you live in a small house?' She furrowed her perfect, no-need-for-threading-here eyebrows. 'Is this an English law?'

'No, it isn't that,' Sonya continued, her lips wobbling. 'I can't have them.' She sighed, eyes glassy. 'I can't have babies.'

Tess picked up her glass of wine and sucked down the contents.

'Because of your small house?' Juno guessed.

'No … because of my ovaries,' Sonya blurted out.

'Because you are overseas?' Kira's frown deepened. 'I do not understand this UK thinking. They do not let you have babies?'

'I would like nothing more than to fill my entire house with babies,' Sonya continued. 'Lots and lots of gorgeous, icky, sticky, sweet as syrup, lickle babies …'

Had she said 'lickle'? She didn't want Sonya to live through this again here, in such a public arena. She had to do something, say something and quickly.

'Well, *I* don't want babies!'

The words were out of her mouth before she had thought too much about it. And there was that gasp again but this time louder. Loud enough that conversation on the male relatives table stopped too.

'But you must have them!' Kira exclaimed, rising from her chair. 'You *have* to have them!'

'I don't think I do,' Tess stated. 'I mean, no offence, but I don't really have time for babies in my life. I work really hard and that takes up all the time.' She laughed. 'I mean, I don't even have time for a relationship.'

She got to the 'p' of 'relationship' and realised just what she had said. She opened her mouth to backtrack but Banshee Kira was already on it.

'But what about Andras?'

All female eyes were on her and she felt the prickling on her bare skin like a whole team of mosquitos were Greek dancing across her shoulders.

'Except for Andras, obviously,' Tess responded.

'But, Andras wants children,' Kira continued, leaning ever closer over the table. 'Andras has *always* wanted children.'

She was now realising that it may have been better to let Sonya carry on with her true-life heartache. She had opened up a can of ... she was going to think worms but it actually might be Corfiot snakes and lizards. She shuddered and then noticed that everyone was *still* looking at her.

'Well, we haven't really been going out that long,' she began.

'But you are in love,' Juno said. 'You travelled all the way from England to visit him.'

'I know but—'

'You need to talk about this with him,' Kira interrupted, pouring some more wine into her glass. 'It is very important.'

'Well, I expect, we will talk about it, if we need to,' Tess replied, picking up the glass of wine Kira had filled.

'You need to,' Juno stated.

'Yes, you really need to,' Kira agreed.

'Why does she need to?' Sonya asked, coming back into the conversation. 'You're making it sound like if she doesn't talk to him about it then the world might ... explode or something.'

Juno looked to Kira. Kira looked back at Juno and the other women at the table suddenly found their dinner plates/laps/children/the air away from Tess ridiculously interesting.

'You tell her.' Juno directed the order at Kira.

'It is not my place.'

'It is your place more than anyone else here,' Juno insisted.

Kira said something in Greek Tess wasn't sure she really needed translated to get the gist of.

'For God's sake, just tell me,' Tess begged.

Kira shook her head. 'Because Tess,' she began, 'that is why Andras and Elissa broke up.'

Before she could even swallow that piece of information the women were talking again.

'You only had to look at that girl to see she was never going to have children.'

'Always eating like a bird. Always the dresses from boutiques. And her fancy job.' There was a unified tutting.

'Well,' Tess started. 'I'm sure we can ...' She wasn't sure why she was so desperate to explain a fictional future.

'I will be having a job,' Kira stated.

There was another collective gasp but Tess clung on to Kira's words and pressed the conversation onwards. 'Oh, what are you going to do?'

'I want to start my own business when we are settled on the mainland. I have experience in cooking for rich people, mainly rich English people.' She looked at Tess. 'I am going to set up on my own, with some staff in the future.'

'But, Kira, you won't have time for all that,' Juno said.

'Why not?'

'Well, Spiros will be beginning his new job and you will need to be there for him. And we have just talked about the babies,' Juno continued.

'I am a little young to start having babies yet,' Kira announced.

Another gasp went up and all the men turned their attention to the table of women again, the only sounds the faint lilt of the lute and *bouzouki*, the clink of china and glass from Taverna Georgiou and the slow, soft waves of the sea.

'Does Spiros know this is your plan?' Juno questioned. 'Or Isadora?'

'You make it sound like it is something bad, something I should not be doing.' Kira swigged at her wine. 'You have your own business, Juno, and you, Agatha. Why not me?'

'Yes!' Tess exclaimed. 'Why not you!' She was willing to jump on this extremely worthy bandwagon. Why couldn't Kira have her own business?

'I started my own business when my husband died,' Juno said.

'And,' chipped in the woman called Agatha, 'I started my business when my husband left me.'

'Ah,' Tess said, pointing a finger across the table. 'And that's where the problem lies, for all of you ladies.'

She gazed around at the bemused looks on the Greek women's faces. 'You, all of you, are waiting to see what your husband does before you decide your own future.'

'My husband did not have much choice. When God decided to come calling he had to go,' Juno stated.

'But, looking back,' Tess said. 'Could you not have started your business when your husband was still alive? What was stopping you from doing it earlier.'

'Thanasis was a farmer,' Kira informed her. 'He would leave early in the morning and he would return late at night.'

'Leaving the whole day free for your business,' Tess said, directing her gaze at Juno.

'But he always needed food prepared and—'

Agatha interrupted. 'My husband left me for someone who had their own business.' She sighed. 'Maybe, if I had been a little more like her then he would not have felt the need to look for something else.'

'Well, I didn't mean ...' Tess started.

'But you didn't really supercharge your career until after Adam,' Sonya blurted out.

Tess held her breath for so many reasons. She hadn't yet told her best friend that Adam was about to pledge his future to someone else. Because she didn't want to think about what that meant. How this woman could possibly be 'the one' when, after so long of being certain, she had ended up being 'the won't'.

'Adam?' Kira queried. 'Who is Adam?'

'No one,' Tess said quickly. She would kill for a Dr Pepper right now.

'He is a love rival for Andras?' Juno asked.

'No,' Tess said. 'He is nobody.'

'Andras is nobody?' Kira said, turning her head and raising an eyebrow.

'No, Adam.' She didn't really want to even say his name. '*He* is nobody.'

'Did he want children? And you did not?' Kira continued the questioning.

'No, nothing like that.' She was feeling hot now, her cheeks like they had been pressed against a roasting *gyros* grill.

'Excuse me.'

Tess looked up. A man was stood in front of her, smiling and seeming to have directed what he'd just said at her. She had seen him in the church today. He was another one of Andras's cousins or something. He had that archetypal dark hair and olive skin but that's where the similarity ended. Andras had nicer eyes and his lips were fuller, more genuine, and sexy. She swallowed and gave the man a polite smile.

'Nikos, what are you doing?' Kira asked him, standing up and reaching for another bottle of wine. 'You are supposed to be with the men.'

'For the dinner,' Nikos said, leaning a little closer to Tess. 'The dinner is now over and we are to dance.' He held his hand out. 'Patricia, may I have this dance?'

'Nikos!' Juno said in warning tones.

'What?' He held his hands up with apologetic undertones that Tess wasn't at all sure were sincere. 'It is just a dance.' He ducked his head a bit closer to hers. 'What do you say? Shall we?'

If she was honest with herself, right now she would have done pretty much anything to get away from the table and the conversation about weddings and babies and … Adam. She took hold of Nikos's hand and let him pull her from her seat. 'Yes,' she agreed. 'Yes, let's dance.'

# Fifty-four

Andras was just serving a table of ten their main courses when he heard the music start down on the beach. He had been backwards and forwards from restaurant to family table all evening before sharing a rather stilted conversation over a meal at the private table with Marietta. But now he was not thinking about his cousin, his attention was with Nikos, leading Tess over the stones towards the wooden jetty.

His throat dried as he watched. Nikos had always been the ladies' man. He swallowed. Perhaps that was unkind of him to think that; since Elissa, he too had been playing that game until recently. But this just felt … wrong. Seeing Tess with Nikos, him helping her up on to the lantern-lit jetty where a couple of Kira's relatives had already started to dance together … He hated it.

'Andras.'

He turned at the sound of Marietta's voice. She was just behind him and reaching out, she touched his bare forearm. Immediately he took a step back.

'Marietta, I am sorry. I know we have a lot to discuss but—'

She smiled. 'We do not always have to talk.' Her cheeks began to take on a little colour. 'Sometimes it is easier to just let things happen.' She paused. 'Let actions speak for us.'

'Marietta …'

She bobbed a curtsey, dropping her head a little, then catching his gaze again. 'Dance with me, Andras.'

Now he was torn. Dancing with her would surely give her the wrong impression, false hope of their relationship progressing into something other than kinship if she tried hard enough. But if he danced, got up on the pontoon too, then he would be able to keep an eye on Nikos and Tess.

'It is a wonderful night, no?'

He stopped thinking completely at the sound of his mother's voice. A strong hand came down on to his shoulder and the scent of her heavy, floral perfume filled his senses.

'It is a wonderful night,' Marietta quickly agreed. 'The perfect start to the wedding festivities.'

'I remember this night for my wedding,' Isadora said, her eyes going to the clear night sky. 'So many friends and family, all uniting in being united.' She turned to him then. 'And it seems, Andras, that your girlfriend is enjoying being united with Nikos.'

He couldn't help his gaze travelling across the beach to the wooden jetty. Nikos was holding Tess's body close to his, their hands interlocked in a dance hold, swaying over the uneven planks of wood, the sparkling water beneath them.

'I was just asking Andras—' Marietta began.

'Come,' Andras interrupted. He reached for his cousin's hand. 'We will dance.'

He didn't care what message this gave to Marietta or his mother. The only reason he was thinking of dancing at all was to ensure that Nikos kept his hands to himself in respect to Tess. He rushed over the stones, Marietta struggling to keep up his pace, then leapt up onto the boardwalk.

'Andras,' Marietta called, a little breathless.

He turned his head, saw she was needing help to clamber up, given the length of her dress. He offered her a hand and deftly pulled her up alongside him, causing their bodies to touch as she tried to regain her balance. She smiled, pressing a little closer. This had been a mistake. Now what was he going to do?

'You are very beautiful,' Nikos whispered into Tess's ear.

This guy was more forward than England's Harry Kane, or any of the men she'd dated in the past six months. And he had a sleight of hand that BGT winning magician, Richard Jones, would have been proud of. Already Tess had felt the need to add several impromptu shimmies into her dancing when Nikos's hands had wandered across the bottom of her backbone.

'That's jolly kind of you to say.' *Jolly?* Why had she said that? She sounded like she was in *Call the Midwife*.

'It is the truth,' Nikos continued, breath hot in her ear.

Was that his tongue she'd just felt? She swayed her head in a move she was sure she had seen Ariana Grande perform on MTV, removing the target. 'And I am spoken for.'

'Andras … he is not the right man for you,' Nikos whispered.

'No?' Tess asked. 'And why would you think that?'

Nikos drew his head away from the crook of her shoulder and looked at her intently. 'He has been married before, you know.'

'I know that,' Tess agreed.

'And things did not work out.'

'I know that too,' she answered.

'I would not treat you that way,' Nikos continued.

'And how do you know the way he treats me?' Tess wanted to know.

'He will treat you the way he has treated every woman since Elissa left him,' he said. 'Like you are disposable.'

Tess looked over Nikos shoulder, saw Andras and Marietta coming up the dock. Were they going to dance? Together? Her stomach did a swan dive at the thought of that. She had already spent the entire evening watching them share an intimate dinner on the shoreline, the table Isadora had turned into Romance 101. She shook her head, forced her eyes away. This was all ridiculous. This was all fake.

'Perhaps being disposable is the best way,' Tess answered with a sigh.

'What do you mean?'

'Well,' she answered, slipping an arm around Nikos' neck. 'If everyone knows where they stand in the disposable stakes, then no one can really get hurt, can they?'

'Excuse me.'

It was Andras, standing next to them, with Marietta at his side.

'You are coming to dance too?' Nikos asked, pulling Tess into his body.

'I am,' Andras answered. 'With Tess.'

Tess looked at Nikos with a shrug of the shoulders and a helpless smile but, in truth, she was relieved.

'But you are with Marietta,' Nikos said, holding his ground *and* Tess's hand.

'But in fact I am with Tess,' Andras answered firmly.

Tess deftly removed herself from Nikos's arms and smiled at him. 'Thank you for the dance.'

'Anytime,' Nikos answered gruffly.

'Shall we?' Andras asked, holding his hand out to Tess.

'Andras!' It was Marietta.

Tess watched Andras turn his head to look at his cousin.

'Your mother ... she ... she will not be pleased,' Marietta stated.

He nodded and Tess felt his hand tighten in hers. 'I know,' he replied. He bowed a little to his cousin before turning away.

Then he began to lead them further up the jetty, past the other couples, until they were standing right at the end of the platform, only lanterns and the stars above lighting the way and nothing but ocean in front of them.

# Fifty-five

So naturally, Andras slipped his arm around Tess's waist, drawing her into his body, his other hand finding hers and holding it tightly.

'I am sorry about Nikos,' he spoke, beginning to sway them gently to the slow tempo of the Greek musicians on the beach.

'Oh, you don't have to apologise. I was grateful for someone to get me away from the girls' table.'

'I am sorry for that too.'

'I had to sign shoes,' Tess admitted. 'What is that all about?'

'Did they also make you spit on the floor?'

'What?' Tess laughed. 'Is that a Greek thing too?'

He nodded, smiling. 'For luck.' He shook his head. 'You must have realised that everything is about luck around here.' He sighed. 'Luck and duty.'

Tess swallowed. It was so nice here, in Andras's arms, living this pretence, being a couple, under a Corfiot sky. Despite the way Andras felt about his family, to her, there was no real pressure as to how anything was going to go. Because there were no rules. No promises. No expectation. But she still itched to know the truth after everything the women in his family had said.

'Did you split up with Elissa because she had a career?'

He stopped dancing then and, still holding her hand, he looked deep into her eyes. 'What?'

'Sorry, I know that it's none of my business but Kira and Juno and … Agatha, I think her name was … they all said that the reason you split up with Elissa was because she wanted a career and you just wanted her to have babies.' She swallowed. 'And I … just wanted to hear that from you.'

A low sigh left him and he loosened his grip on her hand, letting it go and dropping his to his side. 'Is that what they all think?'

'It was my fault,' Tess jumped in. 'I was trying to steer the conversation away from something Sonya had said that was going to make her cry an ocean's worth of tears so, to change things up, like you do, I told the whole table that I didn't want to have children.'

Andras sucked in air through his teeth and shook his head at her, a hint of a smile on his lips. 'I can guess what reaction you might have had to that.'

'Yes, well, it was too late to backtrack, and then the women were on a roll.'

Andras smiled, nodding at her. 'Sit down with me?' he asked, indicating the wooden floor.

Only a few days ago, if someone had asked her to sit on bare boards in a dress that would usually have cost over three hundred pounds if it hadn't been from the British Heart Foundation, she would have pulled a face and refused. Now she found herself bending down almost eagerly, steadying herself as she lowered her body on to the slats, feet hanging over the side, only inches from the sea, a slight breeze buffeting her hair. Andras sat close, his legs swinging over the water, shoes almost touching the ocean.

'Elissa and I didn't split up because she wanted a career or because I thought she should stay at home having babies,' Andras spoke.

'If I really was your girlfriend I would be very relieved right now.' She swallowed. She *was* relieved. Genuinely relieved. But not at all relieved that she felt that relief.

'Tess, I have never told anyone, not one soul, why Elissa and I really broke up.'

Now she didn't know what to say. She turned her head to look at him more closely. She could see so many different feelings etched on his face. She had seen some of them reflected in her own expression in the days and weeks after Adam. Pain, hurt, misunderstanding, sorrow.

'Elissa was pregnant when she left,' Andras stated. He blew out a heavy breath that seemed to take some of his life force with it. She watched his knuckles tighten as he scrunched his fingers up into fists against the wooden platform.

'So ...' She knew her voice was shaking and she had no idea why or how to control it. 'So, you have a child?'

Immediately he shook his head and gasped. 'No.'

'No?'

'The baby ...' He stopped, the word seeming to catch in his throat. 'The baby wasn't mine.'

'Oh my God.' It was an instant reaction. Complete shock brought her hands to her mouth. 'Sorry ... I shouldn't have said that.' She breathed. 'I shouldn't have said anything.'

He shrugged then. 'It has taken me a long time to come to terms with it, but I have had to come to terms with it.' He looked at her. 'But still, I don't seem to be able to tell my family that my wife, the woman I loved, the woman I knew my mother didn't approve of, had cheated on me ... and that she was carrying another man's baby.'

'I am so sorry,' Tess said softly.

'*Ochi*.' He shook his head. 'No, you do not need to be sorry.' He looked out over the water. 'When she told me, every piece of me began to die inside, but I still wanted her, wanted them both. I still believed that our marriage could recover. I said I would stand by her. That we could leave Corfu and make a new start wherever she wanted to.' He breathed. 'Do whatever she wanted to.'

'But she didn't want to?' Tess guessed.

'She hadn't just betrayed our vows, she had fallen in love.' He sighed. 'What do you say to that?'

Tess mused on the sentence for a moment until she made her reply. 'At least you got to say something.' The sea breeze suddenly made her shiver. She wanted to say something now, to him. She wanted to tell Andras. And as that emotion toyed with her, inside she felt herself slowly begin to unravel.

She took perhaps the biggest breath she had ever taken before letting the words tumble from her lips. 'My fiancé didn't come to our wedding.'

'What?' Andras whispered.

She nodded. 'He left me spinning around in the wedding car outside and then ... when I couldn't bear seeing any more of the village or the desperate look on my mother's face, I got out of the car and I walked up the aisle expecting him to spontaneously materialise like the genie in *Aladdin*.' Her breaths were coming thick and fast, heart pumping. 'I stood at the front of the church, waiting, looking at my family, his family, just standing my ground, thinking that somehow this was going to turn out all right, if I just didn't move. If I stayed right there, right there where I was supposed to be, where *he* was supposed to be.'

'He didn't come.'

Tess shook her head. 'No. I stood there, with the vicar making small talk about spiritual growth and nurturing, and then my dad started to come down the aisle towards me and … my mum stood up and then, I knew, then it finally sunk in that Adam wasn't coming.' Her shoulders shook as she drew up her head like she was somehow fighting for air. 'And I still didn't want to hear it. I had my mum and my dad just a few feet away, heading towards me, Rachel looking at me with tears in her eyes, all of them wanting to comfort me, wanting to make things better and I couldn't stand it.' She started to quake, suddenly feeling so cold, lips trembling, shoulders wobbling. 'I put one bare foot in front of the other and every single flagstone felt like it was a bed of nails, so I ran.' She let out a breath. 'I sprinted up the aisle and out of the church, nothing on my feet, and I didn't stop until I got home.' She swallowed. 'Two point four miles of not feeling my feet getting cut to ribbons.'

Now it was all becoming clear. The not walking barefoot on Kalami beach, still wearing her designer shoes when she jumped off the boat into the sea on that very first trip, and at Agios Spyridon with the dog. This was the reason why she didn't want to ever be barefoot. Why having her feet strapped into something at all times was necessary for her. Right at that moment, Andras wanted to find this Adam himself and hurt him like he had hurt Tess.

'He is not human,' Andras whispered. 'To do something like that, on what should have been such a special day.' He slipped his arm across her shoulders, wanting to wrap her up, wanting to take her pain away. 'To leave you there.'

Tess sniffed. 'My sister Rachel kept telling me it would have been worse if he had gone through with the marriage and left me afterwards but, I don't know … This way it was so humiliating for everyone and there was nothing tangible to show for our relationship, just Breville sandwich-makers and a cheeseboard set and bloody scallops.'

'You should not feel humiliated,' Andras spoke gently. 'You did nothing wrong.'

'But I don't know that. I will never know that.' She raised her head to look at him. 'Because Adam never spoke to me again.'

'What?'

'I tried to call him. Text him. Email him. Just for an explanation and, like you, I suppose I hoped we might be able to somehow work it out ...'

'And he never explained himself?'

She shook her head. 'No.'

'And all this ...' Andras began. 'All this is why you date, not love.'

'Like you,' Tess replied. 'With your flings with holiday-makers so you can't get hurt again.'

He nodded his head in acceptance at his own situation, so desperately similar to hers. 'Except it does not always feel the way it should, does it?'

He looked across the shoreline where some of his family were starting a conga line across the stones, shouting *opa* and laughing their way into a circle.

'No,' Tess admitted hesitantly.

He turned his attention back to her and began to feel that now all too familiar sensation whirring in his psyche. There was something here, something between them, that wasn't cheap or disposable, and it was bubbling and burning its way to the surface the more time they spent together.

He took a breath, his fingers finding the fine gold of her hair and trying to tame it into position as he gazed at her.

'I have spent such a long time being afraid,' he admitted. 'Of making other poor choices, of misinterpreting my own feelings, of getting hurt again, but I think ...' He smoothed her hair back, his fingers contacting the slight curve of her neck. 'I think that even if you try to guard your heart, even if you try to lock it up so tightly, there is going to come the moment ...' He paused. 'There is going to come the moment when someone arrives with the key.'

Her eyes, the colour of the sea, were looking back at him, her full lips slightly parted, her scent, the heat from her skin, everything about her was calling to him. He shifted slightly, leaning a little forward, slowly, taking his time, not wanting this to be about lust and libido but something else, *everything* else. And he didn't want to push her like he felt he had in Kassiopi, when he had been jealous and crazy and ...

Her lips met his then, softly, slowly, her mouth working delicately over his in the sweetest, most sensuous way he had ever experienced. He felt her hand cup the back of his head and he deepened the kiss, welcoming her tongue, tasting her desire. This wasn't a throwaway moment. This was one of the best moments of his entire life.

She broke the kiss, leaning away, touching her fingers to her lips, eyes wide. Was her expression surprise? Shock? He didn't want to say too much. But he knew he needed to say enough.

'Tess ...' he began.

'What was that?' She seemed to be questioning herself as well as him.

'It was ...'

She started to get to her feet, apparently not wanting to hear his answer. 'I have to go. I have to go and find Sonya.'

'Tess ...' Andras began again.

'Tomorrow,' she blurted out, upright now, her teeth juddering together. 'I'll see you tomorrow. A Greek eight o'clock.'

There was nothing left to say right now. He just had to let her go. He nodded his head. '*Kali nichta.*'

'Goodnight,' she answered, rushing down the jetty.

Tess wasn't shaking, she was shuddering, actually internally quaking like a volcano ready to erupt and spew lava, melting its way down a mountain trail. Her legs could barely hold her weight as she stumbled down the pontoon. What had she done? Why had she kissed him like that, like it wasn't just about her neglected G-spot but about ... She couldn't even bear to think the words that were popping up, all of them synonyms to a four-letter word beginning with 'L'.

She blinked back confusion and tears and ... there was Sonya in front of her. Thank God. Someone sane, someone from London life, not Greek life with all its holiday, relaxation and escape connotations. She put on a smile, urging her limbs to move faster. And then she saw the expression on her friend's face.

'Sonya?' she said, hurrying up to her, own emotions camouflaged.

'I ... I called Joey,' Sonya whimpered, face dropping its sun-kissed look from earlier and seeming to pale by the second.

'You got hold of him. Well, that's good,' Tess ventured. Still Sonya's expression wasn't looking hopeful. 'Isn't it?'

Sonya shook her head. 'No,' she breathed. 'I didn't get hold of *him*.'

Tess swallowed. 'You didn't?'

'No,' Sonya said, this time with the tail of a wail at the close of her sentence that led to her putting a shaking hand to her lips.

'Son, what's happened?'

'It was a woman,' Sonya blurted out as tears fell from her eyes. 'A woman answered Joey's phone.'

# Fifty-six

Tess passed Sonya the ouzo bottle and watched her friend swig back a good glug of the aniseed-flavoured alcohol. That was a great thing about Greece. Siestas in the afternoon just meant the shops opened until late at night for necessary grocery purchases, like the ouzo and the oregano crisps they had just purchased from one of the mini-markets.

Now they were sat crossed-legged on the shore in the dark, only the ambient light from the beachside tavernas casting a glow enough for them to see, the lanterns and fairy lights from the wedding dinner far enough away to make them virtually invisible. And that was what Tess wanted to be at the moment. Invisible. She gazed across at the mountainside, framing the cove of Kalami, pinpricks of light plotting the course of buildings among the tall trees to the pinnacle of headland. It was so picturesque. So peaceful. So filling her head with romantic thoughts she had no idea what to do with …

'I should have said something,' Sonya stated, resting the bottle on her lap, fingers clutching the glass like it was a life preserver.

'Maybe,' Tess responded.

'I mean, it could have been anyone, couldn't it?'

'Yes,' Tess answered. 'It could have been anyone. Like … his mum?'

Sonya vigorously shook her head. 'No, it wasn't his mum.'

'How do you know?' Tess asked. 'Just how much did this woman say?'

'She said "hello",' Sonya explained. 'His mum talks with a posh accent, even though she's not posh, and if it was her it would have been "hell-ooo", not "hello".'

'Well ...'

'And that's weird too, isn't it? To pick up someone else's phone and just say "hello" as if it were *your own* phone you were answering, or someone's phone you were really comfortable answering, like a close friend ... or a lover.' Her voice cracked a little. 'If I was answering someone's phone, as a random woman who happened to be near the phone, I would say, "Hello, this is Joey's phone." Why didn't she say, "Hello, this is Joey's phone"?'

'What you really needed her to say was "Hello, this is Joey's phone, I'm Ceri, a totally platonic, battle re-enactment acquaintance."'

'Well ... yes, but ... do you think it was Ceri?' Sonya asked. 'Do you think he *is* in Margate with her now? Not at home pretending?'

Tess sighed. 'Oh, Sonya, I really don't know.'

'You don't?'

'I don't, and I'm sorry, but I am probably *the* worst person to ask for relationship advice.'

A beat went by before Sonya spoke again. 'I don't know. Perhaps, you're the one who has had it completely right all along.'

'What?' Tess pulled the bottle of ouzo away from her friend and began to unscrew the cap.

'Well, all this time, while you're been going through Tinder and Shacking Up ...'

'Hooked Up,' Tess corrected.

'All this time, I've thought that it can't possibly be fulfilling to have a different man every six weeks. It can't be the type of relationship that wholly satisfies a woman's needs, not just tiny designer dinners at Jamie Oliver's or *Fifty Shades* sex, you know … to feel loved and cared about and … secure, like you're walking around in Ugg boots and a big, thick fluffy blanket all the time … but …'

Tess swigged back the ouzo and waited for Sonya to reply. Her friend let out another sigh.

'But?' Tess asked, looking at Sonya.

'But maybe, you're right and all my ideas about lifelong love and partnership are wrong.'

Hearing her friend say that shot a bolt of fear right through Tess. She began to shake her head. 'No. That's not true, Sonya.'

'Isn't it?' she asked. 'Because right now I can't think of anything better than never feeling like this again.'

'Sonya, listen to me, you don't know anything yet. You need to hang on in there. You need to see Joey, face-to-face, when you get home. You need to tell him about the baby situation, no matter what that means for your relationship, and you need to just get it all out there, how you feel, how much you love him and just … just be honest.'

Where had that come from? Her truth-telling on the jetty with Andras? She had spent her whole life since Adam avoiding honesty, wrapping everything up in Italian meals, trips to the opera, and one really, really bad biker pub.

'Or I could be like you,' Sonya suggested. 'I could swallow all this away and I could start afresh. I wouldn't have to tell *anyone* about my faulty ovaries, or *anything* about myself, I could just enjoy some male company and some nice dinners and—'

'And you would end up just like me,' Tess said. 'Soulless.'

'But … you're happy with it. You've told me so many times how happy you are with it no matter what I've said and … perhaps I should have listened more.'

'No,' Tess stated. 'You shouldn't.' She let a breath go and, straightaway, there was the taste of Andras's lips, the touch of his fingers in her hair, the smell of his light aftershave mixing with the sea breeze and the sand …

'But you were so sure …'

'I am sure, at least, I was …' She closed her eyes, trying to block out the haunting lilt of a mandolin that was seeping its way inside her.

'Has something happened?' Sonya asked, reaching to drag back the ouzo bottle.

Had something happened? Whether she wanted to freely admit it or not, something *had* happened, *was* happening with Andras. A man she had only just met. A man she had been thrown together with. A man who would probably score ridiculously badly on shared interests on the Hooked Up rating score. A man who seemed to understand her and accept her so easily.

'I kissed Andras,' Tess stated.

'I know,' Sonya said. 'On our first night. Oh. Are you still thinking about it?' She put her fingertips to her lips. 'Was it *that* good?'

'I kissed him tonight,' she breathed. 'On the jetty.'

'Oh my!' Sonya exclaimed.

'And outside Passion, after he got all jealous when someone tried to chat me up.'

'Oh my!' Sonya said again.

'So, I broke my single for the summer vow and … I'm sorry about that, I really am, but—'

'Tess—'

'No,' Tess broke in. 'You don't understand.' She was struggling to breathe now, the combination of the humid air and the ouzo clagging up her throat. 'There's more. It's much, much worse.'

'It is?'

Tess nodded. 'Much worse.'

'Double swig of ouzo worse?' Sonya asked, passing Tess the bottle.

There was no backing out now. She had to tell Sonya the truth. If only to stop her giving up on Joey and thinking that she wanted to commit to a life of meaningless liaisons.

'It's worse because … I'm pretty sure it meant something.'

'It meant something?'

'I think so. I mean it felt different. From all the other kisses, since Adam.'

'Oh my!' Sonya said again. '*You're* feeling something! You're *feeling* something!'

'Shh,' Tess begged. 'It can't be real though, can it? And … I don't *want it* to be real, do I, for all the reasons you just said. The potential loss, the heartbreak when it happens, the starting over again, the weekends of going back to doing something with someone that means nothing.'

'Is that … is that what it really feels like?' Sonya asked. 'Weekends filled with everything, which mean nothing?'

Yes, that's what it felt like. That's what it had felt like for so long. That was the path she had chosen to ward off any permanence: loneliness. Publicly she was the woman with a man on her arm and a great career; privately she was still completely alone in every single respect. She had decided dating with zero expectations was better than dipping her toe back into something else, but now Andras had talked about hearts and keys and she had told him about Adam …

'Adam's getting married again,' Tess blurted.

'Bloody hell!' Her friend reached for the ouzo bottle.

'And apparently my mother doesn't hate me,' Tess concluded, snatching the alcohol back and putting the rim to her lips.

'You spoke to her?' Sonya asked.

Tess shook her head. 'No. Rachel called.'

'Well,' Sonya said, grappling for the ouzo. 'All of those things – you feeling something with Andras, you talking to your sister, Adam moving on with a skunk, because she has to be a skunk if she isn't you – these are all good, good things.'

Tess put the bottle down on to the beach and took hold of Sonya's hand. 'Joey loves you, Sonya. He really loves you. Hold on to that while you're here and I'm sure when you get back all this can be sorted out.'

Sonya nodded. 'I hope so.'

'I hope so too,' Tess replied, giving her friend's hand a squeeze.

'So, what are *you* going to do?'

Tess let out a breath, her eyes travelling over the beach to the wedding-party tables. The sounds of laughter, music and Greek life travelled on the night air. 'According to the Georgious all you really need to do to be happy is spit a lot.'

'Really?' Sonya exclaimed.

She smiled. 'If only life were really that simple.'

'So?'

'So, I'm going to finalise the Black Velvet designs and I'm going to see what tomorrow brings in Corfu Town.'

Sonya slipped her arm through Tess's and leaned her head on her shoulder. 'I want to be Greek,' she said a little sleepily. 'I want to buy a little house by the sea with flowers everywhere and blue and white tables and chairs. And I would hang those decorative evil eyes all over it and fill it with cats. Well, perhaps not fill it with cats because they would probably try to chase all the lovely lizards away, but there will be cats, and maybe a bird, if they can get on together. I've always wanted a canary, and I could crochet a cover for the cage and ...'

Tess closed her eyes and let Sonya talk about her dream house in the sun, all the while wondering if her life back in London was ever going to be the same again after this holiday.

# Fifty-seven

# Taverna Georgiou

This was ridiculous. Why had he put on a tie? Andras put his fingers around the knot of black material and tugged it away from his neck. It was a twenty-five-degree morning and, being accustomed to the heat, it really shouldn't be bothering him, but today was his last chance. If the bank said no to the idea of a loan then he had two choices: to stay in the business with his mother or to sell his share to her or someone else and … he didn't know what came after that. He hadn't thought that Spiros getting married and leaving the island was going to have such an effect on *his* life, but it was.

'Andras, we only have ten tomatoes.'

It was Dorothea, stood at the kitchen door with two tomatoes in each hand, as if exhibiting proof. This was all he needed. And what was happening to his stock? He always carefully controlled it and Hector had been in his pen when he'd left the house.

'Good morning, Dorothea! Good morning, Andras!'

It was his mother, Marietta at her heels again. He checked his watch. He needed to pick up Tess and Sonya in less than ten minutes.

'We have no tomatoes,' Dorothea said in Isadora's direction, offering out the ones in her hands.

'You have no tomatoes!' Isadora exclaimed.

'I am dealing with the tomato situation,' Andras said, brushing down a tablecloth on his way towards them.

'I took some last night to make the feta and tomato dip but I thought you would have more,' Isadora stated.

'You took some,' Andras said. 'From the restaurant kitchen.'

'The *family* restaurant kitchen,' Isadora added quickly. 'The restaurant that will soon be half mine again.'

'Mama, I have to account for all the stock.'

'So, I cannot use tomatoes for my own son's wedding dinner?'

He gritted his teeth. He didn't have time for this. Babis and Victor would be here soon to continue setting up the tables. He needed to get in the car with the notes he had made late last night and head to Kalami Cove Apartments.

'I have to go,' he said, pulling the tie from his neck and pushing it into the pocket of his trousers.

'Go?' Isadora queried.

'I have a meeting in Corfu Town this morning.'

'What sort of meeting?' Isadora inquired.

'A business meeting.'

Isadora folded her arms across her chest and pinned him with a furious look. 'You are meeting Patricia.'

'Patricia – Tess – is coming with me, yes. And Susan, I mean, Sonya.'

'So, what sort of business is to be done with two English people with you?'

'Mama, Tess is a businesswoman.'

'Is this business to do with the restaurant?' Isadora didn't wait for him to make any reply. 'It is, isn't it? This is just what I was saying, about her wanting you for your business interests. Well, if it is to do with the restaurant then I should come with you.' She banged her stick on the flagstone floor.

He didn't want that. He couldn't have that. He was nervous enough about the meeting without having his mother breathing down his neck. And then there was how things were with Tess, his feelings for Tess. He had no idea how that was going to change things today, and for as long as she was here on Corfu.

'I will tell you all about it when I get back,' he said, stepping away from the group. 'Dorothea, call Giannis. He will know where to get tomatoes at short notice.'

'Andras!' Isadora exclaimed.

'Isadora, we do have to meet with the florist,' Marietta spoke.

'Andras!' Isadora shouted again, banging her stick.

He waved a hand and called over his shoulder. 'Relax, Mama, focus on the wedding.'

# Fifty-eight

# Kalami Cove Apartments

Tess brushed her hands down the sundress she was wearing and looked at her feet. She had opted to wear the plain flip-flops Andras had bought her from Agios Spyridon. And as he came to mind, her stomach abseiled down to somewhere near her French-manicured toenails. She had stayed up late last night to finalise the Black Velvet designs and in every keystroke, every pencilled line she drew, was Andras. Her vision for this brand had changed since she had been here. To begin with, she had thought ultra-contemporary had to be hard, bold and fierce to compete on the high street and in the chain's marketing. But, with the new company name – albeit unapproved – had come the realisation that the wine bars were offering relaxation, escape, perhaps not quite in the same way Taverna Georgiou was, but Destination Unwind all the same. She smiled to herself, hugging Andras's laptop to her body. She had put together projections for his bank meeting too and that seemed to be making her ridiculously happy.

Sonya let out a sigh and dropped her mobile phone down from her ear.

'Still no answer?' Tess asked softly.

'No,' Sonya replied. 'It just goes straight to voicemail now.'

She slipped an arm around her friend's shoulders. 'Don't worry, remember?'

'I know,' Sonya said, nodding. 'I've got lots of sightseeing to do. The two forts, the esplanade, the bust of Gerald Durrell.'

The blast of a horn startled them both and Tess shielded her eyes from the sun to look down the road. Fotis's truck was heading towards them.

'Oh, it's Fotis!' Sonya exclaimed, waving at the approaching vehicle.

'He's stopping,' Tess said as the truck drew to a halt.

The window wound down and Andras's face appeared from the cab. '*Kalimera*,' he greeted.

'Oh!' Sonya exclaimed. 'You're not Fotis.'

'No,' he replied. 'My car would not start again and Spiros, he needs his. Something to do with ropes and one of the blue caves on his lists.'

He looked sizzling hot in another bright white shirt, his hair perfectly in place, his gorgeous lips that could do special things … She swallowed. She needed to pull herself together. 'Do you have a licence to drive a lorry?' she called up to him.

He smiled at her. 'We have to get to Corfu Town, no?'

# Fifty-nine

# Corfu Town

Tess took in the busy, bustling, vibrant city as Andras navigated the truck around the town looking for somewhere to park. There was something here to delight every sightseer, from the two forts (Old and New), to the residential area of Cambiello with its four- or five-storey ancient buildings guarding the labyrinth of winding streets, laundry on lines across the narrow lanes, dogs and cats sitting beneath archways of cream and terracotta enjoying the heat of the day.

'My book says it is best to park at the Old Harbour and walk into the main town,' Sonya commented, head in the pages of her Marco Polo while they bumped along at pace.

'Yes, but it will be full now,' Andras answered.

'It's only a little after nine,' Tess said, checking her watch.

'To be in with a chance of parking in Corfu Town you must arrive before seven o'clock,' he responded. He turned his head slightly and smiled at her. 'An English seven o'clock.'

'So, what are we going to do?' Tess asked. 'You have the meeting and ...'

'Do not worry,' he answered. 'For today we are just going to pretend we are a coach.'

Andras parked the truck behind an exhaust fumes-spewing coach that looked as if its best days were behind it and Tess followed Sonya in the most inelegant disembarkation known to woman. Once on the ground they were treated to a spectacular view of the Old Fort. Sonya had her camera out before the dust had settled under her sandals.

'Wow!' Sonya exclaimed. 'Look at that … it looks like a beautiful, crumbly, historic cake sat on a bed of sparkling ocean.'

Tess breathed in the humidity and sunshine, letting the heat prickle her skin as she gazed at the Venetian architecture. It was layer upon layer of greying stone interspersed with greenery climbing up its walls, all surrounded by the aquamarine sea, yachts with their tall masts bobbing at the bottom of its steep walls.

'It is special, no?' Andras said.

Tess shivered, now realising how close he was and her whole body immediately reacting to that.

'It's beautiful,' she replied. 'But then, the whole island is beautiful.'

'*Ne*,' he said, nodding.

'You can go now!' Sonya called, heading closer to the wall, camera still focused on the fort.

'Go?' Tess inquired.

'Yes, to the meeting at the bank.'

'*Andras* has a meeting at the bank,' Tess replied. 'I was going to sightsee with you.'

'I don't need you to sightsee and you don't like museums and I won't want to go in the designer shops … besides, don't you need to show Andras the projections?'

'Well, yes, but …' Tess faltered.

'You have done the work for me on my accounts?' Andras asked her.

She nodded. 'Yes, but I was just going to go through it with you quickly so you could present it to the bank. I don't need to be there and—'

'Going now!' Sonya called. 'I'll text you!'

'Sonya!' Tess yelled at her retreating friend.

'I have maps! Good luck!'

Tess swallowed. She knew what her friend was doing. This was because she had admitted she had feelings for Andras. Sonya was trying to do a bit of matchmaking and now she was backed into a bit of a corner.

'It is OK,' Andras said. 'You do not have to come to the bank with me.'

'No, I … it's just …' She didn't really know what she wanted to say. She batted a mosquito away from her face and blew out a breath. A few days earlier she might have screamed about the insect. So much seemed to have changed. 'I just didn't want to leave Sonya on her own or turn up to the bank with a whole entourage but, seeing as she's left me to rub Gerald Durrell's bust or something …' Tess smiled. 'Can we get out of the heat? I fear your laptop might melt if we don't and then where would we be?'

He smiled at her and slipped his hands into his pockets, drawing something out. 'I have paper.'

# Sixty

'This place is so buzzy!' Tess remarked over the street sounds of mopeds, traffic and a red-and-white uniformed brass band playing under the ornate bandstand. 'But nothing like London.' She looked across at Andras. 'I meant that in a good way.'

'What is London like?' Andras asked her.

'Hectic and stressful, but eclectic ... and wonderful all at the same time.'

'You have lived there a long time?'

'No, well, since Adam.' She swallowed. She'd said his name again and it seemed that now she had started saying it here in Greece, each mention hurt just a little bit less. She cleared her throat as they carried on walking up the esplanade. 'I come from a small village.'

'Like Kalami?' Andras inquired.

'It isn't quite as lovely as Kalami,' she admitted. 'And it has more cows than goats and tortoises.'

Andras stopped walking and took a deep breath. Tess turned her head then, and saw the sign: Beta Bank.

'We are here,' he stated. 'We will have time to go through the numbers on the computer and then ...'

'Don't worry,' Tess urged. She wanted to touch him. Take his hand or put *her* hand on his shoulder and just connect with him. Let him know she knew how important this was for him. Instead she held steady. 'Everything is going to be OK. You have a great business and so much potential.'

'But not enough tomatoes,' he said, sighing.

'What?'

'It doesn't matter,' he replied. 'Come on. We will go in.' He pushed at the door.

Andras could remember the last time he had felt this nervous. It was meeting up with Elissa at the lawyer's office to complete the paperwork for their divorce. Her pregnant swell had been obvious then and, as he signed his name to the end of their marriage, it was an extra dart to his heart to know that she was literally starting a brand-new life without him.

The all-marble office was cool and air-conditioned, for which he was grateful, and he led the way to approach the desk.

He spoke in Greek. 'Andras Georgiou to see—'

'Good morning, Mr Georgiou, Mr Giantsiorhs will see you now.'

'What?' He turned and looked at Tess. Wetting his lips, he turned back to the receptionist. 'My appointment is not for another half an hour.'

'What's happening?' Tess asked. 'What is she saying?'

'Mr Giantsiorhs is running ahead of schedule so he can see you now,' the receptionist repeated.

'He can see me now,' Andras said to Tess.

'Now?' Tess exclaimed. '*Now* now?'

He nodded. 'What do we do?' He lowered his voice, eyes locking with hers. 'I haven't looked, or prepared, or ... I have to make this work.'

He felt her take hold of his hand then and that spiral of something he still couldn't quite explain shot through him. Fear, excitement, nervous tension, all began to whip up a tsunami of emotion. He needed to get his head together.

'Then we see him now,' Tess stated calmly.

'Your work, on the figures, in English. I don't know how to ...'

'Then I will present them,' Tess replied. 'And you will have to translate.' She nodded like she was completely at ease with this situation. 'OK?'

Her question was because he was floundering. He needed to keep control, keep the faith. He knew his business. He *believed* in this business. And that was all he needed to know.

'OK,' he answered. 'I am ready.'

Mr Giantsiorhs looked like he had eaten rather too many knuckles of lamb, but he had a nice smile and a firm handshake that Tess got the benefit of as well as Andras. She was going to treat this just like a meeting at McKenzie Falconer. She was going to build Andras's brand right in front of Mr Giantsiorhs' eyes, wow him with the restaurant figures and get an agreement in principal to the loan. This Greek bank manager was just like a client needing direction towards signing on a dotted line, nothing more.

She put the laptop on the table and, instead of sitting in one of the chairs opposite the banker, remained standing.

'Good morning Mr G—' Shit, there was no way in hell she was going to pronounce his surname. She smiled and spoke to Andras out of the corner of her mouth. 'Translate.'

A flurry of Greek ensued until Andras spoke again. 'He wants to know who you are.'

'I am Mr Georgiou's business representative.' She lowered her voice. 'It sounds so much better than fake girlfriend, doesn't it?' She smiled as she flipped open the laptop lid and moved her fingers over the touchpad.

'Mr ...' She really needed to stop addressing him by a name she couldn't say. 'Sir, we are here to offer you, and your establishment, a fantastic opportunity.'

'We are?' Andras queried.

'We are.' She nodded, for her own benefit more than anything else in the hope it would instil confidence. 'Andras, translate please.' She cleared her throat. 'We would very much like Beta Bank to be partners in bringing this locally renowned restaurant in Kalami on to the international stage.'

'Tess ...' Andras stated.

'Don't worry,' she whispered. 'I do this all the time. We are going to show him, right here, just what you're going to be doing with the loan, how it's going to progress your business and increase its profitability tenfold, and how that loan is going to be paid back *before* the term even finishes.' Tess waved a hand. 'Picture the scene.' She turned the laptop around to face Mr Giantsiorhs and a photograph of Taverna Georgiou flashed up on the screen. 'This individual, traditional but contemporary restaurant has been drawing locals and holidaymakers to its tables for centuries ...'

'Centuries?' Andras exclaimed.

'Aren't you translating?'

Andras said something in Greek and Tess, on a roll, continued.

'The souls of Greek warriors speak from its walls and the sides that ... aren't walls ... have an unprecedented view of Kalami Bay.'

'Tess ...' Andras tried again.

'Mr Georgiou has been running this business for five and a half years and in the last two years he has seen a significant rise in turnover, and this after a rather erratic Greek financial position within Europe.' She nodded knowingly at Mr Giantsiorhs. 'We all know all about that, don't we?'

'Tess,' Andras said. 'I don't think you need to say all of this.'

She looked at Andras. 'I'm outlining the business and in a minute I'm going to move on to the plans you have for your events and …' She turned her attention to Mr Giantsiorhs then, before looking back to Andras. 'Why aren't you translating anything I'm saying to him?'

The banker cleared his throat. 'I actually speak English.'

Suddenly the air conditioning was inadequate to subdue her flaming face. She sank down into the chair, wobbling a little. Why hadn't Andras stopped her? She swallowed. She hadn't let him get a word in. This was his business meeting and she had hijacked it – with the best intentions, granted – but she didn't know Greek business and he needed this loan to keep the restaurant his and keep his mother at arm's length.

'I'm sorry,' Tess said apologetically.

Mr Giantsiorhs waved a hand and reached for the laptop, pulling it across the desk towards him. 'It is no matter.'

'Mr Giantsiorhs,' Andras said. 'I am looking for a loan of twenty-five thousand euro.'

'Mmm,' the banker replied, his fingers jabbing at the keys.

'The figures are all there,' Tess said. 'You'll find on the sixth PowerPoint slide is quite a convincing flow chart.' She really did need to shut her mouth now.

'I have plans to create some additional space – more covers – but first, I would like to try some small events. However, I cannot do that without a little capital for initial outlay and advertising to kick-start things.'

Mr Giantsiorhs was now writing things down on a piece of paper, his other chubby hand reaching out for an ancient-looking calculator. Was he really going to make his decision using something so ... analogue? She was nervous on Andras's behalf.

'He can afford the loan repayments,' Tess blurted out. 'I mean, based on the rate you offer on your website page.' As she said this she wondered whether the man even knew what a website was. 'And the taverna itself ... wow, it is really something special. You really have to visit it to see the—'

'View of the bay?' the banker asked, looking up from his paper. 'Or to hear the souls of Greek warriors speaking to me from the walls?'

Why had she said that? She blamed Sonya for all her Corfu guidebook talk on the way here.

Mr Giantsiorhs pushed his calculator away and took a deep breath, elongated his rotund frame into the back of his deep leather chair. His body language was saying no. She didn't want him to say no.

'Your brother is getting married, no?'

Andras's heart dropped. This had been his main fear. To come here and use a white lie to get the money he needed had always been a risk on this small island where everyone knew everything about everyone. He knew, if he had been honest and said he needed the money to pay out his business partner then the application would be immediately denied. But now it looked like he had tried to pull the wool over Mr Giantsiorhs' eyes. And dishonesty, no matter how slight, was not something that would be accepted.

'Yes,' he answered. 'My brother gets married in two days.'

'And he is leaving Corfu.'

'Yes.' He swallowed. 'He is.' He could feel the anxiety invading his shoulders. 'I will be honest—'

'Mr Giantsiorhs ...' Tess swallowed, having just about managed the pronunciation. 'The truth is, Andras wants to make a new start with this business when his brother leaves. You know what it is like, growing up with a big, Greek family, there is always someone wanting to do something one way and another wanting to do quite the opposite.' She smiled. 'Now, Andras wants the chance to take the taverna in a different direction, not forgetting all the great times his family made there, but forging something new, taking what works really well already and building on that, creating something even better.'

The air seemed to still and Andras surveyed the banker's expression, hoping to garner some indication of what he was thinking. Tess had stopped him from telling the truth about the loan. It was still prickling his conscience. And this man wasn't stupid.

'Your brother does not need money for his share of the business before he leaves the island, no?'

Andras's chest tightened. How could he possibly lie to a direct question like that? He steeled himself, his lungs expanding in preparation for admitting everything.

'He does need money to leave the island,' Tess blurted out. 'But I've covered that.' She nodded.

'Tess ...' Andras said.

'And why would a business advisor do that?' Mr Giantsiorhs asked. 'Or, what else did you call yourself? A fake girlfriend?'

Andras wanted to drop his head into his hands now. This was a disaster.

'I know how this must look to you,' Tess began softly. 'I know that I came in here and said some stupid, perhaps a little over-the-top things, but I did that because I am passionate about the taverna and I am passionate about Andras. He is the most solid, dedicated, trustworthy person I've ever met. More than that, he's highly intuitive and understanding, not just of his business but of … life.' She took a deep breath. 'He has been putting everything and everyone ahead of his own needs for such a long time, now it's his turn.' She stretched forward, pushing the laptop towards Mr Giantsiorhs again. 'You really need to look at the figures and the projections before you make a decision, and why not come and have dinner at the taverna one evening. Come and see what makes it so special for yourself.'

Andras couldn't take his eyes off her. All those things she had just said. Was that really how she felt about him? Or was that just for the benefit of the banker? To ensure he got the loan? He swallowed, finding himself really wanting to believe the former.

'OK,' Mr Giantsiorhs spoke finally.

'OK?' Tess asked. 'He gets the loan?'

'No, OK I will print off the figures and I will make my consideration.'

'You will?' Andras asked.

'I will need to put this all into a system and it will need to pass to the head office and … we will see,' the banker concluded.

'Thank you,' Andras said, getting to his feet and extending his hand. 'Thank you so much.'

'I'm so happy I could kiss you!' Tess exclaimed. 'But I won't,' she said quickly. 'But maybe we should spit.'

Mr Giantsiorhs looked a little wary of Tess's suggestion and Andras quickly butted in. 'Thank you so much for your time.'

# Sixty-one

The sunlight hit Tess's cheeks and the humidity swept through her body as they burst out of the doors of the bank on to the street. She turned to Andras, clasping his hands and squeezing them tightly.

'Oh my God! I really think he's going to give you the loan!' Her whole body was alive, singing with this fresh, ridiculous, utter joy.

'Because of you,' Andras said, smiling at her, his fingers entwined with hers.

'It almost wasn't. Why didn't you tell me he spoke English?'

'Why didn't you tell me I had warrior souls in my walls?'

She laughed then. 'Well, perhaps that's an angle we can work on for one of your events. Greek Ghosts and Ancient Stories.'

She stopped, her smile slipping slightly. She had said 'we'. She had said it like she was a joint taverna owner about to spend the rest of her life event-planning by the sea. 'Andras, I'm sorry I lied about having money to cover Spiros, but if you had told him what you needed some of the money for, then …'

'I know,' Andras stated. 'I know why you did it and I also know that *you* know I was going to tell the truth.'

'Sometimes you have to keep the truth from people to protect them, as well as yourself.' She swallowed. This was all a little close to home and the fine hairs on her arms were standing to attention as they continued to hold each other's hands.

A phone tone erupted from her bag and she broke contact to unzip it and retrieve her device.

'It's Sonya,' she informed him, looking at the screen. 'She's on a boat to somewhere called Vidos Island. Where the hell is that?' She looked to Andras. 'Is it still in Greece?'

He laughed then and nodded. 'Yes, it is just a short ferry ride away. Would you like to go?'

'What's there? Lots of lizards and things that are going to sting me?'

'Some very nice beaches,' Andras said. 'We could take a picnic.'

'Now it's sounding more appealing,' Tess admitted.

'Come,' Andras said. 'We will pick up some food and head to the port.'

# Sixty-two

# Vidos Island

Just a ten-minute trip across the water and the small ferry had docked at the island of Vidos. Already, just from observing the greenery and rocks, Tess knew this was some sort of Sonya haven. She could practically smell the animals ready to pounce as she stepped off the boat on to concrete land.

Andras passed her a bottle of water. 'You should drink,' he said. 'It is very hot today.'

She accepted the bottle and took a welcome swig as, around them, the rest of the ferry passengers disembarked, bags of summer sun paraphernalia swinging from their arms. She passed the bottle back and grabbed her phone as another text came in.

'Sonya says she's had lunch with a German couple and they're going to see the bird and wildlife sanctuary.'

'You would like to go there too?' Andras asked.

'To be honest, I would really rather find a nice beach and eat the picnic,' Tess admitted.

He smiled. 'Then we will go this way.'

Andras knew exactly where he was going. At the far side of the island was the best beach. It was tranquil, not a place where there were sunloungers or facilities, just the rustic simplicity of the sand and pine trees all around. When he and

Spiros were children they had gone camping on Vidos Island, spending a few weeks in the summer with their school friends, enjoying what had felt like endless days where the sun always shone and nothing bad could ever touch them. It all seemed so long ago, but the memories were good ones and he wanted to share that place with Tess.

'Spiros and I used to come here when we were children,' he said as he led the way down the winding track they were travelling on. 'Sometimes with our parents. Sometimes with summer camp.'

'And what did you boys get up to?' she asked.

'Swimming, making camp fires, fishing.'

'I don't want to fish,' Tess said.

'No? Why not?' Andras asked.

'I love eating fish, I just don't really like how they feel.'

He smiled. 'No lizards, no bees, no fish ... are there any animals that you do like?'

'I picked up Hector all by myself and I'm not opposed to the odd cat or dog or—'

'Beetle?' Andras asked as one scurried across the dirt in front of them.

Tess let out a shriek and jumped so her feet were nowhere near the insect, perhaps worried a trail of its family would follow.

He laughed. 'Come, the beach isn't far.'

Within a few minutes the track opened out, the trees and brush fanning out to reveal a taupe-coloured beach, a turquoise ocean bubbling in front of it. It wasn't like any of the other beaches she had seen on the island. There was nothing but the sand, the sea, towering palms and pines and flowers all the colours of the rainbow. Across the water, Tess could see Corfu Town and, even from this distance, was able to clearly see a docking cruise ship and pick out lemon-hued bell towers.

'It is a good beach, no?' Andras said.

His low timbre so close to her ear set off that internal merry-go-round of feelings again. Feelings she had spent all night re-conjuring up only to attempt to dismiss them again.

'It's a great beach,' she answered.

'Let's find somewhere to sit and eat,' he replied.

There was no one else around and they had their pick of spots. Andras led them to the far edge, away from the main path they had taken, a space half in sunlight, half in shade, the trees making dappled marks across the sand.

Tess dropped to the ground, eager to rest and stretch out, the walk in the heat having sapped her. She closed her eyes and stilled her mind, focusing on the warmth and relaxation that had become such a part of this holiday in Corfu. Right now she was so grateful for Tony and her second scallop-clad proposal. If she hadn't been in the very middle of that crisis, she would never have been open to going away with Sonya. And that would have meant she would never have even thought of going to Greece. To have not experienced every happy, completely crazy moment of this trip was completely unthinkable now.

Something tickled her face and she snapped open her eyes and let out a screech.

'Relax,' Andras said. 'It is only a butterfly. See.' He indicated a pair of yellow and white wings fluttering off into the distance, away from the noisy, mad Englishwoman who had disturbed its peace.

'It's not natural to like insects like Sonya does, you know,' Tess spoke. 'My sister Rachel has to fly-spray anything with more than four legs in her house.'

'So, it is an inherited condition? This hatred of creatures.'

'I don't hate them. I just don't want to share my private, up-close personal space with them,' Tess stated. 'It's all about boundaries. They stick to their habitat and I'll stick to mine.'

'And if your habitats collide?' Andras asked. 'You are, after all, in a land that is a little foreign to you.'

'If they promise just to exist and not to attack then I can give them that same assurance.'

'But what if they get too close? Perhaps almost unintentionally?'

He was blurring the boundaries now. Was this conversation about to turn into something other than wildlife? A sliver of heat wound through her spine just at the idea of it.

'Are we still talking about animals?' Tess breathed.

'I do not know,' he admitted. 'Are we?'

She was hot. She was on fire with desire as she looked into those chestnut-coloured eyes. She couldn't reply. She was afraid anything she did say would be as pornographic as the Blackberry Boudoir branding.

He smiled. 'I am sorry. Here.' He offered out a plastic container to her. 'Feta cheese?'

She swallowed. She didn't want him to be sorry. She wanted him to kiss her again. Why couldn't she just say that? Tell him. Show him. Like she had started to last night?

'Andras ...' Shit, now she had said his name she had to follow it up with something else. But what?

'It is OK,' he said. 'I know what you are thinking.'

'You do?'

He nodded, putting a piece of the white, crumbly, rich cheese into his own mouth. God, she couldn't watch him eat. He ate like he had a degree in sexy.

'You are thinking that there is no one but us on the beach ...' he began.

Did he have wine in that bag of supermarket goodies he had shopped for? Anything alcoholic at all? Didn't Sonya's Marco Polo mention some really good aperitif made out of kumquats?

'We are celebrating a small breakthrough with the bank ...'

He needed to stop talking now, because with each accented word, her nether regions were beginning to warm up like Louie Spence before some high-kicking.

'You are thinking about sex,' Andras stated finally.

'Fuck!' Tess said as her wedge of feta cheese fell out of her hand and down her front.

'Yes,' Andras said. 'That.'

'No, I mean, yes. Perhaps ...' She breathed out. 'Maybe?'

He edged closer to her then, until he was by her side, a little facing her, just close enough that her libido woke up. She wanted to feel those lips dance all over her ...

'I told you before that I do not want to have sex with you, Tess.'

Immediately crushed, she bit on her bottom lip. She knew that. He had always been so honest with her. He was being a gentleman. He had never treated her like she was incidental. That was why their fake relationship had worked so easily.

'I know,' she answered with a resigned nod.

'I *cannot* have sex with you,' he repeated. He reached out a hand, his fingers touching the underside of her wrist, tips moving delicately in a figure-of-eight motion that was causing all sorts of eruptions inside her.

'I know.' She swallowed again. 'You said.'

His fingers began a slow walk up her arm to her elbow. Right now she was considering making a mental erogenous zone map because 'inside of elbow' had never been on her radar before.

'Tess,' he breathed, his head moving closer to hers. Getting closer was an odd way to give someone the sexual brush-off.

'Yes,' she answered.

'I don't want to have sex with you,' he said. 'I want to make love with you.'

If it was possible for your heart to explode yet still be beating, then that was what had just happened. Feelings began to cascade like a thunderstorm of hot summer rain, soaking her, drowning her, forcing her under and then swimming her back up again.

'Say something,' he begged.

His beautiful voice was laced with both fear and thrill and it hit her all at once. This was real. For him *and* for her. Here, in this moment, they were in love. She was in love. Tess Parks was meant to be staying single for the summer but Tess Parks was *in love*.

She placed the flat of her palm against his cheek and rubbed the Cupid's bow of his top lip with her thumb.

'Say something, please, Tess.' He kissed the pad of her thumb.

She paused but her reply was as definite as it ever could be. 'I want to make love with you, too.'

# Sixty-three

Andras took his time, just to look at her after she had said the words, the words that had made every part of him ache with a longing he had never admitted to owning before.

She parted her lips to speak and he tensed, scared that she would suddenly take back what she had said, that all this would sift through his fingers like the fine sand they were sitting on.

'Andras,' she whispered. 'I don't know how this has happened … it shouldn't be …'

'I know,' he replied. 'I feel it too. That the circumstance of us meeting was so …'

'Ridiculous,' she offered. 'Crazy.'

'Beautiful,' he added, his fingers reaching up into her hair.

He couldn't wait a moment longer. His whole body was so wired, desperate to express exactly what she had grown to mean to him so quickly. He drew her towards him, lips seeking hers, longing to feel the heat of her mouth on his and, as they connected, a sound came from her that had his arousal deepening further still.

Their lips together, mouths entwined, he lowered her down on to the sand, his body resting over, until finally he withdrew, making a distance to just look and admire her.

'Don't stop kissing me now,' she begged.

He smiled down at her. 'Do not worry,' he said. 'I have only just begun.'

Despite the sizzling temperatures, Tess was shivering, every centimetre of her on the highest of alerts. Her back flat against the heat of the beach, her nipples grazing the inside of her sundress, she had never felt so utterly in the moment and it was both ecstasy and agony because of how unfamiliar it felt.

She drew her arms up off the sand, her fingers reaching for the buttons of Andras's shirt. She wanted to see him, feel him. She slid back one plastic button, releasing it from the white cotton, until he caught her hand in his, aligning their fingers together but stopping her from performing the task she wanted to perform.

'*Arga*,' he whispered.

'What does that mean?'

'Slowly,' he replied.

She closed her eyes, letting him guide her hand to each button in turn, helping her pop them loose. She felt her fingertips touch his skin and she couldn't do it blind any more. She wanted to look. Opening her eyes, she took in every sinew of that magnificent body she had seen at close quarters since she arrived on the island. Firm pecs moved to tight abs, honed olive skin covering each defined muscle. She put her hands on him, smoothing up from his stomach to his shoulders, pulling him closer to her, wanting to engage with his mouth again.

Then, as he kissed her, she felt his hand moving against her skin and the straps of her sundress. So gently, he edged each spaghetti strand down until she had no choice but to move her arm up and out. As soon as she was free she re-found his hair, diving her fingers into it and pulling him closer, strengthening their kiss.

She writhed as his fingers traced down her arms, over her ribs, before brushing teasingly close to her now bare breasts. She just wanted him to touch her now the passion and intensity was welling up so thick and fast ...

His ripped his mouth away from hers, breathing hard and heavy, as those deep brown eyes gazed at her. She had never been looked at like that before, like she was the only woman in existence, like he was having difficulty with the 'slowly' he had suggested.

And then his mouth found one of her now olive-sized nipples and she was taken to a whole different level of turned-on. His luscious mouth licked and teased and delivered perfect strokes of heaven to her already aroused skin as she both gave in and fought over it, bare back shifting in the sand, fingers whirling in the hair at his nape.

She couldn't wait any longer. If she knew the Greek word for 'fast' she would have been shouting it for the whole of Vidos Island to hear. She sat up, shifting him away from her, her fingers reaching for the waistband of his trousers, wanting to tear the things right off him.

'Tess,' he said, palming her hands.

'No,' she answered, feeling for the zip.

'Tess,' he repeated, an undisguisable edge of heat to his voice.

'Take them off,' she ordered. 'I want to see you.'

Her words stung Andras in the sweetest, most sensual way and it was all he could do to stop himself from doing exactly what she asked. But he had to. He needed to commit to this with everything he had, with his heart and soul. Because, despite them living in different countries, this was not like anything he had had before. He wanted to savour every moment.

'What's wrong?' Tess asked, looking at him with concern painted on her expression.

'Nothing,' he answered, his eyes locked with hers.

'Then ...'

'I do not know how this will work, Tess,' he admitted. 'But, I do know that I want this, what we are about to do, to mean ... everything.'

He kept watching her eyes, trying to see or read what she was thinking.

She reached out, taking his hand in hers. 'Andras,' she said, 'it already does.'

She leaned forward, lightly kissing his lips, her fingers moving to touch his body again, fingernails teasing his skin from the top of his core to his navel.

He got to his feet, standing up, his back to the ocean, the sun licking the skin on his shoulders and put his hands to his waistband. His eyes on her, he slowly pulled down the zipper. Inching the material down over his hips, he let his underwear come too, sliding both down over his thighs until they pooled at his feet. He stepped out and onto the sand, all the while watching her.

Before another thought could enter his head, Tess was up off the sand, slipping off her panties and moving towards him, jumping up into his arms, her mouth finding his with a desperate urgency.

He held her tight, her legs swinging around his hips, her heat so tantalisingly close to his arousal he could barely breathe. His kissed her hard, his arms holding her up, securing her against him.

'In the water,' she breathed, her lips close to his ear. 'Make love to me in the water.'

Andras was carrying her like she weighed nothing, across the sand, towards the sparkling water, her nakedness kissed by the Corfiot sun, her heart thumping a rhythm she didn't recognise. She wanted this moment more than she had wanted anything else. Nothing before had been like this, she had meant that, not with any of her Hooked Up liaisons, not even with Adam. This was something completely indescribable.

The water hit her toes first, then, as Andras walked them in deeper, she felt the cool lapping of the waves on the rest of her skin until she couldn't be passive any longer. She wanted to get down into it, feel every part of the ocean on every part of her. She slid down out of his grasp, submerging herself, her shoeless feet uncaring for what lay beneath. The water was so clear, such a tonic not just to her skin but to her soul.

She turned to face him, smiling, with everything she had, beckoning him towards her. There was nothing else to say. No words were needed any more.

Andras stood before her, waist deep in the sea, beads of water sparkling across his bare chest, and she wanted nothing more than to feel him inside her.

She looped her arms around his neck and let him raise her up until she could feel the length of his arousal. She held his eyes, dipping her body slowly until she felt him push forward a little. She gasped, feeling him enter her, and then he drew away, denying her, teasing her. She tipped her hips towards him again, wanting the connection back, needing it.

'Andras,' she breathed.

'What?' he asked, breathless himself. 'What do you want?'

'You.' She shuddered. 'I want you.'

And then she felt him, all of him, firm, solid, slipping inside her, the waves aiding her to rock back and forth against him. Clinging to him, she closed her eyes, letting her other senses take over – the smell of his skin as she breathed in, the taste of the saltwater on her lips, the sound of the ocean, the touch of his hands at the base of her spine.

'Tess,' he whispered as their moved in perfect unison.

'Call me Trix,' she said, smiling.

# Sixty-four

'You drew all of this?' Andras asked.

Lying on the beach, grazing on the picnic of feta, juicy, sweet tomatoes, olives and fresh bread, Tess had just shown Andras her Black Velvet branding. She snatched up another olive, popping it into her mouth as she nodded at him. His trousers were back in place but he was still deliciously bare-chested owing to the fact she was wearing his shirt.

'Obviously, your laptop didn't have a drawing app and it was so slow to log into my work system, so I had to download a free program that's probably corrupted everything digital you own and draw the rest.'

'It is amazing,' Andras said, scrolling over to the next design.

'I'm pleased with it,' Tess admitted. 'At short notice and, given what I had to design with, it's actually some of my best work.' She smiled. 'And quite a lot of it is down to Corfu.'

'It is?' Andras asked.

She nodded, then pointed at the screen. 'See the name? Well, ordinarily, I would have gone for something with straight lines, thick, bold, shouting out, the way the "b" has a tail that connects to the "v" and in turn swirls to the icon of the glass, that was inspired by everything I've seen here. It's like a flag fluttering from a boat or those eucalyptus trees at Agios Spyridon beach twisting in the breeze. It says "relaxation perfection".'

He smiled at her. 'And is that how you feel now?'

'Are you referring to our "swim"?' She felt the need to make the quotation marks in the air and, as she did that, she felt her cheeks heating up as her mind rewound to thirty minutes earlier when he had melted her in every way.

'I am referring to the moment when I felt happier, more complete, than ever before,' he whispered.

'Andras ...' she breathed.

'I am sorry,' he said, leaning forward and kissing her lips. 'I do not want to make you feel afraid.'

She shook her head. 'I'm not afraid, just processing.'

'For me too,' he admitted.

She kissed him again, then flipped the laptop shut and turned around onto her back, gazing up at the azure sky above them. 'So, do you want me to help you with some branding for the new, improved Taverna Georgiou?'

'You would do that?'

'Of course,' she said, turning to look at him as he settled next to her, lying on his back too. 'I know I'm not here for much longer but ...' And there it was. The reason why this was never going to work. Because she was on holiday, and he wasn't.

'You know, the restaurant, it was never really my father's,' Andras said, changing the subject.

'What?' Tess exclaimed. 'But I thought it was one of those family businesses where it passed to the sons and you took over, and now Spiros is leaving, that was why your mum wanted to be involved.'

'The restaurant was my father's dream. He had worked in restaurants all his life and wanted to be the one in charge of his own place. He worked and he saved and then, finally, he got enough money to buy the taverna. But three weeks after it was his, before he could even open, he died.'

'I'm so sorry,' Tess said, reaching for his hand.

'And that's why Mama always hated the restaurant. She would become my business partner to help Spiros, and to think that she was helping me, but she believes the restaurant killed my father. The pressure of taking on a new business, the hard work he had to put in to save the money. She wanted us to sell it on again but I didn't want that. I wanted to make it work, in my father's honour, and I have.'

'Yes, you have,' Tess agreed.

'But now it's time for a change,' he said.

'With your new ideas for events.'

'Not just that,' he said, turning over on his side and looking at her.

'No?'

'The restaurant is everything to me but, after my divorce, it became an obsession,' he admitted. 'I don't want it to be an obsession any more. I want it to be a passion again.' He took her hand. 'Seeing the island again, with you and Sonya, it has shown me how much I have been missing, locking myself into work all the time, not having time for anything else, not *making* time for anything else. I need time away from serving meze to make these plans for expansion and entertainments and I need time to finish building my house.'

'So, what are you saying? You're not going to wait tables any more?'

'Not all the time, no,' he replied. 'I am going to appoint a manager.'

Tess disconnected their hands and stifled a laugh. 'It killed you to say that.'

'It did not,' he retorted. Then immediately he relented. 'OK, maybe a little.'

'I think it's a good idea,' Tess told him. 'No one can survive on work alone.' The sentence echoed in her own mind. If she believed that, she wouldn't be spending every waking moment when she wasn't dating at McKenzie Falconer.

'And what about you?' Andras asked.

Rumbled. He knew her far too well already. She smiled. 'I think we were talking about your restaurant plans.'

'Hellllllooooo!'

Tess sat bolt upright at the sound of Sonya's voice. 'It's Sonya,' she said, her eyes already scouring the sand for her dress. She dipped a shoulder out of Andras's shirt before she remembered she wasn't wearing a bra today. She chanced a glance over in the direction the voice had come from, then snapped her head back. 'I think she's with the German couple!'

Andras caught her hand in his. 'Relax,' he said. 'Your dress got wet in the sea and you needed my shirt.'

She swallowed. He knew that she wasn't ready for the world to know what had happened between them. She felt bad about that, as if she had given him everything in one minute and then taken it straight away again the next.

'Andras …'

He squeezed her hand. 'It is OK.'

'Oh my! It's sooo hot, isn't it? Isn't it hot, Hans?'

'*Ja*,' the man, presumably Hans, replied. 'It is very hot for walking.'

He looked at least six foot three, had cropped ginger hair with a beard that almost reached his chest. Next to him was a tiny woman, her jet-black hair in plaits. Around both their necks were expensive-looking cameras and a set of binoculars.

'Sorry!' Sonya exclaimed. 'How rude am I, not introducing you all.' She waved a hand towards Andras and Tess. 'Hans, Elsabeth, this is Tess and Andras.'

'It is nice to meet you,' Andras said, getting to his feet and holding his hand out to Hans.

'You too. Your island, it is so wonderful,' Hans said, shaking Andras's hand.

'We have almost trekked the whole length of Corfu,' Elsabeth informed them, settling herself on the sand next to Tess. 'Today we came here for one special reason.'

'The Great White Egret.'

'I think you'll find he's the new president of America,' Tess answered.

'It's a bird,' Sonya said, sitting down. 'There are lots of them on Corfu but here, on Vidos, Hans and Elsabeth were hoping to catch them in action.'

'In action?' Tess queried.

'Mating,' Hans announced, dropping his large frame to the beach too. 'You know …' He grinned. 'In, out, shake it all about.'

Elsabeth laughed and Tess could feel Andras was looking straight at her.

'They do a dance,' Sonya said, picking up an olive and slipping it into her mouth. 'The male rises up on its legs, bright white feathers fanning out at the bottom and spiking up at the top and then he bobs and bows … up and down, down and up … Then finally he starts swooping his swan-like neck around.' Sonya laughed. 'Hans showed me a YouTube video over his *loukanika*.'

'His what?' Tess asked, finally looking up.

Andras smiled. 'Greek sausage.'

Tess baulked. Thirty minutes earlier and … no, she didn't even want to contemplate it.

'So,' Sonya asked, nudging Tess's arm. 'How did it go with the banker?'

She nodded quickly, toying with the buttons of Andras's shirt. 'It was really good, in the end.' She looked to Andras who was offering out some picnic to Hans and Elsabeth, sunlight gleaming off that gorgeous body. 'There's no firm decision yet but we're, you know, quietly hopeful.'

# Sixty-five

# Taverna Georgiou

Andras stood, his back against the wall of the restaurant, surveying everything before him. It was the start of evening service and tables were filling for their always sold-out Greek night. Pride coated his insides as he watched the staff he had trained over the years running things like clockwork. It was going to be a hard job to decide who he was going to give the position of manager to. He hadn't really groomed any of his waiters or waitresses for the role and he was starting to realise that was a mistake. Had he really not thought that one day he would want to grow and expand, not just the business, but himself? He supposed he had been holding back for so long, feeling he *had* to hold back, needing the solidity of what had grounded him after Elissa had left. He had been afraid to even think of new opportunities until he had been pushed into it by the departure of his brother and been shown something else by Tess.

'Help me.' It was Spiros's voice in his ear and he turned his head, seeing his brother at his shoulder. 'I have Mama telling me she expects a grandchild within six months and I have Kira telling me she wants to run her own catering business when we get to Parga.' Spiros shook his head. 'I do not know which one I fear more, and I am sure it takes longer than six months to grow a baby.'

Andras put a hand on his shoulder. 'There is nothing to be afraid about. Kira wanting some independence is a good thing.'

'It is?' Spiros asked, sounding very unsure.

'Of course.' He smiled. 'If she has a business to look after she will not have time to get bored with you.'

Spiros scowled. 'This is not the time for jokes. My wedding is tomorrow.'

'And it is going to be a beautiful day,' Andras assured him. 'Perhaps I will soon have good news for you too.'

'You will?'

'I went to see the bank today. I am hopeful for a loan from them.'

'Oh.'

There was something about Spiros's tone that spiked at him. He did not seem excited or particularly interested about this development.

Andras continued, 'I know that it will take a week or so for the money to come through, if they agree, but—'

'Mama has given me the money.' Spiros dropped his head.

'What?' Andras exclaimed.

'I'm sorry, Andras. We needed some cash to pay some bills on our new house and Mama was there and … I could not say no. I could not afford to say no. But no papers were signed. That is between you and me. We will work it out.'

As much as he wanted to be angry about this development he had held out on his brother for too long. He knew that. He would just have to speak to his mother. Ensure that she realised that the money she had given Spiros was just a loan, that he intended to pay her back and keep control of his business.

'It is OK,' he told his brother, patting his shoulder.

'It is?'

He nodded. 'Mama and I will work it out. You just concentrate on your wedding and the move ... and Kira.'

'I have nothing to be nervous about, right?' Spiros asked, putting his hands into the pockets of his jeans and looking rather like someone heading for Death Row.

'Nothing at all,' Andras insisted. 'Except maybe what happened to Uncle Dimitri if you put a foot out of place tomorrow.'

'Tomorrow I am going to ask her,' Spiros announced.

'Ask what?'

'I am going to ask Mama what happened to Uncle Dimitri.'

Andras smiled. 'Then you must tell me if it is worse than any of us have imagined.'

Spiros nodded and jostled Andras with his elbow. 'Very soon you will be free of Mama's plans for you and Marietta. She will be going back to the south of the island soon.' Spiros laughed. 'No more fake girlfriends, huh?'

He smiled but it didn't reach his eyes. Should he tell his brother the truth? That he had feelings for Tess, feelings that he had never believed would be possible.

'Spiro ...' he began.

'Spiro!' It was their mother, standing in the centre of the room and beckoning her younger son.

'What have I done this time? The donkey is well again, I have been pinned and measured a thousand times for my costume, my hair is cut shorter than I would like and I have arranged for the pharmacist to make a herbal remedy to try to stop Helena fainting.' He shook his head. 'As every day goes by I come to realise why you didn't get married the traditional way, Andras.'

Andras clapped a hand to his brother's shoulder. 'One more day, brother ... and everything changes.'

'Spiro! Come here, your Auntie Tadita wants to dance with you!'

'Auntie Tadita,' Spiros said to Andras. 'Have we met before?'

'I think she is the one who squeezes a little too hard,' Andras answered.

'Andras, they all squeeze too hard.' Spiros let out a breath. 'Rescue me if I am not released in fifteen minutes.'

# Sixty-six

# Kalami Cove Apartments

'I've had a really, really brilliant day!' Sonya announced, slicking lip gloss over her lips.

The women were sat outside on their terrace, an open bottle of retsina on the little table, a half-empty bag of oregano crisps alongside it. Tess's eyes were on the photo of her and Andras she had taken on that first boat trip, the one she still hadn't shared on social media.

'Did you have a brilliant day? After the boring banking?' Sonya asked.

'What?' Tess looked up from her phone.

'You're not on Hooked Up again, are you?' Sonya looked to Tess's phone. 'Oh that's a lovely photo. When did you take that?'

'At the start of the holiday, you know, Andras's first day as our guide man.'

Sonya sighed. 'We've done so much here, haven't we?'

'We have,' Tess agreed. 'It's been …' She sought for the right word. 'Special.'

'So,' Sonya started. 'Have you thought about Andras? Whether there might be something real there?'

She had done nothing but think about him since they had made love on Vidos Island. On the boat back to Corfu

Town, surrounded by Hans, Elsabeth and Sonya with binoculars trained on the wildlife, she had watched Andras, strong hands holding the side of the boat, dark hair moving in the breeze, his shirt covering that taut torso. They hadn't had a chance to talk about what happened next, but perhaps neither of them had any answers.

'I don't know,' Tess replied. She picked up her glass of wine with a smile and put it to her lips. 'Not everything has to have a plan, does it?'

'No, I suppose not. Although I do find a plan helps focus you on what's important.'

A rap on the door of their apartment drew their attention to inside and Tess looked at Sonya. 'Are you expecting someone?'

'Maybe it's Andras?' she suggested.

'We said we would be at the taverna for eight for the Greek night, and whatever craziness Isadora has in store,' Tess reminded her friend.

'Perhaps it's Alex with some more towels. I did ask him for some more towels when we went past the bar earlier.' Sonya got up. 'I'll go.'

Tess looked back to her phone and pressed on the contacts icon. Her last calls. Rachel and those missed calls from her mum ...

A scream from inside had Tess's phone tumbling to the table and she shot up off her chair ready to attack whatever had made Sonya shriek, even if it was a carpenter bee.

'Sonya?' Tess called.

'What are you doing here?' Sonya exclaimed to the door of their apartment.

Tess's mouth dropped open as she made it inside and saw who was standing there. Tousled blond hair, stone-coloured

cargo pants and a T-shirt declaring 'Eat, Sleep, Civil War'.
'Joey.'

'Hello, Tess,' Joey greeted soberly. He turned his attention
back to Sonya. 'Sonya, can we talk?'

# Sixty-seven

# Taverna Georgiou

Joey was here in Corfu. Tess hadn't really known what to do and neither, it seemed, had Sonya. There had been a lot of opening and closing of her mouth before any words had made it out. And the very first thing her best friend had said was, 'I'm sorry, the air is artificial in here.'

There had been an awkward moment with Joey's backpack – whether to put it down, whether to leave it on his shoulder – and then Tess had decided to call the shots. Ushering them both through to the terrace, she grabbed a fresh glass, another bottle of wine from the fridge and made them sit at the table. They needed time to talk, without any spectators, and, telling Sonya she was going to Georgiou's and she only needed to call/text/send a carrier egret and she would come back, she left them alone.

Now, having taken the beach way, Tess was stood outside the taverna, looking up at the fairy-lit, wooden picture window frames, pots of riotous buds of colour spilling over the stone-work, just as she had that very first evening on the island.

'Excuse me. Would you like a table?'

She smiled to herself before she looked up, the voice sending delicious ripples through her. Andras was stood at the top of the small flight of steps, dressed in his uniform of black trousers and white shirt, a little open at the neck. It was a modern-day

Shirley Valentine scene but she didn't care, because to her it wasn't clichéd, it was pretty much perfect.

'Yes, please,' she replied, moving forward and stepping onto the first step. 'For one.'

'For one?' he queried.

'Sonya's boyfriend, he's here. He just turned up at our apartment.'

'And they do not want to eat?' Andras asked as she took another step up.

'It's complicated with them at the moment. I've left them with wine and some crisps but I hope, when they've talked, they will come down here.'

She stood on the last step, finally right next to him, and breathed in his scent. Citrus, pine, mixing with jasmine in the air …

'A table for three then,' Andras responded. 'We will remain hopeful.' He trailed a finger down her arm and immediately goosebumps she couldn't control broke out. He finally clasped her hand with his, gently brushing her skin with his thumb.

'I really want to kiss you,' Tess blurted out. She couldn't believe she had said that. Her heart was literally beating out of her chest from just standing next to him, holding his hand.

'You do not need to ask,' he replied softly.

She leant forward and brushed her lips against his, feeling that immediate spark of passion flow through her.

'There is no Susan?'

Tess flew back from Andras at the sound of Isadora's voice. She cleared her throat before answering. '*Kalispera*, Isadora. No, Susan is with her boyfriend tonight.'

'Her boyfriend. Is he Greek?'

Tess shook her head. 'No, he's English.'

'Then you will sit with us,' Isadora announced.

'Mama ...' Andras began to protest.

'You do not want me to get to know better the woman that you claim to love?' Isadora queried. 'Everything is arranged for the wedding. I have time tonight.'

Another night being scrutinised like a rare species for not having babies and devoting her time to business. Or, perhaps, simply enjoying the ambience, the food and the company and not thinking too hard about anything else.

'That would be lovely,' Tess answered. 'Thank you.'

'Good,' Isadora stated. 'Come, you can help me match up Marietta with Victor. He is a good boy and he has very nice eyes.'

Tess looked to Andras, an expression of surprise on her face. He shrugged and picked up a menu.

Andras delivered platters of tzatziki, olives, taramasalata and houmous, together with griddled pitta bread, to table ten then looked over to the table his family were dining at. Tess was smiling, laughing with his mother over something and Kira was joining in, showing the women something on her dress. He picked up a jug of water and made his way over to them.

'It is for luck,' Kira said, fingering the brooch. 'It was my grandmother's. It is solid silver she had from when she was a child.'

'It's very pretty,' Tess remarked.

'It is for luck,' Isadora stated.

'I know,' Tess said. 'Kira said. There are things we do for luck in English weddings too, you know.'

'There are?' Isadora asked.

Tess nodded. 'We have a rhyme, well, like a rhyme, it goes ... something old, something new, something borrowed, something blue.'

'What happens after you say the song?' Kira asked.

'Do you spit?' Isadora inquired.

Tess shook her head. 'No. The bride has to have all these things, so something old – like your brooch from your grandmother, Kira – something new, the dress maybe is new or shoes; something borrowed, one of your wedding party could lend you something to wear on the day, a ring or a clip for your hair maybe ... then something blue.'

'What can I have that is blue?' Kira asked, eyes wide like not having the blue item was going to scupper her entire wedding plans.

'More water?' Andras asked, leaning towards empty glasses and filling them up.

'Well, in UK weddings brides tend to have a garter,' Tess said.

'A garden?' Isadora asked.

'A what?' Kira added.

'It's a, well, it's a piece of lace really, elasticated lace, that you put ... on your thigh.'

Andras made that the moment to get close and pour Tess's drink.

'You tie something to your leg?' Isadora asked. 'It sounds ridiculous.'

'Yes,' Tess said, nodding. 'It is a bit crazy. And they itch quite a bit.'

'You have worn one?' Kira asked.

'You have worn one for a *wedding*?' Isadora snapped.

'I ... well ...'

'Tess, could you come with me?' Andras said, putting his hand on her shoulder and encouraging her away from this pit of fire she was about to fall into.

'You have been married!' Isadora continued, shock coating her voice.

'Tess, come on,' Andras ordered, pulling her chair back for her.

'No,' Tess answered, her voice shaking a little. 'I haven't been married.'

'Tess ...' Andras begged. He knew how it felt for her to talk about this and he didn't want her to have to go through it again.

'My fiancé left me at the church,' she said. 'He decided not to marry me.'

Kira shook her head, picking up her glass of wine. 'And that is why you throw yourself into work, work, work, all of the time, because you cannot get over the shame and the devastation.' She patted Tess's hand. 'And that is why you have all the other men and pretend to be Andras's girlfriend.'

Andras gripped the chair and closed his eyes. Spiros had told Kira. And now Kira had blabbed the truth after too much wine.

'*Pretend*.'

The word was said by Isadora and was directed straight at Tess. He wasn't going to let his mother attack her.

'I am sorry,' Kira said, putting her hand to her mouth. 'I am sorry, I am talking with the wine and—'

'OK, that's enough,' Andras said.

'Enough of what?' Isadora asked, turning in her chair and looking up at him.

'Kira is right,' Andras sighed. 'It is true. Tess isn't someone I met earlier in the summer, in Paleokastritsa. She is someone I simply met when she turned up at the restaurant and we struck a deal. She would pretend to be my girlfriend and I would give her a tour of the island and unlimited Wi-Fi.'

'I do not believe this!' Isadora exclaimed. 'You have lied to us. Lied to all of your family.'

'Because you made me!' Andras shot back. 'With your constant pushing with Marietta. I had no choice.'

'You could have told the truth,' Isadora slammed.

'You do not want to listen to the truth. You just want people to do as they are told. All the time. With this wedding. With the restaurant that does not even mean anything to you. I could not breathe. I am always the one you think made a mistake marrying Elissa. The one who does not know what he wants and needs to be told. Well, that isn't the case, Mama, I do know what I want.' He took a deep breath. 'I want this business to flourish, I want to finish building my house, I want some balance in my life and ... I want Tess.'

A collective gasp went up from the table.

A gentle Greek tune began to emanate from the musicians at the far end of the restaurant but all Tess could concentrate on was Andras's words. *I want Tess*. She didn't know what to do. She was glued to the seat of her chair, feeling the eyes of Andras's family on her. Should she get up? Should she stay where she was? How did Andras's declaration make her feel?

'Mama,' Andras carried on, 'in a way, I need to thank you.' He rested a hand on Tess's shoulder again. 'If you had not pushed and pushed and backed me into a corner, then I would never have made a connection with Tess. And to think about not having her come into my life, well, I cannot even imagine it now.' He took a breath. 'I do not want to imagine it.'

'What are you trying to tell me, Andras?' Isadora asked. 'That you meet this Patricia last week and you are in ...'

'In love with her,' he said boldly. 'I am in love with her, yes.'

Something inside her was shifting again. Making love on the beach was one thing but this, these words, in front of his whole family, in his taverna, this was something else. It was filling her to the brim with a euphoric feeling she had never known before, but was it real? Could it be hers? Did she want it?

'I am sorry, Tess,' he breathed. 'I should not be saying this to my family before I say it to you.' He squatted down so he was level with her and took her hand in his. 'I know there are so many questions to be answered, but I know what is in my heart and for once, I am listening to it.'

'Andras ...'

'You do not have to say anything here or at all. I just don't want to pretend we are pretending any more,' he whispered. 'I want my feelings for you to be clear.'

How much clearer could he be? He had worshipped her, body and soul, on Vidos Island, and he was doing it again now, finally telling his mother how he felt, telling everyone how he felt about her.

'I feel the same,' she whispered tentatively. 'And it makes me so happy, but so frightened ... and I don't know what to do about it.'

He took both her hands then, squeezing them tight, before bringing them to his lips and kissing them. 'Dance with me?' he asked.

She nodded and got to her feet.

'Andras,' Isadora called.

Spiros came behind his mother's chair and put his hands on her shoulders. 'Mama, let them dance. There will be time for talking later.'

# Sixty-eight

Tess rested her head against Andras's chest as he swayed her in time to the heavy lament of the *bouzouki*. Right now she wanted to stay in this moment for ever, wrapped in his arms, not thinking about anything else but how perfectly content she felt, here under a Greek sunset in this pretty little village, with this gorgeous man.

'I am so sorry!'

It was Kira, swinging up to them in Spiros's arms, hair whipping Tess's shoulder as they began to dance next to them. Tess shook her head. 'It doesn't matter. It wasn't your fault.'

'No,' Spiros said. 'It was mine. For thinking my wife could keep a secret.'

'I am not your wife until tomorrow,' Kira responded stiffly.

'Stop this,' Andras ordered. 'If anyone is to blame then it is me. I am the one who made this situation. But, on the whole, I am thankful for it.' He tightened his hold on Tess.

'It is unbelievable,' Spiros said, a smile on his face. 'My wedding brought you together with someone from England.'

'*Our* wedding,' Kira corrected, playfully cuffing his arm. 'Just because you are a man, not everything is just yours.'

Spiros held his hands up. 'I surrender. I will do as I am told. I know my place.'

Tess raised her head from Andras and looked up, drinking him in. 'This is almost where it started,' she whispered. 'Here, dancing to the *bouzouki*.'

He nodded. 'I remember.' He smiled. 'I remember you drove a hard bargain for your Internet connection.'

'And hardly had time to use it,' she answered.

'Tess,' Andras said.

'Yes.'

'It is Sonya.'

Tess looked to the restaurant entrance and there was her friend and Joey. They were holding hands and Sonya was wearing the biggest smile.

'Go to her,' Andras said, stepping back from their embrace. 'Tell them we still have food.'

Tess smiled, squeezed his hands and headed off across the stone floor.

She raced towards Sonya, hoping against hope that everything was all right, that the smile was genuine, that their talk over the Greek wine she had left them had ironed everything out. She didn't have to wait long. As soon as Sonya saw her she let out a shriek of excitement and bounded forward, gathering Tess up in a tight squeeze.

'I'm engaged!' Sonya exclaimed. 'Not *almost* engaged, actually, properly, engaged! Look!'

Sonya shot out her hand and on the ring finger of her left hand was a beautiful gold ring with a diamond centre stone and three rubies above, creating a crown shape.

'It's Georgian,' Sonya said. 'It's from the 1780s and it's a symbol of a triumphant love.' She put her hand to her chest, as if emotion was about to burst out of her every pore.

Tess gripped her hand. 'I am so, so happy for you.' She looked over Sonya's shoulder at Joey then whispered, 'So, everything is all right, with Margate and …'

Sonya nodded her head. 'He wasn't in Margate, just like you said. One of his battle re-enactment pals – Eddie Red

Beard, always a bit of a pain in the gluteus maximus – thought it would be funny to take Joey's phone. Then he lost it, probably at that hotel, which is why a woman answered it when I rang and didn't say "Joey's phone".'

'So, Ceri being tagged ...'

'Eddie Red Beard went to school with her, before either of them chose battle re-enactment sides. But he knew very well what rumours that would start.'

'No merger plans then?'

Sonya laughed. 'No.'

'And the needing space, and the baby thing?' Tess ventured.

'We talked it all out. He told me how he had been feeling. I told him ... I told him I couldn't have children ... and it changed everything.' Sonya looked to Joey who was standing a little awkwardly, hands in the pockets of his cargo shorts. 'He's hit thirty-five and had a bit of a pre-mid-life crisis. He was worried that Dunelm Mill was one step towards whole weekends in B&Q, retirement and, well, death. I told him all the things we've done here, how I wished he had been here to experience it with me – no offence – and how I am open to absolutely anything! Just because I like mooching around craft stores and tea rooms, doesn't mean that's what I want to do all the time, I'm all for new interests and different ...'

'Positions?' Tess offered with a grin.

Sonya blushed. 'Well, yes, and he said that when he mentioned children he wasn't really sure that was what he wanted *right* now, but he wanted it to be something we thought about.' She sighed. 'Tommy Blue Jacket's just had a baby and it was palmed around the re-enactment society trussed up in a leatherette and lace Babygro looking very cute a few months ago. I think that was the catalyst.'

'Do all the re-enactment society members have coloured nicknames?' Tess inquired.

'Joey is Joey Jade Horn.'

'Good Lord!' She wasn't sure she was going to be able to look at him the same way again.

'But he said one thing he knew he didn't want was the space he thought he did want. And he wanted me.' Sonya heaved a gigantic breath. 'And that's when he got down on one knee, between the chair and the trailing bougainvillea, about three tiles along, and asked me to marry him.'

'I'm so happy for you.'

'And so, talking about babies is on the table, for the future maybe.' Sonya let out a contented sigh. 'Either the adoption route or the Elton John route, and everything is going to be perfect ... if we can get some food. I'm so hungry!' Sonya looked around at all the half-empty plates as diners got out of their places to join in with the Greek dancing.

'Come on,' Tess said. 'Let's find you both a table and teach Joey all about a proper Greek meze.'

Sonya grinned. 'I'm afraid we ate all the crisps. Oh, and Hector's in our garden again. Alex put a box over him.' She linked arms with Tess. 'So, did I miss anything here?'

'Nothing much,' Tess answered. 'We had lovely food, wine, a bit of dancing. Oh, and Kira told Isadora I was Andras's pretend girlfriend.'

'What?'

'As I said ... not much.'

# Sixty-nine

His hair damp with sweat from the Greek dancing, Andras joined with his restaurant clientele in applauding the professional musicians who, like every week here, had put on an amazing show. Tomorrow the restaurant would be closed for the first time ever for a private event: Spiros and Kira's wedding.

He shook hands with diners and nodded at others as he made his way through the restaurant to begin the task of clearing up. Tess was sitting with Sonya and her boyfriend at table seventeen, coffee grounds burning in a pot next to the candle after the man had been savaged by mosquitos within a few moments of sitting down. Kira was sitting on Spiros's lap at the family table, brushing back his newly shorn hair, then squeezing his cheeks and laughing at the comical results. It was then he saw his mother, quietly making her way towards the exit, leaning a little more heavily on her stick than usual. He swallowed. Despite the formidable exterior, she was getting older, and they really needed to talk.

'Mama,' he called out as he got closer.

She didn't turn around. 'I am tired, Andras. It is a busy day tomorrow. I need to get home to bed. Fotis is coming to collect me.'

'In his truck?' Andras queried.

'Yes, in his truck.'

'But, Mama, how will you ...'

'I have been getting into trucks for years, Andras. Your father had a truck if you remember.'

He did remember. He remembered how much fun it was, clambering up into the lorry with Spiros and going out for the day in this huge wagon with space for everyone, but not at all conducive to the Corfu roads.

'Mama, please, stop,' Andras said, taking her arm as she descended the steps to the beach.

'I said I am tired, Andras.'

'And disappointed in me, I know,' he replied, releasing a breath. 'Please, Mama, sit down with me?'

With his arm, he indicated one of the beachside tables ahead of them, clear of crockery, but with a candle still burning from the previous diners. For a moment he didn't know if his mother was going to agree, but then she moved, stick leading the way, stabbing at the shingle and sand.

He pulled out a chair for her.

'Why are you fussing around me, Andras? I am as capable of sitting in a chair as I am climbing into a truck.'

'I know. I am just …'

'About to get your heart broken again.' Isadora let out a furious sigh that somehow turned into a sob and had the Greek woman grabbing at the handbag over her arm and searching its contents.

Andras took a napkin from the holder on the table and passed it to her. She snatched it quickly and covered her nose, letting out a tremendous 'honk' as she blew into it.

'This is all your father's fault,' Isadora stated, screwing the napkin up in her fist.

'What?'

'You are the same. You have feelings so quickly. You do not think about the long-term consequences.'

'What are you talking about?'

'With your father it was *this* place,' Isadora exclaimed, eyes going to the lit-up exterior of the taverna. 'This restaurant. He loved it. He wanted it. And it killed him.'

'Mama, the taverna is a success. I am going to make sure it becomes *even more* of a success. As *my* business.' He sighed. 'Spiro told me you gave him the money. You didn't need to do that.'

'He needed it now. What sort of mother would I be if I did not help him?'

'I know. But I am arranging a loan with the bank. I will pay you back.'

'Before you leave for England?' Isadora snapped.

'Mama, I am not leaving for England,' Andras said.

'No? That is not what comes next after this week of deep and meaningful love that was fake at the beginning, but is now everything you have been waiting for all your life?'

'Mama,' he swallowed. 'What I feel for Tess is real, no matter how it came about.'

'Like with Elissa? Trying to get you to leave the island with her. Always wanting something bigger, something better, just like your father with this restaurant.'

'If Elissa had asked me to leave the island with her then I would have,' Andras informed him.

'And if Patricia asks you to?'

'Her name is Tess, Mama,' he breathed. 'Just Tess. And she won't ask me to leave the island.'

'Why not? Because she will move here, marry you, take half the restaurant and wait for you to die through working too hard?'

He shook his head. 'No.'

'Then what?' Isadora demanded to know.

'Because both of us are too scared to even talk about a future together. Because, a man left her at her own wedding and she never loved again and ... because Elissa ...' He stopped talking, emotion burning its way up his throat. Could he really tell his mother the truth about the way his marriage had ended? 'Because Elissa ...' he began again.

'Fell in love with Stamatis Alexopoulos and was carrying his baby,' Isadora stated.

The breath flew from Andras and he crushed his hands together. 'You knew.' He swallowed. 'You knew, all this time.'

Isadora nodded, tears in her eyes. 'And every day I would see you so broken, so heartbroken, working and working and paying too much attention to holidaymakers and it was breaking my soul into pieces because of what she did.' Isadora gasped. 'I did not like the girl. I did not want you to marry the girl. But you made your choice and no matter what I thought about it, I did not want my son to be so ... torn apart like that.' The tears fell from her eyes like the waterfalls at Nymfes, and Andras reached for her hands, shielding them with his.

'You should have told me,' he said softly.

'No, Andras,' Isadora replied. 'It was up to *you* to tell *me* ... but I knew you would not and I do not blame you. I had put up the barriers when I told you how much I disapproved. I just ... did not want you to leave. Selfishly, it has always been about not wanting you to leave.' She took her hands back, wiping at her eyes. 'Spiro, he needs to leave, to learn, the boy does not have your independent nature. He needs Kira as much as she needs him but you ...'

'You made me independent, Mama. *You* are independent. Look how you lead the women of the village, look how you have got on with things since Papa died, look how you have planned the whole of this wedding tomorrow.' Andras squeezed her hands. 'You are part of who I am, not just Papa.'

His mother did not reply, still sniffing.

'But you have to know that I will always make my own choices. In life ... and in love.' The sound of the lull of the waves on the beach made him pause. 'I am no more right for Marietta than she is for me. You must know that. You must see that.'

'I know that she would do everything she could to make you happy.'

'But, Mama, that is not the kind of relationship I want, or the type of relationship *anybody* wants. Where is the partnership? Where is the equality?'

'Can you see Tess picking the olive harvest and making *stifado*?' Isadora asked.

Andras smiled as the image came to mind. Tess dressed simply, plucking ripe olives from trees, shaking the branches, twigs getting caught up in her hair. He shook his head. 'I can see it, but it would be a terrible idea.'

'See!'

'No, it is a good thing, Mama.' He leant back in his chair, stretching out his legs. 'Because I don't want Tess to pick olives or make me dinner. Those are not reasons to have someone in your life. In fact, they are the least important reasons to have someone in your life.'

'But ...' Isadora began, leaning forward a little.

'Was that why Papa married you? For your cooking?'

'Andras, you know that your father was a far better cook than I am.'

'So, you married *him* for *his* cooking?'

She shook her head, but there was the beginning of a smile at the corner of her mouth. 'We fell in love,' she admitted.

'There was no way I was going to let him be taken in by my cousin Leda's bottle-blonde hair.' She tutted. 'That girl was always such an attention seeker.'

'Mama, I do not know what will happen with Tess,' Andras admitted. 'Perhaps nothing; perhaps everything. But whatever does happen, it will be *our* choice, because we came together by chance and somewhere along the line, despite all the odds, we fell in love.'

'Andras,' Isadora said, her eyes once again full of tears. 'I just want you to be happy.'

'I am happy, Mama,' he answered. 'Happier than I have ever been.'

# Seventy

# Andras Georgiou's home

The moon was full and almost as round and fat as the tortoise Andras had carried up the mountain to his house.

'How does he get out?' Tess whispered as they made their way across the lawn to the pen Andras had built.

'I do not know, but if my mother catches him anywhere near the restaurant ...'

He didn't need to finish the sentence for her. 'Uncle Dimitri?'

Andras smiled at her. 'Spiros swears he is going to ask our mother exactly what happened to Uncle Dimitri tomorrow.'

'You mean no one actually knows?' Tess asked.

He laughed. 'No.' He put Hector back into the wooden home, making sure the latch was secure. Then he moved over to Tess, taking her hands in his. 'You are sure you want to stay tonight?'

She smiled. He was always so concerned for her feelings, not wanting to push, never expecting anything. She leant forward, lightly brushing her lips with his. 'Yes, I'm sure. Besides, I could hardly stay in the apartment with a newly engaged couple, playing a very awkward raspberry.'

'Or blackberry,' Andras added. 'Like your clients.'

'Exactly,' Tess replied.

'Then I will make coffee,' he said, leading the way to the property. 'Or something stronger?'

'Still no Dr Pepper I presume?' Tess asked, hopefully.

'No,' Andras answered. 'But I do have Coke.'

Andras couldn't keep his eyes off her. He had made coffee and every so often, as he waited for the machine to brew, he had looked through his sparse, unfinished kitchen, just to gaze at Tess, sitting on his sofa, shoes off, bare feet up on the cushions, staring through the full-width windows to the moonlit view of the sea beyond. It seemed surreal. To have someone sharing his space, someone he already cared so deeply about.

'What?' Tess asked, smiling as she took the Coke he handed her.

'Having you here.' He sat down on the sofa beside her.

'Yes?' she asked.

'I like it,' he replied, finding her hand and entwining his fingers with hers.

'You do?'

He nodded, edging his body closer to hers. 'I do.'

'Be careful there, Andras, you'll be getting very close to repeating Spiros's wedding vows.' She gave him a soft smile.

'The wedding is tomorrow,' he reminded her.

'I know. Isn't the whole village in lock down and a whole Greek armada sailing to the church?'

'Something like this,' he agreed. 'Then the day after ...'

Her fingers tensed next to his and she shifted, reaching forward to put her glass on the coffee table.

'I go home,' she said.

He swallowed, in reaction to how those words hit out at his heart. He wanted to say so much but part of him was still holding back, not wanting to address the inevitable.

The silence was deafening. She was looking at him, those azure eyes affecting him in so many different ways. What did he want to say?

'Tess ...'

'Andras ...'

'Please, you speak first.'

She shook her head. 'No, you can.'

He took a breath, readjusting his position on the sofa, one arm resting on the seatback, fingers closing over the fabric. 'I know that we do not live in the same place but that should not mean that we cannot be in the same place for some of the time ...' He sighed. 'I am not making this very clear.'

She shook her head. 'I know what you're trying to say.'

'You do?'

'Yes.' She nodded. 'You want us to try to see if we can make this ... this connection between us ... something more than just for this holiday.'

He nodded. 'I would like to try that, but what do you feel?'

He was almost holding his breath as she released hers. What if she did not feel the same? What if the moments they had shared on Corfu were going to be the only ones they had together?

'You know everything about me, Andras,' she said in a voice that was barely more than a whisper. 'You are the only one who has ever known everything about me. And there is a reason for that. I just ... I don't ... that is, I'm not very good ... at making commitments that last longer than six weeks, and ...'

'I know,' he replied, squeezing her hand. 'I understand.'

'When I get home, when you're here without me, neither of us know how we are going to feel,' she said. 'What feels real here, under that perfect sky, with all the cray-cray family stuff going on, it might feel different when there's some distance between us.'

She was being wholly honest and he valued that. He knew his feelings for her were strong, but she was tapping on the brake, being sensible, and it was entirely the right thing to do.

'Andras, I've given you more than I've ever given anyone since my wedding-that-didn't-happen. That means everything to me.'

'It means everything to me too,' he reassured her.

'I think, what I'm trying to say is, let's make the most of how we feel now, and let the future take care of itself.'

Had she really said that? It sounded like a TV commercial for over-sixties life insurance and Tess's heart was drumming like the baseline of a Tinchy Stryder track. She wanted to be all in. She felt all in. She wanted to tell Andras that she was falling in love with him, words to back up her actions on the beach when she had literally hummed with ecstasy. But her psyche, the defence mechanism she had so maintained so beautifully, was still urging caution.

'Andras ...' It felt like a brush-off and she didn't want that. She hadn't said nearly enough.

'You do not need to say any more,' he insisted, still holding her hand in his. 'We have both been through difficult times, both thinking that these feelings could not be for us in the future.'

'There's more to it than that.' She sighed. 'I need to put some things right at home before I can even think about moving on.'

*Moving on*. Was she really going to finally be able to do that? It had always seemed so impossible and maybe it still wasn't clear cut, but the one thing she did know was she *was* going to speak to her mum. She was going to actually have a conversation with her about the wedding-that-wasn't, about what happened afterwards, about how sorry she was for the loss of all the money and how she had tried to go some way towards saving to pay it back to her and her dad. Even if it didn't rescue their relationship, she will have done everything she could.

'I want to try, Andras,' she said. 'To move on.'

'Me too,' he responded.

She looked into those chocolate-brown eyes, then shifted her gaze a little lower to rest on those sultry lips. The only moving on she wanted to engage in right at this moment involved her on top of him sans clothes.

'Show me some more of the house,' Tess purred.

'What would you like to see?' Andras asked, bringing her hand to his mouth and dropping hot kisses on her fingertips.

'Does your bedroom have a sea view?' she asked.

# Seventy-one

The view from Andras's bedroom was stunning, but the light streaming through the glass as the sun rose had woken Tess early. Now, a cup of steaming coffee in her hands, she took in the baby-blue sky, small white scudding clouds moving across the horizon, the sea shimmering with sunlight as small fishing boats bobbed and dipped amid its undulating peaks and troughs. And nearer, on Andras's thick, green lawn, there was Hector, a large paw pushing at the latch of his cage.

'*Kalimera.*'

Tess turned away from the window at the sound of Andras's greeting and held her coffee mug in the air. 'Morning. I made you coffee. It's by your side of the bed.'

*Your* side of the bed. She had slept here one night and had claimed a side? 'On the bedside table,' she corrected.

'Thank you,' he said, pushing the sheet down off his body and shifting on the mattress.

Tess watched every abdominal muscle tweak with each minute movement. It was like having your own up-close-and-personal Calvin Klein ad.

'You are wearing my shirt again,' Andras commented, taking a sip from his mug.

'You want it back?' Tess asked, prowling towards him, eyes heavy with seducing intentions she hoped he was taking note of.

'I think I might,' he responded, his eyes darkening.

She sprung, catlike, on to the bed and slipped a hand either side of his frame, holding herself above his body, just as she had last night.

'Then take it back,' she teased, voice low as her erogenous zones started having a party.

He moved to kiss her and she jerked her face away and out of his reach. 'Oh no, not fast,' she mimicked. 'We are going to do this very, very slowly. What was it? *Arga?*'

'Tess,' he breathed, voice straining as his hands began to wander to the buttons of his shirt on her body.

Who was she trying to kid? She wanted his lips on hers more than she was craving drinks from the Coca-Cola company. She pressed her mouth to his then felt him spin her around and over on to the mattress until his frame was on top of hers.

'I want to rip that shirt away,' he breathed. 'And then I want to kiss every part of you.'

'Yes,' Tess said, her body quaking with anticipation.

He held her wrists, dropping another sizzling kiss on her mouth. 'But ... it is past eight o' clock.' He let her go and vaulted from the bed, stretching his arms in the air and elongated his torso like he was doing it for her personal viewing pleasure.

'Andras, please,' she begged. 'A Greek eight o'clock. We can wait for a Greek eight o'clock, you know, the one that doesn't really exist.'

He grinned. 'We have to meet Spiro at my mother's house. I have to shave him and the other men have to help him to get dressed.'

Tess sat bolt upright. 'Did you say *shave* him?' She blinked. 'Like remove all his body hair?'

'No,' Andras laughed. 'Just his face.'

She pouted, feeling a little frustrated. 'And what do I do while you're shaving?'

'Anything you want,' he replied. 'You can stay here, make some breakfast, sit in the garden, relax ...'

'What time do I have to be by the boat for the church?'

'Eleven o'clock.'

'And you're sure your mother isn't going to ban me from the vicinity like she has banned the tortoise?' Tess asked. 'I mean, all Hector has done is raid the restaurant kitchen, he hasn't ever lied to her.'

'Or said that he does not want babies,' Andras added.

She grabbed a pillow and threw it at him, watching it cuff his shoulder. 'That's not funny.'

He was moving back across the wooden floor towards her then, that body of perfection shifting closer, igniting her arousal and sending her stomach into KitchenAid mode.

'My mother knows how I feel about you,' Andras said. 'I told you, we have talked.' He kissed her shoulder.

'And Marietta isn't going to be putting some Greek ugliness hex on me or anything?' She shivered as Andras's lips reached her collarbone.

'I will still love you even if you end up looking like Medusa,' Andras responded.

'*Love* me,' Tess whispered, the words feeling unfamiliar.

Andras stood back a little, keeping his face level with hers. 'Is that too much? To say that, in this moment?'

Was it? He had shown her in so many ways how he felt and said so too, just not with that four-letter word beginning with 'l' that always seemed to put a different slant on it. She shook her head. 'No.'

'No?' he queried.

'No, it isn't too much,' she answered. 'It's nice. I like it.'

He kissed her mouth. 'Good,' he responded. 'Because, when I mentioned Medusa, I felt sure you would be focused on the snakes.'

She hit his arm playfully and he recoiled, laughing.

'I have to shower,' he said, walking towards the door.

Just the thought of that delicious torso under hot running water was enough to make her labia throb. She picked up the pillow and hugged it to her body.

Then Andras put his head around the bedroom door. 'Tess,' he called.

'Yes?'

He smiled. 'I have a double shower.'

She had never run so fast.

# Seventy-two

# Kalami Bay

'My engagement ring changes colour almost every time I look at it,' Sonya announced. She held out her hand, twisting and turning it in the sunlight like it was some sort of heat-activated mood ring. 'See how the rubies are dark now, like Morello cherries, and now ...' She moved her hand again. 'Lighter, like rose wine.'

'Is Joey OK?' Tess asked, waving a hand in front of her face to ward off the heat that was stifling, here on the wooden jetty on the beach. Joey was stood a few yards away, carefully positioned in the only bit of shade available from the overhang of a sign advertising boat hire.

'It's the heat,' Sonya answered. 'We had to get five fans for the bedroom last night. At first, given the stale air issue, we were going to try without anything, but then Joey's bites started itching and he started scratching and I said cooling him off was the only way to ease things.'

'I was hoping you would be hotting things up in the bedroom, not cooling things down,' Tess remarked.

'Oh, we did that, twice, before the itching and scratching – and a little bit before I introduced him to ouzo.'

'Here they are,' Tess announced, her eyes going to the beach.

'Oh my!' Sonya exclaimed. 'Kira looks so beautiful.'

'Now you have to spit,' Tess ordered.

'What?'

'According to Greek tradition – Andras filled me in – every time someone compliments the bride today you have to spit.'

'What, here? On the floor?'

'I have no idea.'

'Let me get a tissue,' Sonya said, unzipping her handbag.

'Apparently she also has a lump of sugar under one of those gloves and a gold coin in her shoe,' Tess added.

'Goodness!'

Kira *did* look beautiful. Her abundant hair was plaited back off her face, flowers threaded into the design and her dress was simple, long and white with a lace cape over her shoulders. On her feet were the shoes all the women had signed at the pre-wedding family dinner.

Spiros led the donkey, Andras by his side, so handsome in royal blue suits, white shirts and waistcoats. Tess's skin prickled in reaction to her lover's gaze as he made his way towards the wedding guests waiting by the two large boats that would take them all on the short cruise to Agios Spyridon.

'I think I'm going to cry,' Sonya said, the tissue she had got out to spit in now serviced in wiping at her eyes. 'I wonder where she got that lace cape ... do you think that would look good on me?'

Suddenly, Tess's arm was not her own and she looked to see Isadora at her side, in the process of linking their arms together.

'You will sit with me,' Isadora stated.

Tess looked to Sonya for some sort of assistance or a get-out. This could not be good.

On board the boat, filled with both families of the wedding couple, Papa Yiannis led some holy chanting to which everyone seemed to know how to respond. Sonya and Joey were sat at the very edge of the boat, hands locked together. Tess's arm was still being softly crushed, Greek style, by Isadora, who hadn't released her grip since they had set sail.

'My son says that he loves you.' Isadora spoke low in Tess's ear.

She wasn't sure what to say. She had a feeling this was going to be a little bit like watching a sex scene on television when you were thirteen and your parents were in the same room. She opted for nodding her head.

'Andras does not love easily,' Isadora continued.

'I know,' Tess replied.

'He might seem like the strong Greek man who can take on the world but ... there is much more than that.'

'I know,' Tess repeated. 'Isadora, I should apologise for pretending to be something I wasn't when we first met. I didn't think enough about it and, before I knew it, I was in the middle of it and then ... well, here we are.' She didn't know if she had ever said as many words and said absolutely nothing at all.

'My boys,' Isadora said, shaking her head, eyes going to Andras and Spiros at the head of the vessel. 'They will do and say anything rather than tell a truth I do not want to hear and face the consequences.'

'If we are talking truths and parents,' Tess began, 'I haven't been able to tell my mother anything that wasn't about tea or mackerel hotpot for a year.'

She felt, rather than saw, Isadora's turn of head, the weight of the Greek woman's gaze on her.

'I think it is in all children,' she sighed. 'A deep despondency when you know you have done something to disappoint the ones that love you most, and you're sorry, but suddenly, somehow everything has changed.'

'You must speak with your mother,' Isadora ordered.

'I know,' Tess answered. 'I'm going to.'

Her arm was squeezed again, but this time more a reassuring pinch than boa-constrictor-on-a-mission.

'I see how Andras is with you,' Isadora said. 'And this time … I hear what he tells me.'

Tess didn't know how to respond. She looked across the boat at the main players in the wedding, watching Andras talking with his brother, then smoothing down the shoulders of his jacket.

'You make him happy,' Isadora admitted. She sniffed. 'Perhaps that is enough.' She sighed. 'I have always only wanted for him to be happy.'

'He makes me happy too,' Tess finally replied, smiling as Andras looked over at her.

'Good,' Isadora answered. 'Then today we will all be happy!' She dropped Tess's arm and stood up with the aid of her stick. 'Everybody sing! Come on! This is a wedding, not a funeral! We will sing and we will dance! *Ela!*'

# Seventy-three

# Agios Spyridon

Light from dozens of candles filled the holy space as the bride and groom stood before the priest, their family and friends, a donkey, a goat and three chickens (an odd number for luck) to become man and wife.

'What are they doing next?' Joey whispered to Sonya.

Sonya leafed through the book on her lap, eyes scrutinising the writing within. 'I'm not sure. Did they do the exchange of crowns?'

'Yes,' Tess said. 'Didn't you see? Three times of swapping.'

'It says something here about a common cup,' Sonya stated.

'I think you'll find that's called a mug,' Tess replied.

'No, there's a cup that the priest fills with wine that symbolises life and the couple each take three sips out of it to signify how they will share their life together.' Sonya looked to Joey. 'This is so traditional and lovely. Maybe we could incorporate that into our wedding.'

'Three sips of Davey Black Friar's mead,' Joey suggested.

'Oh yes! He does make a lovely mead,' Sonya agreed.

'They're walking around the table,' Tess pointed out.

'Are they?' Sonya asked. 'With candles and the Bible?' She shifted her position, looking around the large frame of Fotis who was stood in front of them.

'It looks that way,' Tess answered.

'How's Helena holding up?' Sonya asked. 'I can't see her from here.'

Tess leaned out a little. 'I can see the top of her flowered hat. I think she's still standing ... oh, they're coming down the middle of the church.'

'Did they do it?' Sonya asked. 'Are they married?'

'I think so,' Tess said. 'Everyone is smiling.'

'Kira's Uncle Timon has been smiling since we got on the boat. I think he has a hip flask of *tsipouro*.'

'What's *tsipouro*?' Joey inquired.

'A bit like mead,' Sonya said, patting his leg.

'Or battery acid,' Tess added.

Andras now had a sister-in-law and his little brother was married, about to embark on a new adventure on the Greek mainland. He couldn't be happier for him. It had been a beautiful ceremony, his mother had cried happy tears and as the prayers and traditions were being shared, he had thought only of Tess, his deep affection for her and how their meeting had changed him.

The bright sunshine greeted them as they stepped out of the church to almost an entire village full of people cheering and clapping their hands together. It seemed Agios Spyridon, like Kalami, had all come out to celebrate the wedding Greek style.

As people pumped his hands and Helena and the other young children gave out sugared almonds to everyone, he searched for Tess. He had something he wanted to give her.

'I am married!' It was Spiros, grinning like a man who was destined to spend the rest of his days with the love of his life. 'Married!'

Andras clapped him into a brotherly hug, holding him tight. 'Congratulations, Spiro. I am so happy for you.'

Spiros held Andras away from him, eying him sincerely. 'And I am happy for you, with Tess.'

Spiros shook his head and brushed some imaginary dust off his brother's suit jacket. 'She is going back to England soon.'

'She is?' Spiros inquired.

'Of course,' Andras replied. 'That is where she lives.'

'You do not think to ask her to stay?' Spiros asked. 'I know what I said before, but the way you are with her, it is like me and Kira.'

Andras smiled. 'No one is like you and Kira, Spiro.'

'I get it,' Spiros said. 'You do not want to talk about your feelings with your brother.' He opened his arms. 'But now I am married I have been bestowed with counselling properties.'

Andras let out a laugh.

'Do not mock me; ask Papa Yiannis.'

Andras drew Spiros back into a hug, squeezing hard. 'I am so proud of you, my brother.'

'Stop now, please, Kira is desperate for the photographer to capture all these crazy "emotional" pictures. I am planning to be in none of those!'

Andras stepped back and, as he did so, there was Tess, standing under the large eucalyptus tree seeking shelter from the direct sunlight. The cream, light fabric dress she was wearing moved with the gentle sea breeze, her hair too, that beautiful hair …

'Go to her,' Spiros ordered. 'Give her that candle I saw you put into your pocket.'

Andras smiled at his brother then stepped towards Tess.

The wedding had been so different to a traditional English wedding. There had been no exchanging of vows, just the priest making blessings and a lot of chanting, but the symbolism, the things done for luck, had been utterly charming and captivating. This was all on the cards for Sonya very soon. Her best friend was going to be putting that scrapbook of wedding plans to the test very soon.

'Tess.'

And there was Andras, looking super-hot in that suit, a sliver of olive chest exposed beneath the unbuttoned white shirt, stood beside her.

She smiled. 'The wedding was lovely.'

'Could you see? There were so many people in the church *I* could hardly breathe.' He smiled.

'We were behind Fotis,' she answered. 'But we made it work.'

He reached into the pocket of his trousers and drew out a taper candle, simple, no Jo Malone, its wick black where it had been lit. He held it out to her.

'What is it?' Tess asked. 'I mean, obviously it's a candle but ...'

'It is one of the candles that was lit during the wedding ceremony,' Andras replied. 'It represents everlasting love and Kira and Spiros will keep the candles until they are all burned right down to the end.' He gave her the candle. 'Except this one. This one I want to give to you.'

'Andras ...' Tess said.

'You do not have to say anything. I just want you to have it and to take it back to England and maybe light it and remember Corfu.'

She wrapped her fingers around the candle. 'I won't forget Corfu, Andras.'

'Andras!' It was Marietta calling, beckoning furiously from a few yards away. 'It's the donkey!'

'Go,' Tess said, sniffing away her emotion as best as she could. 'Go and be the *koumbaro*. Did I say that right?'

Andras nodded. 'Yes.' He kissed her quickly. '*Sagapo*.'

'What?' Tess exclaimed as Andras made off, the donkey appearing from the right adopting speeds of a steed Frankie Dettori might have mounted. 'What does that mean?'

She slipped her free hand into her bag, determined to ask Google Translate the answer, but checking the home screen she saw she had three missed calls, all from the same person. *Mum*.

It was time to face the music. Her stomach in knots, she pressed the screen. Closing her eyes she listened to the number eventually connect and then:

'Hello.'

There was her mother's voice, sounding more poignant than ever before.

Voice choking up, Tess replied. 'Hello, Mum, it's me.'

# Seventy-four

# Taverna Georgiou

Joey threw a plaster-of-Paris plate as hard as he could at the floor of the restaurant as, all around the bits and pieces of crockery, the wedding guests swerved and jigged and hopped and skipped their way across the room in time to the Greek band. It was evening and the celebrations were still continuing. The food, as always, had been divine – dips and bread, olives, fresh fish, rosemary-coated roast potatoes, green beans and a selection of puddings Tess had liberally dipped into. It was such a wonderful culmination of everything they had enjoyed during their Greek holiday.

'He's been wanting to do that all evening,' Sonya remarked, seeming to marvel at Joey's smashing skills.

Tess smiled and took another sip of the sweet white wine they had been drinking since the afternoon, with plenty of water in between to counteract the alcohol and the heat. 'I spoke to my mum.'

Sonya gave Tess her full attention then. 'You did?'

'I did,' Tess replied, feeling lightness fill her up as she recalled their talk.

'And … how did it go?' Sonya asked.

'Better than I could ever have hoped for,' Tess said.

There had been so many tears as she had leant against the eucalyptus tree telling her mother how sorry she was about the wedding, how for so long she had hated herself, blamed herself and how she had been saving long and hard to make things right. And her mum had listened, just listened, until Tess was completely spent and then there had been tears from her too. Sadness that Tess had ever felt that way and promises that their connection would never be lost again.

'I'm so glad, Tess,' Sonya said, chinking her glass with her friend's.

'And I'm going to pay for her to go to New Zealand. She told me she didn't want the money I've been saving, that Dad could do without it too. The loans are all paid off, but I'm not going to let her give up on her dream.'

'You could go with her,' Sonya suggested.

Tess shook her head. 'No, I couldn't. I've just had this holiday and I need to get back to work. I had an email earlier, the Black Velvet branding seems to have gone down really well so I need to push that through and ...'

'And there's Andras,' Sonya added.

All the time she had been pretend-thinking about work and saying all the right, sensible things, all she had been really thinking about was Andras. Corfu. How many weeks she needed to be back at work before she could have another holiday. Perhaps she couldn't tell him she loved him yet but she was aching to visit again before she had even left.

'Tess,' Sonya said, waving a hand in front of her face.

'Sorry ... I was miles away.'

'Were you?' Sonya asked, patting her hand, her eyes going to the ceiling, fairy lights and wedding bunting hanging from the beams. 'Or were you right here?'

'Mama!' Spiros shouted across the table, his words slurring a little after a day of celebration. 'Mama! There is something that I have to know.' He started to stand up, pointing a finger before Andras dragged him back down to his seat.

'This is my husband,' Kira announced, hair now loose from its confines, looking as wild as ever. 'My husband who is going to be too drunk to be of any use to me tonight!'

'That is not true!' Spiros insisted, rising from his chair again.

'Spiros!' Isadora said, banging her stick. 'It is time for you to start listening hard to your wife.'

'Yes, I will,' Spiros answered, raising a hand to his eyebrow in a mock salute. 'But first, Mama, there is something I want to know.'

Andras poured his brother a glass of water. 'Drink this.' He held it out.

'Wait!' Spiros said, waving the glass away. 'Mama, please, you must tell us ... what happened to Uncle Dimitri?'

All eyes, including Andras's, turned to his mother, like she held all the answers to the Grexit crisis.

Isadora took a long, slow breath in and then released it out fast with the words. 'He died.'

Everyone at the table inhaled at once and some of his relations made the sign of the cross over their torso.

'But how?' Spiros asked. 'Why?' He took a sip of water. 'All these years we have had to imagine just what his fate was. I have thought of wolves eating him alive or holidaymakers in Kavos eating him alive or a sea accident involving hundreds of jellyfish, but I do not want to wonder any more.'

'Hundreds of jellyfish!' Kira remarked. 'And wolves? You watch too much television.'

'Mama, you need to tell us,' Spiros begged.

'He died,' Isadora repeated. 'That is all you should need to know.'

'Andras.'

It was Dorothea tapping him on the shoulder, a special white wedding-day handkerchief over her hair. Her tone had an urgency like the entire kitchen might be on fire. He got to his feet and followed her quickly.

'Is everything OK?' he asked as they arrived at the desk. 'Is it the tortoise?'

'No,' Dorothea stated. 'It is the telephone.' She picked it up and held it out to him. 'It is the bank.'

He took hold of the receiver and put it to his ear. 'Hello.'

As Mr Giantsiorhs made his introductions, Andras's eyes went to his taverna and all his family and friends enjoying the wedding festivities. That's what he wanted from this business. More and more nights like this, as well as making money, making memories.

He swallowed as the words the banker was saying hit home. 'I see ... yes ... I understand.' He nodded on instinct. 'Thank you. Of course.' He replaced the receiver and took a deep breath. Dorothea was still there, looking at him, wringing her hands nervously.

'Is everything OK, Dorothea?' he asked.

'I heard Spiros asking about your Great Uncle Dimitri.'

Andras smiled. 'He is intent on getting to the bottom of the family mystery before the night is out.'

Dorothea nodded. 'Dimitri did die,' she confirmed. 'But he was one hundred and two and still had his own teeth!' She folded her arms across her chest. 'Isadora was always about the drama, even at school!'

Andras shook his head. 'Do you think we should tell Spiro?'

Dorothea looked towards the table where Spiros was sat, hiccupping into someone's hat. 'I think if you tell him tonight he will not remember in the morning.'

Andras nodded and put his arm around the cook. 'Go and have a drink now, Dorothea, relax. You have worked so hard.'

'You too, Andras,' she answered. 'Perhaps a dance with Tess, no?'

He smiled. He wanted to share every last moment of Tess's holiday with her, he just needed to work out how to tell her about the bank.

# Seventy-five

# Kalami Beach

Hand in hand, Tess and Andras walked along the sand and shingle away from the taverna, searching for some quiet space, both knowing that Tess's hours on the island were dwindling fast.

'It was a lovely wedding,' Tess said.

'You have said this, many times,' Andras replied.

'I know.' She did know. She just knew that the things she really wanted to say weren't coming easily. 'I just …'

'We should not pretend,' Andras said, stopping walking and turning to her.

She was facing him now, their hands engaged, the moon casting a warm glow over the rippling water of the sea. 'Pretend?' she queried.

'That when tomorrow comes things will not change.' He sighed. 'You are leaving.'

'I know,' she said, heaviness weighing down her tone.

'Do not be sad,' he told her, squeezing her hands. 'You have to go to be able to one day come back.'

'One day.' She swallowed. One day sounded like a whole galaxy away.

'I had a call from the bank,' Andras told her.

'You did?' She was holding her breath now, so wanting to hear good news.

'They will give me only half of the amount I asked for.'

It took her a second to react. 'Half?'

He nodded. 'It will be just enough to pay out Spiros, but it won't be enough to make improvements.'

'Oh, Andras, I'm sorry ...' She swallowed. 'But that doesn't have to be the end of it. I mean, there are other banks, or you have time now to start saving and making firm plans for extending and for the event nights.'

'I do not know.' He shook his head. 'Maybe this was a sign.'

'A sign?'

'That my dreams were too big.'

'No,' Tess insisted. 'Don't say that. It isn't true.'

He cleared his throat. 'It is OK. It is irritating, but there is nothing I can do about it and ... I do not want to think about business tonight.' He let go of one of her hands to run his fingers through her hair. 'I want to think about only you.'

The way he was looking at her was making her insides crumble like the ruined castle on the headland of Kassiopi. Those soulful dark brown eyes were drinking her in and all she wanted to do was wrap herself around him and never let go.

'Listen, Andras, I have some money, unexpected money, money that had a different destination until tonight. I could ...'

Before she had finished the sentence he was already shaking his head. 'No, Tess, I do not want your money.'

'I know you don't. Just like I'm not the gold-digger your mother pegged me as when we first met.'

'Tess ...'

'No, listen, I wouldn't be giving the money to you. I would be making an investment. Investing in a lovely Greek taverna by the sea with exquisite views, inside *and* out, depending on whether there's a hot restauranteur hanging half-naked from the beams pulling himself up and down like Stephen Amell.' She took a breath, excitement and lust mixing around in her chest. 'And, if I made an investment, I would need to come back here, right here, to Kalami, perhaps staying at the house of the restauranteur to keep a very close eye on my investment and ensure proper conduct was being maintained ...'

'Proper conduct,' Andras said, inching his body a little closer.

How did he make something so bona fide sound so damn sexy?

She nodded. 'Yes, I would need to know that the wine was being cooled to the optimum temperature, that you had managed to secure a supplier who could provide you with Dr Pepper for all those English holidaymakers desperate for it and that, well, standards were being kept up.'

'I have high standards already, Trix,' he reminded her. 'Very high standards.'

'I know,' she breathed, practically losing herself in his eyes as he lowered his face to hers. She broke the spell quickly, putting a hand to his shoulder and edging him back. 'Wait.'

She held on to his shoulder and, one by one, she pulled off the flip-flops on her feet, embedding her bare soles onto the sand and taking a deep breath.

'Now,' she said, lifting her face and holding his gaze. 'Now you can kiss me.'

His lips stole the breath from her and, as she clung to him, on the shoreline of the perfect Greek village, she knew there was no way in the world she was ever going to pledge to be single for the summer again.

# Epilogue

## Five weeks later

### McKenzie Falconer Offices

'So, I was thinking, for the TV ad, we could have the Alannah Myles song "Black Velvet" playing in the background, a bit retro, I know, but retro is cool. Then, I thought, a lone female could ride a horse along the surf and stop at an upmarket bar to order a bottle of ... Black Velvet Blackberry Crush Pinot.' Craig produced the bottle from behind his back like he was a magician.

Was he serious? Tess sat up in her seat at the boardroom table and stopped doodling Greek flags on her notepad. She was distracted, highly distracted. Because it was six weeks. It was exactly six weeks since she had first met Andras and the enormity of that was overwhelming. Six weeks was the rule she had lived her life by for so long. Six weeks had always been like her own personal waiting-for-Armageddon. And this was it. Six weeks with Andras. Timed out.

'Craig, I don't mean to be rude ...' She did. She absolutely did mean to be rude. 'But that sounds very much like an advert for sanitary towels.'

Craig's face began to redden like lava from Etna.

'Tess!' Russell exclaimed.

'What? Is sanitary towels a taboo subject? Didn't we have the account for Female Form at one point?' If they still had it, she might suggest Craig be the portfolio manager. She shook her head. 'The whole branding is meant to be relaxation. The horse and the song, it's too distracting. The advert needs to be cool, sophisticated. We need an instrumental soundtrack, something the audience is instantly going to pick up on as "escape", "unwind" …'

There was a knock at the boardroom door and Sally, Tess's secretary, appeared.

'Sorry to barge in …' Sally looked at Tess and raised her eyes, rolling them a little and nudging her head to the left.

'What is it, Sally?' Tess asked. 'This is a really important meeting. We're on a very tight deadline.'

'I know. I just …' She had dropped her voice to a stage whisper everyone could still hear. 'I've got something for you and … it's a bit strange.'

'Got something?' Tess asked. 'What, like a parcel?'

'Smaller,' Sally said.

'A letter?'

'Smaller still.'

'What is this?' Russell asked. 'Charades? We need to get this underway, Tess.'

Tess knew she had been the one to hold up this whole branding process with the name change.

'Sorry, Russell,' she said. 'Sally, just give it to me.'

'Now?'

'Is it rude?' Tess asked. She almost hoped it had something to do with Tena Lady, just to see the look on Craig's face.

'I … don't think so,' Sally said, stepping into the room.

Now Tess was curious. She swivelled her chair out from under the table and turned her body towards her secretary, waiting for her to cross the room.

'At first I thought it was a joke but apparently it isn't,' Sally stated. 'Here.'

Sally's outstretched hand contained something small and plastic ... a maroon red colour. Tess took it. It was a bottle top. A bottle cap from a 500ml bottle of Dr Pepper ... but the writing was in Greek. Her breath shortening, she rolled it around her fingers and, as she did so, it flipped over, revealing a number 6 written on the inside. She was up out of her chair, heart pummelling her chest wall.

'Where did this come from?' she panted. 'Where did you get this?'

'There's a man,' Sally said. 'He's in reception.'

'Tess, we really need to ...' Russell started.

Tess didn't hear him. She wasn't thinking about anything else apart from the glorious hope that the person downstairs was the only person she wanted to see more than anyone in the world. She fled from the room, the bottle top clutched in her hand, willing to sprint down all nine flights of steps if she had to.

In Andras's hands was the topless bottle of Dr Pepper he had spent a few weeks tracking down. He could have bought one here in the UK, but it needed to be from Greece. It was important, to go with everything else he had in mind. But he was nervous. He checked his watch. Perhaps coming here, to Tess's work, had been the wrong thing to do. She had an important job, he knew she was busy. Maybe this would look like an invasion rather than a romantic gesture.

'Excuse me.'

He looked up at the sound of her voice. The voice he had been listening to on the phone and over Skype for the last month sounded even better echoing around this ultra-modern reception area so unlike anything in Kalami.

'Do you have an appointment?' Tess asked.

He could tell she was catching her breath, but she slowed her pace as she took the final steps down to him.

He shook his head. 'No, Trix, but I do have a Dr Pepper. All the way from Corfu.'

She ran then, landing in his arms, the drink sloshing out all over the floor as she hugged him close, mouth dropping eager kisses on his lips.

'You are such an idiot,' she breathed, kissing him again. 'You brought this all the way from Corfu.'

'It had to go in the hold,' he answered, kissing her back.

'How? Why? You didn't tell me you were coming,' she said, finally letting him go and gazing up at him like he was her whole world.

'I had to come,' he said with a smile. 'It is our anniversary. Six weeks since we first met.'

'I can't believe you remembered,' Tess said, hands going to her mouth.

'I have come here to make sure we make it to six weeks and one day,' he spoke. 'Then six weeks and two days and then maybe … for ever.'

She gasped as he picked up a box from the burgundy-coloured reception chair and held it out to her. 'It's a new laptop,' he announced. 'That works very well with the new broadband I have installed at the restaurant and my house. Corfu misses you, Tess, Hector misses you, I miss you. I can stay here for a few days but after that I will have to go back to the island.' He swallowed, knowing he was going out on a limb here. 'Come back with me. We can work things out. Some time here in the UK, some time in Corfu …'

'Yes,' Tess interrupted. 'The answer is yes.'

'Yes?' he queried.

'Yes,' she repeated. '*Sagapo*.'

He felt his whole body move at the sound of that small word coming from her lips. 'You know what that means?'

She nodded vigorously. 'I googled it.' She kissed him. 'I love you.'

This was what he had hoped for. This was what he had thought about the whole way over on the plane. She was taking steps forward and putting her faith in him, in *them*.

'Oh my! Eyes are closed! Eyes are closed!' Sonya exclaimed, appearing from the door to the post room. 'Is fornication allowed in reception? I'm quite sure it isn't in the company manual.'

'Hello, Sonya,' Andras greeted. 'We must have a meeting. Maybe tomorrow?'

'A meeting?' Tess queried, holding his hand.

'Sonya and Joey are going to get married at Taverna Georgiou,' Andras informed her. 'We need to discuss their plans.'

'What?' Tess remarked. 'You didn't tell me!'

'Well,' Sonya began, 'it wasn't definite until a few days ago. Joey wanted to hire this medieval castle but it cost a small fortune and then his mother got involved – she wanted everyone to dress up like Morris dancers – but then I suggested Corfu and Andras's restaurant and reminded Joey how perfect Kira and Spiros's wedding was and … it went from there.'

'Are you going to be able to cater for a whole team of battle re-enactment enthusiasts?' Tess asked Andras.

'In Greece that is just like a family dinner,' he responded, kissing the top of her head.

'Come on,' Tess said, pulling him towards the stairs. 'Come and meet everyone. I want them all to see the man behind Black Velvet.'

'That sounds like a James Bond film,' Sonya said with a giggle.

'OK,' he answered, pulling her to a stop and dropping another kiss on her lips. 'But after that … I want you all to myself.'

Her lips curved into a smile and she reached up, palming his cheek, her thumb brushing over his top lip. 'I promise,' she whispered. 'And I can guarantee, there will be absolutely no need for faking anything.'

# Acknowledgements

Thank you to my wonderful agent, Kate Nash. You do need a medal for dealing with my randomness on a daily basis! But I think we're a dream team!

Thanks also to my new, and rather wonderful editor, Emily Yau. I am so thrilled to be working with you and Ebury and I'm so excited for whatever is coming next! Here's to more wine and some Greek food!

Thank you to my best writing friends in the whole wide world who are a constant source of inspiration, hilarity and kick-ass when I need it:

Rachel Lyndhurst
Zara Stoneley
Sue Fortin
Linn B Halton

Thank you to my lovely street team, The Bagg Ladies! You are all so amazing and I appreciate every single tweet/share/conversation over crazy ideas.

Thank you to the wonderful book blogging community. You ladies and gents are our lifeblood and we couldn't publish and promote books without you! Keep reading, keep *loving* reading and keep telling the world about your passion for great books!

Thank you to all my Greek and Anglo-Greek friends! I do love researching Corfu as often as I can and your ideas, stories and general ouzo-infused loveliness never fail to hit the spot.

Last, but not least, thank you to my husband, Mr Big, because without you this story would be missing that vital touch of realism. True Happy Ever Afters take love, friendship, commitment and a whole lot of laughter. And we're still winning!

# Letter from Mandy

Did you enjoy your holiday in Kalami, Corfu?

I had so much fun writing *Single for the Summer* and I really hope you loved every single second of Tess and Andras's story.

Who was your favourite character? Were you cheering on Tess? Did you like Sonya? Did you fall for sexy Andras? Did the story make you want to book a holiday to my favourite Greek island?!

I love to hear from readers so if you loved the book let me know and sign up to my new release newsletter.

Twitter: @mandybaggot
Facebook: mandybaggotauthor
www.mandybaggot.com

Mandy xx